MW00879223

All the Seasons Never Lived

Judy Hovis

First Edition

PAGE PUBLISHING, INC.
Conneaut Lake, PA

First originally published by Page Publishing 2021

ISBN 978-1-6624-3022-0 (pbk)
ISBN 978-1-6624-3692-5 (hc)
ISBN 978-1-6624-3023-7 (digital)

Printed in the United States of America

Reflecting on my life and family—particularly some of the women who came before and will come after, it became clear we are made of hearty stock. We are like women across the world and throughout history. Along the way, we either grow and develop or pull back and die; not physically but mentally. It is our courage that keeps us moving forward.

So begins the story of Clarice, my great-grandmother. We were born almost a century and continent apart but our struggles bind us together.

Only enough of my story is told to connect the challenges faced by Clarice with my own and how we remain intertwined. An almost fatal accident transported me back to the late 1800's. It was France, 1889 and I was living Clarice's story as if my own.

Jackie

Acknowledgments

THE JOURNEY HAS been long and there are many who stuck with me throughout the fifteen years. My gratitude to those who believed, inspired, and encouraged me when I was ready to give up. I include in this group those who graciously listened every time regaled with more about the book.

I'll begin with my family. My biggest supporter was my soulmate and husband Robert, who encouraged me every step of the way. My children, Lloyd, Lorrie, and Dawn always believed their mother could do anything and for their love and support I'm blessed. Thanks to their spouses, Jennifer, Mark, and Mickey, who also had to hear about the book more than once. Even my sister, Bonnie, and brother, Joe couldn't escape the "book talk" and remained supportive throughout. Of course, my wonderful grandchildren were always cheering me on.

My diva friends, Elizabeth, Kathy, Kimberly, Peg, Patricia, Lucinda, Marcia, Betty, Marguerite, Linda, Shelagh, Sherre', Terri, Vicki and Wanda were my cheerleaders. Also, a special thanks to Peg Dowgwilla who spent considerable time reading my book and making several important suggestions to improve the reader's experience.

I owe a great debt of thanks posthumously to my dear friend Fran Parker, who as my "senior advisor" was one of the first people to read my book and encourage me to go to the finish line. As a well-read English major, her opinion of my writing skills gave me the boost I needed.

Thanks go to Michael P. Fitzsimmons, Professor of History Emeritus, Auburn University Montgomery, publisher of many books on French History, who unselfishly spent several months editing my book and also making sure that any historical events were accurate.

My deepest appreciation and gratitude go to Tom Gill, author of four books including *Return to Emerald Isle.* Tom graciously agreed to read my book and then took the time to do an in depth edit. Not only did he spend a year with me going back and forth on the best ways to present certain passages, but was my official mentor throughout this process. His patience and insight helped me finish the journey. I will be forever in his debt.

PART ONE

Jackie

The Beginning

Her life, by all accounts, had not been easy. Instantly, she was once again transported to another time, another generation, another country.

She was outside with Aiyox, her beautiful German shepherd, playing in the yard, and then suddenly pulled over the wall away from Aiyox, away from the light and being carried into the forest. There was heavy breathing and then the calm. Where was she? It was so dark, and the branches were stinging her legs as she was being carried through the bushes.

I want my daddy!

She liked the candy the nice big boy gave her. But he looked mean now; she'd thought they were going to play. When would he take her home?

The dogs were barking in the distance as she began to cry. She had been left alone for only a few minutes when she saw him. *Oh, there's my daddy! He's coming to get me.*

But, Mommy, he was my new friend and gave me candy. We were running in the woods. Why is Daddy crying?

Too young to understand, it wasn't until she was older that Jackie found out she had been kidnapped.

Years later, she would learn the incident had taken place in April 1947 in Marburg, Germany. Her father was one of the first US Army officers sent to a war-ravaged Germany after the peace treaties had been signed. His small family had happily accompanied him and looked forward to this new adventure. Little did they know the pitfalls awaiting them.

The war had been hard on the German people leading many to thievery, kidnapping, and even murder; times were tense. There had been no peace during the Nazis' reign of terror. Even the young were recruited into the gestapo where they learned hatred—even for their own families.

After the war, it was because of these lost souls that a black market grew to massive proportions and thrived on people's desperation. Within that atmosphere, there also was a more sinister element of evil: the trade of children became a lucrative business.

Jolted back to the present, Jackie Hancock gazed out the bedroom window. How long had she been in the other time and place? These flashbacks were happening more frequently, and she couldn't help but wonder what it meant. Not only her journeys back in history but more perplexing were those journeys back to the time of her great-grandmother, Clarice. It didn't frighten her but gave her more to think about. *Somehow, we are connected through time with more than our DNA.*

Back in the present, she could relish the start of the day, beauty emerging like a newly formed blossom on a vine. Despite the briskness of that November morning, it felt as if they were cloaked in the sun's embrace, keeping everyone warm during the solstice of winter. Gloomy days are quickly forgotten by the brilliance of the sun on a clear winter day!

We really should seize every day (carpe diem). Wasn't that what any good therapist would say? Later today, I'm going to tell my story to several hundred women who are privileged to be part of an elite award-winning women's business group. How I became one of these special women is beyond me but I'll happily go with it. Several years ago, I was fortunate to be selected to become part of the inaugural group in spite of any misgivings that I may have had regarding my so-called talents and success.

As I dress for my big performance, I'm struck with many thoughts. How do you tell a story that is so profoundly personal and yet has merit in the telling? How much can you cut out and still get the point across? Will I help other women who have come through adversity? I'm still struggling with the idea that, in five hours, I will be standing up in front of my peers, not only sharing my insight as an experienced business woman but interspersing with personal vignettes; some causing me great concern.

My nerves were tightly strung much like two rubber bands holding together a frayed manuscript. There were many reasons—not the least of which is the last time I told some of my story back in 1999, everything went downhill from there.

What would my grandmother have said? "Jackie," spoken with her cute little French accent, "you will be magnificent. Tell your story from your heart and everyone will hear you!" Well, perhaps if she could see or hear me now, she would say something like that or maybe she'd tell me to use discretion. A little mystery where I'm concerned is a good thing!

Bringing her thoughts to the present, she looked in the mirror. "Gosh, I look old," Jackie said as she applied her makeup. Talking out loud somehow made her take more stock in her appearance. The years had been kind to her even through her many trials and tribulations.

Her shoulder-length hair, trimmed in recent years as she aged, was a beautiful shade of rich brown with golden highlights that seemed to blend with eyes that, at times, were green, amber, and gold. Those eyes spoke volumes about what they had seen and experienced. "I wonder what my children would say if they could hear my little speech." *Children* was a loose term since all three had been adults for at least twenty years. It was funny how they had come so far and had finally settled with her, each in their own unique way, a kind of bonded truce born of blood.

Just then, Craig came in the bedroom and called to her. "How are you doing, babe? Have you been practicing your speech in front of the mirror?"

Jackie wrinkled her nose and said, "Uh-huh, but I think my speech is way too long and needs to be cut back some. All I need is to drone on and on, boring everyone to tears."

"I doubt seriously that anyone will be bored with what you have to say. Your charisma draws in an audience and keeps their attention."

She started to respond, but memories of the past flooded her mind like cacophonous waves crashing against the shore. Against her will, she found herself reliving the time twenty years before when she lost hope. Always the resilient, eternal optimist, a trait her friends considered to be naive and somewhat frivolous, she had fallen into an abyss of despair.

After suffering through the loss of her home and business that left her virtually homeless, she thought nothing mattered anymore. She arose each morning and mindlessly pushed herself through the day, if only to carry on for the children, oblivious to her surroundings.

Jackie stifled her negative thoughts and the memories they had evoked. Shaking her head and looking in the mirror helped her return to the present. Ever mindful of the power of positive thinking, she quickly changed the direction she had taken. They say depression is a jealous lover, always fighting for a part of your soul that, once given, you cannot replace. Jackie chose to keep her soul intact.

"You don't look so bad, even for a middle-aged broad," she said to her reflection. As if to reinforce a more positive flow of thought, she broke into a big smile that made her laugh at the face looking back at her. *No one ever accused me of not being able to laugh at myself,* she mused. In fact, she had a way of being self-deprecating that pulled people to her, as if embracing a long-lost friend.

Her mind switched back once again. Thinking about the stories of Clarice, her great-grandmother and the women who came before fascinated her even today. It was on this tapestry where her inner soul was woven. She felt such a deep connection to a past so rich—the many generations of unique personalities providing a plethora of extremes. It also served to diminish the memories of her often-painful childhood.

Sadly, the time spent living near her grandparents was limited to a year here or there when her father was sent somewhere across the world, usually somewhere his family could not accompany him. When she was older, Jackie's parents allowed her to live with them. From a child's perspective, those were wonderful, peaceful times. She could certainly breathe easier when living with them, and the problems that she normally shouldered seemed far away.

Once an adult, Jackie's perspective changed when she realized her grandmother had the same problem the females in this family always seemed to have—sacrificing their independence and sense of self to the men they loved. This was the weak link in a long chain of very strong and capable women and somehow managed to diminish the positive energy and self-confidence they all had carried with them.

Jackie thought back to her childhood and the incongruities of her parents' marriage. The relationship between her mother and father was like converging two classics: War and Peace and the fiery story of Anthony and Cleopatra.

It was a wound that never healed; the poison in their marriage fueled most of the inner fears and demons she spent her early life fighting to overcome. Even now, married a second time to a man whom she truly loved, there was still some thread of longed-for independence that managed to keep her from yielding to the totality of selfless love. Perhaps remaining interdependent yet separate could be accomplished, but she didn't understand how to make that happen without giving up the one piece she managed to salvage from her first marriage.

Craig was her knight in shining armor, dashing and handsome, always glib and charming—even in discouraging times. He was her passion and could wring out every ounce of emotion from within, leaving her drained even at the best of times. Recently, they had to face the mounting debt from yet another round of borrowing intended to keep the bank at bay and her new floundering business afloat. He had hinted that maybe they needed to take a break, a revelation that brought her to tears.

Enough of this, Jackie thought. She didn't like this train of thought either, so as quickly as it began, she shut it down. She did make a promise that before too much time passed, she would find the key to unlock the historical drama that continued to play out through the generations of her female ancestors. Thoughts of Clarice Pontifi, her great-grandmother, and the life she lived drifted into her mind once again. But what about Clarice? Was she really any different from the women who succumbed to the charms of a man only to lose sight of their dreams and the pursuit of a greater purpose?

The story of her great-grandmother's life was one of unbelievable dimensions. Maybe that's what this deal called life is all about—struggling, surviving, and, maybe, just maybe, winning in the end. She had heard multiple times the bits and pieces of her very intriguing French heritage, sometimes delivered with intense emotion and always exceeding any anticipated story.

The murder in Paris, complete with its mystery and intrigue, always fascinated her. Plus, the fact that this was her own history stoked her penchant for sleuthing. If Clarice could live a life so full after suffering the early hardships she had to endure, then certainly Jackie could put aside these small inconveniences and get on with the business of living life to her highest expectations. Before too much time lapsed, she would dig into the family past in more detail.

More so than any intrigue, though, was the part of her history that remained fragmented with unanswered questions about what drove the women to pursue the unknown risking everything. She needed closure for why she had this wanderlust for life, never satisfied.

That she could possibly risk her security for the pursuit of that unknown force scared her. Was it a wild streak that they all had in common? What was the missing link?

Glimpse of the Past (*Fall 2004*)

Jackie was still reminiscing over the past ten years and had a brief moment of sadness. It was already the fall of 2004, and life seemed to be flashing by with no time to slow down the clock. Driving more slowly, she was determined to soak in this entire experience.

The drive to Ketner Auditorium on the Queens College campus took Jackie through some of Charlotte's finest neighborhoods. Since she had plenty of time, her chosen route was more circuitous, allowing her to enjoy the deep emerald lushness of the evergreens and the remainder of late autumn iridescent gold-painted scenery in a city known for its magnificent landscapes. It also gave her time to reflect on her speech and practice once again what she would say to the group.

As she rounded the bend on Sharon Road, she decided to play the speech in her mind one more time. There would be interesting revelations—some bordering on shocking—to most of the group. One of the stories she planned to share with them would certainly be talked about later. If only they knew the half of it. She was planning to unveil only snippets of information to minimize her exposure.

Traffic abruptly stopped, snapping her attention back to the road. She could see children playing in a yard nearby. *Such unbridled happiness and energy*, she thought longingly. With the window down, their laughter was unadulterated and free of any outward pain that a childhood lost too soon could bring to a young heart.

She gazed at the beautiful manicured lawns that were characteristic of the Myers Park scene. Majestic great southern oaks lining the streets provided a canopy so lush as if to declare its rightful place as guardian of the noble estates, shielding the homes' occupants from intruding eyes. Grand homes stood sentry for the families that embraced the lifestyles defined by comfort and wealth. She imagined what it would be like to grow up in such a place. Coveting other people's lives was not in her nature even though, regrettably, she never experienced what she imagined the children to have—a normal childhood!

Her peace with the past came slowly but never wavered once it had taken hold, filling some of the early voids with love and laughter, much like what she imagined the children were enjoying as they played in their yards. The inner strength she developed served her well later in life.

Thinking back to her parents and some of the difficulties facing them as an American military family thrown into Germany right after the war, it was easy to see they did the best they could to provide a normal routine. Jackie's kidnapping could have ended in the worst way but instead proved to those around her that she was born to do something special and that God's grace had spared her.

Doris and Clayton Dade, Jackie's parents, had no idea what was in store for their young family. The road to Germany took them first to the small, quaint city of Marburg, nestled in the Bavarian Alps. The postcard-perfect scene could not have foreshadowed the ensuing drama to come, nor would it have changed the outcome.

As the captain of the US-based military police, it was doubly ironic that Clayton's own little girl would become the victim of one of the lost souls and of a society that had just come through a madness of extreme obsession that changed the world forever.

* * *

The day started without the usual crowd of workers moving in and out of their rented four-story house. And what a house it was, practically a fortress built with double reinforced stone and adorned with hardwood timbers four inches thick that crisscrossed at every window intersection, making the home impenetrable. Perched on a hill overlooking the quaint village of Marburg, the manor stood as a reminder that even the mighty can fall. They christened their majestic new home *Guten Tag*, or "Good Day" in English, as if to send out a welcome to their new German friends.

Helga, the number one maid in the ever-revolving staff, had managed to implant herself permanently in Doris's good graces. She knew the young mother had plenty to cope with now that the new baby boy had arrived. It bothered Helga, and she thought it strange how Doris seemed detached from little Jackie and barely held the baby boy! It was her decided opinion that both of these precious children needed her big chest to lay their heads on.

"Maybe these Americans don't understand how to mother their babies," she snorted to herself. Was there anything better than the sweet smell of a baby's skin, freshly washed and powdered? If she had anything to do with it, there would be many hugs and kisses for both of them.

It was a beautiful sunny day, the clouds floating like puffs of cotton in the azure blue sky. Helga let Jackie and Aiyox out into the six-foot fenced-in yard to play, comfortable in the knowledge that the perimeter was secure with fortresslike fence posts surrounding it—and of course the giant German shepherd to protect her precious *Liebchen*. Occasionally she would look out and check on the duo frolicking in the morning sun, smiling to herself in wonder at the innocence and freedom of youth.

Her attention had been pulled to the baby boy, Billy, and his incessant screaming. Goodness, that Liebchen cries too much. She was unsettled once more by thoughts of the young mother and her lack of interest in the baby.

At that moment, Doris came running up the stairs, yelling the whole way, "Helga, Helga, where is Jackie? She's not in the yard. Aiyox is barking nonstop and running back and forth along the fence. Where is she?"

Helga's heart fell as she ran to the window in disbelief. "Augh, my Liebchen must have come in and is hiding in the basement. I'll just run down there and find her!" declared Helga.

"No, she's not down there. I've already looked all over the lower level, including the wine cellar and pantry. What have you done? Why weren't you watching her?" Doris yelled.

Helga clasped her chest as the throes of desperation engulfed her, and she realized Jackie was, in fact, gone! Scurrying around and flapping her arms in panic did nothing to dispel the dread and fear hanging in the air. To see the large woman jumping around would have been comical under normal circumstances, but the seriousness of what could possibly have taken place was all too sobering!

Doris turned on her heels and ran out the door, down the hill to the military police station where her husband was the commanding officer. He would know what to do; as always was the case, his broad shoulders supported her in times of trouble. He would lead his company of military policemen and they would find her daughter, she kept telling herself over and over.

In between the panic and trying to maintain control of her emotions, Doris wished her so-called beloved husband was home more. It was a desire that invariably came whenever she needed his counsel or felt lonely, as so often was the case now. Her hopes for a normal family routine that included her handsome husband generally did not materialize.

Helga, in the meantime, buried her head in her arms, distraught and in a state of despair over her lapse in judgment; leaving the three-year old alone for any length of time was unforgivable! It occurred to her that while she was judging her employer for her shortcomings, Doris was the one who knew when Jackie was missing, and there was no mistaking the level of distress in the young mother's voice!

After what seemed like an eternity, Clayton and his crew of military police found the frightened girl deep in the forest surrounding Marburg, unharmed except for minor scrapes and bruises.

In a fashion reminiscent of a great rescue, the troops, led by her father, tracked the kidnapper through the thick underbrush until, in desperation, he abandoned Jackie by a big rock and fled farther into the forest, trying to evade the angry group. It didn't take long for the military police to capture him.

Clayton scooped her into his arms, soothing her by telling her, "Daddy's here now, sweetheart," a move that would later become the basis for her hero worship of him and carry her adulation of him through darker times.

They later found out she had been kidnapped by one of the angry young men who roamed the streets in search of black market goods or of young girls which they could barter for a much larger prize. Though little physical harm had come to her during the ordeal, it did change the framework of her life, at least throughout her early years and set the stage for a dramatic life.

The serenity of earlier days was radically changed in the household, replaced with a type of obsessive behavior that developed from fear. Her parents' overprotectiveness manifested itself in a variety of ways—not the least of which was quarreling over Doris's inability to keep Jackie safe.

At the same time, her mother's unnatural fear of staying alone at night was growing more incessant with every passing day, transferring to Jackie a sense of foreboding that bore a hole into the fabric of her very being and carving out a part of her sense of security and exposing it as her weakness.

Glaringly obvious to those close to them, Clayton began to retreat emotionally from Doris. Rather than listen to her incessant tales of intruders and fears that were, for the most part, unfounded, he poured all his attention onto his troops and military duties in Marburg. His impatience with Doris's weakness and constant criticism fueled a need for more and more distance, pushing him to spend late hours at headquarters or at the Officer's Club with his buddies.

Courageous

CONTINUING HER DRIVE to Queens, Jackie thought about those formative years and how she often sought comfort within the recesses of her mind. Her fertile imagination sufficed to give her the playmates and missing "little girl" joy that actual living could not mimic except in rare moments.

As she moved through adolescence, she started reaching out to the memories of her ancestors and the love and care that she received from her own sweet grandmother. It wasn't that her mother didn't love or nurture her but rather suffered in silence to her own pain-filled life, inevitably short-changing those she loved. In spite of all her faults, including this enervation of spirit, she, at times, was warm and loving. Aside from occasional dereliction of motherly duties and a general disassociation with the realities of motherhood, Doris's heart was in the right place.

During the next few years of moving between military bases in the US, life was generally lived without incident except for the exposure to the dysfunctional relationship between her parents and the scars left on all of them from constant fighting.

It was at this time Jackie gained a confidence level and adult persona beyond her young years. Innately recognizing the need for calm and serenity, she became the peacemaker and often the go-between with her bickering parents.

Imagine what it would be like as a child to witness two people you love, your supposed role models, screaming out vile descriptive words at each other. Jackie witnessed such behavior and did her best to push these difficult encounters to the back of her mind to cover up disappointment in her parents.

In spite of a growing personal confidence, there was the fear she balanced, best described as a continuous dull ache in the middle of her soul, never abating for long. Years later, she protected her brothers from the very belligerent renderings of her parents' battles that were played out almost daily on the stage of human indignation.

As she matured, Jackie developed a humorous, sarcastic way of looking at her parents which helped her deal with their shortcomings. She decided the only benefit her parents gained through the continuous yelling was in keeping their lungs clear.

Suddenly, honking horns brought her back to the present. Jackie shook her head as she moved forward and focused on the road. Assessing her thoughts of the past few minutes, it was her strong level of confidence and belief in her ability to overcome the odds that helped her through that unstable upbringing.

Try as she might to stay focused, her mind continued to wander. How had she survived? She thought about the positive influencers in her life aside from her grandmother and stories of her great-grandmother, Clarice. Even her parents, and certainly her own broken mother, had attributes that contributed to her growth in a positive way. Doris was tough when the chips were down.

Her vivid imagination and the time she spent alone in thought helped her move through the legacies of those women who had paved the way. It would be part of the fabric of her future and drive Jackie to find the common bond that defined the women who came before—frail in some respects but stronger than the historical depictions of women, especially those surrounded by successful men.

Some of her role models were women she only knew through books—those who defied the odds in a man's world risking everything to prove their equality. Jackie admired them for different but equally strong reasons and planned to mention a couple of them in today's speech.

She emulated Amelia Earhart, a woman fearless enough to go after what she wanted. At the same time, she could identify a similar pattern Amelia demonstrated that had derailed Jackie and the other women in her family. After working as a telephone operator to earn money for an airplane, Amelia crashed only a few months later and had to revert to what was traditional women's work at that time. Nevertheless, her enthusiasm didn't waver as she pushed forward, instead of trying to force herself into the stereotyped molds available to women.

Another one of her early personal heroes was Susan B. Anthony, a champion of temperance and an early advocate of abolishing slavery. She believed in equal pay for equal work and fearlessly devoted her life to organizing and leading the women's suffrage movement. It was with deep regret that Jackie acknowledged never actively following through on her own desire to help the oppressed, and it proved to be a major void throughout her life.

Her solace came from the knowledge that she befriended the oppressed and many others over the years when caught in difficult situations and especially when tensions were high. Other people may have avoided them, but she became an outspoken advocate.

The Accident

"Thank God for some of the early adversity in my life," she said out loud, realizing she was back in Charlotte, sitting in traffic. "Boy, I have to keep my mind on this so-called upcoming speech. At the rate I'm going, the meeting may well be over by the time I get there."

It's funny how this speech has affected me, she thought. *It certainly has opened up my mind to the past again. Some of the joys but also old demons have rushed in to torment me further. Well, I won't let the negative parts of my life overtake the good that dwells there.*

After the holidays, when everything settles down, she continued to muse, *it may be time for me to learn more about my ancestry and take the time to discover the common thread that not only bound these women together, but lessons learned along the way that were passed on to successive generations.*

Speaking out loud again, she said, "Yes, if I can make a difference in other women's lives by learning what those common traits are, perhaps I can steer them toward lives of full intention, lives devoid of fear and insecurity. In doing this for others, I will heal myself and feel fulfilled."

She was moving now after having waited through another traffic light. Closing in on her destination, making her last turn onto Queens Road, a slight glint in the rearview mirror caught her eye. As she moved to glance toward the light, out of nowhere came the truck, bearing down on her. Horns were honking and the squeal of brakes against metal struck a nerve.

This can't be happening, her mind screamed.

With little time to react, she jerked the wheel just as the front wheel well of a large concrete mixer truck crashed into the right rear side of her Volvo, pushing thousands of pounds of reinforced steel toward her. In that shattering moment, all of Jackie's life surfaced and a feeling of deep regret blazed in her conscious mind as the darkness tried to sweep over her.

* * *

Flashing lights seemed to be buried in her head, fighting with the darkness, trying to keep her from sleep—blissful sleep. Voices were shouting now, interrupting the rhythmic melodies playing in her semiconscious state, refusing to let her float with the music. Amid it all, she could hear a siren wailing. *Why won't they shut up*? she thought. *I'm so tired and they keep waking me.*

"Keep her awake, John, at least until we get to the hospital," shouted a commanding male voice. "If she passes out, we may lose her!"

Jackie could not quite pull the words together to make sense of the gibberish. But even in her semiconscious state, she understood the tonal crescendos rising to feverish heights might signify something to worry about.

Later, it was learned the truck driver ran the red light and early tests had indicated he had been drinking, blowing almost twice the legal limit on the Breathalyzer test.

Jackie should have died instantly, but as happened other times in her life, she survived. This time, a small crater was carved into the steel frame of the steadfastly safe Volvo, enough to spare her from the certain death of being crushed by several tons delivered at full speed. It amazed even the hardened patrolmen that anyone could survive such an impact although they were sure the driver wouldn't make it once delivered to the hospital.

If only her brain would work. She could hear the voices of her family—the worried concern of those she loved and loved her in return.

Why are they worrying? She heard words like *critical, may never come out of the coma, may not be functional again*, and she wanted to holler out to reassure them she would be just fine.

Then her mind drifted back—back to stories of Clarice, the women who followed her, and the men who helped them become empowered. There was the mystery that embroiled the family in murder and intrigue. In struggling to clear her mind, Jackie could hear her mother's words: "Forget about the Germans. It's all about the family secrets hidden at the old estate."

PART TWO

Clarice

The Early Years (1889)

THE SOUND OF the train winding through the Swiss Alps was comforting to Clarice. Soon the whoosh-whoosh of the wheels as they turned would lull her to sleep. Night had come too soon for Clarice and Andre. Both were young and filled with excitement; they were going to see their most favorite cousin, Jacques. They had left Milano earlier that day for their annual pilgrimage to the family's summer retreat. The Pontifi family would be in residence there for the summer. What could possibly go wrong?

The trip was just one reason for their joy. Anyone who had been around them could plainly see there was the added anticipation of seeing their father, especially since they had been unable to hide their excitement for the past two weeks! After all, wasn't this the reunion where they could finally capture their father for the summer? To see Jacques and all the others was but second place, wasn't it? Clarice continued to ponder what lay ahead as the train moved tirelessly over the miles of track. There was a comfort to the sound, and the happiness she felt right now could hardly be contained.

Before falling asleep, Clarice thought about the reunion they had that morning on the platform while waiting for the train to Mulhouse and the final leg of their trip. Were they really all together again as a family? The rest of their extended family, except *grand-mère*, would all be waiting in Mulhouse. She had told Clarice she would be along soon after taking care of some family business. Her grandmother was a very interesting woman indeed, and she wanted to be just like her when she grew up! In her mind, she was just about the most interesting person in her life, except Papa, of course. She overheard her mother telling her friends that Marie Chevais (*grand-mère*) conducted business like a man and worried someday she might end up in trouble. She wondered if her mother was embarrassed for people to know that Mrs. Chevais was her own mother. *Guess I'll ask her when I get older*, Clarice decided.

Papa had been gone so long it was hard to think of him as being part of their routine. Is it possible he was going to stay this time? Oh, to have him for more than a week at a time. She was, after all, the apple of his eye and knew that he would always be there for her in spirit no matter where his travels took him. Mama said he had to travel to keep up with his business ventures.

"What could be so important," she had asked her mama last week, "to keep him away so long?"

"Your father is a very important man, Clarice, and he must always be available for his people."

Humph, his people don't need him as much as we do, she thought. *And it seems as if Mama is always crying when he is gone.* It made Clarice want to weep for her mama's loneliness.

Aurelia was lost in thought herself, thinking mostly about Augusto. He was a handsome man, his dark hair and eyes attesting to his heritage—Italian with a little bit of French thrown in. Sometimes Aurelia would look at him and wonder how she could be so fortunate to have such a wonderful man. Yet the very traits that characterized his noble bearing also kept him from being entirely hers. He was a man for his people.

She couldn't help but worry about what Clarice had said to her. She was very insightful for a girl so young. At only age nine, Clarice was aware of her mother's pain and loneliness. Her mother said she was too old for her own good, and other adults she came in contact with would tell her parents out of earshot that she was too independent and smart for one so young. Augusto, her proud papa, would tell them she was *spirited* and that it would serve her well one day. It did concern him that she was so beautiful! His little Clarice, with her amber doe eyes and long dark silken hair, which somehow always seemed to escape the braids her mother would weave every morning. She would grow up and make some young man a fine wife.

Aurelia knew Clarice did not understand and sensed her own loneliness for Augusto. Now she had fallen into a role almost pathetic in its weakness in spite of the lofty intentions she had of maintaining her own identity. Suffice to say, Aurelia came from hearty stock with Madame Chevais as her mother and mentor.

Yes, Aurelia had to admit that she was critical of Ma Mère, as Augusto so readily pointed out once too often, but that was part of the troubling aspect of her new persona. While she wanted to emulate her mother, this role in which she had been self-cast muted and vilified what could have been vibrancy in her own right. Aurelia found the role demoralizing, but even more offensive, it was capable of producing jealousy disguised as self-righteous behavior.

Certainly, Augusto was not responsible for making her feel inadequate. By nature, she was not a jealous woman, but the past couple of years, with his frequent absences, her confidence had gradually eroded. As a strong virile male in French and Italian societies, women and men alike would naturally single him out for shared confidences. If she happened to be standing there, all the more apparent the snub to her own intelligence and independence of thought.

Well, her mother never seemed to have those issues and could hold her own with the best of men.

Aurelia made a commitment that she would get to the bottom of her unhappiness and live life in the way her mother had guided so long ago. She suspected Clarice, whom she knew loved her, did not have the same measure of respect for her as she did for *grand-mère*, and she could not blame her daughter for having those inclinations.

Clarice interrupted her mother's self-analysis just then. "Mama, will he have to go again soon?"

"I don't know, Clarice. We will just have to enjoy him every day and pray that he will stay the summer with us."

Augusto had been born to a long line of Italian aristocrats and winemakers in 1860 in a small village in the Tuscany region of Italy. As the eldest son of the "wine baron," his destiny had been carved before birth. He traveled extensively from countryside to city, frequently crossing the border into France and back into the villages of Northern Italy. His mother was of French heritage and family land holdings merged the two borders.

Moving through France to Paris increased the sense of mystery that fueled his reputation as a debonair man of the world. With threats to political stability in France becoming very real, especially in the years following the downfall of Napoleon III's government in 1870 and the establishment of the republic, Augusto was groomed by a very astute father to learn all that he could to protect himself and his family.

By the time he turned twenty years old, he had become a scholar of the unsettled French political scene and understood the role, even though minor, Italy had played during this period. This knowledge allowed him to arm himself with the information necessary to maneuver among the people and countries to which he held allegiances. It was then that he began to travel regularly between the family estates and business holdings.

Augusto's father, having been a supporter of Camillo Benso, conte di Cavour, the prime minister of the Kingdom of Piedmont-Sardinia, imbued within his son a love of France and Italy. Italy's relationship with France gave Augusto more reason to play the role of worldly diplomat.

He remembered how, at bedtime, his father would share some of the detailed history with him in the form of a story. As a young man, he found that he looked forward each day to their tradition of history time. It was during these sessions that Augusto's guiding principles were formed.

Augusto was most aware of the impact the loss of Alsace-Lorraine to Bismarck had on the people of the Alsace region, one with strong ties for the

Gervais and Pontifi families. Augusto's motivation was born of love: a quest to reassure his people and reconfirm his love and support of them, whether in the Alsace region, Italy, or the center of France—the great city of Paris even with all its strife.

The politics of the republic had been stirred during the years of 1870–1879 by the then commander I and V French Corps, Patrice MacMahon, duc de Magenta, himself a monarchist.

It was this recent history of war and violence in their beloved region of Alsace where Aurelia's fears and anxiety were bred. It was not in her nature to be a recalcitrant woman, for, after all, wasn't she a Chevais?

Back in the moment again and agonizing over what kept him so long, much of Aurelia's concerns centered on her husband's travels and long absences, preordained before his love of her and certainly before the current unrest.

She remembered so well when he came waltzing into her mother's showroom during one of her breaks from the University of Paris. Aurelia liked helping her mother even amid the criticism of her peers.

There was a certain freedom and sense of rightness in working among the LeMonde of French society—a constant reminder that Madame Chevais did not care what was said about them behaving like common women of the wharf!

Unlike her other potential suitors, Augusto was aloof, focusing his attention on a diamond her mother had on display in the center showcase, clearly deep in thought and not aware of Aurelia's obvious beauty, or so she thought.

"May I help you, sir?" she asked Augusto.

Leveling his fire-braised, charcoal eyes to look at the girl who spoke to him, he said, "You must be Madame Chevais's daughter. She has spoken often of you and your talents."

"You know my mother?" she inquired. Immediately, her interest in this stranger, acting so aloof and much like a partner in some mysterious plot, was piqued. The reserved gentleman's knowledge of her mother also intrigued her. It wasn't until much later that she found out the full truth of just how the relationship with her mother wove their bands through all their lives. In the following year, when Augusto came back to Paris, she learned how much Marie Chevais depended on him and the extent of that dependence, particularly since the death of Aurelia's father.

What she hadn't realized in the year that passed was how very much she looked forward to seeing Augusto again.

Their whirlwind courtship started from the moment Augusto laid eyes on her for the second time. Unknown to her, he had inquired of Madame Chevais as to the status of her beautiful young daughter.

Aurelia, aware that she had drifted to another time, abruptly turned back to Clarice to reassure this precocious girl of Augusto's love of family, only to see that she had vanished, probably off to see what she could learn about the excitement taking place all around her. She was convinced that her very self-assured daughter understood well how much her father adored her, a thought that moved Aurelia to melancholy.

Clarice, meanwhile, made a silent promise to the Blessed Mother that she would do everything she could to please Papa in the next few days. If only Mama would smile and laugh as she used to when Papa was there most of the time then he would have to stay with such a loving family.

André was still young, only six, but always eager to have Papa play with him. Surely, he would behave if only to win his father's approval. Yes, she would do everything in her power to keep her father with them for the summer. Then Mama would be happy. She dozed happily off into her own little dreamworld where people were laughing and singing all the time.

"Wake up, my sweet little Clarice," her papa said. As she opened her eyes, she could see the sun coming up behind the figure of her father. He bent over her and lovingly kissed her forehead. "Clarice, look at the beautiful morning sky! We are almost to Lucerne, and the sun is starting to rise. There's a rainbow of gold and orange and red. It is a sign of the beautiful summer to come. We will have such a good time together as a family."

Clarice prayed that it would be so, but she had an uneasy feeling that her happiness would not last. Her mother would scold her for sure, admonishing her that she was too serious for her own good. Well, she would stop thinking those thoughts when Papa finally stayed in one place—with them. Years later, she knew those *thoughts* were part of her intuitive gift—or curse, as was often the case.

The train moved fluidly through the Swiss Alps, around each bend a new vista emerged to please the senses. The shadows cast by the rising sun created an interesting display on the landscape. A nearby lake was shimmering brightly as the ducks and geese were preparing to take off for a day of exploring. "Such a beautiful sight. I know there is no other place in the world like this, Papa!"

"Clarice, when you grow up and become a young woman, you will always hold this piece of paradise close to your heart. But I promise you, there will be many roads that you will travel and on them beauty will abound. You are the sunshine, sweet Clarice, and everywhere you go, the world will be a wondrous place."

Mulhouse, France

The Unsettling

SUMMER STARTED OFF with a bang. When they arrived in Mulhouse the next day, Aunt Marcella and Uncle Jonque were waiting anxiously at the train station. Curiously, her young cousin, Jacques, was missing. Jonque had a very concerned look on his face, and his wife looked even worse. "Merde, Augusto, there is much to tell you." He pulled him aside and whispered, "Antoinette has been beside herself with worry." Antoinette was the official family matriarch, Clarice's great-aunt and her grandmother's older sister. "We must make immediate plans for a trip to Paris for time is of the essence!"

"What nonsense are you speaking, Jonque?" Augusto's stomach was slowly forming a knot in his midsection, giving credence to some of the recent information he had been given. He hoped that Aurelia had not heard the menacing comments from her brother. He knew she was anxiously awaiting the arrival of her mother in a few days. Madame Chevais was Aurelia's anchor, and lately she looked like she needed some mothering.

An angel in the form of Marcella had her cornered, bending her ear. Thankfully, Clarice and Andre had run ahead to see about Jacques and engage in friendly chatter with Bernard, the family caretaker, nanny, butler, and sometimes chauffeur. He could pass as the patriarch of the family and certainly had the level of respect reserved for that position.

"Speak softly so your sister does not hear you!" Unlike her mother, Aurelia was very delicate and easily frightened at least it seemed so in recent years. "We have just arrived and would like to enjoy our first moments in Mulhouse without the rush, rush that we left behind in Cannes," he said to lighten his brother-in-law's mood. Jonque was known for overreacting to any slight problem that might arise.

"Mother has taken ill and is calling for us. She is very weak and may not make it through the night."

"What happened, Jonque? She was in the best of health when I stopped in Paris last month. How could it be possible that such a thing has happened so quickly?"

Jonque hesitated, trying to decide whether he should tell his brother-in-law the truth or wait until after they had a chance to be totally alone. "I will explain more when we arrive at the manor. Perhaps we should have the carriage make the first trip to the manor with the women and children while you and I make the plans for the trip to Paris. I have checked the schedule, and the best we can do is leave first thing in the morning. There is a train to Paris that leaves at eight twenty-five and arrives there around one thirty. We must go."

"Slow down, Jonque. You still haven't told me what's going on," said Augusto. "Aurelia cannot hear us now, and before I totally disrupt our family holiday, you must explain. Has she been ill and we did not know?"

"It…it's not illness, I'm afraid," said Jonque. "I only said that in case Aurelia could hear me. Mother has been the victim of an attempted robbery. She was in the midst of one of her annual audits and consolidations when this happened. We have warned her of the dangers in the past, but you know my mother and her stubbornness and now—oh, dear God." He started to cry softly. "I can't believe this has happened to *Ma Mère*!"

Madame Chevais, as her many loyal workers referred to her with obvious adulation and respect, was also her immediate family's matriarch. Unlike her sister, she was very independent and fearless. Not only was she the keeper of the family history and secrets, but she was also the administrator of the family fortune. It was rumored that the family had amassed a fortune in crown jewels and priceless antiquities beyond anyone's imagining.

Augusto remembered the letter that he had received from the madame two weeks ago. She had shared with him that there were family issues of great importance that she must talk to him about. At the time he received her first letter, he thought it odd that there had been no mention of this when he stopped in Paris the month before.

Unwilling to alarm her sensitive children, Madame Chevais turned to her son-in-law in times of need. Augusto Pontifi was enough of a thoroughbred Italian to be fearless in nature—unlike her own children. Her confidence in her son-in-law calmed her fears. Enough so she had also assured Augusto that this latest piece of family business could wait until later when she joined the family for holiday in Mulhouse.

Aurelia came hurrying over when she saw her brother in the state of panic and despair. "Jonque, Jonque, what is wrong?" Marcella tried to stop her, but it was too late.

"It's Mother, Aurelia. She is in a bad way. I did not want to tell you just yet."

"What do you mean?" Aurelia demanded as Jonque managed to utter that their mother had been badly injured in a robbery attempt. "What are you saying? No, it cannot be!"

Augusto grabbed Aurelia just as she was falling. "Aurelia, my chérie! Jonque, help me lay her down. Marcella, get me a cool rag please. And hurry."

Jonque, flustered and frightened, tried to continue with his explanation of the events that transpired in the past thirty-six hours. "Augusto," he stammered, "you know how Mother insists on personally auditing her business holdings once a year on the last week before summer holiday. The details are sketchy, but Monsieur Duvalier's assistant tried to reach me and ended up sending a messenger instead. The messenger arrived last night on the last train from Paris. He left Paris before many of the details were known, but apparently Monsieur Duvalier found Ma Mère unconscious on the floor when he arrived at the shop for their monthly meeting."

"What happened then, Jonque, and how serious is this?" demanded Augusto.

"I only know what the messenger told me, which was not much, but he is back at the inn in the village, waiting for the return trip in the morning," Jonque continued to stammer.

"We must pay him a visit immediately," said Augusto. "I will demand an accounting from Monsieur Duvalier when we arrive in Paris. Marcella, please take the children and Aurelia back to the manor." Augusto was calmly barking orders now, the natural leader in a time of crisis. "And, Marcella, when Aurelia comes to, please tell her that Ma Mère is injured but will be fine and that I will fill her in with the details later."

Marcella stopped short, confronting Augusto with her usual fearless manner. "What if she demands answers from me before you return? She can be a very strong-willed woman, you know!"

"She will, but you must plead ignorance and assure her that Jonque was overreacting. Tell her we are getting the details from the messenger and I'm making arrangements for us to leave on the morning train to Paris."

Clarice, in the meantime, noticed that there was a commotion taking place on the rail platform and decided to check it out. "Come along, Andre. Let's find Mama and Papa." Before she reached the halfway point, her uncle Jonque turned and rapidly approached them.

"My precious Clarice, I'm going to give instructions to Bernard to take you and the other children to the manor, along with your mother and aunt Marcella. They will be here momentarily."

Paris

The Duvalier Link

THREE DAYS BEFORE *the Pontifi family started their trek to Mulhouse, the family lawyer, Joseph Duvalier, realized that Madame Chevais has discovered some discrepancies in the family books.*

He assessed the current situation much as Napoleon's hangman might before tightening the noose on his helpless victims. *Soon it will be too late for any of Madame Chevais's sniveling children to prevent the inevitable ending to their self-indulged lifestyle.*

Joseph's anger always seethed just below the surface like molten lava in anticipation of the great eruption—soon to eradicate any obstacle in its path. It gave him great satisfaction to think he had the power to reduce life to a lower state of existence!

Joseph Duvalier instinctively knew he would never be totally accepted as one born to the elite group of French society that bordered on royalty. But as the titular head of Duvalier, LaFranc, & Menuet Law Firm, he convinced himself that by conducting noble business on behalf of his many well-heeled clients, somehow his less-than-desirable avocation was elevated through this interaction.

That Marie Chevais enjoyed high society stature by birth continued to irritate him to the point of exasperation, antagonizing him at times when he could ill afford to let his personal feelings interfere with his master plan.

"A farce," he muttered out loud. "I will make sure she will never again see the Louvre on the eve of the Holy Day!"

Born in Luxembourg to a family of struggling peasants trying to eke out a paltry, threadbare existence, the young Duvalier was left to survive on his own gut instincts. Joseph, or Rubin, as his real name had been before the *transformation*, was nonetheless molded into a tough fighter. But where a sense of morality and determination might encourage a young man to approach a chivalrous existence, Duvalier's mind twisted in the ways of the unloved; he was never comfortable in his surroundings.

A Prussian by birth, Duvalier, as a young man, had managed to ingratiate himself to the family of Monsieur De Morny, a close personal friend of Napoleon III. Through this relationship, Duvalier expressed an interest in moving to France which would become his adopted country. In 1862, at the early age of fourteen, he moved to the city of Mulhouse.

There he studied all that was French, but by the time he reached manhood, the Franco-Prussian War had broken out with Germany, laying claim to the Alsace-Lorraine region of which Mulhouse was part, further confusing Duvalier's loyalties.

His adopted family fled to Paris in 1870, leaving all their worldly possessions in the care of the young German. Here began the twisted journey of young Joseph Duvalier.

Managing to use his brilliant mind long enough to pursue studies at the University of Luxembourg, Duvalier acquired the education he needed to become a first-class barrister, enabling him to wind ever tighter the web of deceit and dishonor that would later become the framework of his life.

Standing here now, admiring his image in the mirror, he effected a pirouette, curtsied, and pulled his fingers ever so slightly across gnarled lips, blowing a kiss to his reflection, as if to declare his right to a princely title and all the accoutrements that royalty afforded. The fact that he was only royalty in his imagination had not deterred him from pursuing his latest interest.

Marie Chevais had everything he desired but never could quite capture for himself. It served her right that he would ultimately control her and all the Chevais fortune.

Years later, it was whispered among Parisians that Duvalier had been driven to attack the Chevaises not for altruistic motives, which could be those manifested by a sense of honor in protecting his German ancestry, but by lust. His weakness was the jealously of and lust for Marie and all the trappings he so often denounced publicly.

He had an uncanny ability, however, to justify his actions to those who trusted him, often before they could realize where his madness would take them. In the guise of igniting the mechanism for radical action, which he had already primed, Duvalier prepared for his final move.

It would be easy to protect his reputation as an upstanding French citizen if any of his illegal activities with the Chevais and Pontifi families were uncovered. He had to be sure that as he moved against them, his future plans would be secure.

Paris

Two Days Prior

Aristocratic in appearance, Marie Chevais appeared like many other well-heeled Parisians of the day, but there the similarities ended. Envied and feared by some but respected by most among the powerful elite, the LeMonde, Madame Chevais commanded her own destiny. Bold, daring, and outspoken, she somehow managed to keep her femininity intact—at opposite extremes from her business persona.

At a glance, she looked almost like a beautiful white stallion with a spattering of black in the mane of curls and waves that fell as ringlets to the midpoint of her back. Her toned and fit frame, the result of years of hard work, belied her sixty years. Many a suitor had come under her spell, but there was only one man, other than her beloved Marcel, who captured her heart so many years ago. She sighed, thinking back. There were no regrets, only an occasional painful memory that she wouldn't trade for any amount of love and attention from the current breed of men.

Looking over the pile of records on her desk, she wondered how to get through this latest batch in time to catch the train to Lucerne and then the carriage on to Mulhouse day after tomorrow. Her family was expecting her, and Clarice particularly would be disappointed if she didn't show up on time. She must remember to spend extra time with that dear girl. Aurelia also had acted peculiar lately—letters arriving at rapid rate to ensure that her mother would be coming were a bit unusual, even for her daughter. Everyone's nerves had been on edge—the depressing Prussian Wars and this ugly business of the political unrest, even pulling at family loyalties to each other.

Madame Chevais was reconciling the books in the back of her main showroom. Opulent by any definition, the four-story brownstone appeared chiseled by hand. Magnificent lion heads adorned the four corners on each floor, giving the building its regal bearing. She remembered, as a young woman, bringing Angelo here to meet her parents. The living quarters took up the third and fourth floors while the shop and showrooms could be reached handily from the street. Located at Twenty-Five Rue la Paix, the address added an element of class to the business, along with a sense of built-in security that only resided in the best places in Paris. The ultra-elite within the glittering world of fine jewelers found their place on the Rue la Paix.

To be born into a family such as the Chevaises was a blessing never to be taken for granted as only one who stood on the outside looking in could attest, much like peering through shimmering glass, colored in streams of light-reflected rainbows.

Marie, unlike her peers, had understood at an early age that to be of the elite carried a responsibility to be engaged in the moral rightness of humanity to her fellow man regardless of his station.

Even so, gaiety and fun were the order of the day. Moving beyond the *l'affaire* where Parisians were divided by Nationalists and Revisionists, the sense was that time was being wasted and each man must find his own happiness beyond the politics of the day. Any Frenchman would be the first to tell you the importance of living life to its fullest pleasure. Parisians were known to have their proclivities—among them a certain lust of the flesh.

Art and literature moved hand in hand to solidify Paris's standing in the world as the center of refinement and the educated elite. Very real material and technological advances were being made in the last decades of the nineteenth century. Replacing gaslight, there was electricity, gramophone; there was a functioning telephone by 1879 and, incredibly, a Jules Verne-like wonder, the pneumatique, which allowed people to send each other billets-doux flying through subterranean capsules through the city—one end to the other within an hour.

Marie was thinking about how Aurelia had been spared the bourgeois trappings of Paris when Augusto took her away to his beloved Milano to live shortly after marrying the very young bride. With Marie's blessing and Augusto's prodding, it was easy to make the decision to join him in Milano.

It was on a brief trip to visit with his family a couple of months prior that Augusto asked the somewhat shy Aurelia to marry him. He then accompanied the smitten young woman back to Paris to ask Marie for her hand in marriage.

Aaah, the wedding, an affair to remember! They decided to move the whole thing to Mulhouse, away from Paris and Milano to contain the crowds of curious onlookers. The Pontifi and the Chevais families were equally well established in the glittering society of their respective cities.

Marie remembered how beautiful Aurelia looked in her hand jeweled gown, floating like a princess down the aisle of the cathedral.

It was a fairy-tale wedding, and even though they had moved to the country estate for the festivities, the crowd was estimated to be over one thousand strong, spilling out of the cathedral into the streets of Mulhouse. The entire village was invited, along with family, friends, and the political powerhouses of the day.

The guests traveled from Paris, Milano, and within Mulhouse to pay their respects to the couple. It was to the villagers that the family gave the seats of honor in tribute to the many generations of Chevaises who had grown up living among, playing with, and employing the people of Mulhouse.

She and Angelo, Augusto's father, had been lovers in every sense, souls forever entwined. That they did not marry was of their own doing—Marie understanding her need to stay in Paris to carry on the family business and Angelo betrothed to a distant cousin.

There was no mistaking the fire that burned, molding them forever as one. They could walk away and remain friends because the memories of what they had would endure. And so it was fitting that Aurelia would become Augusto's bride.

Somewhat reluctantly, Marie shifted her focus back to the present. The sun was moving farther into the horizon, casting a muted light and deepening the furrow in her brow. Sitting there brooding, Marie was worried more than ever at the recent turn of events. And for several months, she had noticed inventory items from her shop had been missing yet had not been reconciled to the sold-items lists. Most disconcerting was the fabled Monchartrain Diamond could not be accounted for in the standard records or in the ultra-secure main vault.

And her message to Monsieur Duvalier this afternoon had left her with more questions than ever. He was "too busy" to send a response, leaving the messenger waiting for two hours before giving up.

More disturbing than the disappearance of valuable artifacts and jewelry, Marie had the uneasy sense that key papers were missing—papers outlining all the land holdings and wealth of the Chevais family. They could lead a shrewd manipulator like Joseph to Switzerland.

The family land holdings were vast, and it would be most difficult for him to penetrate at every level given the safeguards that had been built in. Just the same, she knew she must stop him from finding the key to unlock the core Chevais treasury housed separately from the main Swiss cache.

"The scoundrel," she said out loud. "I will catch him at his game. It will just be a matter of time!"

Fifteen years before, she had hoped that Joseph Duvalier was the answer to the Chevais dilemma, solving a mystery mired so deep that the answers were buried within a Swiss bank, the location at that time known only to Madame's late husband, Marcel.

Joseph Duvalier had come to her rescue when Marcel died suddenly. Brilliant at handling the business side of their vast holdings, Marcel had only just begun the process of grooming Marie to handle the erudite details of each facet of the Chevais estate. Not only would she have to manage the day-to-day activities and reaches of a very robust business empire, there were all the holdings housed in Switzerland that needed her attention.

It didn't help that the situation in Alsace-Lorraine interfered with her communication; the easy access back and forth through Basel and back into Mulhouse, France.

After Marcel's death and laden with unbearable sorrow, Madame had set out to find the life raft necessary to keep the estate operating at full speed until such time as she could once again look at her surroundings without weeping.

Marcel had come along a couple of years after her relationship with Angelo had ended. Determined to build a successful career in the business of her parents, she was content to live without the love she had shared with Angelo, certain that no one could bring her the joy that they had shared during their courtship.

Oh, but she was surprised to find in Marcel all that she had with Angelo and yet more, much more. Able to separate herself from Angelo for the good of her career, she could not imagine a life without Marcel.

He was a funny little man, charming her and winning her affections while drawing her respect for his business acuity. He was kind yet commanding in his ways.

Despite being small in stature as many of his family were, he exuded a giant presence. When he walked in a room, all eyes turned to see this man who garnered so much attention and respect. The fabric of the man was written in his eyes, eyes showing immense kindness and love not only for his Marie but also those who came to him in need.

It was easy for Marie to trust people especially with the type of support system she had with Marcel and all those who loved and respected her. Her natural inclination to be inclusive with those around her did not extend to Robert Duvalier. Recommended by Marcel's good friend, Paul Marchand, she held her cynicism in check and agreed to employ Monsieur Duvalier. Whereas Marie was warm and friendly with people as a general rule, there was some undeniable element to him that led her to be more cautious. Ever alert to a woman's intuition, she seldom let down her guard and never discussed the secrets that had yet to be uncovered in Switzerland.

It was Angelo whom she had taken into her confidence a year later. After Marcel's death, she turned in desperation to the man who, many years earlier, long before Marcel, had filled her life with such joy!

She presented her problem to him as a child would come to the father. Angelo, a name that she could only bring to the surface on the rare occasion when her mind was in free flight, unafraid of the consequential pain that the memory would evoke. She let it consume her for the next few moments.

Angelo Pontifi, afraid to leave his own problems, decided to send his son to help Marie on his behalf. It was then the friendship between the young dashing Augusto and Madame Chevais began.

She remembered the day he had entered her shop, how taken aback she was at the similarities in appearance between father and son. It was like losing her loved one all over again, and remembering the loss caused her to gasp.

After what seemed like several minutes, she managed to catch her breath enough to whisper greetings to this younger version of Angelo.

Now thirteen years later, sitting at her desk, she wished that Augusto was here. Her children, Aurelia and Jonque, always thought her eccentric to do a monthly consolidation of all her inventories. They would have opted for Monsieur Duvalier to complete all the tasks, along with his management of the family's entire estate. Her instincts would not allow such folly.

There was something about Joseph that she could never totally trust. He was, by all accounts, a respected member of one of Paris's finest legal establishments. Perhaps she had trusted him too much already.

Housed in the old Paris mime theater, the firm of Duvalier, Menuet, & LaFranc evoked splendor and grandiosity, complete with doormen and a red carpet upon which to enter the grand hall. Those Frenchmen who aspired to show the city their measure of success, even if ill-gotten, could be counted on to employ the services of one of the many barristers on hand.

There was at the core a group representing the well-heeled, genuinely elite segment of the Paris society. Of course, Joseph Duvalier represented the elite and, more subtly, the criminal element when it served his purpose.

Joseph was visibly excited when Paul Marchand called, expressing the need for his services in aiding his good friend, Marie Chevais. A golden opportunity for him to weasel into the Chevaises' inner circle, it was as if his every wish had come true. As with any fledgling relationship, whether professional or personal, they spent countless time together fine-tuning, reinforcing, and cataloging all the family documents. The problems began shortly thereafter.

The business relationship appeared normal in every aspect, except for the obsessive attention Joseph continued to display with regard to Madame's personal schedule and whereabouts. It could be said, and often whispered in and around her circle of friends, that Joseph Duvalier became enamored of the beautiful Marie Chevais to the point of obsession, but that would barely describe the situation. Joseph's motivations extended beyond greed and lust.

Madness and politics worked maliciously within him, creating the perfect tempest waiting to destroy all who came in his path. He had learned well from his gypsy ancestors.

The Incident

ONLY TWO WEEKS ago, she had sent a letter to Augusto, now her son-in-law, expressing her concerns of recent events without going into any detail. Spare him the rhetoric if this turns out to be an old woman's imagination, she decided. Through several messages, they agreed to have a business meeting sometime during the family holiday.

Now she turned her attention back to the books. Strange, there were several entries on the ledger from last October that appeared to have been altered. She made a note to question Joseph about this as well.

Her uneasiness was growing as she proceeded to look for the Monchartrain Diamond. All gems and precious antiquities valued at greater than five thousand francs had been double tagged, and the recorded location addresses were housed in a special vault at the offices of the Duvalier, LaFranc, & Menuet Law Firm.

Every quarter, Marie Chevais would pull inventory randomly and move it to one of her other locations even one unknown to Duvalier himself. It was said that the noble, horn-rimmed owl looking for prey could not compare to the keen awareness Madame Chevais had in all manner of her arrangements.

Aware of the pitfalls in trusting her attorney with all the family secrets, she protected the vast estate in as many directions as possible but could not possibly avoid all intrusion. Diversifying the financial holdings within the estate ensured keeping the control where it should be—with her and her son-in-law, Augusto.

Monsieur Duvalier, be damned. He must never find out about the Swiss account; she swore to herself. It was there among several of her dummy accounts, those created to throw off any would-be intruders, where all records were kept along with certain "grants."

Just then she had the ominous feeling of being watched. Her natural sense of security was altered in that moment—under attack from an unknown source. Brushing the thought aside, she arose from her desk and made her way to the hall door. Marie was unafraid but tentative in her movements toward the door. "This is ridiculous," she bravely exclaimed out loud! "Why am I even taking the time to explore noises that have always had residence here along with the spirits, particularly those of my late husband, Marcel? Merde, what an old fool I have become."

With much bravado, Marie maneuvered through the dimly lit hall toward the showroom, checking in rooms along the way, reassuring all was well.

At that moment, as if caught in the slow motion of an orchestrated act of dramatic impact, an arm reached out and grabbed her around the neck, forcing her back through an open doorway into one of the storerooms housing her fine art collection.

In the flash of enlightenment, Marie knew too well that her fears for her family and the well-being of the Chevais estate had been well-founded. Brutal was the reality, but she fought valiantly, determined not to give up willingly. Mindful that her death would be imminent if she succumbed to the darkness, her will to survive gave her Goliath-like strength.

She managed to pull away from the masked intruder and run for the connector hall, all the while trying to reason her mind to calmness and clarity. Looking for any semblance of a weapon with which to defend herself, she remembered the scabbard hanging just inside the door to the Palazzo Roma Room at the other end of the hall.

So close now, she could feel and smell the stale breath of the intruder on her neck reaching like a viper to snare his prey. He had already injured her in the scuffle to get away, but she was strong, managing to scratch his face and rake her thumbnail across his eye, causing him to scream in pain.

This time, Marie knew she would have to make it count. Moving toward the sword, she grasped it and swung around as hard as she could, striking the intruder with all her might!

It might have made a difference if she had connected with the blade rather than having it deflected by his arm. *She knew that time was running short, and she lunged at the man with all her might, knocking him to the floor but not before he had cut his head on the mahogany armoire standing sentry next to the door. Even in his pain, his rage pushed him to jump up and grab Madame Chevais and thrust her fiercely into the fireplace.*

He stopped as quickly as he had moved, assessing the scene, confident that he had taken care of the problem. Joseph and the others would be pleased. Well, the others would have to understand that this was just an unpleasant "accident"—necessary to keep all their secrets.

The irony was that the "group'" wanted to conduct this little raid but take all measures to ensure that Marie would not be harmed. The idiots thought stealing and dismantling the estate bit by bit could continue without her knowledge.

Joseph had other plans. There was never any doubt that Marie was the target of this little excursion.

Quickly, the intruder, moving silently like a hunter through the brush, worked to remove any trace of recognizable, identifying evidence from the room. After finishing his kill, he made his way out of the area.

Unknown to Robard, he had not finished his assignment as planned. Critically injured and with little strength left in her battered body, Marie tried to move toward the door. Her movements, akin to pushing a boulder up hill, were labored and her breathing hampered by her crushed ribs and mangled arm.

Even in her dazed state, she could sense the stillness in the room. "God help me. I must find the document for Augusto," she rasped. "I must move to the armoire. I must." With her life in imminent danger, Marie pulled her broken body across the expanse to the chest, and from underneath, she reached for a rectangular envelope taped to the bottom.

Tucking it in the only place she could find, Marie gasped one last time and whispered, "Where the spirit has will, so also I live for my heart is yours, my darlings, for all eternity." At that moment, she felt a sharp pain and then nothing.

Paris

The Day After

In a section of Paris known for the exchange of goods and money through nefarious channels, a meeting was taking place that would forever alter the lives of the Chevais and Pontifi families. The innocuous-looking building on Rue de Rainier was a good front for a business enterprise that may not otherwise have qualified for the term *legitimate*.

Alive with activity in a small parlor on the second floor, an assemblage of characters was having a lively discussion about the subject at hand—the question of why they were called together at this early hour. It could only mean trouble! The infamous Monsieur Duvalier was holding court as usual. But this time, he had very important matters to discuss with his cohorts—or coconspirators as was the case.

"Monsieur Duvalier, what could possibly be so urgent that we must meet before daybreak?" said one elderly gentleman, looking somewhat disheveled in the hastily clad attire he managed to throw on. "My bed was nice and warm!" Olivier would have passed as the most gentile of the band of conspirators.

"I have come from a nice warm woman myself," grumbled a younger strapping version of Mr. Duvalier. Pierre Duvalier was Monsieur Joseph Duvalier's younger brother.

"Pierre, you can keep your pants buttoned long enough to hear what I have to tell you," said Joseph Duvalier.

"This could not wait until later in the day when it would attract less attention?" Paul Marchand asked plaintively after listening intently to the banter. Paul could be classified as the critic of the group. Always the pragmatist, he ventured on to declare to anyone who would listen that "we are risking much by meeting this way."

It was a known fact that one of their group, Robard, was a renegade bandit wanted by the French government. There were signs in the past month that the Parisian gendarmes may have been watching the activities of their close-knit little "community."

Monsieur Duvalier called the meeting to order. "We have had an incident! Our timetable must be changed. You all know that one of my clients, Madame Chevais, has been one of our points of interest. I have personally worked with her for the past fifteen years, long enough to gain her trust, which I must tell you, was not easy. Aside from the fact that she is stubborn and very independent, her brilliance in business is indisputable. She is not like a woman, rather like a shrewd businessman. In this case, however, her instincts may not have served her well!

"Last evening, one of our own, Monsieur Robard, paid a visit to Madame Chevais's showroom. I had asked him to conduct a preliminary scouting for us so we could execute the next phase of our little operation. Unfortunately, he was supposed to go later in the evening—after my meeting with Madame Chevais. She was in her office and heard Robard enter from the rear door in the alley. Normally I come to the front door and she gives me entry into the office."

Paul said, "Why in the world would he enter her building without being positive that no one was on premises?" Sensing that something significant had occurred, he confronted Joseph. "What has happened to Madame Chevais?" Becoming very alarmed, he shouted, "You were not supposed to let any harm befall her!"

"Unfortunately, when Robard entered the building, Madame came to investigate the noise he made upon entry. You know how fearless she is, particularly when defending her property and so-called principles! I'm afraid there was an altercation, and in the scuffle, Robard hit Madame. This caused her to fall into a metal sculpture, seriously injuring her."

An elderly gentleman spoke up, "Do not speak of such a thing. Only madmen would harm Madame Chevais! You assured me she would be treated with respect and not manhandled like some common patsy."

Standing beside him, Monsieur Paul Marchand was visibly distressed and not pleased with the occurrences of the night before. Collecting himself momentarily, he asked, "How badly hurt is she, and will she be all right?"

Olivier also was disturbed at this news. "I warned you that Robard was too rough, just a common criminal, not of our ilk! This is a dangerous business, breaking and entering into a respected woman's property, let alone causing her injury and possible death!"

"I regret that she has sustained serious injuries and is, at this moment, undergoing surgery at the hospital." Joseph did not bother to tell them that his only regret was Robard's failure to kill Marie as originally planned. The witch had fought as a man, wounding him in the process, enough to save her life.

"This is unconscionable!" Paul sputtered. "Where is Robard anyway? Has he gone mad?"

"Robard is temporarily out of commission, and we will not speak of him if anyone asks. In the meantime, the courier is already en route to Mulhouse to inform the family."

"That is convenient, isn't it, Joseph?" Paul spat out. The hatred they had for each other seethed openly now.

Joseph gave him a look which clearly was a warning, not just for Paul but anyone in the room who dared question the great Duvalier!

Leaving Mulhouse

AUGUSTO SIDLED THE horse and carriage over to the stables adjoining La Rue Blanc Inn, wasting no time in formalities. Addressing the attendant, Augusto asked, "Please tell me, where is Monsieur Gerard, the innkeeper? We must see him immediately."

"Of course, Monsieur Pontifi. He is expecting you." Augusto was well-known in the village; the years of summers spent at the manor, along with his benevolence to his servants, all of whom were villagers, endeared him to all the townspeople. He, after all, had married their precious Aurelia.

Along with a level of reverence, there was an unwritten code they would protect their beloved Chevais and Pontifi families. Word had already arrived, most likely from Bernard, that the messenger from Paris must remain until Augusto's arrival.

At that moment, Monsieur Gerard arrived with the man known as Claude Molyneux, a courier sent from Paris.

"Monsieur Pontifi, my condolences on the disturbing news of Madame Chevais's, shall we say, mishap. Monsieur Duvalier would himself have traveled to inform you of the recent events but must stay to manage the affairs of the Chevais's estate, as you must know."

Augusto looked at the man in disbelief, knowing full well there was much more to this story along with the troubling feeling that Claude, representing himself as the courier, was more than a mere messenger. It did not assuage Augusto's feelings of uneasiness that he appeared nervous and anxious to avoid any conversation.

"Monsieur, what is your name?" asked Augusto.

"Claude Molyneux, at your service," intoned the courier with an air of importance.

"Well, Monsieur Molyneux, why don't you tell me what has transpired in Paris? And don't leave out any of the details."

"As I told Monsieur Jonque Chevais, I am only the lowly messenger for the LaFranc, Minuet, & Duvalier Law Firm. Apparently, a common thief broke in to the Chevais property and unknowingly came upon the madame. There was a scuffle. She fought back mightily and, in the ensuing melee, was severely injured. Uh, the point—"

"How do you know this, Monsieur?" interrupted Augusto. His voice became as cold as steel, setting a trap for the unsuspecting courier.

"Ah, Monsieur Pontifi, as the center for Paris' premier diamond and precious gem dealers, you know how vulnerable the House of Chevais has become, uh, since the demise of Monsieur Marcel and…" Hesitating, Claude realized he had said too much. Augusto prodded for further comment by agreeing with the imbecile.

Trying to smooth over his statements, he proceeded. "Well, you know word gets around, giving encouragement to all manner of low-life to take advantage of the situation where they might not have otherwise taken." Augusto observed that this last bit of idiocy was spoken by a member of the low-life scum.

It only took a few minutes of conversation with the hapless man for the cold reality to hit Augusto, the blast of ice forming in his gut the answer! It would serve no purpose to show his hand now. Claude was only a pawn in a much larger game! He could contain the rage building, the warrior waiting to avenge a wrong, as long as needed to save Madame Chevais.

There was a gnawing at his very core, the fear gathering momentum, waiting to consume him and anything in its path. He was pretty certain Joseph Duvalier had orchestrated the so-called mishap with the madame.

How could he have missed the thinly disguised desperation in Madame's last letter, covered up by her staunch stoicism? He should have recognized the need to take immediate action and not have allowed himself to fall into a trap of becoming ambivalent to danger—an omission only an amateur would have allowed. Time was of the essence; he must get to Paris as quickly as possible.

There was no time to lose, of this he was certain. At that precise moment, Jonque came around the corner. It was better he had finished his business with the courier, lest he ask too many questions.

"Augusto, where is the messenger? I wanted to ask my own questions. How is Ma Mère, and what happened?" The questions rushed at Augusto like a charge of the bulls pushing through the square in Pamplona, Spain, where he had spent some of his youth.

"Jonque, he does not have the answers. He is a mere dangling puppet of the Duvaliers. We will sift through and get to the bottom of this."

Adept at maneuvering around his brother-in-law, Augusto avoided answering the question about Madame Chevais's state of health. The very thought filled him with sick dread. He loved her like his own sweet mother, maybe more, certainly at a different level. Heroine worship had stayed with him from the first moment he understood her.

They met through unusual circumstances. It was thirteen years ago when he had been summoned suddenly by his father. Indicating an emergency, Augusto hurried back to Milano, expecting the worst, hoping his own frail mother had not taken ill. Arriving in Milano, he made his way out to the family estate, winding through deep emerald-green blankets of the leaf-borne trees of the olive groves. Being surrounded by the sweet-and-sour blooms of the majestic olive trees, always gave him a sense of oneness with his ancestral home! If he could capture this scene and the reminders of the beauty therein, he would forever have his heaven on earth.

As a young boy, he often spent hours every day riding through the groves, pretending he was the prince of his own kingdom, complete with intriguing hideaways, one of which was nestled in the thickest part of the olive grove on a patch of land known as the Thirty Miles. It had been created through an aberration of olive tree vines that formed a tunnel just the right size for the adventurous boy.

Augusto shook off the nostalgia and continued on his task. Mindful of the urgency in his father's message, he could not luxuriate in the beauty of his surroundings. Often on his visits home, he would stop and sit on the hillside and look over the vast expanse of the olive groves, soaking in the pungent aroma of the oil-laden fruit and filling his senses with the bounty that he was sure God bestowed upon the Pontifis.

The hour was getting late and his father was waiting on him. Rounding the last turn, he could see the villa ahead. Resplendent in a rustic coat of aged stucco, the old Pontifi villa had borne four generations of sons and daughters to carry on the many encoded layers of tradition only those of the blood could peel away. Palatial in appearance with four massive rooms, Villa Venetta carried the centuries of wear as only an ancient structure of the stone-embedded stucco could, wearing her wounds with pride for her history and standing majestically with the promise of her future.

He remembered how as children they enjoyed moving stealthily through the halls, pretending to be the gallant warriors defending their castle. As was often the case with big Italian families, the children were prized above all else, encouraged to be playful in their actions and even spoiled.

Still reminiscing, his attention was drawn to a lone rider there in the distance, framed in muted light, rapidly coming toward him. As the rider neared, it was clear that, whatever crisis was upon the Pontifi family, it had escalated.

"Hello, Father!" Before he could continue with his greeting, the burly figure of Angelo Pontifi came within twenty feet of his son. Jumping from his horse, he quickly ran over to Augusto, addressing him with the formal style of business partner to business partner, absent the warmth they normally shared on greeting each other after a long absence. Mutual respect modified by the urgency left no time for niceties—at least for the present.

"Augusto, my son, you must go to Paris. My old friend, Marie Chevais, is in need of our help!"

He knew what that meant: his father's first love would only call on him when there was an emergency and no one else in which to confide.

"Come to the table now and let your mother see your face. She will want to make sure you are well-fed, my son. You must understand we will only speak of this now and leave it to the olive branches as we make our way back to the villa."

"I do, Father. No need to worry Mama."

With those words spoken, Angelo finally embraced his son in the grand Italian fashion embodied in the spirit of two men with the same blood.

"Ah, Augusto, it is so good to see you, my son. We have so little time together, but what you are doing now is very important to me. Thank you, my son."

The evening was festive and filled with love of the family for one another. His mother made sure to spoil her eldest son. Good food and wine gave way to hours of shared memories from the large family, often moving them to laughter and, occasionally, tears. It gave Augusto a warm feeling to know he came from such a place.

The next day, he started his trek to Paris, arriving the afternoon of the second day. Paris was not part of his normal travels, so this would be an exploration not only of his mind but also of his senses once he accomplished his mission.

Winding through the narrow cobblestoned streets, imagining the early damage seen in the aftermath of the Paris Commune caused Augusto to reflect on the changes taking place. It was to his relief that the filth and disease that was rampant in Paris in the earlier part of the 1800s was gradually being cleaned up by Haussmann and his team. Albeit unsettling to see, he reasoned that the destruction of the buildings and moving the poor out to other areas was necessary. It reminded him, once again, of his home near Milano and how fortunate they were to have escaped the ravages of war and destruction.

To The Manor

THE RIDE TO the manor sufficed to keep the very active children enthralled while whispered conversation continued between Marcella and Aurelia.

"Look, Jacques, the geese are gathering over Fontana pond!" exclaimed Clarice. "This is a magical place, isn't it?"

"I bet we could fly over the pond, just like the geese, Clarice!"

"Oh, Jacques, you are so silly!"

When Jacques looked disappointed that his little game wasn't to be played, Clarice quickly said, "Well, perhaps we could pretend to swoop down, touching the lily pads and landing on the water just like the geese. But remember, it is the ever-majestic swan, moving silently and smoothly, that calls to us, reminding us of all the birds. He is the most graceful. We would become like the swan, gliding over the pond, never worrying about coming to shore. When our waltz ended, we could soar up into the sky and never come back." She paused. "You know, Jacques, we could even fly over the oceans and see the world."

Clarice was getting carried away with her own dreams of flight. Much to her cousin Jacques's delight, she became totally enraptured with their little charade.

"Now who is silly?" said Jacques as he pulled Clarice's braid.

"Ouch, you beast," she laughed.

Andre wanted to join the fun. "Who's flying, Clarice? Can I pretend too?"

"Of course, you may, my little brother. But you know pretend means we really can't fly. We just, well, play-act that we do." She always had a soft spot for Andre and mothered him too much. Frail like a small bird, she worried about him. He was like their mother in so many ways—fearful of life and weak of health, driving her to overprotect him.

Thinking of her mother brought Clarice's attention back to the present. Peculiar, she thought, that Papa and Uncle Jonque remained behind. Some feeble excuse about making train reservations for travel later on was the best they could do. She suspected another reason but couldn't get an answer from her mother.

Like the veil of darkness, an unexplainable feeling of doom settled over her and the merriment of a few minutes ago left as quickly as those geese taking flight, frightened by the sounds of unknown intruders.

There were times when her intuition served her well, but right now it only made her nervous. Looking over at her mother and Aunt Marcella did not help. They were definitely upset about something.

Stealing glances, it almost looked like her mother had been crying. Yes, in fact she was sure of it. She moved over to her mother at the other end of the carriage and spoke softly, out of Jacques's and Andre's earshot. "Mama, whatever is wrong?" she practically begged. "You must tell me right now," she demanded.

"Oh, Clarice, ma chérie, it is Ma Mère. She has, well, been injured in a fall."

"Mama, no, it isn't so!" Clarice could feel her heart beating heavily. Aurelia's words were like weights nestled in Clarice's stomach. The young girl tried to understand what her mother had just said.

"Clarice, it is even worse than that. Forgive me but I cannot lie to you." Aurelia was really beside herself now, not helping the situation. "Your grandmother was injured when someone broke into the studio two nights ago. Apparently, there was a scuffle and knowing Ma Mère, she fought like a tiger."

Aurelia tried to calm herself after seeing the look on her daughter's face. She mustered as much bravado as she could but still stammered. "Ma chérie, she will be fine. You know the strength of your grandmother."

Clarice was absorbing the shock while trying to pull her thoughts together. Unlike other girls her age, she possessed an inner strength on which she could rely. A combination of her grandmother's characteristics, along with the driving need she felt to protect her mother, compelled her to force back any tears or hysterics that a normal nine-year-old might display.

There will be time later to cry, she thought. *Right now I must help my mother!*

"Mama, you are right. Grandmother is not like others. She will fight like a queen, not unlike the great queen, Eleanor of Aquitaine."

Clarice thought of her dear Ma Mère fondly. All her dreams and aspirations were fueled by intimate fireside chats or garden walks with Marie Chevais during family holidays. A bold woman, she was unafraid to speak out sternly, particularly on matters of importance to Clarice's own parents but was soft and gentle with her grandchildren.

Oh, how she wanted to be like her someday! Grand-mère really listened when Clarice would describe her desires and wishes for the future. It was a convergence of the minds—the old, Marie's, and the young, Clarice's—that ignited her ambitions in life. That she wanted to dance might not have appealed to her mother, but Grand-mère was so excited and encouraging that Clarice wanted to scream for joy! She always believes in me!

The bond between them was strong, and Marie had a special place in her heart for Clarice. As a toddler, she would follow Marie around, never losing sight of her. It was comical at times to see the miniature of the great woman shadowing behind, walking as her grandmother walked—assured and in control, yet not out of nappies.

Clarice, wise beyond her years, reflected now on the conversations overheard. She had a sense that this intrusion must have been serious because her grandmother would never have taken any chances unless forced into action.

PART THREE

Jackie

The Aftermath (January 2005)

SHE HEARD A name through the fog. "Jackie, Jackie, wake up. Please, honey… It's Mom."

If only she could focus. Not clear. Why couldn't she open her eyes?

Doris was gazing at her battered daughter, a fractured shell of the beauty she had once been. How could she have survived such a force? the hospital staff whispered. They didn't know her daughter and the strength of will that seeped through every cell and fiber, healing and mending this broken body.

"Dammit, Jackie, I know you're in there! Can you hear me? Answer me!" she yelled. The crusty old woman smoothed down her daughter's hair like a mother does with a new baby, trying to groom the little sprigs that seemed to sprout up in odd little places.

Christmas 2004 had come and gone, an endless parade of friends and relatives passing through, a testament to Jackie's heart, one that embraced so many with warmth and love. This last week her son-in-law could barely make it through the stress as day after day there was no change, so Doris took matters in her own hands.

She made him take a break, sending him home after only an hour each time he came up to the hospital. After the first three weeks, he could no longer look at his wife lying there in a coma. To save his sanity and keep the business going, he limited his time to one hour per day knowing his mother-in-law would send out an alarm if he needed to be there.

As she fussed with her little girl, a low mumble came out of what looked like it could have been a mouth.

"Ma-Ma, when are we going to be in Paris?" she whispered coarsely.

Doris almost jumped out of her skin with joy, not quite comprehending what Jackie had mumbled but quite sure that she had just witnessed the breakthrough everyone had been praying for over the past two months.

"How many more miles, Ma-Ma?"

After Doris calmed down for a minute, she ran for the doctor, panting as she caught up with the attending physician who was making rounds. "Dr. Jamison, come quick! She's talking. I believe she's about to wake up!"

They both ran back into the room, and to Doris's deep disappointment, Jackie had not opened her eyes. The mumbling started again. "Mom, are we close to Paris? Where are Uncle Henri and Aunt Paulette? We must find them."

Dr. Jamison looked puzzled but compassionate, nonetheless, as he posed his question to the "sometimes difficult" mother of his critically injured patient.

"There's a good chance that her mind is pulling data from childhood, filed away in the anterior lobes of the brain."

"Does that mean she isn't waking up?" the very distressed mother pressed.

"It only means that she hasn't awakened yet, but this could be a good sign. I'd like for you to keep talking to her. Find out where she is in her development and try to bring her forward. You'll have to prod and pull the data or, more specifically, her past recollections each step of the way. Don't give up even when Jackie resists, and she most certainly will balk at the constant intrusion. If we can move her through to her current time frame, we should see a marked change in her cognitive abilities."

Exiting the room a few minutes later, Dr. Jamison left a very excited Doris to *work* on the woman, who slightly resembled the beautiful daughter that was once Jackie, lying in the bed.

Doris didn't care that people thought her ignorant and just a little emotionally unstable. She had long ago given up any of the trappings of the breeding to which she had been exposed while growing up.

Her sweet dear mother, Giselle, her French name but called Pat here in America, was the quintessential French lady so often defined by poets in their musings of the perfect woman—well-bred and versed in the ways of the rich and genteel of French society.

Giselle had tried to shield Doris from the tyrannical father she had the misfortune to irritate on a daily basis. It just wasn't fair that she was singled out as the difficult one, but that seemed to be her lot in life.

Paul Perry was a good man in many ways, and Giselle had followed her heart to marry him and come to America so many years ago. His belief system mirrored what many young men raised in Ohio farm country subscribed to which was that women were meant to stay in the home tending to the family. To his dismay, his unruly middle child did not go along with his way of thinking!

Yes, Giselle had been a naive young French maiden, but it was World War I, after all, and times were difficult. He was the handsome young driver for General Pershing, parked and patiently waiting outside while the general paid his respects to Clarice and Henri, Giselle's parents.

After multiple visits, it was obvious the young man had fallen for the beautiful young woman. Doris's grandmother, Clarice Bonnebeau, was taken with Paul and gave her blessings to them. Henri, on the other hand, was somewhat reluctant to let go of his little girl. It was only after Clarice had pleaded with Henri that he finally relented.

The war was still waging although winding down in Paris. His son, Henri Jr., could take on the family business when he came of age, allowing Giselle to leave the country and not feel as if she was shirking her family duties.

She was so beautiful, like her mother, he mused. Oh, the memories of Clarice, a vision to his eyes the first time he spotted her on stage at the Folies Bergère!

It wasn't easy bringing her around, and much of the baggage she carried still weighed heavily on her to this day! He only hoped his beloved little Giselle could be happy living in a new country called America. These were strange times with the instability of the war, so Henri reluctantly decided that he must let her go.

Jackie

PARIS (April 1954)

JACKIE SAT IN the back seat of the car, looking out at the scenery while her parents were busy talking in the front seat. She could hardly contain her excitement at the thought they would be entering Paris in about four more hours.

Her uncle Henri and aunt Paulette would be waiting eagerly for their arrival. They were really her great-aunt and uncle—her precious grandmother's brother and sister-in-law. She thought about her grandmother with longing. There was a special connection between them. She wasn't sure exactly why, but Gram always seemed to understand and give her extra affection whenever possible. Her father was a military officer so they were always moving around the world. Seeing her gram was rare.

She loved her parents too, but they were part of the reason she felt so detached at times. At ten years old, Jackie was still considered a child, but she considered herself a grown-up. Old beyond her years, as one of Mother's so-called friends had said. The old biddy was gossiping about her parents as usual. It was hard to keep anything quiet in military housing, and the walls were really thin. If she could just pretend that it didn't bother her! At times it was possible, but only when she pretended to be invisible. Life in her house was different from her friends', so maybe that's why Gram made certain to show she was loved.

Jackie certainly felt like the mother in this family, taking care of her younger brothers and keeping them from hearing everything. What she heard when her parents were fighting would have made them cry, but she was tough. She knew Bill, her brother three years younger, had heard a couple of their fights, and she would always hurry to hold him in her arms, soothing him until he quit crying.

"Jackie, you're a million miles away!" her mother said as she turned around to look at her.

Jackie studied her. She was a beautiful woman in her own way. Doris had a mysterious dark look which was, as she heard her father say too many times, seductive to men. After checking it out in the dictionary, she figured out that her mother must be attractive and looked at by other men. Of course, she flaunted it all over the post, according to one of the bigmouth neighbors. Jackie suspected they may have thought her hard of hearing or, perhaps, too naive to understand. No wonder her father often seemed angry and much of the time anxious to keep an eye on her mother.

There was no doubt that Doris was absolutely, madly in love with Clayte, her husband of twelve years. He was tall and handsome with movie star looks, which did nothing to dispel her mother's feelings of insecurity. She heard her mother say more than once that he was enticing women to throw themselves at him. Of course, that was usually at a shout when they were fighting.

Where her mother was dark and pretty, her father was blond, blue-eyed, and handsome—at least in Jackie's mind. She guessed her mother was also very jealous of all the women who were too friendly with her father.

Her father was bigger than life—a hero to all who appreciated the sacrifices made by their military men. He was always being appointed to do special things for the military. She remembered that, just last year, he was selected from all the men on the base—officers or enlisted—to escort Linda Darnell, the famous movie star. During her tour of Europe, Miss Darnell had been brought to their military base and the general had personally asked

Clayte to escort the beautiful actress. Boy, that sure didn't settle well with her mother.

"What are you thinking about, Jackie?" her father asked. "If you don't come out of that trance soon, we'll be in Paris and you'll miss all the sights." He worried about her, aware she shouldered more than any young girl should ever have to. It hurt him to realize he was partially the cause for her current detachment. Maybe someday she would forgive him and understand what caused the constant bickering between him and Doris. Of course, he wasn't sure that he'd ever understand it totally.

It had been a long journey—and often through hell—with Doris. He tried to be patient, but she knew how to get him going. If only he could contain his temper! No child should ever be exposed to the kinds of battles that were going on in their house. Only he knew the reason for Doris's instability, and he'd be damned if the children should ever find out. If she ever acted normal for one day, he'd be shocked.

When he had time to think about his role in the battleground, Clayte had to admit to himself that he couldn't handle the liquor and Doris too. It was his escape from the constant bickering.

Jackie looked up at her father and acknowledged him with a smile. "I'm just looking at everything, Dad, and the countryside is so peaceful here."

Peace was something she always looked for in her young life. They had lived with her grandparents at least three times when her father was sent by the Army to some remote place. Even though she missed him a lot when he was gone, life was easier and more peaceful with her grandparents.

Better still when she lived with them and her mother was gone too. Staying with her grandparents for more than a few days and having them all to herself happened only a couple of times, and when it did, life seemed normal—maybe even like what other kids her age experienced.

It seemed when her mother and father were together, they were either fighting or making up. When they made up, everything would be okay for a while—in fact, really grand! There was no in-between for this family. Their mutual jealousy kept them always on edge.

This last episode was really frightening, with Jackie intervening to keep someone from being killed. Her mother had the capacity to make her father furious, and when he lost his temper, he was a different person. She was afraid of him at those times.

She suspected the reason they included her in this trip to Paris was because they felt guilty about the last big fight and what Jackie had witnessed. She wanted to bury it so deep in her mind that the pain would go away forever. But the harder she tried, the worse it got. If Bill-Bill, her affectionate name for her little brother, hadn't been exposed to this last episode, she thought perhaps she'd feel better—but maybe not.

How could a young sensitive boy withstand the emotional upheavals taking place in his family environment almost daily? He seemed so nervous all the time, a constant reminder to Jackie of the need to protect him.

Austria

Two Months Prior

Her thoughts drifted to a couple of months earlier, back to their apartment in Austria. They had been cooped up for several days because of an unusually severe snowstorm. She could tell her parents were ready to get out and she would be stuck babysitting as usual. Not that Jackie really minded because it was nice when she was left with the responsibility of taking care of her brothers. The only thing was, how would they be when they came home? She tensed up thinking about it. At least with them gone, she could help control the temperament in the room.

She got her wish and, soon, had the freedom she wanted. Most of the evening she read stories to Bill while rocking Joe. Finally, she put the boys to bed in the back bedroom. When she checked later on, they were sound asleep like little angels.

She later went to bed, concerned that her parents had not come home yet. "Of course, having them home would just mean more yelling and fighting." She sighed. Her bedroom was right off the dining room and had sliding translucent glass doors separating the two rooms so she could hear everything in the whole apartment from front to back. Jackie slept fitfully. Finally, she could hear the clock gong in the background, signaling that it was 3:00 a.m.

Where were they, she wondered. It certainly was late—later than they normally stayed out. Oh well, it would be quiet as long as they were gone. At that moment, she heard Bill come running down the hall. "I'm scared," he said. "I saw a ghost in the closet."

"Well, come on in and get in bed with me! You probably had a bad dream, Bill-Bill."

Jackie knew he had bad dreams every night, and it broke her heart because he was so frightened all the time. She was angry at her parents for always fighting in front of him, and she was fiercely determined to protect him.

Bill had settled in the bed with his sister and was soon sound asleep. She had started to drift off herself when she heard a loud commotion, which could only mean her parents coming home. It was possible everyone in the building heard them come in. As usual, they had been drinking way too much.

Her heart started to pound furiously as she tried to cover Bill's head and ears with his blankie, hoping he wouldn't wake up. But it was impossible to keep him from hearing their yelling, and he began to cry.

After listening to them screaming at each other and hearing objects hitting the wall, there were a couple of seconds of silence. All of a sudden, the wall of glass that separated her bedroom from the dining room shattered!

Quickly, Jackie scooped up her brother and ran down the hall to put him in the bedroom with the baby, Joe. Bill was sobbing and holding on to her for dear life. "It's okay, honey. Mommy and Daddy were just playing and accidentally broke the glass," she explained to a hysterical little boy. About that time, Baby Joe started hollering. Boy, she had her hands full this time. After a few minutes of soothing and petting Bill while holding Joe, they both went to sleep.

She vowed that *they* would never scare Bill again if it was the last thing she ever did—her vow to protect him made with all the bravado she could muster. She immediately marched back down the hall to the living room to confront her parents.

She never expected to see the scene before her eyes. At first glance it looked as if her father was dead. He was lying on the floor with his eyes closed and blood pouring from an open wound on his head. Her mother was rocking back and forth, crying and pleading for Clayte to wake up.

"What have you done to Daddy?" she yelled at her mother, forgetting all about the boys. "You killed him! You killed him!"

"No, no he's just knocked out. I didn't mean to hit him so hard. I...Oh dear, what have I done?" She shook him. "Wake up, Clayte," Doris cried and then started sobbing.

"You're drunk," Jackie said sadly. "Daddy's drunk too, isn't he?" Her mother calmed down and looked at her.

"I'm sorry, honey," she slurred. "We were just having a little discussion." Jackie noticed her Mother's eye was black. Suddenly aware that her mother had been defending herself in the fight with her father, she softened.

"What happened to your eye? Did he hit you again?" Her mother was crying softly now and nodding yes. "I'm sorry about your eye, Mom, but why can't you and Daddy act like other parents?"

With that, she ran out of the living room and back down the hall to her brothers. She wanted to forget everything about this evening. Jackie's disappointment in her parents was an ever-unyielding weight, determined to crush the very life out of her, like a boulder that had to be moved up the mountain on the backs of those who carried the weaknesses of others.

Finally, huddling up with her brothers and secure in the knowledge that the worst was over, as somehow it always seemed to evolve, she slept for a few hours.

The next morning, in spite of the turmoil from the night before, everything appeared to be calm. It never ceased to amaze her that her parents could wreak such havoc and then act all lovey-dovey. She noticed with unbridled astonishment that there was a huge bouquet of flowers on the coffee table.

Jackie was unable to understand how such a violent fight could so easily be swept away with a few hours of sleep and a silly bunch of flowers. "How disgusting! I'm going to do everything possible to make sure Billy and Joe-Joe don't have to be afraid again," she vowed out loud.

Doris

Secrets (April 1954)

JACKIE SNAPPED BACK to the present as they rounded the last turn on the Rue de Montague. All of a sudden, there in the distance, they could see the large imposing structure, rising up, towering over all the others. It looked like a perfectly shaped silver Christmas tree, but as large as a mountain. "Wow, what is that over there?" she asked excitedly.

"That's the Eiffel Tower," her mother said. "You can actually ride up to the top in an elevator and see forever."

"Oh, Mom, Dad, can we do that please?"

"Sure, honey, I don't see why not. This trip is for you too. Dad and I want you to enjoy yourself. We'll see all the great Paris landmarks while we're here. I have a little surprise for you. There are some interesting facts that I just happened to have written down for this precise moment. The Eiffel Tower is 986 feet high and was constructed between 1887 and 1889. At one time, it was the tallest structure in the world. Most French people know the contractor was a gentleman named Alexandre Gustave Eiffel, a French engineer. What they don't know is he also designed the internal structure of our Statue of Liberty!"

Doris looked over her shoulder to see if her daughter was still paying attention and was pleasantly surprised at the excitement expressed on the precocious girl's face, prompting her to continue.

"One more item you might be interested in and can use for your next school project is the reason it was built. The French government commissioned the Eiffel Tower as part of the Universal Exhibition and to celebrate the centennial of the French Revolution."

"That is so interesting." Jackie exhaled and, in the next intake of breath, blurted, "What about Uncle Henri and Aunt Paulette? Will they be able to come too?"

"Of course, dear, if they have time," Doris said.

Doris couldn't help but think how refreshing it was to hear Jackie sound like a young girl instead of an adult burdened with too many of life's problems.

Life, it was funny how it twisted and turned much like the branches on a beautiful rose bush—filled with the promise of new buds yet covered with thorns, poised to sting if moved the wrong way. Sometimes when one disease took hold, it killed the whole bush. She wondered if that's how their lives had become—diseased and withering on the vine.

God, how she hated that she contributed so much to Jackie's problems! Peace seemed to elude her, and the turmoil in her mind seemed endless. If only Clayte loved her the way she loved him, life would be so much better for all of them. His wandering eye kept her on edge all the time. Doris knew for a fact that he had been philandering for over a year, maybe more. The first time she found out about another woman, she could have cut his heart out on the spot. After that, Doris became jaded and somewhat desensitized to his philandering ways, but not entirely!

She sighed. Damn him! It made her mad all over again just thinking about the hussy Clayte had been involved with recently. He even promised her that it would never happen again, but she knew differently. Doris had told him that she'd leave if he did this again, but in her heart, she knew that she was too weak to pull that off.

Her mind drifted off to another day, a nightmare in the making. She was busy at her job as secretary to the medical supply captain. In typical military fashion, she was holed up in a small corner of the large supply warehouse. Certainly not the most glamorous spot, but her boss was great. Aside from the kids, this job was the one bright spot in her depressing life.

She and Clayte fought all the time these days. His jealousy over her boss, unwarranted but nevertheless relentless, kept things stirred up at home. Clayte would drink every night when he was home. When he got drunk, he became even more belligerent and abusive. The kids were suffering, particularly Jackie. *Someday*, she thought, *I'll have to do something about it.*

Just then, the telephone rang and jarred her out of the madness that was consuming her. "Hello, Forty-First Medical Supply Unit, Doris speaking."

"You don't know me, Mrs. Dade, but I think you'll be interested in what I have to say," a low sultry voice whispered in the phone.

"Who is this?" Doris asked, a little wary and sensing that she was about to hear more than she wanted.

"It doesn't matter who I am, just what I have to tell you."

"This really isn't a good time. If you need my boss, he's out of the office right now," she declared.

"No, you're the one I need to talk to about my *little* problem."

"Problem? What kind of problem do you have, Miss…What was your name again?" Doris was becoming very anxious now as she tried to maintain her calm.

"For the past six months, Mrs. Dade, your husband and I have been seeing each other. I'm sorry to tell you this, but he loves me and you just need to back away. You can't hold him against his will, you know!"

"You are out of your mind! My husband would never risk losing his family for an obvious home-wrecker! I don't believe a word of it, and I'm not going to listen to this anymore!" All the while she knew that every word the woman had spoken was true.

"It is true and if you don't believe me, I'll tell you where he has a beautiful little strawberry birthmark."

This was becoming much more than the other encounters Clayte might have had in the past. Doris thought that at any moment she might throw up but managed to keep her cool while her mind moved a hundred miles a minute. It was clear that Clayte was up to something, but she was not going to play this game anymore. If the bitch thought she could move into her territory, she was sadly mistaken!

She could feel the hair at the nape of her neck standing on end. In spite of outward appearances, she had the capacity for great strength and the ability to respond when confronted with danger—and this was certainly danger! She was used to it in her almost daily fights with Clayte.

"So you think, Miss Whoever You Are, that you can call me and threaten my marriage? You must think I'm a patsy."

"Clayte loves me, and he told me you're not willing to give him a divorce," said the mysterious woman.

"Is that so? Well, let me tell you that you are barking up the wrong tree with your personal problems! Clayton and I are very happy, and in fact, we'll be leaving on a second honeymoon soon!" She couldn't resist the dig and knew her comment had hit its mark. There was silence on the other end of the line followed by a long sigh. At that precise moment, Doris hung up the phone.

She put her head down on her desk, and the tears started to flow. Before she could pull herself together, Dan, her boss, came in.

"What's the matter, Doris? Can I help?" Dan was such a caring person and she appreciated his friendship so much. She suspected that his interest was more than just on a friendship level. "Did that husband of yours upset you again?"

"No…no," she stammered. "I'm fine. It's nothing, just a bad day."

Doris got up from her desk and gathered her things. "Dan, if you don't mind, I need to take the rest of the day off."

"Well, certainly, Doris. You work hard and do a great job for us. If you need some time, by all means you deserve it. But you worry me. Are you sure you're okay?" He knew that things were difficult at home and even though he tried not to allow his personal feelings to interfere, it just wasn't possible where she was concerned.

She knew that Dan was a good listener. Hadn't she dumped on him before? This time, she needed some space not only to sort through everything she just heard but also to figure out where her life, particularly with Clayte, was heading.

One thing she did know was that she would confront Clayte about his extracurricular activities. This time, he had pushed her too far. He wasn't going to talk his way out of this so easily. Her gut told her that he was guilty as charged. God, how could he do this again? Hadn't they been through enough in their marriage?

The tears welled up again, and she just let them flow. There was no sense in trying to be stoic. She'd been in this position before and the first time she had actually thrown up. In spite of everything, her husband's multiple indiscretions and now his obvious affair, he was her weakness. For that reason and that reason alone, she always ended up forgiving him.

They had met on a blind date right after she had broken off a two-year engagement to Marty Simpson. Clayte was the most handsome man Doris had ever laid eyes on. After a whirlwind courtship of only three months, he asked her to marry him. God, she remembered, as if it was yesterday, the feeling of overwhelming love! If she'd had wings to propel her, how she could have danced on the stars that day!

Sighing, she could feel her resolve to banish Clayte forever dissolving as quickly as her anger had come. Whatever else he was, he did love her and the kids and, in spite of his weakness of the flesh, was always there for them.

Just then, a nagging voice interrupted her train of thought. "Mom, Mom, did you hear me?" said Jackie. "What were you thinking about for so long? Dad and I were just discussing Henri and Paulette and you never even said a word!"

Clayte looked over at her with an all-knowing look. He was used to her lapses of time and could only imagine what was going on in that head of hers, as usual imagining his indiscretions. Dealing with her paranoia was becoming unbearable. Yes, he had strayed but not to the extent that she thought. He was going to have a serious conversation with her when they returned to Germany.

He hadn't considered this small recent indiscretion to be anything more than just that. Hmm, I may have to check in with Mary, he thought.

Clayton

The War

AT THAT MOMENT, Clayte interrupted Doris's train of thought. "Well, ladies, take a good look around you. We have officially entered Clichy, a suburb of Paris! We will be in the heart of a city, its beauty unrivaled anywhere in the world, in less than an hour. Jackie, when we leave here, you will never think of Paris as an ordinary place again. It will forever leave an imprint on your mind, one of reliving history, moving among the great military leaders, and the significance of how the last big war shaped the city's framework."

Inquisitive like a baby just learning to crawl, Jackie couldn't contain the many questions she had of her father. The times were few and far between when he shared war stories with her, but those were times when she felt the closest to him. "What happened when you rolled into Paris, Dad? And where were Uncle Henri and Aunt Paulette? Did they leave Paris during the war?"

"I'll answer your first question last. Henri and Paulette managed to stay in Paris most of the time during the war. There were times when they managed to escape to the old summer hideaway near Lucerne, Switzerland. You're still young, but you can understand the need to stay because Uncle Henri had a successful business. It was important to move his profits to Switzerland periodically. Otherwise, the Germans would have confiscated all his money."

Before he could finish telling Jackie the story of the hideaway, Doris interrupted, "It's all about the family secrets, not the Germans! Supposedly there were all kinds of secrets hidden at the old estate."

"What secrets, Mom?"

Still angry from her memories of his recent shenanigans, Doris was smug in her knowledge and secretly happy to take the attention away from Clayte. Doris continued with the story.

"It all started with Clarice and the first Chevais secret! Chevais, as you may remember, was your great-grandmother's last name. It was the summer of 1889 and most of the family was in residence at the manor house near Lucerne," explained Doris.

"Tell me about the manor house. What did it look like, and was it big and…" Jackie gasped, totally out of breath and unable to finish the sentence.

"Whoa, first things first!" Doris interrupted. "The entire clan, Chevaises and Pontifis, always summered in Mulhouse. They were a grand family with predictable habits and close ties to each other."

Jackie's mind wandered to a tranquil setting where families gathered in a place that would look like a picture out of the French countryside with rolling hills and castles in the sky. Daffodils and tulips were blooming wild and free with their colors providing a canopy of beauty. She could almost smell the sweet gardenia bushes smattered throughout—a joy of delight to her nostrils. Cascading water flowing into mountain streams supplied the local lakes and ponds; it provided the perfect backdrop for the painting in her mind.

She imagined they were much like a flock of majestic birds flying south for the winter; all of them came to the manor to escape. The normal, mundane routine in their respective environments captured them for nine months of the year, except, of course, for those wonderful holidays.

Jackie was so impressed with the way her mother had presented the facts on the Eiffel Tower that she ventured to beg. "Please tell me about Clarice, Mom."

"I will in time. Have patience, my dear." Building up the drama of the family story was more in keeping with Doris's nature, and she proceeded slowly, drawing the young girl's attention as she spoke.

"Unknown to the family, this particular summer would evolve into much, much more, a summer they would never capture again. All their lives would be transformed, altering their destinies and those of future generations."

"Good grief, Doris," interrupted Clayte. "You don't have to drag this story out just to prove a point."

"I'm getting to the point now, if you don't mind," she replied. "You should try to see the beauty and drama in the family' history. It would broaden your perspective and give you an appreciation for the hardships and the joys that my family endured."

Doris expected another sarcastic diatribe from Clayton, but he was uncharacteristically silent.

"Anyhow, Jackie," she proceeded, "unfortunately the change that occurred was the result of traumatic events taking place in Paris that summer and the mystery of the missing Chevais estate, or at least part of it. Your great-grandmother Clarice, who was nine at the time, had to bear the brunt of the tragedies that unfolded, all within a short period of time. It was this difficult period of time that formed the basis for her later actions and sometimes misunderstood deeds. Before I tell you those stories, I will say that the first secret had its core in Paris."

Doris started telling Jackie the story of Marie Chevais and the events that were transpiring in Paris as the rest of the family was in residence in Mulhouse.

Transfixed, Jackie did not utter a word, except to gasp a couple of times. Toward the end of her mother's story, she practically cried, "What happened to Clarice and Andre?"

"Well…" Doris hesitated as she saw Clayte's expression. "Just wait until you are older and let your grandmother pass down some of the family history since she can do it in more detail."

"Why can't you tell me now?" asked Jackie

Realizing that she had stepped too far, Doris backtracked by saying, "There are some things that really are intended for adult conversation, and besides, it would not be fair to your grandmother! You know how she loves to sit and tell you stories."

Petulantly, Jackie confided, "Grams did tell me a little bit about Clarice, my great-grandmother! She sounds so interesting, but Grams couldn't remember all the details about what happened during that last summer Clarice was at the hideaway."

"Hideaway? What do you know about the hideaway?" Succumbing to the pressure applied by her persistent daughter, Doris said, "Maybe Uncle Henri can fill in the blanks."

The car became quiet, and Doris realized for the past few minutes that Clayte had not been part of their little conversation.

As if on cue, Jackie piped up, "Finish your story, Dad. Were there any people out along the streets of Paris?"

Clayte proceeded to describe in detail how the French people had cheered and greeted them with almost-divine adulation. It was still hard to believe that barely more than ten years later, they were practically in a cold war or at the very least at a standstill in building a strong relationship with France because of the current political climate. De Gaulle was in self-imposed political withdrawal and his many loyal followers were not happy with the current government.

Clayte's mind went back to a different time—a time of anticipation. It was 1945 and they were billeted outside Paris. Troops were waiting for word of the German surrender in Reims in Northwestern France.

As the story unfolded, some months before his battalion, part of the 101st Airborne's 'the Screaming Eagles' had parachuted behind enemy lines and succeeded in cutting off supply lines. In the process, they were surrounded by Germans, fighting hand-to-hand combat in blizzard conditions so intense to rival that of wind tunnel-blown pelts of ice. Could anything equal the hardships endured by the soldiers?

He had just made contact with good Mother Earth when rifle fire whizzed overhead. Ducking into the heavy forest underbrush, Clayte heard the approach-

ing tanks. German, he surmised. His buddy, Hal, had parachuted right in after him but caught his chute in a grove of tall hardwoods.

Clayte tried to help his buddy as rapid fire of the AK-58s ricocheted off the trees like buckshot seeking its prey. The screams came from deep within, lingering like the fog on a marsh, heavy in its veil. If he lived another fifty years, he would never forget the sound that Hal made as he hung dying in the trees—an unfit graveyard for a brave soldier.

What was it that drove men to fight their brothers?

The great Battle of the Bulge took a toll on the American soldiers, selecting all the young and ever brave to add to the casualty list. The world would never forget the toll of the Second World War.

"Dad, you haven't finished the story yet!"

Caught off guard by Jackie, he decided to backtrack and tell her some of the history. It would give him a chance to squelch any emotions he might have displayed while remembering the sorrow he felt over Hal.

Reminding himself that Jackie was very mature for her age, he addressed her question directly. Taking a more formal tone, he started, "You are old enough to understand this, so a bit of history about the war first. After the D-Day invasion at Normandy, our 4th Infantry Division, along with those of us in the 101st who parachuted into France, teamed up with the French resistance and liberated Paris on August 24, 1944. Yes, it was a grand celebration but knowing there was so much more yet to come, it was tempered by a sense of unease. Our soldiers were facing more hardship than they had ever experienced. For those of us part of the American forces, little did we know at that time what was waiting for us. Most of us fought in the last big German offensive, the Battle of the Bulge. It was one of the bloodiest battles of World War II with nineteen thousand Americans dead."

Clayte drifted for a few minutes, thinking back only to be jolted by Jackie's voice.

"What happened next, Dad?"

"The American troops moved forward throughout the Ardennes region, which is covered in dense forests, giving them cover from the enemy. The hills rise from 1,100 feet to over 2,100 feet in the boggy moors of the Hohes Venn region of northeastern Belgium. The region has steep-sided valleys carved by fast-flowing rivers. Of course, these valleys also gave the enemy plenty of cover to carry out their offensive.

Other than Verviers in Belgium and Charleville-Mézières in France, both exceeding fifty thousand inhabitants, the Ardennes region is sparsely populated, with few of the cities exceeding ten thousand inhabitants.

Soldiers were subjected to tremendous hardships, enduring incredible cold, crossing rivers that were blocks of floating ice and suffering with the indescribable pain as their hands and feet became too frozen to use. They had to move cautiously every step of the way to avoid land mines and snipers hiding in trees. Now you can see why it was even sweeter the second time we arrived in Paris!"

"Gosh, Dad, no wonder you don't like to talk about the war!" Even though she couldn't see her father's face in the front seat, Jackie could sense he had moved into the dark world where they could not enter.

What a sight before them. The trucks were rumbling into Paris, squeezing through the tight avenues from every direction. As they moved from the outskirts into the city, they could see the scars of war etched on every street corner with an occasional swastika still painted on buildings. There was no hiding the raw beauty of Paris—even with all her battle scars. The Eiffel Tower represented a symbol to all that Paris was still standing and not even war could bring her to her knees. The magic was there albeit under a surface of dust—the dust of a war that had lasted too long.

The troops were moving freely now among the crowds, cheering along with the Parisians. When they approached the Champs-Elysees, the swell of thousands upon thousands of Parisians could be felt as if they were moving the trucks along with the sheer force of their energy. All the while they lined the streets shouting, "Vive les Americains, Vive les Americains, Vive les Americains." Even the pain of a war so brutal could not quell the enthusiasm etched on each and every Frenchman. The weary faces of the troops now had been transfixed with big smiles—incredulous about what they were witnessing. The Arc de Triomphe stood sentry as the Americans pulled into the center of the city.

Clayte could taste it and feel it even now as he drove into Paris with his family.

Turning onto the Champs-Elysees, his muscles tensed as if preparing for a surprise attack. Relaxing enough to calm his nerves, the jolt of what he just felt weighed heavy on his mind. Clayte's demons wouldn't die easily! Every day there was some reminder of the years spent in France and Germany, but it was becoming easier as time passed.

His attention was drawn back to the present when Jackie suddenly spoke up. "Isn't that the old building where Grandma grew up? It has the number on it, 1807 Avenue des Champs-Elysees."

"Yes, it looks much different than it did when we were coming into Paris back in August of 1944. It was a time when the people of France were grateful for what the Americans—and all Allied troops for that matter—had sacrificed. We helped free them from the Nazi regime controlling France. Not fighting the Nazis was never an option for the Americans. After the discovery of the concentration camps and the horror of what was perpetrated on the Jewish people, no country of conscience could stand idly by and do nothing."

His mind wandered again—back to the battlefields, the miserable days of frozen feet, no food and clothing that alternated between extreme dampness and icy stiffness. More of his men were falling in the face of such hardships. Clayte tried to save them all, pulling them behind him, even dragging at times until they fell off—one by one.

Perhaps worse than the physical misery inflicted on them was living with the smell of death. The stench bore through his nostrils, invading every pore with rotting flesh of those once his comrades in arms. It was a smell which took him years to forget.

God, how he hated this war and himself, even though he was barely out of his teens, for letting these boys die so far from home.

"Dad, listen to me," Jackie demanded, breaking into his thoughts once more.

Henri

Paris

A TREK THROUGH Paris was like watching a Technicolor movie. Colors of the rainbow dominated the landscape like the surreal French impressionist paintings that could be purchased on every street corner. Unlike any other city, there was drama in the very buildings and streets that claimed Paris as home. A sense of history along with the marvels of the new contemporary France gave inspiration to painters and poets alike to create the greatest works of their time. No one could say that Paris wasn't where the world started and would ultimately end.

As if on cue, there sitting around the turn was the old Paris Opera House, still regal in its bearing yet humbled with age. Yes, they were getting close to the shop, Uncle Henri's hat shop, and Jackie was becoming more excited every minute. "It's been so long since Uncle Henri came to visit. He's so much fun, just like Grams," said Jackie. The car turned the corner and Doris pointed to the building ahead.

"Look, there's the shop, Jackie." Clayte pulled the car around the curve and parked in front of a magnificent brownstone building. Etched in every cornerstone was an old lion head carving balancing each of the four stories, as if keeping watch. Wondering what they had seen could keep an imagination like hers busy for days! The carvings were reminiscent of the France of old. Jackie imagined they had been there in the days of Clarice.

She decided anyone lucky enough to share such a dwelling with her *special* uncle had her interest. The one thing she knew about herself was that she was curious about people, particularly those living in another world from her own. Did they have family secrets? Underneath the facade of the brownstone, wrapped in layers of intrigue, were the burned-in memories of past generations. Like the burnished and washed patterns of a handmade quilt, each square had been infused with its own story. *If only she could learn all the family stories, then she could be assured of who she was.*

Underneath her little girl exterior lurked a shrewd manipulator. Jackie was already plotting how to get the rest of the story out of anyone she could. Her mother had almost given up a piece of the secret but stopped short because of her father's intense, scolding hot gaze. She always knew when things started to turn in the opposite direction.

"Jackie," Clayte said, "why don't you take some pictures before we go in? You can walk over there and get just the right vantage point." He was determined to scold Doris the moment Jackie got out of earshot.

"Just exactly what did you think you were doing when you told Jackie to ask Henri about Clarice? She is not old enough to comprehend what her great-grandmother had to deal with as a young girl. Certainly, it is not your place or mine to discuss Clarice and her proclivities, if you know what I mean!"

"And you think you're more capable than I am of deciding what she can and can't learn about her own ancestors? You certainly are one to take the high moral ground, aren't you?" Doris practically screamed.

"Keep your voice down. She's right across the street, for God's sake!" Clayte pleaded.

Just then, Jackie walked around the other side of the car, startling them, as if catching two naughty children in the throes of vandalizing their surroundings. Verbally, they were doing just that.

It figures they had to have something to quarrel about, particularly since she was beginning to let her guard down and enjoy the trip. If only our lives could be as happy as what we have experienced over the past few days—driving leisurely through the country, taking time not only to look at the sights but also to talk as well, she thought.

But as if on cue, the demons started dancing their rhythmic steps around in her head, causing the otherwise excited and happy girl to shield herself, as if preparing for a sudden lightning strike. Where were her senses anyhow? Every time she trusted them, she was sorely disappointed.

At that moment, Henri came bounding out the door of the Brownstone. "My chérie amour," he declared. "It has been so long." He hollered as he scooped a nonetheless excited Jackie up in his arms. The sight brought laughter to the whole group. There was Henri, the short, fat, balding Frenchman, barely tall enough to lift his great-niece over his head, let alone twirl her around. They fell on the ground in merriment as they continued to laugh in delight!

The atmosphere was charged, but this time with joy. All the previous tension seemed to disappear as the climate went from hurricane winds to balmy breezes.

Henri, ever the consummate Frenchman and charming gentleman in residence, had immediately sensed the tension between Doris and Clayte and seized the opportunity to dismantle an otherwise volatile time bomb. *Humph,* he thought to himself, *some things never change. I must protect Jackie—at least while in Paris—and make sure she has a simply marvelous time.*

"We are so pleased that you have come to Paris, especially during this busy time!" Henri allowed. "My chérie Jackie, we will have a très bon time while you are here. There is so much to tell you about Paris and your family tree. Your grandmother would be so pleased to know that you are well taken care of, ma chérie!"

Henri was nothing to look at, but if personality could paint a picture, his would be like the pièce de résistance. Short and somewhat rotund, his persona embraced the French mystique in ways that could not be defined by mere words. Charm and savoir faire were just two of the adjectives that came to mind. It was obvious that he had what women wanted—a smoldering sex drive bordering on the risqué. His wife, Paulette, laughingly joked about the way women fell all over him because they couldn't help themselves. One thing was for sure: he made every woman he came in contact with feel she was the most beautiful woman in the world.

"Come, let's go inside. Paulette has been very anxiously awaiting your arrival. I'll have Martine get your bags and take them to your rooms, but first, a little toast to your safe arrival!"

As they entered the grand hall, Jackie couldn't help but gasp at the beauty surrounding them. "Uncle Henri, it's so pretty and I've never seen so many paintings except in a museum."

Surprised, Henri said, "Jackie, I forgot that you have never been here to the grande dame. You were very young when you last came to Paris, and this place was still under repair from the ravages of the war. It is a magnificent place, is it not?"

Paulette came charging around the corner at that exact moment, exclaiming her joy at seeing her grand-niece. "Oh, let me look at you, dear child. Ma chérie, you are so beautiful!" One could say that Paulette was a female carbon copy of her husband, but with hair—lots and lots of hair. In fact, her hair was like a neon sign, the bright orange kind, announcing to all who did not know her well that this was a unique individual.

She and Henri never had their own children, a loss that still wounded them during the holidays when friends gathered round with all their loved one—children, grandchildren, and assorted add-ons. She had to settle for add-ons herself and adopted several loving pets to fill the void.

But oh, this child was precious to both of them—a blend of Henri Sr. and Clarice and, of course, Jackie's own parents. The eyes always looked as if they could see a greater vision, much like the old fortune-telling, mind-reading gypsies who moved in bands across Europe these days.

She herself had her fortune told by a crafty old woman that had left her shaken for weeks. In spite of her cynicism, the gypsy had accurately told of previous misfortunes only a true mind reader could have known.

Paulette was in a hyped-up state—excited about life and capable of disarming even the most volatile of situations, even the one she sensed right now. Charming to the core, Paulette could divert anger in most people and channel it so it would seem more of an intensity of spirit, or rather spirited as she would call the person who was the object of this attention.

After what seemed like several long minutes of squeezing her, she released the breathless Jackie to move over and embrace Doris and Clayte.

"Oh, you beautiful darlings, let's get you inside and we will open the *special* champagne, no?"

Doris was relieved that the tension had been broken. At least for now they could move into the easy chatter between loved ones. She could have kissed Paulette right then!

Day two brought more excitement and expectation of events to come. Henri and Paulette were well-known for their hospitality and frequent entertaining. Even throughout the war, they were able to enjoy some of the good life in spite of the German's occupation of Paris.

The secrets and mystery of Paris lured even the less adventuresome to open their eyes in anticipation as each new day began. Cobblestoned courtyards nestled behind closed gates concealed the lucky Parisians' magical homes but also allowed glimpses to those passing who appreciated the opportunity to peek inside.

Paulette conspired with Henri to create the ultimate adventure for their guests, complete with tidbits of family mystery.

They started off their tour the next morning by making a visit to the Shoppe Le Chapeau, a top Parisian hat designers' showroom owned and operated by Paulette herself. The comical group paraded into the front parlor followed by Paulette, who immediately commanded them to take their places while she would handle the rest.

"Come in and sit right here, Jackie. There is a surprise waiting for you!"

Henri picked up the elated girl and set her on the large counter facing the front of the store, turning her so she could watch the show that was about to begin.

"Bring out the models, Paulette, and start the music," hollered Henri, who was feeling very full of mischief—as usual.

Paulette, in her best impression of a French model, came out first prancing around as if her life's career path was to emulate a prima donna in drag. A hat tilted on her head, the plumes shooting in every direction, brought hoots of laughter to the excited group.

Jackie clasped her hands in glee, enjoying every minute of her own private show. Somehow, they had talked her mother into modeling a diminutive pillbox hat, wearing it in a way that evoked sincere admiration from the small group of critics for its elegance.

Elegance was not a description typically inspired by her mother's demeanor and presence but, on occasion, could be found lurking beneath the surface. This was one time the appreciative group would have to agree that Doris had stepped into another dimension. The hat itself was small, made of beautiful off-white brocade, piped with a band of black velvet. Framing her mother's face in a way that Jackie had never seen, she couldn't help but notice the beauty beneath the otherwise pained exterior.

Maybe for today, Mama could enjoy her time together with all of them, including her father, she thought.

She caught a glimpse of her father, and even though Jackie, in her youth, might not have comprehended the depth and complexities of adult love, the others could see a look in Clayte's eyes that told a story of a man fighting with his mixed emotions. There were those memories of a love from yesteryear still apparent in his eyes, of the woman who captured his heart a long time before, offset by some distant, indescribable void hanging in the imbalance of a fractured relationship.

Looking further, a professional could also see the glimmer of anger lying just below the surface, fighting with the loving thoughts and setting a stage for the confused feelings that contributed to easily ignited outbursts.

From her vantage point and tuned into the less subtle nature of her parents' mood swings, Jackie also sensed the underlying anger in her father, forcing her to conclude that if being married caused such constant aggravation, she just didn't need it!

PART FOUR

The Road To Paris (June 1889)

After a very long night, Aurelia, Augusto, and Jonque arose early the next morning, readying them for the long trip to Paris.

Bernard brought the carriage around.

The atmosphere in Chevais Manor had turned from gaiety to gloom in a matter of hours. The anticipated homecoming had been dampened by the events that had taken place in Paris the past twenty-four hours. Under normal conditions, the two families would be sitting in the Grande Parlor, catching up with all the usual family gossip. The children were playing underfoot, becoming reacquainted with each other and anticipating their first meal together in the family dining room.

Unlike the more formal, almost austere in comparison, Grande Dining Hall—Cook's Heaven as it was affectionately called—exuded warmth and familiarity. The lingering smells of freshly baked pies reminded even the least hungry man of past rumblings of youthful hunger unfed. In the cold chill of a winter's day, the fireplace blazed, sending out a message to loved ones ambling by that here was a room filled with warmth and love from generations of the past.

The walls were adorned with ancestral paintings, announcing the Chevais lineage to all who passed by. At one end of the room stood the old French woodblock table long enough to seat sixteen hungry souls, along with ample room for additional guests.

Overstuffed sofas and chaises were strategically placed on the opposite end of the room from the dining area and even around its perimeter walls. There was enough comfortable seating to eagerly accommodate an afternoon of reading for all of the dining crew if they chose to pull out a book from among the hundreds of shelves lining the walnut paneled walls. Many an afternoon you could find a member of the family or guest napping in the Cook's Heaven.

Spring and summer entered the room through the open screens that covered the large glassed-in atrium extending from one end of the room. Beautiful bougainvillea and clematis looped over the trellis ceiling of the atrium signaled that life was being born again through the ever-growing vines. Trails of ivy and vinca vines with occasional bursts of bright color could be seen weaving their way in and out of the side trellis panels supporting their posts. It was warm enough to signal the heat of summer was soon to be upon them. The early-morning breezes were flowing through the atrium into the family dining room and beyond.

Augusto pulled in a deep breath as if to soak up this moment, preserving it for a future time when his emotional reserves might be in a state of disrepair. The smell of eggs and freshly cured ham wafted through *petit coin de paradis* (little piece of heaven), arousing not only hunger pangs but a sense of belonging rooted in the history of the manor. There were the lives it touched and the hidden passions it bespoke from other days.

Permanently entrenched was a kitchen staff that would serve the Chevais and Pontifi family with love and care, as if preparing each meal for the royal family. The staff's roles and honored professions were passed on from generation to generation with pride. Family members worked side by side, lovingly preparing the food that fed "their other family."

There was a resolute quiet among the staff this day, an understanding that something had happened to change the happy, balanced environment within the manor.

Now everyone had gathered in the upper chamber, the adults sequestered at one end, while Bernard was attempting to entertain Clarice, Jacques, and Andre with card tricks. Normally, his magic kept them enthralled for hours, and they begged for more when he tried to leave. The somber mood covered the room like a canopy, stifling any attempts at the small talk and frivolity that were the norm for this evening.

Even the young Andre, with all his boyish charm, could not bring a smile to their lips. Aurelia was the first to break the silence, turning to Augusto in despair.

"What are we to do when we arrive tomorrow, Augusto? How is it that we will function?" Her voice barely a whisper, she added, "What can we do to help Ma Mère? She can't die! If only she had come two days earlier as planned, this terrible mishap would never have befallen her."

He didn't have the heart to tell Aurelia that any change in schedule could not have prevented this blatantly obvious attempt on Madame's life. The forces of evil driving this attack were already at work in a scheme that would probably catapult them all into the fight of their lives.

Precautions have been taken, he reassured himself, but danger lurked and his first priority must be to protect his family at all cost. Saving the Chevais fortunes would have to take a lesser role in this battle.

If he had harbored any doubts of Duvalier's intentions, they had been dispelled in the course of the events of the past couple of days, including the weak attempt by his courier to distract Augusto.

Sometimes knowledge casts its cloak in such a way that covering the obvious becomes moot—and so was the situation with Augusto. He knew too much to believe that it was a poorly timed robbery attempt that caused the injuries to Madame or a mere coincidence that the thief would enter the building while she was immersed in her work, not realizing her presence.

Augusto continued to pace and finally stopped in front of the adults, addressing them authoritatively, as if he were speaking to his children, "We all must try to sleep, for morning will be here too soon, but not soon enough to be at Marie's bedside, to be sure. Please repair to your rooms, and I will coordinate with the staff for the care of the children."

Jonque tried to protest, but Augusto had already turned, disappearing down the Grande Hall stairs to the servants' quarters below.

Train of Despair

They were crammed into what was commonly referred to as the elite cattle coach—the only space left in the morning rail trip to Paris. Circumstances forced the anxious family to accept whatever hastily arranged accommodations could be made on such short notice.

Bernard had, as usual, taken great pains to manage the care of his family, the only people he truly loved and, instinctively, as a new baby clings to his mother, knew they felt the same for him. Subdued in his dealings with others, his passion and the pains he took in his care of the Pontifis, particularly Augusto and little Clarice, were nothing short of hero worship.

He watched as the train left the station, the great sense of loss pervasive in the atmosphere, like waiting by a loved one's deathbed, hoping to change the natural course of events. "May God keep them safe," he mumbled. "They deserve better than this."

Augusto had come to him last night and taken him into his confidence, certainly an honor for Bernard but one weighted heavy with the responsibility he bore.

"Dear God," he cried, "how could life take such a turn with a family devoted to such kindness and love of all mankind? Gratitude for this family soaks into every fiber of my being and as long as my breath continues, I will forever be in Augusto's debt!"

The children were in his care, and he took this role seriously. Clarice, the adultlike child, unnerved him to the extent that any story he told to the others would have to be substantiated many times over to become even slightly plausible to the extrasensory gifts she possessed. Augusto had cautioned him that her perceptiveness bordered on witchery, to everyone's amazement, including the clairvoyant reading her palms under the tent at the village festival.

He now believed anything told to him about Clarice, particularly after the way she had cornered him just yesterday with all her questions regarding Madame Chevais. Possessed with a perceptive mind, Clarice was not a normal child by any standard, proven by her uncanny ability to grasp and understand adult innuendoes and subtleties.

The extent of Madame's injuries could not be hidden from this precocious young lady. It was almost as if the two were connected as one soul, bound together on another life plane.

At that moment, Clarice was pacing the floor, trying to control the jitters that were threatening to overtake her good sense. She was waiting on Bernard to return from the train station since her parents had insisted on not disturbing the household as they left on their journey. The tension was more than most children her age could absorb.

On his way back to the manor, Bernard reflected on the fragility of life, and he hoped that in conveying Augusto's last message to Clarice, she would not take more from it than was intended for her to understand.

Interim Peace

Disoriented, her breath coming at a fast pace, she awoke from the nightmare that seemed to envelop her with its clammy yoke. Unsure of her surroundings, every movement was tentative as she rolled to the edge of the bed. The relentless nightmares wouldn't stop their pursuit of her mind. Over and over they lingered into her consciousness, filling most of her waking days with pain. She would try to reconstruct those last days before the darkness.

Mama and Papa, Aunt Marcella, and Uncle Jonque arrived in Paris the afternoon of June 15, 1889. She would remember that date for all her days. Bernard and Clarice received a wire upon their safe arrival and was relieved to know that the journey was without incident.

Bernard was peculiarly quiet, almost morose, when the wire arrived, which was in total conflict with the personality they all knew and loved. More reason for Clarice to be worried, nothing added up in her way of thinking. It was time to corner him and explore more fully the events in Paris leading up to the injuries of her beloved grand-mère and the hasty departure of her parents.

Andre and Jacques, her cousin, came running excitedly down the stairs at that moment so her mission would have to wait.

"Clarice, the sun is shining and it's a beautiful morning! You know what waits for us in the stables. Please say yes," cried Jacques.

She could not avoid the reasonable request by Jacques, so in spite of her mood, she agreed to take the boys exploring back to the pond, a starting point through the wildlife preserve on the edge of the village. They were all comfortable riding their own horses, and this might be just the medicine she needed to calm her nerves.

"Okay, Jacques, Andre, we'll take the horses after you've eaten a good breakfast! We can't have you starving if we go into the wilderness!" The boys' eyes got large at the mention of the wilderness, and Clarice chuckled. She couldn't resist a little tease. After all, they were so gullible!

"I'm just talking about the preserve, silly. You love seeing the wild birds and animals at play, and we will pretend that we are animals too!"

They loved Clarice when she was play acting and the gaiety of the moment was quickly lightening her mood as well. Clarice, at her dramatic best, was a delight to behold. When in the moment, she could deliver an award-winning performance.

In the meantime, events were unfolding in Paris that would forever alter their lives and leave an imprint on the heart and mind of the perspicacious Clarice.

At this time, though, the children were guaranteed the simple joys of childhood as they ran from the manor.

"Hurry now, boys, or I will beat you to the stables!" Clarice shouted with glee. As the door slammed shut after the boys, Bernard exhaled visibly. His move did not escape her, and Clarice, in her all-knowing voice, said, "Bernard, you will tell me everything later. You know I'll get the truth out of you." She chuckled.

If only she didn't have to know the truth, Bernard thought to himself. *Innocence is so easily lost, and the young should never be deprived of theirs until such time as they become older and wiser.*

After mounting her favorite mare and positioning in front of the boys on their own ponies, Clarice slowly moved to affirm her place, leading both of them wide-eyed and excited to be part of any adventure that included her.

Clarice evoked awed adulation from anyone she encountered, whether child or adult. Questions of why and how someone so young could command the kind of attention, saved for so few, were answered simply with, "She's so much like her grandmother!"

Flinging her long braid over her shoulder and feigning a dramatic belle grand ingenue attitude, she commanded, "It is time to depart for our safari into the jungle, gentlemen."

The merry band moved fluidly through the goldenrod-crusted meadow with a purpose-driven speed, anxious to move into the fringes of the vast preserve. From the distance, it appeared as a dark mass rising toward the sky, moving with the mountain swell, thinning at the crest.

For the less adventurous, the appearance of the thicket edging the preserve would be a frightening prospect. Clarice, ever the fearless explorer, had no such thoughts at this moment, having conquered her fears of such foolishness in years past—at least the layer anyone could see.

Andre, peering through his heavily lashed eyes, glanced at his sister.

"Clarice, do you think there are tigers and lions in there?" he hesitantly asked.

"Most certainly, my little brother," she confidently answered.

Riding hard now, the experienced trio maintained the gallop in a rhythmic cadence reminiscent of soldiers marching in step on their chestnut-glazed stallions, bracing for the unknown yet bravely ready to face whatever fate had cast for them.

For the children, with faces aglow and freshly tinted by the chafe of the wind, the excitement was building with the promise of adventure in a wild kingdom of their own making.

Could they imagine at that time their lives would be so drastically altered and forever changed?

The Arrival—Twenty-Four Hours Later

"Orient Express Special," called out the conductor, "arriving now on Track 13. You will disembark to the right, leaving through the South Gates."

The surreal scene awaited them as they descended the stairs leading from the coach. There was nothing quite like Paris in the summer—bustling streets, beautiful cobbled courtyards complete with sculptures posed behind closed gates. On either side of the Seine high walls shut off ancient monastic gardens, which could only be imagined by the masses of people passing by each day. The full-throated birdsong in their treetops were the only telling sign of the beauty that was contained behind the walls.

Augusto quickly assessed the crowds to see who might have an interest in their arrival. He had enough concern that he left the group to skirt the edge of the rail line at the back stockyard, looking for facial signs to identify those with enough interest in the group to be considered suspect.

Not finding anything of significance, he made his way back to the station posthaste to transport his family as quickly as possible to the hospital. And as expected, they were anxiously awaiting his return, a fact Aurelia pointed out rather impatiently to her errant husband.

The carriage ride to the hospital was marked by a stillness and calm that reminded Augusto of a murky pond still in its wait for the unsuspecting wanderer to stumble into its depths. He occupied his mind by allowing his focus to move back out onto the streets.

Paris was still divided by loyalties, the Alsace-Lorraine factions demanding Germany to release their land. Alsace had been French since 1681 and Lorraine since 1766, so German influences prior to 1686 did little to persuade loyalty in a populace predisposed to embracing all that was French.

Demand for the return of the region to France was running high. Even those with a penchant for peace at all costs were known to be grumbling. The educated classes were inclined to look toward France for their value system, particularly the Catholic people of Alsace-Lorraine. The Alsatian Jews were particularly pro-French. It was for this reason they fled to the west toward Paris to escape Prussians and conscription into the German Army.

"If we yearn for all that is French," Augusto blurted out, "why do we continue to embrace our lifestyle in Mulhouse, impervious to changes happening around us? We cannot discard our German brothers, Jew and non-Jew, to proclaim this French elitist attitude, yet a German is never invited to a proper Parisian's table! How are we to live in peaceful harmony if we continue to rebuff our brother?"

The others in the coach looked at him as if he had lost his mind but quickly realized Augusto was occupying himself with intellectual discourse.

"My husband," Aurelia interrupted, "you know many Frenchmen have divided loyalties, even within families. It's not possible to declare our loyalties one way or another but rather remain French while in Paris and a Lorrainer while in Mulhouse!"

Aurelia continued, "Just be thankful we have had peace since the end of the Franco-Prussian War and the fall of the empire of Napoleon III. And except for the unfortunate Commune situation, Paris has been free of strife."

He was happy to see that Aurelia was interacting in a conversation of the mind. "After all," Jonque interjected, "our staff family is all of mixed blood, including Bernard, who is of the Jewish faith. We could only hope to have such loyalty from a Parisian, don't you agree? Speaking of which, I'm not so sure we can trust Duvalier and we must look to dear Augusto for guidance."

"Jonque, there are some things we must discuss later," he whispered. "You are right to be wary of Duvalier. If anything happens to me, please make haste back to Mulhouse and protect the children."

"Of what do you speak, Augusto?" A sound of approaching panic gurgled in the back of Jonque's throat.

"Calm down, brother-in-law. I will explain all later—away from the women!"

He knew all too well that Jonque would only be mollified for a short time before charging head-on to Augusto for answers. Marie Chevais was hanging on to life by a thread; it was only her sheer will and the faith she had in her children that fueled her survival instincts.

The carriage arrived at the Pitié-Salpêtrière University Hospital thirty minutes after departing the main train station. Aurelia was wringing her hands as dread encircled like an enemy waiting to pull her ever closer to the death of her mother.

"Oh, Mother Mary, give me strength from our Heavenly Father, grace, and peace to help Ma Mère." She was crying softly now, sure that Augusto would see and cause him more anguish.

Aurelia thought of her beautiful children and managed to pull herself together. Clarice, dear, dear Clarice, would be proud of her now.

A duo of efficient nurses led them through the corridors to the intensive care unit, beckoning them to hurry. Dr. Honoré met them outside Madame Chevais's door.

"I must caution you. She is very weak and slipping in and out of a comatose state. It will be difficult for you to carry on a conversation with her at this stage, Monsieur Pontifi!"

"Talk to her I must, Doctor, but more than anything, we must let her know we love her and will be by her side until the end," Augusto said.

"I understand," Dr. Honore acknowledged.

They entered the room—an austere, sterile setting surrounded by the cold steel of antiseptic equipment poised to do battle to save a life not quite lived to its fullest.

In the middle of the room, against the far wall, was a typical hospital bed complete with railings to keep its occupant safe from falling.

She appeared so frail at this moment, Madame Chevais, a wisp of what once commanded a presence so majestic as to be likened to the greatest of women, namely Joan of Arc and Olympe de Gouges. Here lay a genuine lady of France—inspiring, fearless, yet hovering on the verge of death.

Oh, the dismay for the waste of a wonderful mind and true humanitarian, one whose drive for respect and parity helped forge the path for strong women, those not afraid to reach out and challenge the old customs of the male superior society. Madame Chevais managed to break the barriers of male domination while still preserving a feminine grace and sensuality that even in these later years drew male admirers from every walk of life.

That Marie could be lying there near death was too difficult to comprehend.

The Plan

Duvalier's Evil

Sequestered in his office, word had reached Duvalier that the party had arrived at the hospital as planned. At first glance, his office appeared to be an elegant and serene haven for a serious legal mind—walls of books lining three sides and a magnificent Louis the Fourteenth desk centered at one end, the backdrop for a canvas depicting the Paris scene through the windows lining the wall. If he peered out his corner window, he could see the Seine from one angle and Notre Dame from another view. "Yes, it is fitting that I should have such an office," he said to himself.

He had been diligent in his preparation of the papers and felt assured that it was only a matter of time before he could execute the final plan. Joseph Duvalier was pacing as he considered the options available to him—a chore he relished! The pieces were falling neatly into place now.

Duvalier's intent was not so much the actual thievery of precious gems and goods as he had alluded to his *band of rogues* but rather a motive mired in the sick infatuation he had with Marie Chevais. Her rejection of him fueled the madness within him.

"The aloof prima donna will wish she had paid attention to my overtures!" he shouted out. Part of his *vendetta* was relentless desire and a burning need to prove once and for all that Joseph Duvalier was not to be dismissed as a common man, unworthy of her affection.

In the twisted reality of his mind, he could make claim to a grander purpose, as if that justified his current course of action. That he considered himself all-powerful helped to fuel a need to constantly stroke his ego, whether through political gain or winning the admiration of a beautiful woman. He would take great pleasure in ultimately destroying those foolish enough to dismiss him as a mere peasant.

His paranoia carried him into frenzied theatrical motions, much like those of a marionette at the end of a long string. Right now his anger was focused on Augusto and the ever-fueled fire of hate he felt for the son-in-law of the Great Madame. "Huh," he exclaimed out loud, "we'll see who has the last laugh."

It would be too late for the heiress apparent and her precious Augusto to change the course of events. The only disquieting moment came when he found out Madame Chevais was still hanging on to life, his source quickly reassuring him of her vegetative state and imminent death.

On the other side of Paris at the very moment Duvalier was making his final plans, a very weak voice uttered the words *the golden seal.* "The secret location is in the golden seal. You must remove the arch, you must remove the arch." Aurelia was holding Ma Mère's hands and leaning to languish one last kiss on the woman who had given her life. "Ma Mère, she spoke!" cried Aurelia.

Augusto and Jonque came rushing over as Madame Chevais opened her eyes and, with them, implored her loved ones to understand. "You must look to the golden seal for the secret code—the missing link. The arch is…" And with those words, Marie Chevais's breathing ceased.

This information, given in supreme sacrifice of her last breath, was not lost on Augusto. He knew there was a golden seal on the old documents that were the titles to all the Chevais land holdings throughout Europe. They were kept in a vault at the manor house secured with a modern—by 1889 standards—locking system. At first glance, there were no unusual markings on the documents, but upon close examination and with afore knowledge, an astute observer could see an arch was superimposed and raised on the seal. The arch contained a partial code, the remainder of which was held by Madame Chevais in a secret hiding place in Paris. The intent was to keep the code safe if one of the secure places became compromised.

The moment was cast, transcending time, reaching into each one's heart as if to say, "It is well with my soul." Aurelia buried her face in Augusto's strong chest, longing to shut out the world and all the pain of the past couple of days. She was keenly aware that her mother's life had succumbed to this final drama. Somehow, there was a sense of peace and calm within the room—all of them believing that Marie Chevais was with her beloved ones now.

The funeral was scheduled for three days hence in the Notre Dame in a setting fit for a queen. Arrangements were made with Bernard to bring the children on the next train to Paris.

The Aftermath

BERNARD WAS PACING as he studied the wire. How was he to break the news to the children, particularly Clarice? Each agonizing step teased him with the promise of clarity but delivered none. He presented a picture of strength with his stature, the intensity of his demeanor not to be taken for granted. The salt-and-pepper gray in his beard suggested a wisdom born of time.

"Okay," he said out loud, "I'll tell Clarice that her grand-mère is gone but in heaven with Henri. Yes, that will sound better, and then we'll broach the subject with Jacques and Andre." His pacing continued as he delivered his little speech in his mind and worked through the details, practicing all the possible questions from Clarice with their obvious answers.

As he was turning the corner for his last walk around the first level, Clarice came running into him with such fierceness that he could hardly contain his balance.

"Bennie," as she called him. "Bennie, what is going on? You know something about Grand-mère, don't you?" she demanded. "I saw the messenger going down the road as I was coming back from the fields, so I know you received some kind of message!" Clarice was too smart to be deceived, forcing Bernard to make a snap decision even if at an inopportune moment or, in this case, before his nerves failed him.

"Oh, my sweet little Clarice, the news from Paris is not good, and I so wish not to have to tell you this!"

"Bennie, it is Grand-mère, isn't it?" Clarice cried out. "Is she dead? Tell me now!" she implored.

"As I would draw the breath of my firstborn in order to ensure him life, I would also take this truth and the pain you may bear upon my own breast rather than to see you suffer, my chérie!" And with that, Bernard pulled Clarice into his massive arms, enveloping her with tenderness only he could give at this moment.

"Oh no, say it is not so, Bennie, please say it is not so," she whimpered. Laying her head upon his chest, Clarice sobbed tears of a child but with a pain that only the wisdom of age could impart as she let the tide of grief roll over her, bending her to its will.

Her whimpering subsided, Bernard carefully took the limp child, hoisting her in his arms, back up the grand hall stairs to her room, and tucked her lovingly into bed. This poor child was overcome as if by a swell from the ocean's majestic waves had sucked all life form to the sea. She had eventually fallen asleep in his arms with him stroking her hair.

Sitting next to her, watching over his little charge, he reflected again how life was not fair and this child did not deserve what fate had just dealt! Bernard was just coming to grips with the reality himself. That Madame could be gone was almost unfathomable to him, particularly under these circumstances, which were, at best, very questionable. He wished Marcel were here to guide him as he had so many years ago.

How Madame Chevais could have been caught off guard in such a way didn't make sense to him. She was too bright and had an intuitive awareness of her surroundings.

He had deeper concerns, of course, now that the first step in what Augusto had warned might be an attack against the family as a whole had taken place. It would be his responsibility to keep the children safe. And of one thing he was certain: he would lay down his life to accomplish that mission.

First he must busy himself with the tasks at hand—making the arrangements for their journey to Paris the next morning and then dealing with

Jacques and Andre. He didn't relish telling the boys, but it could not be as profoundly sad as it had been in delivering the news to Clarice. Even death could not deter the indomitable spirit that Clarice and her beloved grand-mère shared.

The Funeral

"Why is it," Augusto wondered aloud, "that the thought of death, with its finality, can render normally strong people weak and vulnerable? Dying with nobility is far better than allowing a slow fade into the breach of dishonoring one's true self." He decided not to give any more thought to this truism until they returned to Mulhouse. Augusto's theories often led him to write in his journal as a way to free his mind and still share his wisdom.

Oh, sweet Mulhouse, will we ever feel the same way again? He remembered the first time Aurelia had taken him to the Chevais family retreat, a day much like this day. The sun was shining, breezes were blowing, and there was a hint of change in the air. Unlike today, however, there was a promise of the wonders tomorrow would bring, along with the cherished dreams of youth.

She was so beautiful perched upon the seat of the coach that he had ached to hold her close and feel the sweet touch of her silk upon his skin. They had sought each other in passion, only holding back until the time they could finally be joined in marriage under God. To have tasted her lips was enough, and if left to chance, they would have been lost in their lust for each other.

Once they became one, what joy they had together. He thought no other man could be so lucky, every day an adventure in loving and living life to its fullest! Aurelia was everything a man could hope for in a wife and mate for life—soft yet strong, feminine but courageous.

It had changed, not overnight but slowly as the criticism and veiled threats toward their family had increased. The same outside influences that had undermined Aurelia's sense of security, pulling at the happiness she had felt and to a certain extent causing the fear she now manifested, were once again at work.

Here they were faced with yet another invasion to their harmonious existence, Marie Chevais's death and the possibility that she had been murdered! Marie Chevais! Augusto drew comfort from remembered advice his father had once given him.

"*It is in death of those we love that we find the clues to life, and along with that knowledge comes a profound understanding of the fragility of our existence. To waste a day becomes a sacrilege to the whole idea a life should be sanctified.*"

Marie had not wasted precious time on the mundane and knew from where she came and understood the greater glory of God. To that end, her family could take solace and comfort in knowing Marie Chevais was now with her beloved Henri in the arms of God.

The funeral procession was long—fitting of the renown that Marie Chevais had in Paris and regions beyond. To say that she was wildly popular would be to understate the reach of a great and fearless woman—ahead of her time yet engrained in her world of the day.

Clarice, Jacques, and Andre all arrived that morning from Mulhouse with Bernard, who hovered like a mother hen watching her chicks. It was a day of profound sadness tempered by a renewed sense of purpose—that of pulling together as a family during this difficult time.

As he had expected, Augusto was not surprised that Clarice became the stronger of the young trio and even managed to keep her brother and cousin shored up during the funeral proceedings. It always amazed him to watch her and the way she could transcend any difficulty.

The procession rounded the hill, not an ordinary hill but one molded into the surroundings like Venus de Milo sculpted onto her pedestal. The hill stood as a reminder to all who passed its way: Life is fleeting and to waste one day was more than a travesty. It spoke to humanity of wanton selfishness and a misuse of all that God had provided.

As they looked over the cemetery, the party could see the gathering crowd waiting apprehensively for the family of Marie. A more beautiful and fitting day could not have been mustered up for this solemn occasion. The lilacs and roses were blooming in the background, an appropriate stage for a lady of Paris in her departing act.

How fitting that the meadowlarks were singing joyfully as if to acknowledge Marie deserved their special attention. Somehow, along with the sun, seeing the flowers with their rainbow-inspired arms reaching toward the sky and hearing the melodious birdsong gave the grieving family a sense of peace.

All had been caught up in the somberness of the ceremonial aspects of the funeral and transported to another time—the old-world markings etched forever on the grave stones surrounding them like sentinels at post keeping watch over the dead.

Many a Parisian had been buried here with the ceremonial grandeur afforded those of a certain station in life. The cemetery's recent history bore the pain of many who lost their lives too soon. The slaughter of eighteen thousand Parisians during the bloody suppression of the Commune of Paris in 1871 created an overflow of human remains that threatened to swamp the cemetery with the blood of those who fought for beliefs never well accepted or appreciated by otherwise civilized Parisians.

Augusto managed to keep one eye strategically directed toward the crowd while mindful of showing the proper amount of respect for his deceased mother-in-law. There was no denying he loved her as deeply as if he had been the heir firstborn, but he was also very concerned for the immediate threat to his family.

There in the back of the crowd, he saw the three men conversing in whispered tones and sneaking furtive glances at the funeral party. He immediately recognized Joseph Duvalier and suspected the dark-haired younger version standing next to him to be Pierre, his brother.

A rough unshaven man was pointing toward the casket being carried from the wagon. Augusto wondered where he had come from. On the other side of the crowd, he spotted Paul Marchand, and although he had no reason to suspect him of wrongdoing in the past, recent troubling information indicated misanthropy toward their family. He now wondered if there was a connection. The irony, after all, was that Paul had recommended Duvalier to Marcel.

His attention turned back to comforting Aurelia and his loved ones. He would address the Joseph Duvalier situation in due time, but right now they would all pay their respects to Marie.

The service was directed by Bishop Giedet himself, a devoted friend of the madame. Often her confidante, he now spoke eloquently of her virtues, love of life, and, most of all, pride in her family.

Finally, the service ended, orchestrated to the symphonic often lamentable drama of the funeral March. All left the cemetery saddened by their loss but at peace with the thought that their beloved was in the arms of those she had loved and lost before.

Mulhouse Bound

Clarice was securely wrapped in her own thoughts as the train left the station bound for Mulhouse. The whistle signaled the start of their journey back to the family's country manor—a place with so many memories, most of which revolved around her beloved grand-mère. Sorting through the disjointed glimpses of years past, along with more recent snippets of time, served to lull her into a state of blissful abandonment.

Bernard was across the way, gazing out at the remnants of Paris as they flew by at rapid speed. Had there ever been a grander city, the marble and stone facades wrapping their arms around the historical structures, bisecting the grand avenues, running down every alley, and colliding with all who might come within? The lilac trees cloaked in purple wonder adorned the vistas beyond the walls, hinting at the splendor yet to come.

It was a different time, perhaps the best of times, when they traveled to Paris and Mulhouse in the years before. Even though he did not spend much time with them in Milano, he knew enough to understand the environment south of France—a comfortable, engaging family atmosphere which always renewed and sent the happy family forth for holidays.

Bernard wondered just how much Clarice knew or sensed of the recent happenings that engaged and then endangered the very core of his adopted family, happenings that moved within boundaries normally impenetrable by outsiders.

The adult Pontifis and Chevaises remained in Paris to tie up loose ends—at least that was the pretense most of the family believed. Augusto had other more troubling thoughts to deal with and soon would have to confront, perhaps even bringing his loved ones into the reality that was enfolding.

Augusto had enough presence of mind before leaving Paris the last time to do some digging into where all the secret family records were being held for safekeeping. Until such time, after he and Marie could decipher the troubling messages that had been intercepted between Duvalier and an unidentified mysterious go-between, to a place only known to them.

Clarice, in the meantime, was sleeping soundly while Bernard kept watch over his brood, ready to protect them at all costs. Robust and stocky, he was considered to be *le gentleman extraordinaire* for his size; he stood six feet two, a giant among the French.

Attributed to his mixed heritage of German and French, his strength proved to be the folly of the man who mistook his gentle nature as weakness. Such a foolish man would certainly be left with only humiliation if he chose to undermine in any way those whom Bernard loved.

Unleashing the beast was what one young man had hinted when confronted with Bernard's wrath over inappropriate remarks made to Aurelia. One grasp of his mammoth hand behind the neck and a person could be thrown quite a distance if propelled with enough strength and anger.

Bernard did not have all the pieces of information regarding the problems at hand but enough to know that they were all in danger. He had been instructed by Augusto to take extra care during their travels back to Mulhouse and beyond that—to follow the other directives upon arrival. He had shielded his adopted family from the ravages of the Franco-Prussian War and adopted a nonpartisan stance very early.

The miles quickly melted into the surrounding landscape, blending one vista to the next with interlocking scenes. Beautiful and untamed, the undulating hills interspersed with valleys, giving way to an occasionally quaint, history-filled village that gave the bored traveler a snapshot into their lives. Merging occasionally into architecturally manufactured cities with their neat row houses reminded one how quickly growth could redefine and change irrevocably the complexion of a region.

Clarice was stirring now. The setting sun proved to be a stronger force than the flimsy drape over the caboose window. Demanding her attention, the colors and intensity of the day's end somehow gave her a sense that she had been caught up in a painting, unlike any she had admired in the many museums visited in the past. Complex yet inspiring, diffuse yet intense, the colors were conspiring to mesmerize her into an altered state of well-being. She had heard Ma Mère discuss the great artists' works of the day and knew she too wanted to understand what inspired them to paint in a way that captured those scenes.

It warmed her thinking of such things. She might not be old enough to understand all the words, but her sense and sensibilities guided her to the meaning.

She really hadn't allowed herself to think too deeply about her grand-mère, but the time seemed right for reflecting on the relationship they had shared. Maybe it was the warmth of the sun, but she was certain that Grand-mère was sitting with her, sharing the scene.

Of one thing she was certain, there would come a time when their paths would cross again and they could once more share their common bond. Until then, Clarice would keep her close. Having all the wonderful memories of Grand-mère would be the driving force throughout her life.

Her own mother had surprised her in Paris by being strong, helping to guide the family when Papa was unavailable. She couldn't quite grasp the whole idea that perhaps she had misjudged her mother, but it was something she would explore in the future.

There was a momentary feeling of euphoria mingled with an almost imperceptible warming flush that spread over her with the idea that maybe, just maybe, her mother was stronger than Clarice had thought. Clarity brought a moment of pride containing a second of insight.

Rogue Movement

BEYOND THE GENTLE musings of Clarice, danger waited in the form of one Joseph Duvalier. In the depths of man's evil where Satan's influence lay wait, Duvalier was organizing the final movement of his plan to dismantle the fortunes of the late Madame Chevais. He quietly assembled the group at the usual place across Paris, on Rue de Rainier, for this last meeting before each would be sent to perform his assigned tasks.

The air hung heavy as the men approached Rue de Rainier. Masked by the dusk twilight, each slithered into place among his own kind, albeit the defiant Duvalier and the aloof Paul Marchand. Still under the delusion that he was merely an innocent victim pulled into a diabolical plan yet unable to disassociate from it, Paul managed to guild his guilty conscience with platitudes of excuse-ridden rhetoric.

The great Joseph Duvalier perceived himself to be above all the others, those who could be found scrambling for their scraps of the fortune. His was a grander mission, and the tasks at hand were only to feed the frenzy of this rebel flock.

Handing over the first of the documents neatly piled in four stacks, he addressed each of them. "Pierre, you have Mission I and the journey to Mulhouse. Please review your instructions now and ask any questions before you leave this room. Once departed, not one of you may contact me or each other until we meet in Lyon on the first of August."

While Pierre was reviewing his instructions, Duvalier called to each of the three remaining in the group, passing out documents two, three, and four, as if to render his judgment to each with the finality defined by a true court of law. There was no discussion among them—quiet to the last man.

It was a bit dramatic to the point of almost laughable even for the likes of Joseph Duvalier, but there was no mistaking his intent and the certainty that they were about to embark on a serious course of action.

Paul groaned inwardly under the weight of this knowledge and his culpability in the bizarre turn of events. Pondering what he might do to escape involvement, his thoughts were interrupted by Duvalier.

"If any of you have an issue or question with your assignment, this is the last time I will allow you to speak of it!" Duvalier declared.

"Paul, you are the one to whom I entrust the secrets of the Chevais holdings. You will have to follow your instructions to the letter with no assistance from me. You are the only one that Augusto trusted and you must pass muster in Mulhouse when this is all over."

Olivier had been pacing while looking over his document. It was quite apparent that he was distressed at the information contained therein. After reading his mission and unable to contain himself any longer, Olivier blurted, "You must be mad. What is this vendetta you have for the family of Marie Chevais? Can you not take your fair share and be done with it?"

"You did not object to our plan while enjoying the spoils of our little treasure hunts. Now you fear that we may pillage the entire fortune and perhaps harm the Chevais and Pontifi families?"

"This is different, Joseph, and though I may offend your sensibilities, I must speak out in protest. You cannot be serious with this so-called mission of yours!"

The hush in the room was crushing with the absence of sound. A friendship of many years became the first victim to fall. In its place remained a face distorted in wrath, shaded as if a dark crimson tide had washed over white sand, coloring it with the stain of blood.

"I say to you, Olivier, leave now and hold your tongue—or lose it!" Duvalier screamed at the startled man.

As shocked as he was, Olivier recognized the strain of madness that haunted Joseph Duvalier. Discretion was to be his savior today, and his future would be spared because of it. He made a hasty exit that gave no time to second thoughts.

Later, through a fit of conscience, he made a strategic decision to distance himself from this whole business. He could not, in good conscience, allow the Chevais and Pontifi families to be further harmed.

Olivier would try to warn Augusto before the plan was executed.

Brave Encounter

Into the Night

The road narrowed as the carriage moved stealthily through dark pockets of a moon-shy sky, pushing forward as if to say, "We'll make our way in spite of the difficulties we might encounter." The occasional blinking of diamond-crusted stars gave the half-sleeping somber group a reflection of the heavens, helping guide them to Mulhouse and beyond.

Navigating over a lesser-traveled route, they were on a road not made by man, black earth blending with the rock as if one, transcending from another time and place beyond the tranquil rolling hillsides. Pathways carved out from wagons and carriages of long ago, and the frequent bumping of the wheels cavorting and teasing the rough cobblestones reminded them they were no longer in Paris but close to their beloved manor.

Bernard sat at guard post atop the carriage along with their driver—a Spaniard named Miguel. Tense and alert, he gazed out over the landscape, straining to see beyond the gray shadowlike figures standing erect, statue-like, at the edge of what Bernard knew was part of the Rhine Valley.

If he held his breath, it was possible to hear the roar of water breaking against the sheer rock cliffs lining the river below. How he wished the moon, in all her majestic brilliance, had not let him down this night. He needed—in fact required—the extrasensory assist from what nature could provide, especially now.

Miguel, a short, stocky fellow, round as much as he was high, grunted to Bernard. "There ahead, señor, something is in the road."

At full attention now, Bernard commandeered the carriage away from Miguel. Miguel understood his boss and the need to be in full control with all his senses heightened in battle mode, ready to face danger. Bernard pulled on the reins with all his might, jockeying between the ruts in the road and control of the carriage as the horses fought to be free of their constraints.

To the right of the path, disaster awaited, the drop descending some three hundred feet to the raging river below, over razor-sharp, centuries-hardened shale, waiting to impale the misled traveler.

Even with the help of Miguel, the horses were almost too much for Bernard. He could hear the heartbeats of the magnificent animals, muscles straining and sinew stretched to the maximum, as they fought to regain control.

"Whoa! Whoa!" cajoled Bernard, continuing to pull with all his might, both thumbs bleeding profusely as the leather reins cut into the outer layers of his skin.

"Miguel, grab the other rein and twist it around the carriage seat. Quickly now!" commanded the gentle giant.

As if in slow motion, the carriage rolled to the edge of the cliff, coming to a complete stop. They pulled up just short, also avoiding a boulder that had mysteriously rolled onto their path. By now, the sleepy young riders were fully awake and anxiously asking questions of their crew.

Visibly shaken, the men managed to calm down enough to give comfort to their charges, assuring them they had never been in danger.

The children and their nanny were obviously shocked and frightened from the nearly disastrous accident, and as to be expected, they huddled together, shaking from fear yet trying to seem brave. Even Clarice was at a loss for words.

The first one to speak was Clarice. All she could manage was a whisper, "Well, I'm sure this would never happen again. As you can see, we are all fine."

She had broken the tension by speaking up, allowing for the boys' questions to come at a rapid pace now. After satisfactorily answering their questions, Jacques, the oldest boy in the group, bravely hinted that he could have saved them all if fate had taken them over the edge.

"Oh, you say now, Jacques," Andre derided half-heartedly, still in shock at what almost happened.

Clarice interrupted them from their silly banter, "Be quiet, both of you. Just because you can swim does not mean you could do anything about the jagged rock below, Jacques. This is not a matter to be discussed now."

She instinctively knew this was not normal, that something was amiss and she intended to find out all she could from Bernard later, out of earshot of the others. Even as young as she was, she couldn't shake the sense they were in danger.

Miguel and Bernard were unable to move the boulder more than a foot, but that was enough to allow the carriage room to maneuver around, making their way on to the manor.

More troubling to Bernard was the knowledge that only a couple of people knew their route would be changed to the secondary road. He had to assume malicious intent from whoever was trying to prevent them from reaching their destination. He vowed to stay on full alert, mindful of the danger in their path.

Luckily for them, their would-be assailant was so sure of the success of his plan and the ease with which he could carry it out that there was no backup in the event of failure.

It was just after midnight when they arrived at the manor. Even though it appeared all was quiet and remained undisturbed, Bernard was as attentive as a lion watching guard over the entrance to his cave.

Unsettled Times

As THE NEXT day unfolded, it became apparent that their drama from the night before was just the beginning of many tumultuous and agonizing days of waiting, wondering whether this abject normalcy was all they could expect. Was it all a dream, forever lost, along with a young girl's innocence?

Years later, Clarice played these scenes over and over in her mind until the inevitable clammy feeling would envelop her once again, claiming any peace she might have.

Arriving at the manor and making their way through the hallways in the early hours of morning, the group moved as though encased in a delicate shell, ready to break with any misstep taken. Bernard's sense of impending danger did not provide him any feeling of security. Even though he tried to shield his mood from his children, they knew something was amiss.

He was ever mindful of man's weakness of spirit and willingness to jump ship, straying from standard mores, especially when put to the test. The current climate, one brewing like a steam pot within France, supported undermining the long-held Frenchman's code of honor.

Bernard began to think freely of the numerous possible ways the information of their whereabouts and the route they would take was leaked to Duvalier's men. Top on the list of possible informants was the long-ago jilted boyfriend of Aurelia, the low-spirited, spineless Paul Marchand. Bennie never trusted him even though Paul had won the trust of Madame and Marcel. And he had spent enough time with them at Mulhouse to know of the different possible routes. He was certain that Paul was the one who would wish harm to the Chevais families, perhaps not physically but by undermining their family fortune.

Bernard had taken the children to his wing, tucking them into what he considered his safe haven. His *children* would be sequestered here until such time as he could decipher what was transpiring behind the scene; one that seemed to be painted as if in a bizarre kaleidoscope.

The question of who gave away their secret route nagged and consumed him, but not as much as what part this all played in the events of the past week.

Caution dictated that he conceal the whereabouts of the children temporarily, and even though Clarice did not like this latest turn of events, she judiciously obeyed Bernard's command. Her role became that of a hawk protecting her nest—keeping watch to ensure that the younger children were never out of her sight.

Not exactly a hidden apartment, Bernard's hideaway, nonetheless, kept the children away from the other staff and any unexpected visits from strangers—at least until he could be alerted.

Within his private space and behind a facade of Oriental screens flanked on all sides with native flowers and banana trees the size of baby palms was a door that appeared to be the entry into an unused potting shed with an exit to the outside. Unknown to the casual viewer was the old tunnel running behind a bank of shelves housing the family's old pottery. The tunnel had originally been built to connect the atrium to the fields and gardens.

This generation of the manor staff had no knowledge of the tunnel, except an acknowledgement that Bernard had his private area. It was an unspoken code of respect to leave any questions of secret tunnels and mysterious passage ways unasked. The hierarchy of the servants had been rooted in place for thirty years and, although curious about recent events, was not going to change their habits now.

Storage areas filled with old pots and rustic garden tools were in abundance within the side rooms. A distinct aroma of earth served to remind them of where they were. Just before the end of the main corridor was a light-filled sanctuary, created from the oversize grain storage bins of the last century.

In the center of the room were overstuffed sofas and chairs as comfortable as old slippers. It suited Bernard to spend his off days right in the midst and under the nose of his family—unbeknownst to all, including the children. The one exception was, of course, Augusto. "A fail-safe escape for times of trouble," Augusto had said when he and Bernard completed the renovation several years ago.

Clarice had followed him to his hideaway last year, and he had to swear her to secrecy then. Now even though this was at first exciting, by the end of the second day of this hideaway adventure, the children were straining to escape. Like the broken link in a chain, they were ready to snap their bindings and leap at the first opportunity to escape this temporary prison.

Unlike holidays of the past, this adventure did not have the same festive flair after the second day, and even the little ones sensed a change.

"Surely, we can go into the manor now, Bennie? When are Mama and Papa to arrive in Mulhouse?" asked Clarice. "They will free us from this prison even if you won't," she petulantly declared.

"Your mama and papa, along with your aunt Marcella and uncle Jonque, will be leaving Paris this very evening, arriving here in the first light of morning."

"Oh, thank heavens! Not that we don't love you, Bennie," she cried, realizing how her complaint might have offended the gentle giant.

That Bennie seemed caught up in his own thoughts and oblivious to what she had just said did not escape her. Years later, she would remember, as if yesterday.

Caught off guard for only that brief moment, Bernard cleared his throat and said gruffly, "Until then, please help me keep the boys calm and secured within the tunnel area, Clarice."

Softening at the stricken look on her face, he quietly said, "Oh, sweet girl, we'll go for a walk later when the sky turns to the color of slate and the horizon is like a ripe melon. Do not despair, for despair will only bring you to a place of darkness, my dear. All will be well when the family arrives tomorrow."

She sighed audibly, breathing into her small frame, exhaling to say, "I understand, Bennie, but I want everything to be as it was two weeks ago."

"Clarice, your worries are those of a woman, yet you are still a child. We cannot predict the future, nor can we dwell in the past, for bright days are those that we live in the present, not expecting but enjoying all that life has in store. You are so young and yet so wise. Someday, you will understand the depth of love that dwells within you, waiting to share with those less fortunate and for whom which you will carry their banner."

His words sounded hollow even if he wanted to believe them. But now, when faced with telling this woman-child, Bernard could not keep from spitting them out in rapid fire, hurrying to finish his philosophical musings before losing his nerve.

Satisfied enough with his answer, Clarice busied herself with the boys, careful not to encourage any further exploration. A feeling of impending doom hung like the moss clinging to the tree branches just beyond reach.

Catastrophe

Meltdown

AUGUSTO, ALONG WITH his entourage of family and a few friends, climbed into the comfort of the Oriental Express's special sleeper cars. Exhaustion from the past few days and even weeks made his eyes heavy, coupled with anxiety over what could be happening behind the scenes would not free him to succumb to peaceful slumber.

Aurelia was already in her dreamworld, and he hoped she was finding comfort from the inner peace that only sleep could bring. He could hear Marcella and Jonque quarreling across the tiny space that divided the two sleeping quarters.

"If only she hadn't been so stubborn, Jonque, your mother would be alive today. You must stop blaming yourself for any omission of attention you may think caused this to happen. I won't hear of you berating the honorable man that you are. If there was an omission, my love, it was caused by a lapse in judgment of Marie's own making. She was a beautiful, vibrant woman with the one weakness the women in your family have. Notwithstanding her independent spirit, Marie had a soft spot for the men in her life!"

"Do not speak of my mother in this way, Marcella!"

"It is the truth, Jonque, but even so, there is a grace of spirit in the ability of a strong woman to make mistakes, especially with affairs of the heart. I am not judging her, but mark my words, there is a man who had her confidence, and somewhere in Paris right now he bears responsibility for this vile act."

"Why would she leave herself vulnerable to the likes of a scoundrel of such low breeding?" demanded Jonque. "She did not need a man! Only a foolish woman, and we know Ma Mère was not so, would indulge of the flesh in such a way as to risk losing her control."

"Sweet, kind Jonque, Marie Chevais would not have taken the chance with her business and any interference in the affairs of her beloved family. It may be that this individual had her trust early, worked with her, and perhaps betrayed her in the end. It is quite possible that he may have deserved the trust in the beginning but fell victim to the anti-societal thinking that seems to be prevalent today. There are many motivators that can push a good man or woman into such thinking.

"Right now, even if you are a Republican, you become suspect of being avaricious and selfish of spirit. Marie would never stoop to this type of behavior but, because of her success and the family's wealth, might have been targeted to be made an example."

Jonque sighed at the thought that his dear mother may have been duped into a relationship that superseded all sense of reason because of the heartstrings of a lonely woman.

"I would prefer to think that there was never a disreputable element but rather a passion that grew in her heart that belied the evil of one she trusted." And with that, Jonque turned away to shut out any more words from his all-too-direct but caring wife.

Marcella reflected on the characteristics and traits of the great Madame Chevais. She may not have been born a noble, but proper breeding paved the way for the beautiful woman to capture the limelight within the affluent Paris scene. Ebullient and tenacious, she forged her own place among the literati prevalent among the wealthy do-gooders of the past three decades.

If she had to determine the one trait among the many, it would be the naked, exposed absolute honesty with which Marie conducted her life and affairs. It was this trait that could have served to open the door for an unsuspecting Marie to include a traitorous friend in her private dealings.

The death of her beloved mother-in-law was horrendous enough, but Marcella feared the residual damage that had been done was irreparable, and she prayed that Augusto's efforts would save the rest of the family from the unknown marauders' impending assaults.

Sometime later, Marcella drifted off to sleep. Across the way in the adjacent cabin, a very weary Augusto was calculating the effects of the recent events on the family's business and the steps he had already instituted to protect his loved ones. The estate would remain intact as long as certain strategic plans made over the past few weeks could stop or control the damage already done. His biggest concern was the current physical danger from Duvalier and his business *associates* and how to insulate his family further.

As for his business affairs, he would have to manage them both from Mulhouse and Paris. Jonque would have to assist in this almost unfathomable task, but together they would have the tools to effectively slow down operations to a maintenance level until all the miscreants were eradicated or in prison.

For Augusto, sleep was not forthcoming, but he was grateful for the peace and solitude the cabin quiet afforded him as his family rested. The conversation he overheard disturbed him not so much because of the tone but the content and the surprising information, some of which he had never given thought to.

Only Paul Marchand would have had Marie's trust. The question now was how much information he may have pulled from the unsuspecting Marie, what part he may have kept to himself for future arrangements, and, the most pertinent at the moment, how much he shared with Joseph Duvalier. He determined it was much like extracting a pearl from the sea, which ones you harvest and select for future use may determine the success of your operation.

Duvalier's influence could impact his family for many years, inflicting pain and suffering beyond the death of their beloved grand-mère. It nagged at him as he sought answers to what other traps may await them even now and vowed to untangle the webs of deceit woven around his beloved family.

Augusto's eyes were heavy, and like the others in his party, he drifted off to a sound sleep, impervious to outside interference. This one time he would indulge in the respite, allowing himself a blessed relief from the pressures of his thoughts.

Perhaps it was his sixth sense or a noise outside the door, but Augusto was roused from sleep after only a few minutes of slumber. He made a quick decision to outline recent changes to the family holdings, where the documents had been moved within the Swiss banks, and other safeguards instituted within the past couple of days.

Rather than wait to discuss these important issues with Bernard once safely in Mulhouse, he opted to have the conductor stop at the next station and allow the message to be transported on to Mulhouse via special courier. After imploring the engineer that it was a matter of life or death, he reluctantly agreed to stop. Augusto returned to the sleeper car, but the unease was still with him.

Freight car 7 behind the sleeper cabins had been loaded at the last stop, Troyes. Assured that enough supplies filled the space to last several days, providing his passengers with ample food and the French necessity of good champagne, the engineer had just settled into his routine when disrupted by Augusto. He was grumbling as Augusto left and couldn't shake the feeling of doom. If he hadn't been one of their more important passengers, the engineer might have ignored both the conductor and Augusto.

At the very same time, a lone figure moved around the freight car, preparing for a quick exit. He had carried out his part of the plan and now had to set it in motion. For the moment, time stood still yet rushed him as if scripted for a role in a play. He managed to make his way to the door, disappearing into the night.

It was noted in the *Paris Gazette* the following day that the Orient Express to Mulhouse had met with an untimely accident at or about 2:30 a.m., and in fact, it was thought there were few survivors. Most of the passengers were sleeping at the time of the accident—a blessed relief, according to one journalist who had been traveling on the later train from Paris. His account of the wreck left little doubt that sabotage may have been the basis for the destruction and, to the extent the remains were blown to pieces, could only conjure up the mayhem that must have ensued once the initial blasts leveled the first sleeper car.

Determining who were among the casualties would prove to be a Herculean task that required months of effort by the best forensic scientists from Paris working round the clock.

The stories were told over and over by the few survivors. Each time, the horror of the passengers' last few minutes were always recounted the same way. The first explosion blasted a hole in the side of the main railcar, killing most of the sleeping passengers in the Number One instantly, followed by multiple smaller blasts rocking the very life out of those sleeping in the latter cabooses.

In later years, after many agonizingly painful and sleepless nights, the only solace Clarice had was in believing her parents had been spared the knowledge of their impending doom. Since they had been in the Number One car, it was easy to believe they had not suffered one moment.

Friends and villagers rallied around the Chevais and Pontifi children along with the ever-faithful Bernard. Events were unfolding quickly, and in an effort to spare the children more heartache, they were shielded from all outsiders.

The decision to hold the funerals en masse was based on the belief that since all had perished in the Number One car, they would proceed without positive identification. Even though the villagers conducted the solemn services with total conviction of the deaths of their beloved Pontifis and Chevaises, Clarice knew in her heart that they were still alive. She refused to believe otherwise, and when Bernard had first told her, she walked away. Unwilling to listen further to the words he had uttered, she closed her mind and thus began the next phase of her young life.

The End of an Era

Clarice could pretend with the best of them. She watched the hands of the clock, moving motionlessly around the face, interspersed with the persistent sound of ticking. The words of the priest kept coming at her, yet she refused to open her ears to hear them. *I will never believe his words.*

The days after were like moving through a never-ending, fog-consumed tunnel—winding, winding deeper into an area twisted and dark. She was fighting with all her might not to lose control.

Bernard's voice interrupted her thoughts moving on an erratic pathway, one chosen not by her intent but where she most often found herself now. "Clarice, my chérie, you must accept that your parents are gone. Please listen to what the priest is saying. They are in heaven now, and you will someday be reunited with them." He pulled what he could from his knowledge of their Catholic faith but still couldn't seem to break through this immovable object that once was his beloved Clarice.

She could hear his voice, but she didn't want to listen to his words. If she didn't hear his words, then it couldn't be true! She went back to the blackness, to a mock comfort of being in the presence of nothing.

Bernard was seriously worried about her state of mind right now, among other things. The word from Paris was that Duvalier had orchestrated this successful attempt to destroy the Pontifis and Chevaises and the children were in imminent danger. Once all the properties had been found and confiscated, they would be signed over to Joseph Duvalier. Bernard was sure that he would come after them all.

His duties were clear; even now he could hear Augusto's words echoing in his mind. They had just buried Marie Chevais and Augusto pulled him aside for what would become their last serious meeting. "You must, at all costs, save the children. Do not give heed to anyone or anything. In the event that any mishap should befall the Chevais dynasty, you will follow the orders contained in this envelope. They will guide you if all else fails. I do not expect it to be so, but we must be prepared, Bernard."

"I understand, sir, and you have my oath that the children will be taken care of even if it's in my last breath."

"Bernard, you have been a faithful servant and more, a friend of three generations of Chevaises and then Pontifis. I could not have asked for a more honorable man to have at my side and to trust with my most precious jewels. There were documents missing from Madame's office, and I'm afraid they may have contained the second part of the official family seal—the other half of the code to the Swiss bank accounts. We were not able to find these documents before the funeral, but I don't believe these would have fallen in Duvalier's hands."

Augusto continued, "Because of Marie's great distrust of Duvalier's recent actions, she confided to me that the foundation was secured. Unfortunately, she never made it to Mulhouse and we did not complete our discussion."

The courier carrying Augusto's final will and, most important, the details of where the Pontifi family documents and holdings were kept arrived on the day of the funerals. Bernard was surprised by the visit but humbled by the vision of the doomed Augusto confronting the possibility of his fate while the clock ticked on through the night.

It brought Bernard to his knees in tearful prayer; a man unaccustomed to breaking down, he wept openly.

Dynasty in Shambles

At the same time, Duvalier was instructing his group to implement phase II, the final phase, even as he covered his flank. Now that a big portion of his plan in phase I had failed, thanks in part to Paul Marchand's traitorous betrayal, it was time to regroup and salvage the remains of the fortune to which he could lay claim.

His mood would have been dangerously menacing, except he could bask in the knowledge that the Pontifis and Chevaises had been obliterated. The word from his contact inside the Chevais manor confirmed that the remaining family members consisted of only the children, leaving the long-time French dynasty in shambles.

He could claim most of the antiques, paintings, and other precious jewels as partial payment owed on long-term debts that Madame Chevais had pledged to repay but never followed through with. Forged papers in hand, he was ready to move forward with this part of his plan.

At least the debt allegations supported by the fake papers would be the cover story when his request was heard in court two weeks hence, continuing with the destruction of the family, even attacking and undermining their reputations—justly deserved—as honorable, trustworthy, loyal French patriots.

It could be said that to shred a man's honor would bring the wrath of those ancestors upon the house of the perpetrators. Duvalier had no thought of remorse or even slight concern of such superstitions. To him, their reputation merely represented the Pontifi-Chevais false badge of honor, written on the tablet of time and so openly displayed that it begged to be crumbled with the hammer of doubt.

The weakness in the family could be characterized as their greatest strength—that of one man's humble acceptance of another man, even that of a long-ago enemy.

It was no secret that their loyalties were divided between Alsace and France. Having been exposed to the political beliefs of each in the village of Mulhouse, they grew to understand and empathize with both sides. The villagers were friendly with one another and the Chevais family members without the animosity associated with supporting one cause over the other. They remained neutral and continued to embrace both cultures.

Duvalier knew playing on that theme would be easy, like turning the wheel to increase the flow on an already robust stream of water cascading down the falls, gaining strength and momentum as the pressure increased. So it was when the hearing was held in the Montmartre Judicial District on August 20, 1889.

The travesty of injustice forced upon the family of Marie Chevais could only be viewed as a malicious, intentional repayment of imagined wrongs, brought to bear by unscrupulous means and only allowed to flourish because of the heated emotions that prevailed in France at the time. Normally, any political climate that might take issue with families of great wealth would have easily been diffused, particularly in light of the Chevais's remarkable contribution to the French people.

Even though the treasures were worth millions of francs, Duvalier had to find the documents for the land holdings. There would be no rest until that time, and finding Paul Marchand was his first order of business. Once Paul had disappeared, he had ordered two of his best men to search until they found him, keeping him alive at least long enough to discover information that might give Duvalier enough to find the rest of the fortune. Clues to Marie's daily habits and where she stashed secret papers—and certainly there were many that Duvalier had not been privy to—would lead him to the remainder.

Even in death, Marie Chevais was trying to one-up him but he would have the last laugh. When he finished with Paul Marchand's information, the girl, Clarice, might prove to be worth keeping alive long enough to elicit just the right tidbit to help in his search.

There had been whispers that the Chevaises had a fortune in Swiss banks, but he could not make a determination from what he had illicitly seen in Madame's vaults and among her books. Rifling through her remaining documents did not offer additional information that might confirm this assertion, but he was aware of the holdings through his spy, Paul Marchand.

It was quite a pity that they had to dispose of him, at least so soon and before Duvalier could gather more before they cut out his tongue.

There would be time enough to follow that path to see where it would lead. At times he could be a very patient man in spite of those who might believe otherwise—much to their misfortune. After all, wasn't he the one chosen by Napoleon III to become the leader of tomorrow—a direct result of the persuasion from his friend, Count duc de Morny.

Yes, in time all the pieces would fall into place and his, Monsieur Joseph Duvalier's, greatness would shine through, making his name for all to remember!

PART FIVE

The Beginning (Summer 1892)

Sitting there staring at the rolling countryside dulled her senses. How many seasons had it been? She numbly gave some attention to the changes but couldn't or had no desire to move into whatever landscape was present now.

She could see hawks swooping over a sun-caressed field in the valley below. *I wonder if they are pecking out the eyes of whatever lies in pathetic wait,* she mused. *Whatever bird or beast is lying there had a family, but they are no more.*

When she first arrived at the convent nestled in the mountains surrounding Bern, Switzerland, the hawks were soaring even then, protecting their territory from outside intruders.

The entry drive leading to the convent was hidden from view by the thick bank of underbrush, grown to massive heights and left to the wilderness for centuries expressly for the purpose of concealing any visible access to the *Castle in the Sky*. An astute observer could find the entrance only after diligently searching through heavy brush.

It had intrigued Clarice, the grandeur of the structure upon entering the lower loop—very much like a small castle with outcroppings for the many towers looking out over the beautiful valleys below. As quickly as the thought had entered her consciousness, it disappeared like the wisp of wind on a flapping sail. In her depressed state of mind, she could not quite grasp the grand scale of her new home, choosing instead to move through her days in a numbed state of mind.

The old Clarice would have loved the beauty and accompanying serenity of the *Castle*, and exploring would have been the first order of the day. There was no joy to pull at her curiosity, no interest in her surroundings, just another day in her life. Akin to an accomplished artist, who, upon setting out to paint the Mona Lisa, lost his sight, Clarice felt the same of her new home.

The nuns were whispering again, and in spite of her determination not to listen, Clarice found herself pulled to the voices.

"She's not responding to any of our attempts to draw her out, Sister Mary," said the Mother Superior.

"It has been almost three years since the tragedy. If we don't break through soon, we'll lose her forever," lamented Sister Mary.

Sister Francine, the psychologist assigned to work with Clarice, offered her own assessment. "She's still so deep within the trauma of losing her parents, aunt, and uncle and her way of life it's going to be difficult to bring her around. Even Andre cannot bring her joy, and her rebuff of him when we last put them together was detrimental to our efforts of building his good mental health. My responsibility to Andre is as clear as that to Clarice, so before exposing him to her again in his fragile state, we must work on his self-confidence and coach him in ways to absorb her disdain and rejection of him. He must be comfortable enough to understand that it is not him who must be pitied but Clarice, who is so bottled up with anger and fear of loss that she cannot or will not allow anyone to enter into her life."

Sister Mary, whom the nuns referred to as the Golden One because of the beautiful long blond hair she had upon arrival at the convent, now long gone, was the sentimentalist among the sisters. Her crystal blue eyes seemed to pull at the heartstrings of any who looked her way. She declared, "We all know that Andre is the key to unlock her door, for it was his name she kept calling out from the early darkness. She was his protector, and once she becomes comfortable and secure in the knowledge that he is safe, I believe in my heart that she will draw him in."

"You may be right, Sister Mary, but for now, I am unwilling to take that chance," said Sister Francine in no uncertain terms.

"What about the family dynasty? Has Father Pierre met with the Swiss consul general to see if he has traced the whereabouts of the family land holdings now that he has the official Chevais seal as proof? There is also the question of the numbered Swiss bank accounts," inquired Sister Margaret.

Clarice had been listening intently, but something was stirring within her: anger so strong it consumed her every thought, stripping raw the bare core of her nerve endings. Shaking furiously now, the realization finally hit her that, yes, there had been an ulterior motive at work in the deaths of her parents.

She may have toyed with the idea briefly but always pushed it aside for fear of facing the truth. How could she deny the obvious? It was time for her to think rationally of how to avenge her parents' deaths and the deaths of all her loved ones.

Summoning all her control and pushing the anger aside, she was now determined to pay attention to the nuns. This might be information she needed to make her way to Paris.

"How did Father Pierre acquire the seal after all this time? And what will that do for Clarice and Andre?"

"Shhhhh, Sister Mary, Clarice is sitting by the window over there and may hear you!"

"But, Mother Superior, she has turned a deaf ear. Posing as a rebellious child belies her sadness, but her eyes, oh, her eyes, they tell the truth. Deep within the shell, there is a pain that reflects, as a mirror splintered by brute force, a soul of one who has lost the very threads that bound them to the cloth of life."

"When Father Pierre returns, my hope is we will have some news that could help this family rebuild. Certainly, Andre is young enough that he can overcome the trauma in time. If only we can move Clarice to engage with him again. She will be turning thirteen in a couple of months and will be of an age where her curiosity might pull her toward the truth or at least start exploring her history," said Sister Mary.

Mother Superior noted, "The bounty remaining of the Chevais family dynasty is enough to warrant our careful diligence in the way we preserve our records and calculate the holdings before presenting to Miss Clarice when she comes of age."

Ignoring the discussion of worldly goods and the preservation of the family heritage, Sister Francine, the most self-righteous among the sisterhood, interrupted Sister Mary and the Mother Superior. "The matter of possessions does not interest me, but Clarice's interaction with Andre should become the most important issue we have to deal with! Her rejection of Andre last time did so much damage it took several weeks of counseling and all our efforts in cajoling him to bring him back around. I cannot or will not allow him to be exposed to another round of rejection."

In her fog, Clarice heard what they said. Why do they think she would even care? It's too difficult to love people and then have them leave you. Yes, she could be self-contained—didn't need anyone's attention, love, or whatever else they were trying to push on her! And yes, her impending birthday meant that she was that much closer to leaving and making her way to Paris.

She was more than a little interested in the conversation about Father Pierre and why he went to Switzerland. *I'll pay more attention*, she vowed to herself.

The whispering continued, but the nuns had moved farther away now that she displayed an interest in their conversation.

They thought she couldn't remember what transpired the two weeks after her parents' deaths, but she knew all too well. It was better to keep these secrets from even the nuns. She couldn't trust anyone, except, perhaps, Father Pierre—or at least she had to try and trust him.

The father reminded her of Bernard, the warm familiarity gave her comfort, so much like the big lovable man, capable of great compassion. If only she could find the words to speak to him and win his confidence. She hadn't exactly been open to his overtures and continued to remain a solitary figure within the confines of the convent.

Father Pierre did seem to really care, and what he had done for Andre did not escape her attention. She might act as if she did not love Andre, but nothing could be further from the truth—at least she thought she could remember what that was like, or could she?

As she forced herself to remember, the feeling moved again like a tide, ripping into her stomach, threatening to engulf her, sucking the air out of her lungs, choking her as it did. It was always like that whenever she allowed feelings to move toward conscious awareness.

Pulling her wall back in place, she resumed an objective, albeit cold reasoning process, one she used whenever weakness threatened to overtake her. Now she also had anger in her arsenal. "I'll keep the anger for the fight!" she spoke almost too loudly to herself.

Andre had a chance to heal from the emotional wounds without her interference, and as long as she continued her boycott even though the nuns would try periodically to force him on her, he could continue to progress. Her wounded state debilitated and rendered her emotionally impotent, certainly to the extent that open love for him was impossible.

She spied on him occasionally, watching him at play with the other young boys. Wisps of curls fell on his shoulders, outlining his cherubic face, one that looked much like her mother. As painful as it was to conjure a picture of her, it pleased her to imagine Andre as a young man. He was almost nine years old now, and although still a boy, the day would come when he would be a man.

Perhaps then she could finally open the door and allow him to penetrate the wall she had erected. Her sense of purpose diminished as the fear mounted once again. It was time to act on her instincts and initiate a friendship with Father Pierre. What she had to learn could only come from him, and Bernard had trusted him enough to pass to him the only existing family secrets.

In The Tunnel

The Secret

As if it was yesterday, she remembered that last shattering conversation with Bernard, the one before she left for the convent. Even though he had counseled her before and after the funerals, this conversation was unlike any of the others—more sobering and so final. To realize her parents had possibly been murdered and their lives were in immediate danger was far more than any newly turned ten-year-old could absorb. All that she had loved in Mulhouse had been stripped from her.

Bernard had received advance warning from someone, telling him to hide the children. Even though the manor house had been a safe haven for many years, the recent events had proven that those who wished her family harm had managed to find out all the intricate and detailed family secrets that were hidden within the manor, including the first part of the family seal.

It was no accident or by chance those hiding places had been discovered and passed to Joseph Duvalier. The knowledge of a traitor among the staff had left Bernard shaken but resolved to move quickly to secure all the family's birthright—the long list consisting of properties, estate holdings, and any valuable documents, including the seal.

The conspirator came to the manor in the middle of the third night, after the funeral mass had silenced all the joy, replacing the children's laughter with their lonely tears. What had been the robust conversation of happy people became the hushed whispers of a grieving staff. Cloaked to avoid being seen, he came into the manor through the hidden tunnels, meeting Bernard halfway. She had seen him but could not make out who he was, nor could she hear what he was telling Bernard.

Bernard's face billowed out as if being blown up like a balloon, slowly turning pink and finally a shade of crimson red, ready to burst. Shouting in an angry whisper, his veins protruded like those in a rooster's neck. Bernard poked at the stranger's face menacingly, as if to make a point to the stricken man.

From her hiding place, it was obvious to Clarice that the stranger was in a hurry, but she couldn't hear what he was saying while frantically relating to Bernard the events of the past few weeks leading up to the explosions on the train. He glossed over who the culprits were, but she could tell by the animated way he and Bernard were talking that something was very wrong.

The sound was muffled but hearing them just enough, she had the first of one of her feelings and it made her weak with fear. She felt numb but wouldn't allow herself the right to cry because crying would mean her parents really were gone. It was a thought Clarice had that just wasn't possible, was it? But what if they all were in danger? That would mean leaving her only refuge—the manor.

Surely, Bernard would calm her with his always reassuring reason once the stranger had departed. As she was inching closer, there were sounds from the other end of the corridor.

"Shhh, be still until I can see who approaches," commanded Bernard. The men turned and looked toward the noise building behind where Clarice was hiding.

It was a priest moving quickly toward the duo, obviously in a great hurry, his robes billowing behind him. It struck her even then that his appearance was prearranged and this was a meeting of great significance. She noticed that he was young and seemed somewhat anxious upon being introduced to the cloaked stranger.

Bernard's voice, strained to maintain a level of calmness, broke through to her then. "Father Pierre, please meet Paul Marchand who, up until three days ago, shall we say, was involved with Monsieur Joseph Duvalier, the executor and attorney for Madame Chevais. A close confidante and friend of Marie for many years, he kept secret watch on the Chevais's transactions carried out by the law firm of Duvalier, LaFranc, and Menuet."

His voice still under duress, and threatening to escalate, Bernard gritted his teeth to continue. "Further, Father, Paul accepts some of the responsibility for his role in the deaths of Marie Chevais and her children!" And with that, there was a silence so profound Clarice feared her very breath could be heard down the length of the tunnel.

It took a moment for any of the trio to react to the profundity of Bernard's words. Paul was ashen in appearance, the marker of a man guilty of a sin so wicked even he could not bear the thought of it.

Beads of perspiration rolled down her face as she fought to remain steady in her position behind the trio. Surely she had misunderstood what he said. Afraid to give any more credit to what might have been discussed, she quickly refocused her attention on the men and their conversation.

"Paul, why don't you tell Father Pierre exactly what transpired over the past few days? And don't leave out any details because it's possible there may be something significant that will help us protect these precious children!"

Visibly shaken and distressed, Paul Marchand began his story, "Father, please forgive me because I have failed my beloved Marie Chevais in her greatest hour of need. It was my lack of attention in the last two weeks to the secret meetings that had been taking place that may have contributed to Madame's death."

"Why don't you also admit to Father that you became caught up in the devil's work," Bernard defiantly prodded. "You are also a fool to think we can't see the greed within you!"

"I beg you, please listen to what I have to say. You are right, and for that I must seek forgiveness, but to say greed is not fair. Most certainly there was an element of political correctness, and I may have been caught up in the wave of *anti-German* sentiment," he paused, waiting to see if Bernard would react to his anti-German statement before continuing on with his story.

"Unquestionably, you understand the climate in France as we speak but where I was misled, as a fool to gold, I trusted Joseph's motives for moving against Madame and all that she represented as part of French society. My intent was never to harm Madame, but I fear—"

"Shut up, traitor!" bellowed Bernard, cutting the man off in midsentence.

It was obvious to the young priest that this gentleman was begging for absolution, and even though he could alleviate Paul's guilt, there was no time for priestly duties as the clock was ticking on them even now.

"You can take your penance, sir, as soon as you share all the critical information with us. It is vital for the children's sake that we at least have as much detail as you can possibly relate. We can take care of your soul later." He knew the brusqueness he displayed was not in keeping with a man of the cloth, but he had no other recourse.

Shaken but determined to learn as much as possible, Clarice continued observing from her hiding place, noticing the man in the cloak pull out what appeared to be gold-embossed documents. She could not make out any of the details, but before they moved out of her earshot, there was no mistaking the words *golden seal.*

They moved around another corner, and try as she might to hear, the words were muffled and she could no longer make them out. Frustrated, she tried to move from her position but managed to make enough noise to alarm the trio into moving farther down the corridor.

As the second half of the golden seal passed hands to the young priest, Bernard was pulling a document out of a sealed envelope which had been given to him from a courier dispatched by Augusto. As it was explained later, the handoff could only have been accomplished at the last stop before the explosion.

"Make haste, Father!" cried Bernard. "I will ready the children for the trip before the dawn, and by the twenty-fourth hour hence, they will be within your sanctuary. God be with you and the children's destiny."

As the men ran back out of the tunnel, Clarice confronted Bernard. "What is going on, Bennie, that you are making such a fuss with those men? I heard some of what was said. Tell me now or—" And with that, she burst into tears long held.

Grabbing her and pulling her close in his arms, Bennie said, "Oh, my sweet Clarice, it is time for the truth and you must listen to me. The man who came to us in the cloak was an old friend to Ma Mère but, along the path he traveled, became a spy in the network controlled by a man named Duvalier who would harm her and, further, your mother and father.

"This underground element is controlled by this man, Duvalier. It's possible that he can be tied directly to many deaths, if not by his own hand, then through the activities of those who are his followers. Remember his name, Clarice, for he is the one who is responsible for the deaths of…" He could not say the words.

He paused, thinking of the lame excuse Paul Marchand had given to explain his involvement with Duvalier. It was true there had been the war over the region called Alsace-Lorraine between Germany and France, but it had been over now for many years finally going back to the Germans in 1871. Most Frenchmen and Alsace-Lorrainers were of the same blood many times over. To think there had ever been strife was difficult for him.

"I don't want to hear it again," she wailed. "They are alive! I know it!"

A downtrodden but resolute Bernard quietly said, "Be that as you wish, my love, but in the meantime, we must protect you, your brother, and cousin, Jacques." The time for sentimentality was long gone, and he took command of the situation as only a soldier under fire might.

"There will be a carriage here at dawn which will transport you to a safe haven—away from those who would do you harm. I cannot protect you any longer, and my fear is that when Joseph Duvalier—and make no mistake, he is the evildoer—finds out that there is more to the Chevais and Pontifi estate, he will pursue it at all costs."

With that he turned and walked away, leaving the shaken child to sob uncontrollably. She might have understood his urgency and seeming lack of sensitivity if her mind hadn't blocked the recent events. What sleep she might have had was all but over with the finality of her conversation with Bernard.

They had little time for goodbyes the next morning, but he managed to pull her into his massive arms for one last embrace. Her hurt and anger disappeared when she realized that her beloved Bernard was not leaving with them.

Reflecting on the past years as the trusted steward of the Pontifi family, Bennie allowed himself to once again feel the happiness they had all shared. It was only for a moment soon to be crushed by the new reality.

Life had a way of humbling them when least expected. Sadness can sometimes be described as a feeling of profound loss, and yet there is an understanding at a deeper level, the waning of all the good we have known now becomes part of our past.

Transformation

Peeking from behind the pew, she could see Father Pierre on his knees, moving through his rosary beads in silent prayer. Intrigued by his rhythmic motions and the occasional burst of his escaping breath, she compared it to the wail of the calliope when forced to action. Like a musical street vendor lovingly applying suction to his instrument as he moved through the crowds, the priest had given his full attention to the beads.

"I wonder what he prays for in his solitude," she whispered out loud, realizing for an instant that she was mumbling to herself.

Motivated by her own inner demons, she decided it might be time to approach Father Pierre. She would have to take the risk that this move would open the long-festering wounds for him to see. It would also expose her to the ugliness once again, ripping at her core. Buoyed by her own curiosity and sheer willpower, she made her decision.

"I'll feel him out for any information that will restore my family's heritage. Whatever Bennie gave him in the tunnel may lead me to the truth."

The low husky voice grew louder, bending again in quiet prayer. From her vantage point, she studied the young priest. Chiseled features were hidden behind the cloak of the priesthood, draped so to provide privacy during his confessions of the rosary.

She unwillingly allowed her thoughts to wander back to her parents and the pain of loss she'd endured. It always was the same. They were laughing and planning their summer holiday with family and friends: her father leaving for another trip but ready for the summer to arrive two months hence and her mother happily preparing for the exodus. An agenda for the family holiday always enlivened her mother in ways that were foreign to her the rest of the year.

Those days were infused with joy and the promise of the future—one filled with family remembrances of loving moments past, the fun and frivolity of seeing old friends, their many great expeditionary excursions into places unknown, and that unfulfilled yet expectant anticipation of being together for many years to come.

Just as it always did when she started to warm to the memories, the force hit her again and again, swirling into infinity, as if rewinding time. It left her breathless and weak, threatening to unwind the brittle and frayed edges of her nerves, splitting them into millions of floating particles, never to find their way back to a complete whole.

Thoughts of a future without her parents and Bernard, Grand-mère, and all the others were painful to the point of despair—deeper than any she had known as the waves rushed over her, ready to drown her, bringing her to her knees as she gasped for air.

Unable to change the path of her mind, she abruptly stood up and on wobbly legs, ran from the chapel, escaping into the garden where her sobs could be heard only by the occasional birds landing in the branches of the willow oaks.

Father stopped and, for one brief moment, moved to follow her. He knew she was there, assessing him as he worked through his rosary. Just as he feared, her flight ended any feeble attempt to connect with him. Frustrated as he was to once again lose this opportunity to pull her out of the deep dark place where she had lived since her arrival at the convent, he knew that it would have to be on her terms.

Still confident that Clarice would find the courage to confront her demons, he backed away, hoping the battle would soon be won. Father Pierre continued his rosary, adding a prayer for the small success today—others would say ridiculous but he knew better—and the promise of the future.

He assured himself through his hushed prayers that Clarice was moving closer to confronting her demons and warming to the future by the very way her curiosity pushed to expose the rawness of her past.

The sobbing, muffled by the sound of convent bells ringing, could only be heard by those who recognized it as the cry of a lost soul, not yet healed but beginning to feel life. Her cries were much like the wail of a calf that, as its mother lies dying from the brunt force of a misaligned birth, struggles to stand, instinctively knowing her foundation is gone but wobbly legs anxious to explore the world that waits.

As the sun was moving behind the garden, Clarice sat, quiet now but for an occasional sniffle, watching the amber twilight twisting and moving as the streaks of fiery red followed by brilliant purple moved closer to the earth.

There in the garden, she finally understood what Bernard had been trying to tell her. It was calming to think of him in her current frame of mind, groping to find a balance between the pain and joy of remembering.

Something has changed, she thought. The dark fell, clinging like a dew covered blanket being spread on the moss-covered banks of a meandering river, almost floating on the damp earth. A single wash of light illuminated her spot in the garden, and in that instant she knew. She spoke to the night or to anyone who would listen. "I will survive, learn what I must, understand that which I cannot or will not forget and live my life the way my parents would have wanted."

In the hours following her dramatic breakthrough, Clarice made a promise to herself and to the family she lost: never to forget and never to bend to any man's will! Forever proud, forever strong.

A New Friendship

The *Garden of Light*, so aptly named for the spirit of St. Francis, became the focus of great attention among the nuns. It was said that in the right circumstance and with concentrated prayers directed to one soul, an angel would be revealed in a beam of light as she made her way to the lost one.

It was an interesting theory and arguably hard to dispute based on recent events—the last such event having occurred a century before. The nuns were abuzz these days, describing the miracle of Father Pierre's and their own prayers, positive that the Almighty Father had intervened to heal the beautiful Clarice.

Sister Mary could not contain her feeling of joy at the transformation that had taken place only two short months ago. "Clarice seems to be making progress every day now," she remarked to Sister Francine. "Soon she will be well enough to see Andre again."

"Do not over anticipate her progress just because she has come out of her shell, Sister Mary!" The harsh tone surprised the sister but even Sister Francine had to admit that Clarice was bonding well with Father Pierre.

"Surely, Sister Francine, the breakthrough in the garden was the hand of God, and even you of deep faith understand that the Lord works miracles beyond our understanding and control."

"Perhaps, but consider where she has come from and how quickly she seems to have bounced back—an unnatural state, if you ask me."

"There is a little seed in every soul that can sprout into full bloom, then when subjected to the harshness and sometimes brutal gaze of the sun, wither and die. Another bloom may wilt but rebound under the same conditions as long as it is nurtured with love and tender care, never showing the scars of its difficult growth. Our Clarice is much like the blooms on our rose bushes, stripped bare of its buds after the storm and left with a thorny frame, fragile at best but ready for spring and new life."

Clarice could be found these days sitting in *her* garden writing or talking with Father Pierre. Mindful of her primary motivation now, she was careful not to alarm him or allow him a glimpse into her newfound freedom albeit riveted in following through on her mission.

He was easy to read, and as she plodded along with her mundane conversations, Clarice could tell when she had asked a question that came too close to her quest to find out the truth, thereby raising his suspicions.

As sweet and naive as she had always been, there was no mistaking that an intense sense of survival festered within her and created a depth of understanding far beyond her years. That she could manipulate a man more than twice her age seemed as natural as the skills bestowed on young women coming of age and possessing an innate sense of their own sexuality.

The *vision* she had seen in the garden was as clear today as it had been that night. Clarice replayed it in her mind once more. The angel of St. Frances appeared and she heard "the voice of her father" speaking the words that would bring peace and direction and steer a course for life that would guide her through the darkness to light.

As clear as if he was standing there in the garden, she could hear Augusto whisper, "Clarice, my chérie amour, you must not despair because we are with you always. You will live a life of courage and conviction, uncovering the secrets of your heritage, and along the way, the ultimate truth will prevail. Never fear the unknown, for the path will be troublesome at times, but at the final destination awaits a treasure greater than that which is bestowed on earth!"

Moments transcended time, fear was but a fleeting blush giving way to that raw awareness of a life fulfilled—one dedicated to that of truth and honesty. No matter the consequences of taking a wrong turn in the path if it is well-intentioned and as long as the destination is not clouded because of the deceit and dishonor of others.

From that day, Clarice understood her mission and the truths that were yet to be uncovered. And although she had the loftiest of her father's ideals to guide her, she was determined to use whatever tactics needed to extract information without raising eyebrows.

As the peace settled upon her, a course was charted as if a heavenly guide had moved the stars to form it and soon she would find her own holy grail.

"Father Pierre," she started but hesitated.

"Go ahead, Clarice, speak your mind." It was apparent to him that she had given more than simple thought to what she wanted to say at this moment.

Coyly, like the bashful maiden on the eve of her first encounter with the lad to whom she had been betrothed, shy yet certain that her leverage was in the very charm of the unexpected, she continued, "Well, I was wondering if you could tell me what happened the weeks after we left the manor. I, you know...forgot most everything during the final traumatic days and wondered if you could reconstruct the conversations in the tunnel."

He studied her, softly assessing her ploy but understanding fully the need she had to dig for the truth.

"Well, Clarice, are you willing to open the book to what has long been considered a closed chapter, forcing out not only the truth if it is to be found therein but also the ugliness that prevailed during those days?"

"Yes, Father, I think I'm ready yet, in so many ways, terrified of what might be disclosed through the process, particularly opening up areas that I may have suppressed. With you as my support, there could not be a better time and any knowledge I gain will help find the truth some day!"

"You understand, my dear Clarice, I only know scant information, and for that very reason, this will be a road well traveled before the truth is finally reached. The end is the beginning. Remember this, and it will serve you well in your search."

"What do you remember, Father? What of the other man in the tunnel, the one who handed Benny the envelope? And what was in the envelope?"

Surprised at the detail she remembered, Father Pierre replied, "The envelope contained the other half of the golden seal, one of the most important documents of your family's heritage. It was vital to have it back to preserve not only the Pontifi and Chevais heritage but all your holdings as well!"

"Can you tell me the whereabouts of the entire golden seal and how it came to be? And who was that man? How did he come by it and..." She trailed off, obviously overexcited and becoming winded.

Father Pierre was sitting in stunned silence, waiting for the precise moment when he could frame a response that perhaps might seem plausible to this erstwhile child. Cautiously, he assessed how much and what exactly to reveal at this stage in the revelations. The truth was that he knew enough to understand what he lacked in facts and, therefore, protect not only Clarice at one level but also the nunnery and the children of the orphanage at the same time.

Now a young woman, it was far too soon, even after the dawn of her rebirth, to give Clarice access to this incendiary information, exposing her to danger once again.

"Whoa, my dear, slow down and we'll take it a step at a time," he responded, hoping to stall for time as he regrouped. Even though he knew more than he let on, there were many doors that were yet to be opened. It was dangerous for him to know everything, so it was that he and Bernard made a pact to each leave control and knowledge of certain information with yet a third party, one who could not understand either one until all the pieces were put together.

The Crumbling Wall

Something was missing and Clarice sensed it. Clarice's instincts served her well, and the sessions with Father Pierre over the past year were bringing clarity to her life. She was certain that Father was leaving out some key facts, but to her disappointment, after enough time elapsed, she became acutely aware of his limitations.

Her fragmented knowledge of the events leading up to the death of her parents was enough for her to realize that Father was limited in his knowledge of the details or even a cohesive timeline of the events that took place. During some of their sessions, she had purposely tricked him with information carefully placed to elicit the missing pieces if he had known them.

"Just as well," she said to herself. "If he knew too much, it would just hamper efforts to move forward with my investigation. Plus, it's better if he doesn't know what I'm doing."

Now fifteen years old, a mature young woman had replaced the girl who'd resided in Clarice. The benefits of the road she had traveled had served to imbue Clarice with perceptions and grace far beyond her years. She had overheard two of the nuns discussing how she had blossomed into a beautiful young woman. It meant nothing to her at the time. However, curiosity prevailed and she managed to find a reflective pane of glass to see what they had been talking about. Clarice was momentarily stunned. There stood a tall, attractive girl, not yet a woman. Studying the cloudy reflection, what she thought had been unruly hair turned out to be a mane of deep auburn cascading around her shoulders in gentle waves, framing a face of perfect proportions, except for almond-shaped eyes the color of gold. Etched on her face was the pain and suffering she had lived but, upon looking into her eyes, belied the peace therein.

Reflecting on the recent events aroused her natural curiosity. It left Clarice with unanswered questions surrounding the reunion with Andre only two months prior. But to say her heart was filled with profound joy at reuniting with her brother would be trite at best. Sibling love is so innocent and pure; theirs was no exception.

It was during one of their sessions that Father Pierre asked how she would feel about seeing Andre for what would be the first time in several years. Other than the surreptitious moments she stole to spy on him, usually when he was in the garden with the other children, she had no contact at all.

Sister Francine had been right to keep her from him for so long! Admitting this to herself gave Clarice a sense of relief from the guilt that had threatened to drown her the past several months. It was a guilt borne only to those who understand the role of caretaker within a family dynamic sprung from despair, disaster, or destruction of all or part of the central core.

Once the veil of the past came off, allowing Clarice's feelings to surface, her distress over the neglect and total disinterest for her little brother during this time threatened to undermine any of the progress made over the past year.

She thought about Father's question with slow deliberation, afraid he would suspect she still had ghosts yet to be uncovered. Her psyche was much like an old onion with layers left to peel. Father Pierre had peeled away many layers when they first broke through together, he holding her tightly and she crumpled in his arms, certain her heart would break in two if he prodded any more.

Still at the center was Andre and, if Clarice would allow, the last remaining link in the chain holding the wall together. Her mind in turmoil, fighting the words yet believing in the rightness of his motives, she surrendered any claim left to the self-inflicted pain and sacrifice of not seeing her little brother, holding him, and once again wiping away his tears.

Oh, how she had yearned to see him, touch him, and tell him, "Everything will be all right, my little brother."

As she progressed in her counseling with Father Pierre, these sessions awakened in her all the feelings she had so carefully wrapped away, or so she thought, inside an insulated layer of stone etched with the blood of her loved ones.

It was easy once she started the process—layer upon layer upon layer—piled on like the granite of the old stonemason as he was building his wall, a wall impenetrable to man that stood daring anyone to venture in!

The first time she was approached by the father, after her *awakening* in the garden, Clarice was determined to move forward, propelling her mind to open to the healing she so desperately needed. Whether or not all her motives were clear or even correctly placed mattered not, for the result would serve to open up all that had been hidden from view.

The more she healed, the more she questioned. Soon she was asking about Bernard, her beloved Bernard. Afraid that she might find out that he too was dead, Clarice had avoided any mention of Bernard's whereabouts until the day she could no longer dance around the obvious and blurted out, "I must know about Bernard. Where is Bernard? Is he alive?"

Father Pierre had been waiting for this final breakthrough and prepared his response accordingly. Careful to acknowledge her love and concern yet believing she was not yet mature enough to understand the dangers and double entendres a complete discussion might unearth, he proceeded with caution.

"Clarice, when Bernard handed you and Andre over to my care, he made me vow not to contact him or try to find him, and before you say anything, let me finish my story."

"But, Father, Bennie loved us and…" Her words trailed off as if lost within Father Pierre's intense gaze. Assessing his mood, hoping by his tone that Bernard was in fact alive, Clarice forced herself into a state of mock calmness—at least long enough to allow time to assimilate the facts as he presented them so she could draw her own conclusions.

Ignoring her interruption, he continued, "As you may remember, Bernard made certain to sequester you, Andre, and Jacques within the safe haven of the manor through which passed an underground hideaway built during the seventeenth century. For anyone who knew your family and understood how closely knit the villagers were with all Chevaises and Pontifis, this would have seemed to be a strange move, especially the timing which was immediately upon the return from your beloved Grand-mère's funeral.

"There, Bernard could easily ensure your safety and keep the inquisitive eyes and ears of the staff from learning too much information or assuming there were any problems in Paris. Your father had entrusted him with your safety, and in the event of any mishap, alternate plans had been put into effect, so once word arrived of…" And here Father Pierre's voice trailed off. He cleared his throat, looked furtively at Clarice, and continued, "Well, word had arrived of the train accident and the possibility of casualties, so you see, there also was an even greater need to keep you from hearing more than was necessary."

He hesitated once again before continuing. To his surprise, Clarice had not moved or made a sound after her initial small outburst. Her mind had drifted to the time in the tunnel just before the arrival of Father Pierre. It had occurred to her that the strangeness with which Bernard moved those last few days, paranoid within his familiar surroundings and hiding them like criminals from the very staff and people they loved for so many years, gave credibility to what the father was saying.

Where the children would normally have been deposited with several of the staff to allow Bernard to tend to his business, this time they were immediately hidden within the sophisticated tunnel system that included the hideaway. She had tried to find out why, but Bernard was not going to give her anything in the way of information.

"Bernard was entrusted with not only the critical information surrounding the circumstances leading up to the events of the last weeks before the tragedies but also the details of the location and contents of all key legal papers, including a significant piece that ties the family land holdings together," Father continued.

"You may remember some of the discussions in the tunnel, mostly having to do with those holdings and cash deposits in Switzerland which were separated to keep people like Duvalier from seizing what was not rightfully his. Even a man like Paul Marchand, a close friend of your Grand-mère, succumbed to greed when it came time to choose his loyalties."

"Why was it that the very idea of our rightful heritage became so questionable and almost offensive even to people who supposedly were our friends?" asked Clarice. Pain still resonated in her voice. "Weren't my parents giving and kind to any and all in need?" Her memories of those days were mixed with a blurred haze of emotions worn raw by the shedding of layers upon layers of the healed wounds.

"The vast fortune amassed by generations of Chevaises and Pontifis was like fodder to the greed that thrives as an abscess—never fully drained, yet always festering, waiting to burst and destroy the good flesh with the bad. So it was with your family, Clarice.

"Bernard was the most loyal among all the staff and, beyond his employment, was considered to be a member of the family. To entrust him with the children's care was as natural as if he had been born a Pontifi. It was because of his loyalty that he moved quickly to separate himself from the family in case anyone connected with Duvalier might use him to get to you children. It was for that reason a difficult choice was made to keep your whereabouts unknown even from your remaining relatives in Milano. Until their deaths several years ago, they were believed to be under constant watch and in danger.

"You have been well protected here at the convent, and even though it's possible someone from the outside may hear of new children arriving from time to time, the chance anyone would find out you and Andre were the Pontifi children is remote. Furthermore, Bernard is well hidden himself and has taken measures to ensure his identity is kept a secret."

Clarice had been quietly contemplating this new information and could no longer hold her tongue. “But I miss him so, Father. Is there no way to go to him where he lives and still keep the sanctity of our beloved convent?”

“I’m afraid it is not even up for consideration! There may come a time when the likes of Duvalier will be no more, but until then, we must abide by Bernard’s wishes, my dear.”

The weight of his words fell heavy on her small shoulders, threatening to bend the brave spirit in Clarice. It was with great effort that she rose and said quietly, “I understand, Father Pierre, and will abide by your wishes.”

With that, she walked slowly away into the garden, turning once to look beyond the walls as if to say, “Bernard, all is well with my soul.”

Surprise

Duvalier had been very busy reorganizing and planning his new strategy for a second round with the remainder of the Chevais fortune at stake, along with the ultimate prize, Clarice. "Brilliant," he said out loud to the empty room. "I'll have my last revenge soon enough and, with it, all that remains to pluck away from the heirs." All he needed was a break on finding the young mistress, and his spies were closing in. There was word from a remote sector of France. Duvalier could feel his senses heightened. All he needed to complete the circle was in reach.

March winds were blowing; the early buds had yet to bloom—almost as if they knew the late frost would kill the chance to share their beauty with all who awaited them.

It had been a particularly restless day for Clarice, pacing back and forth through the garden, around the grounds, and back to a statue of Mary standing welcome at the entrance of the convent. Not once, but many times she covered the grounds until the kindly priest summoned her to his office.

Unbeknownst to Clarice, a carriage was moving slowly through the surrounding countryside, cautiously making its way to the hidden entrance of Belfort Convent. Judiciousness was the order of the trip, which is why the passenger carefully scoped out the landscape for signs of being followed.

"Slow down," he commanded the driver, just as the dense forest appeared, casting shadows like a cover of muted green camouflage. "Give me a moment to check out the entrance and"—pausing for an instant, he continued—"Daniel, be mindful of the critical nature of keeping this place secret!"

It was difficult for Bernard to trust anyone, but he had known Daniel's family since the young man's birth and had taken to him immediately. As his assistant, Daniel could lighten the big man's load and, at the same time, replace some of the companionship once provided by his beloved family.

He had received the message from Father Pierre and decided the time had come to risk seeing his dear Clarice. The danger never masked itself for long, and he understood better than anyone the core of hatred that brewed among the enemies of his beloved *children* to the extent that he decided to wait until the week prior to give notice of his journey and time of arrival at the convent.

It had been several weeks since Bernard had received the message, and for all that time, he grappled with whether opening the door to the past and exposing Clarice and Andre to the covert activities of Duvalier and his henchmen was worth taking the chance.

Swift action was needed. Bernard was now certain all his movements were monitored and calculated by those who would be drawn to the family when knowledge of their whereabouts could be obtained.

It had been almost two months since Father Pierre's conversation with Clarice had taken place. Upon finishing the timeline of events leading up to the children's escape and transporting them to the orphanage at the Belfort Convent, Father had taken great pains to detail all he knew of Bernard and his level of involvement in the family. The only area off-limits was Bernard's whereabouts until this day and after much agonizing to himself.

"I have good news to tell you, my dear! Remember, I could not let you go to him, but"—and here Father Pierre smiled slyly—"that did not keep me from asking him to come here."

Once Clarice found her voice, he never thought he'd witness a time when she could be rendered speechless until now. She quietly kneeled in front of the father and proceeded to pray, a sound so soft he could barely hear. After a few minutes, she arose and calmness enveloped her like the angels' wings, lifting her to meet his eyes.

Looking at him, she said, "Father, I will never forget what you have done for me and what you tried to do for my family." Her words moved him so, not for what she said but how the glow embraced her, almost as if the heavenly spirit was speaking to him through Clarice.

Oh, what joyous expectations they all had in anticipation of the gentle giant's arrival. Clarice had been badgering Father Pierre, certain he could detail the collapse of the family dynasty and what had transpired in the dark, twisted days at the end, defining how the Pontifi children would live their lives.

Once he and Clarice commenced the dialogue that unleashed the details of the past, Father Pierre described how an emboldened and angry Bernard orchestrated the escape of the children, protecting them from further harm at the hand of Duvalier. When it was time to hand over the children to the father, the gentle giant ran away, unable to hide his grief at the loss. It was in this description of the big man's gentle side that her unexpected tears threatened to stop his telling of the story.

Following their conversation of Bernard, it was just a matter of time before her persistence wore Father Pierre down enough for him to take the steps to bring Bernard to the convent. That he was alive was relief enough to sustain her until she could find him.

After the initial shock of finding out her beloved Bennie was alive and living near Bern, Switzerland, it was all she could do to keep from stealing away on her favorite horse and finding him for herself. Her respect for the sanctity of Father's promise to Bernard not to reveal his hiding place was the only barrier keeping her in place.

Day after day, she had implored Father to contact Bernard and convince him to come to the convent. Finally, unable to bear her pain any longer, he quietly sent a messenger to the go-between.

It would serve no purpose to expose Bernard and the convent to the elements still in force, those who were waiting for any sign of the whereabouts of the remaining heirs. His plan would have to ensure the safety of all. Reckless abandon, where Bernard was concerned, could lead to a catastrophic outcome.

In relating his version of the events during the days following the train wreck and subsequent funeral, Father Pierre tried to minimize to Clarice the direct attack on the family. Her keen instincts were alerted, however, and remembering the conversations in the tunnel only served to fuel the fire burning within her.

Yes, she had heard enough to know and understand that her parents may have been murdered under the guise of the train wreck caused by *mysterious* explosions. Supposedly this was an innocent series of natural gases being trapped until explosion was the only vent for the combustible mixture. She also knew that the name Duvalier meant something to Bernard—enough to send the otherwise gentle man into a fit of rage at its mention. She vaguely remembered the name, but whatever he had discussed in the tunnel had been blocked out.

When confronted by Bennie, Paul Marchand had blurted out some of the despicable plans that had been crafted by Duvalier himself to bring the family, particularly Marie Chevais, to their knees. There was no doubt of Duvalier's duplicity, and if Clarice had to give her life in pursuit of the truth, then willingly she would.

It was this motivation that kept her going, the knowledge of finding and exposing the truth about the murder—and murder it was—of her parents, aunt Marcella, and uncle Jonque, and her beloved grand-mère. The brutality lingered like a fire out of control, moving across the lush landscape, destroying the living vegetation, and mutilating any animal caught in its path.

There was no escape from the image, wrapping around all who entered as if caught in a flaming inferno.

It was like that for Clarice when it entered her mind for the first time—the pain of the fire touching her skin as if real and the smell of the burn lingered, slowly enveloping her nostrils and threatening to suffocate her.

But those memories were forced into the background, waiting for another time. Now it was time to celebrate. She could barely maintain her dignity, let alone manage to control the many emotions that constantly threatened to overpower her.

It was so exciting; she decided that she must move into position, making certain to be ready the very instant Bernard came into the compound. She started counting down the minutes while setting up her own lookout post at the far corner ridge just beyond the gardens but still within the confines of the convent's grounds. The nuns had given her an old telescope in the first year she had come to the convent, hoping that she could be distracted from her melancholy by looking at the stars.

"Oh, where is he?" she cried out to no one in particular. It was best if she did not alert her little brother just yet in case, well, just in case. She had been disappointed too much already, and there was no use building his hopes until this was a certainty. Now that she possessed her newfound optimism and happiness, risking his mental health was not an option.

Aptly named La Nuaz after the Chilean mountain range, La Nuaz's location high in the Alps had an altitude of over eight thousand feet, casting them above the clouds most days, but not today. There was a smell of fresh air hanging like the dew on the mountain as the road leading up to the convent in La Nuaz twisted and wrapped around like the vine of the wisteria, mysteriously climbing, climbing until it finished its journey.

It always fascinated Clarice to watch through the heavy underbrush the signs of wildlife moving about their day, coupling and nurturing their young. She would pretend that the animals were a family with the mother and father building their nest home while the young were frolicking in the forest. The pleasure of being out here would be hard to give up when it was time to make her move to Paris, she thought.

Yes, today will be a day of remembering and reuniting with the one link to her past which could connect the missing pieces for her future. Even more than that, her beloved Bennie would be here for her to hold on to.

How many days, hours, and minutes had she endured since last seeing him?

Cruelly, she thought at the time, Bennie had forced her to leave him in the tunnel and go with Father Pierre. It had taken a long time to forgive all of them for wrenching her heart out in such a manner.

It was by chance that as she waited and counted the minutes, a movement caught her eye, one of significant proportions to make her take a closer look.

Whatever moved did not look like any animal that lives around here. I must find the same spot to see if it is still there, or maybe it was just my imagination playing tricks on me, she thought.

Her instincts always served her well, and this time was no exception. There off the road at least one hundred feet, hidden by low-hanging branches and braced against a tree, was a lean-to of the sort that might be used by a hunter. It would be virtually impossible for most to see it, but the many years of exploring the grounds gave her a well-trained telescopic view. She could pick out the smallest of plant matter along with most insects or animals.

Talking to herself, she exclaimed, "No hunters are allowed within this region of the mountains, and even if they were, why would they be around at this time of year? I must mention this to Father Pierre later, but right now there is no time to worry about such things with my wonderful Bennie on his way."

There was no further movement among the trees or around the lean-to so Clarice went about the business of watching for Bernard. After what seemed like endless minutes stretching into hours, a carriage pulled through the hidden entrance, making sure to move all the brush placed strategically in its path.

"Please be Bernard," whispered the anxious young woman, now ready to crawl out of her skin in anticipation of his visit.

After pulling through and resetting all the bushes, just so, the carriage moved slowly up the steep and winding road, ever closer to its final destination. A very large man sat at attention in the back of the carriage, carefully surveying his surroundings as they moved up the mountain.

"It must be Bennie!" she cried, overwhelmed with joy. Up from her place now, she raced back up the hill through the gardens and into the compound just as Father Pierre had started on his trek to find her.

"Where have you been, my dear?" asked the father. "We were starting to worry about you and—"

"He's here, he's here! Bernard is here, Father Pierre! The carriage is coming up the mountain right this very minute. Oh, I think I shall faint."

Father chuckled at the drama of the young woman. Still a child he mused, a good sign indeed. "Come, Clarice, let's prepare for their arrival! We can't delay or we'll miss the moment, and we must find Andre lest he miss the excitement."

With that, they both scurried through the gate into the main courtyard with Clarice shouting to all who would listen, "He is here, he is here!" It was marvelous watching her animation and the joy expressed on her face. He only hoped that he hadn't made a mistake in pulling Bernard here.

"Bring Andre quickly now so he may be here to greet Bernard upon his arrival!" The nuns had already quietly pulled Andre into the courtyard after giving him a quick update on what was about to happen. He had been only six when they came to the convent, and his memory of Bernard had faded.

Grand Celebration

Let the Party Begin

Pulling open the large gates, tethered with chain and leather roping, proved to the crowd that in the event of an unwanted intrusion by the outside world, they were well protected. Straining with all their might, Father Pierre, with the help of the groundskeeper, Dominique, secured the gate in an open position just as the horse-drawn carriage bearing the giant man pulled up to the entrance. Unable to contain herself any longer, Clarice rushed to the center of the main courtyard as the carriage rumbled into sight.

"Bennie! Bennie!" shrieked the jubilant Clarice. There were no words he could speak as Bernard jumped from the carriage, not waiting for the driver to come to a complete stop. As soon as he saw her, his heart burst with pride, looking at the young woman standing there in front of all the others. He knew then no matter the cost, he had made the right decision to come.

"Oh, my sweet Clarice!" he shouted as he picked her up and twirled her around. "Not a day has gone by since you and Andre left that my heart hasn't ached, the light growing dimmer with each passing day! Here you are, a child, and yet such a beautiful young lady!" With one fell swoop of his massive arms, he managed to pull her so close she was sure that her breath would stop.

"Bennie, I missed you so much. You must never leave me again!" There was no hiding the melancholy of her words, those tinged with sadness for the loss of her loved ones as well as the loss of time and memories irreplaceable. Those who endure such sadness revel in the hope for what the future might bring, and here was hers, wrapped in a wonderful package called Bennie!

"Ma chérie, you are a sight for an old man's eyes! What happened to the young girl who left me at the manor for a wonderful new world?" They both knew that was a gross exaggeration designed to lighten the fact that their lives had been torn apart because of the deaths and destruction of her family and certainly his.

"Where is that boy?" he bellowed. In the middle of the crowd stood Andre, moving shyly toward the big man but then more aggressively as he made his way through the crowd. "Come here, Andre. Come give Bennie a big hug!"

Clarice had been caught up in her own moment of jubilation and had not realized how frightening this must be for her little brother. Was it perhaps he had no memories of this big man or of leaving the manor and the life they had before? "It's okay, Andre. Bennie is like a father to us," Clarice quickly said, hurrying to her brother's side.

Andre surprised them all by immediately running to Bernard, though not as a boy recognizing a friend but one who would be anxious to see what surprise this stranger might bring to them. Andre stared up at Bennie, trying to figure out just who this man was and why there was such a fuss. There was something about the man that seemed very familiar to him, but he just didn't know what. It may have been the bear hug, the smell of Bernard, but all of a sudden, with a burst of youthful joy, Andre wrapped his little arms around the big man's legs, as if afraid to let go.

Bennie knelt down and gently took Andre's hand, burying it like an acorn caught in the grasp of a bear. "Good day, young Andre! Do you remember me from the manor house when I took you for rides on my back? You were very young, but I always called you little man! We played Army and you would hide from me until I cried *uncle*!"

Just then, with the innocence and acceptance of youth, a big grin spread across the boy's face, and the joy of recognition was heart rendering to Clarice.

It was the moment of recognition for a boy who, being left with no parents at such a young age, had finally found a long missing relative.

Bennie reached over and brought the small boy into his arms. Now he finally had what he longed for all these many years—his family. "Ben-Ben!" shouted Andre gleefully.

"Ah, my rambunctious young man, you have not changed your pace for one moment, and I'm thankful you are still the gregarious boy who played in the manor house from morning until night, never tiring and always, always happy!"

They marched arm in arm up the cobblestoned courtyard to the inner garden, this time without a care in the world. It would prove to be one of the last times the turmoil surrounding the reunion would be held at bay, replaced by the stolen moments of pleasure they found in each other's company. Even the dour old Mother Superior seemed relaxed, and the mood of the day was one of sheer joy for all its participants!

"Let me escort you to my private quarters," Father Pierre said with exuberance. "I am sure you want to catch up, and we will leave you alone to embrace this wonderful occasion. Bernard, we will talk later, but now you belong to Clarice and Andre. They have missed you too long, and for that I am sorry."

"Father, I cannot thank you enough for bringing me back to my loved ones. I will forever be in your debt." Bernard swallowed hard, obviously choked up with gratitude for this precious gift.

Pulling him aside and whispering so softly that even Bernard strained to hear him, Father said, "You are always welcome here, but you may also pay a great price for the risk you took. Mark my words, Bernard, your enemies are waiting for you to make a move, and I fear, together, we may have brought them here to Clarice and Andre."

The exchange may have been out of earshot of the children but did not go unnoticed by Clarice. Unwilling to let the excitement and happiness of the moment be interrupted, Clarice spoke up, "Bennie, come see what I have made for you and then we can eat. The nuns have prepared a great feast in your honor."

"Ma chérie, do you know how long it has been since I laid eyes on you?" He posed the rhetorical question, but it was poignant nevertheless. She knew exactly how long it had been: 1,615 days, 8 hours, and 22 minutes, to be precise.

"Bennie, we have much catching up to do, and there are so many questions I have."

"I understand, ma chérie, and you will, in time, have answers to the unknown parts of your past. It has been a long journey, and I must rest and have some food or fall down dead," he quipped.

It was a very festive evening for the entire convent and orphanage, full of frivolity and more fun than any of them had ever seen in their young lives. Children were dancing to the music the nuns were playing on the piano and accordion. Bernard and Father Pierre were deep in conversation and would look over at the children and smile periodically.

After more music and the great feast to soothe everyone's full bellies, it was time for all the younger children to retire to their rooms. Accompanied by several of the nuns, they made their way back to the orphanage section of the compound, singing as they went. Andre tried to remain with his sister and Bernard but was firmly reminded that even he would have to wait until the next day to continue visiting with his friend.

Clarice and Father Pierre had been discussing life at the Belfort Convent with Bernard, unaware that even as they were sitting here in this beautiful courtyard, safe from all intrusion, there was a set of eyes following their every move.

If Bernard had been less tired, he might have sensed the intruder, but as it was, he had fallen into a happy stupor, full of food and wine and basking in the delight of seeing Clarice and Andre, ignoring his inner antennae.

The sound first came at them, as a shrill wail, debilitating them momentarily with its fearsome tone. "Merde, merde, he has taken Andre," Sister Natalie cried as she ran back into the courtyard.

Bernard did not wait an instant but jumped up immediately and yelled to the obviously distraught nun, “Which way did he go?” Did you see what he looked like?

“I think he went out through the back gate, the one Clarice had come in earlier after watching for our visitors!” With that, he ran out of the compound toward the back gate, Father Pierre following closely behind him. Clarice made up the third in the pack with Daniel bringing up the rear.

Father Pierre hollered to Bernard, “I’ll take a shortcut because he has to cross over a bridge to get down the mountain. You stay on this trail in case he tries to double back.”

“Clarice, you must go back to safety now!” Bennie yelled.

“But, Bennie, I think I know where this intruder’s camp is down the mountain!” Clarice cried, realizing now that she had forgotten to tell them about what she had seen. The excitement of seeing Bennie and the reunion had caused her to forget something very important. She admonished herself briefly before recognizing there was no time for self-indulgent remorse.

Now they were running fast and furiously, following Clarice through the underbrush where she had staked out a place to wait on Bernard. Suddenly, they heard a distant sound, a muffled yell of a child. Oh yes, they were gaining ground and the sound meant no harm had come to Andre.

Suddenly, with the stamina of ten men, Bernard accelerated his speed and left Clarice and Daniel gasping for air. A heroic act for a man of Bennie’s age but understood by all of them. They managed to hear him as he moved closer to the place where he could rendezvous with the intruder and pull Andre back out of danger.

“Dear Lord, please help us to save our boy,” Father Pierre silently prayed. “I will be forever in your debt!”

Just then, the stranger Clarice had earlier mistaken for an animal came bursting through the underbrush, looking for his horse to make his way with Andre. Andre was putting up a valiant fight for a little boy and was not making this easy for the heavyset man.

Bernard managed to startle him just as he broke into the opening, grabbing him with one arm and tossing Andre out of harm's way as much as he could. The stranger was strong, he would give him that, but was no match for the giant Bennie. With one hand he held the intruder to the ground while the others raced into the campsite.

"Here, let us have him!" shouted the leader of the quickly assembled group, most of them men from the village. "We'll show him the folly of intruding in our domain."

Regions of France were divided and often inhabited by tribes of people who were considered hostile to any outsiders. To say that strangers were unwelcome in La Nuaz (the cloud), a literally invisible hamlet that sits in the Beaufortain Alps, was to understate the depth of dislike and distrust they had for anyone venturing into their area.

Having such a lofty perch within the Alps provided them with the isolation they loved. The one who came among them this day was soon made aware of how much they despised intruders. Almost like vigilantes, they started beating him and throwing rocks until the blood ran freely.

Father Pierre, still on his trail, had heard the commotion farther down the mountain and soon came running up. "Wait, let's not become the same type of animal as this beast! Let's put him in the catacomb underneath the statue of St. Mary where he can do no further harm."

"But, Father, we want to make an example of him," spoke the leader, John Paul Broussard.

"No, my son, I cannot condone violence as a man of God, for it is not our place to sit in the judgment of men."

"As you wish, Father, but we will make him talk if you leave his captivity in our hands!"

The Duvalier scout had, by this time, recovered enough from the trauma to understand full well what his fate might be if left to these ruffians.

"Wait, wait, I will tell you everything. Just don't leave me with this mob, Father, I beg of you!"

"All right, John Paul, leave and return to your village with our gratitude for you and your men! We are as always in your debt, but we'll handle this matter now," declared Father Pierre.

It was no small task to reel in the angry bunch, but the esteem to which the villagers held the father now served him and the convent well.

"Mark my words, Father, we will take this matter into our own hands and dole out the kind of justice deserved if we see him outside of the convent grounds," John Paul stated. With that, the group turned and headed over to the village, a long valley and climb away, not suited to men who could not ascend to the high protruding ridgeline of the Alps.

They were a decent group, Bernard surmised, just fiercely independent and determined to manage their own affairs with no outside interference.

The Parting—Fall of 1895

"Be safe, Clarice," said Sister Francine, choking back tears. "The patron saint will be with you." The party of darkly clad nuns along with Father Pierre and one handsomely dressed young man stood at attention as Clarice boarded the train to Paris.

Unable to restrain himself, Andre dashed toward his sister for one last embrace. "Clarice, Clarice, I want to go with you. *Please*," begged Andre.

"Mon chérie, it is not possible now, but I will send for you as soon as possible." The tears were now flowing rapidly in spite of his valiant attempt to keep a stiff upper lip, longing to keep his sister close at hand.

He was on the verge of becoming a young man and trying to be brave, the slight shoulders weighed down with the sadness of years already denied with his beloved Clarice. Wrapping him in her arms while wiping away his tears, Clarice whispered, "Do not fret, dear brother. I will come for you as soon as I can."

"Please promise, Clarice," whimpered the distraught boy. Dramatically waving his arms, he proclaimed, "I have only just found you, and I so missed you while you were away!" They never discussed where she was or that he knew she had been *sick* for fear that her return to him might all have been a dream.

Clarice gently answered, "I'll never let you down ever again." With one final hug, she turned and mounted the steps of the railcar, careful not to turn around for all to see her tears of many life markers—some for joys yet to come, certainly some for joys remembered of long ago. Of one thing she was sure: her future would be inspired by all the memories of a beloved family.

It was her destiny to fulfill the promises made to her dead parents: loyalty to her Mulhouse roots by honoring the many employees tied in their life's work to the community of the Pontifi and Chevais families and to finding a way to bring everyone back together under one roof.

Woven within the heartfelt promise was a contradiction in what had been her core belief for the past few years—retribution as part of her goal. Clarice knew it would have been a direct conflict with what her parents wanted for her and Andre. She tried to embrace the idea that to seek revenge upon those responsible for the deaths of her family would only add to the injustices already perpetrated upon innocent people. Somehow, she had been able to come to a place in her mind that only spoke to the need for justice rather than revenge. Her direction had been formed many years before, and to follow an errant path would only serve to give power to those who sought to destroy everything good in her life.

As the wheels started to move, one spoke driving the next, the train slid slowly over long-traveled rail lines, ironclad and stained with the blood and sweat of Frenchmen many years prior in their quest to connect Paris with its countrymen. Looking out beyond the train station, she could see the herb-strewn fields in the valley below. They begged for those who could venture forth to pick and provide sustenance to all who came upon their paths. She wondered if those early railroad men had at least been well-fed.

The puffed bursts of cotton-like cloud cover sprinkled with colors of gray, blue, and purple appeared from behind the looming mountain vistas, hidden until the last moment among the sharp spires. It occurred to her that here might be where her heart would remain but suspended in a time warp, waiting for her return. For the first time since arriving at the convent, she could reflect on the beauty and think in terms of a life outside both Mulhouse and La Nuaz.

She peeked out the other window in time to see all her acquired "family" waving to bid her farewell. It is funny how life changes before your eyes in ways unexpected and yet not unwelcome. Sighing audibly, Clarice knew it was time to make the break and begin the quest she so earnestly sought.

Sister Francine could not keep the tears from flowing but somehow managed to hide them from Andre. Looking at Clarice for the last time, it struck her that the child she had been was replaced by the woman she would become.

It amazed even Francine that when she studied Clarice, there was this beautiful young woman in place of the gangly girl she had been when she arrived at the convent. She hoped God would keep their young charge safe from harm. The protection and tranquility provided by her life here at La Nuaz would be replaced with the fast-paced life of Paris. There were many temptations for a young woman alone in Paris.

It was interesting to Clarice how events had transpired over the past year, propelling her ever closer to Paris and a destiny with the Chevaises' past, one out of her grasp for so long. Not to be denied, she had begged and prodded the father and any of the sisters who would listen to free her of the life she had known for the past seven years. Ensconced within the walls of the orphanage where she was safe and secure, the pull to follow her heart to Paris was not to be denied to the headstrong young woman.

Reflecting on the past several years, she traced the events leading up to her new freedom back to one year from the day of her awakening and rebirth and, coincidently, six months from her reunion with Andre.

She could isolate the good from the bad and appreciate what she had and subsequently lost. It was easier now to think about the path she had traveled and the loss of her loved ones, but not without feeling the pain.

Isn't it God's way of keeping them close to me? she wondered. If there was no pain in remembering, there would be no feelings of love and closeness to be cherished.

It all started in the summer of 1889 and the promise of a wonderful family holiday. The joy had turned to sadness and despair quickly upon arrival at Mulhouse.

Her beloved grand-mère had perished and along with her, Clarice's dreams of moving to Paris to study. Most of all, she had wanted to spend more time with Marie, but then…

To lose her grand-mère was almost more than she could bear, but to lose her parents, aunt, and uncle right on the heels of Marie's death were unthinkable. From those wounds she could not heal.

She had to acknowledge it was the hand of God and the prayers of the priest and nuns that pulled her through the abyss of despair. If Father Pierre had not persisted, Clarice would have been lost.

It wasn't easy, but this journey to Paris and all the promise of days to come instilled excitement in her about the future.

PART SIX

Glimmer of Hope (March 2005)

Pacing the floor and talking to the still figure for what seemed like days on end, Doris was trying to pull another response from her daughter, the first one occurring two weeks earlier. She had been so certain that Jackie would have awakened from her coma by now and yet still nothing! Time seemed to expand and contract as each day ended with no further response.

Frustrated, Doris circled the room before leaning close, anxious to hear Jackie call out to her or speak even the most insane words, anything to show that Doris's constant chatter was being heard. There was no reason to give up, not now, not ever!

Jackie, sweet Jackie, her eldest child, burdened early in life with too much responsibility. Even her friends recognized she had a special quality, one that transcended the normal, tediousness of everyday life, lending an element of excitement and expectation to everything she did.

She was capable of pulling those around her into this sphere of joy, making them feel special to be her friend. Whatever this special something could be called, it lent an almost mystical element to her life. It begged of stories yet to be told, and it was out of this desire to learn more that they had encouraged her to write a book, one which would tap into her culturally rich heritage.

Doris, on the other hand, could not understand how much the richness of Jackie's early life had helped her. The memories she had were of constant struggle and pain. And now, standing alone in this hospital room, Doris wept for her *girl*, regretting the part she played in Jackie's early trials and tribulations.

She would welcome any conversation, even if it brought to the surface painful memories of years past—a life also defined by the hardships Jackie had to endure.

She could only hope that the very strength with which her daughter lived her life as well as the strength of her ancestors, particularly the women, would carry her over the threshold away from this slow death.

At a glance, the comatose figure seemed at peace, but upon closer scrutiny, an informed professional could tell there were thousands of thought patterns moving through her brain, which, by appearance alone, might have seemed to be dead. Jackie's eyelids were moving imperceptibly, indicating life in spite of all outward appearances.

The old woman decided to tap into her bank of ancestral heroics to prod Jackie back to life. Remembering how Jackie was fascinated by the women in her family tree, particularly Clarice, her great-grandmother, Doris was prompted to start talking once again.

The stories surrounding Clarice's early life and subsequent emergence into Paris society were practically legend. Where Doris's mother, Giselle, was soft and pliable, her grandmother, Clarice, was kind but impenetrable, especially when it came to protecting her family from intrusion by outsiders.

To those who won Clarice's trust, she was warm and ingratiating, extending an enormous level of loyalty.

Clarice was a formidable champion of women's rights—before the days of protests and voting rights allowed women freedom of expression. Of the women in their family lineage, each had their own strengths and weaknesses but none were as similar in character as Clarice and Jackie.

Doris was a character all to her own. A woman seemingly haunted by demons out of her control, she never was the kind of role model Jackie deserved. This was her chance to be more than just weight around her daughter's neck.

She cared not what her critics said, and right now her tenacity was just what the doctors ordered to help bring her precious Jackie around. As if to emphasize her justification for invading Jackie's surroundings, Doris held firm to the spirits of Clarice and Giselle, serving now as a conduit to boost the battered Jackie with stories of the heroics of her female ancestors.

"Listen, darling," whispered Doris. "Do you hear the rallying cry of Clarice? She's speaking to hundreds of women, and they are embracing her every word! Remember those words: We must preserve our honor, our right to serve as any man without fear of reprisal, for in the eyes of God we are also His children. Give us our freedom, wasting not the human impact of the strength gained from hundreds of women bound together in a noble cause!

"I'm going to retell Clarice's story once again and how she came to represent not only her fellow women in trouble, but all moderate and fair-thinking people in a *very unstable* political climate; one which was close to anarchy.

"After she finally left the safety of the convent in La Nuaz to make her way to Paris, she pinned her hopes on building a future for herself and Andre, never losing sight of her ultimate goal of bringing the rightful honor back to her parents' name."

It had been whispered that the Pontifis were responsible for their own deaths in retribution for stealing jewels and artifacts from their countrymen over many years. This, of course, was fueled by the lies strategically shared by Duvalier.

Despite having her own agenda, Clarice was pulled into the turmoil brewing all around her. Paris became a political hotbed for all manner of self-righteous purveyors of the brotherhood of man.

"Clarice had her own goals and master plan which did not include the likes of the politicians. Unfortunately, the truth of what happened to her parents was muddled in the midst of the political unrest during that period of time." Doris, tired of talking, sat down, letting her mind drift to the historical happenings of Clarice's time.

Somehow Duvalier's part in this drama played out as a political statement even if he had other motives. Certainly, the unrest would have provided a good cover for any other illegal activity that may have been taking place at the time. His loyalties were also divided between his relationship to the family that raised him—the de Mornys with their affiliation to Napoleon III and also of Duvalier's German roots.

After Count de Morny died in 1865, his many business dealings and holdings were sold or simply evaporated, leaving little to his heirs or, the least of these, Duvalier. Forced to flee Paris in 1870, Joseph Duvalier began his quest to become a French royal citizen with all the accompanying grandeur. With renewed bitterness, he found it served his purposes to enlist the unsavory soldiers of fortune who helped orchestrate the takeover of the Alsace territories by Germany.

The root problem in the battles between Germany and France existed because of the territory disputes over Alsace-Lorraine. Alsace, with all its grandeur, was portrayed like the peaks of the mountains it supported and the hard-won battles of the past, spilling the lifeblood of its citizens among those hills, forever casting a net of ownership to those who loved the land of their birth. It was a sense of belonging to this special group of people that catapulted the Pontifi and Chevais families into a chasm of divided loyalties to both Alsace and France. Refusing to choose sides had put them in a difficult position and all they loved and supported: the manor, the wonderful people of Mulhouse, and a way of life that had value beyond any material wealth had been held in balance, representing the last frontier between Germany and France.

The Republic, though a longstanding regime, was not the popular party, given the Parisians' fantasies of equality for all laborers. It was the end of Napoleon III's reign, overthrown by the loss to Prussia.

Doris had been talking for at least twenty minutes when she realized Jackie was squirming uncomfortably. Jackie suddenly moaned, moving her lips as if to speak but only emitting unintelligible sounds. Again she tried, but this time Doris could hear the words *c'est toi que j'aime, ma chérie*, spoken in fluent French.

It stunned Doris, so much so that she ran to Jackie's side to see if she was still breathing, thinking perhaps she had had a pre-death experience. "Oh my god, Jackie, you scared me to death," whispered the distraught mother. She scrambled to ring the alarm for the nearest nurse. This was one time she wished she could remember her French, but she believed Jackie had said, "It is you I love, my darling!"

The Wonder of Paris

1895

CLARICE ARRIVED AT the central terminal in the heart of Paris's bustling artist's colony. The nuns and Father Pierre had arranged for her to stay at a special hostel supported by the same diocese that had benefited from the years of Madame Chevais's generosity. This hostel was housed within the convent walls, providing shelter to all who needed a home.

Following Father Pierre's map, Clarice made her way through the congested cobblestoned streets, awed by the sights and sounds of the vibrant city. Every corner held a new delight—the smells of the fishmongers selling their fresh catch, the pungent aroma of the aged cheeses hanging in the open market, and then the refreshing, cleansing whiff of the delicate gardenia bushes and lilac trees lining the Seine River.

Among the marvels of smells was also the promise of an artist's new awakening, there to be admired by all who passed. One piece had stopped her in her tracks: a landscape of a small village, hanging behind the artist's easel and bidding for all to stop and enjoy. Clarice, caught up in the moment, admiring the painting with its beautiful grandeur, soon was jostled to move on. The moment was lost, but she recognized a sense of purpose in the crowd—the waves of people gaily helping her along, most of them intent on their destinations, certain of what lay in wait.

She was almost a veteran traveler of these streets. Her senses had been primed so many years ago with the wonders she encountered during her many trips to see Grand-mère.

The thought of Grand-mère momentarily resurrected pangs of loss that so often accompanied her memories when she moved into that territory. She was determined not to allow those tinges of her loss to interfere with the important work of uncovering the truth of the events leading up to the deaths of her parents.

Arriving at the convent after her journey, Clarice paused to assess her new surroundings, committing to memory the sights of children playing, artists painting their perfect landscapes, street vendors moving their wonderful baked goods through the alleys, tempting all to taste the delectable cakes and pastries. The flowers hanging everywhere, magnificent in their colorful splendor, inviting all to touch.

She could feel the changes taking place within, a blend of soft concern and tenderness for all living creatures tempered with a strengthening toughness, ready to handle any challenge yet to be faced.

"Yes," she uttered out loud, "I can deal with this now, and no matter what lies in store behind those walls, my mission will continue until the time we can resume our rightful place."

The smells followed her all the way to the convent. It reminded her of days past, and a sudden emptiness overcame her again, taking away the good feelings she had conjured on her walk. Pushing them away once again, she knew instinctively that her new life in Paris would be a constant reminder of the good and the bad and her major work would be to battle through it all, arriving at a point where she had ultimate peace of mind.

Her arrival was nearly devoid of any human contact. After banging on the front door, a massive iron and wood structure, for what seemed like ten minutes, a small demure nun opened the peephole to see who could be making such a noise.

"What is your name please?" the shy nun inquired. Clarice had a sense of déjà vu as she waited on the portico fronting the door.

"I am from the convent in La Nuaz. You know Father Pierre? He sent me," Clarice quietly responded in deference to the delicate voice on the other side of the door. "Oh, and yes, my name is Clarice Pontifi."

It almost seemed like the nun gasped but then just as quickly said, "Oh, of course, my dear." With that, she opened the heavy door and let the young woman into the entryway. "Please wait here and I will bring Sister Mary."

She wondered how much these nuns knew of her history, whether Father Pierre had given them details, all of which she had knowledge except for selected information that he pretended not to know. Her prowess in digging for the truth led her into areas which were off-limits.

It was within those walls her new identity was born, most certainly against her wishes. Father Pierre had sent a special messenger to prepare the way for Clarice, assuring the somewhat staid nuns that this special child would be no burden. After all, didn't they owe the Chevais and Pontifi families a debt of gratitude, one that could never be repaid by lesser deeds than this?

Sister Mary was the first to greet the young woman. Taking one look at this beautiful girl, she instantly decided her divine responsibility would be to protect Clarice from those who might harm her.

In spite of her bravado, Sister Mary was keenly aware of the history Clarice carried with her, along with the threats against heirs to the Chevais fortune.

At a hurried meeting that very morning, the Mother Superior pulled them into a circle to pray for guidance in the care of their new charge. Tension built as each knelt to find the proper words to discuss their own fears and yet respect the sanctity of holiness that was to be their guide.

Breaking the silence first, Sister Leonia asked fearfully, "Mother Superior, how is it that we must bear this burdensome child, risking our peaceful existence, when there are many other convents capable of providing better security and care?"

Sister Mary stepped in before the Mother Superior could respond, aware that the Mother's endorsement was shaky at best.

"Sister Leonia, do we not profess to do the will of God and help the burdened lighten their load?"

"We cannot arbitrarily assume these responsibilities and risk our own safety," Sister Leonia replied. "You know how volatile the Pontifi and Chevais names are in certain circles, and might I add, word travels fast in Paris. We risk bringing Duvalier and his renegade factions into our very home!"

"Oh, Sister Leonia, how can we turn our backs on this child, one who is innocent of any wrongdoing, even if the rumors of her parents' activities were founded from truth? It is a political affair, and we should remain neutral. This child has no culpability within these circles."

"But, Sister Mary, you know there is a large share of the land holdings and money that has been held in trust for the children of Augusto Pontifi. It is to be distributed when Clarice comes of age and shared with her younger brother upon his eighteenth birthday. The dowry begs to be stolen from the Pontifi children by the likes of Duvalier and his kind. We are exposing our very lifeblood along with all the good we accomplish every day among the many other needy children of the city. Are you so blind that you would risk all that we do to save one girl?"

Sister Leonia's impassioned plea served to dampen the others' empathy, and the meeting quickly threatened to become contentious.

"Listen, my dear sisters," pleaded Sister Mary. "We don't have to risk anything. We will change her name and swear her to secrecy so no one will be the wiser!"

Mother Superior looked perplexed but allowed the direction of Mary's speech to continue to sink into the group before speaking.

"Here is what we'll do. Your suggestion to change Clarice's name makes sense, and if she is willing to assume this new identity, she is welcome to stay here but, and I emphasize but, only temporarily until she can find employment and her own flat!"

"But, Mother Superior, how can we turn our backs on her so soon after accepting her into our home?"

"It is the only way, Sister Mary! Besides, we are not turning our backs on her. After all, she has resources unlike most of the girls we help. We must look out for the others who make their home here, not sacrifice for one individual. I have no doubt this girl is worthy of more, just as were her parents and grandmother deserving of loyalty and honor from all Parisians, instead of this dishonor forced onto them by misguided politicos."

"Very well, I will bow to your wishes, but make no mistake, finding a suitable flat must be a priority before we send her out of our care or I will leave with her!" Mary angrily declared.

Sister Mary, often a very vocal minority of the sisterhood, had always been an independent thinker, not given to following the pack. That she became a nun was as much in defiance of her family as making a statement for her love of God. She would defy any who would keep her from defending a principle, one for which she would fight and die.

Any chance her parents had of pairing her with the village's wealthiest landowner had disappeared as quickly as Mary. Her first impulse was to flee to Paris and immerse herself into the counterculture of the Left Bank's forgotten colony of artists. It was never her goal to become one with her Lord even though, as a devout Catholic, Mary's silent musings were often in a dialogue with Him. It was better she had decided to trust that He had given her the wisdom to determine what was right for her.

Circumstances, including a brush with one of Paris' unsavory characters, drove her to the convent where she now found her peace. It was her street experience that made her keenly aware of the dangers presented to an innocent girl like Clarice.

Yes, she would definitely become the protector of this woman-child, arming her with knowledge as well as watching out for her.

New Awakening

Clarice found the next days were busy with the work of settling into her own space, making adjustments to the convent's routines, and planning her next move, part of which was to secure a position and look into classes at the university. Finding a flat would come quickly once she could show secure employment to a prospective landlord.

Her loneliness was almost gone, replaced with a newfound spirit of independence, along with the adoring attention of Sister Mary. They had formed an immediate bond, not unlike what she had with Father Pierre. She dared not dream of her mother and the relationship they might have had but could hope this might lead to a close second.

Then there was the business of changing her name. With great reluctance, she agreed to be referred to as Cherise from this point forward. "Sister Mary, why must I hide from all that is my history, burying outward signs of affection and the memories of the love of my wonderful parents and grand-mère?"

"Cherise, my heart is heavy for the losses you have suffered already, but it is wise for you to remain undercover with this new identity."

"But, Sister Mary, it's so unfair that I cannot live freely to glorify and honor my parents, they who sacrificed so much to those less fortunate, fighting for the rights of their countrymen, even those whose ideology might not have been in the favor of those in power!"

"Sweet Cherise, my dear girl, I do understand and empathize with you, but the smartest course of action is for your whereabouts to remain unknown to those who would wish you harm. There are many misguided souls who covet a chance to destroy all that you represent. The smartest position is to present a neutral, noninvolved face in the crowd, and the time will come when you can work to exonerate and glorify the Pontifi and Chevais names. Until that time, it is imperative you follow the course Father Pierre prepared for you."

"Oh, Sister Mary, why is life so difficult? I'll bet if I was a man, all would be different!" pouted Cherise, once again showing her age.

"Be that as it may, the smart course is the one you must take now," Sister Mary declared. The duo settled into a routine that could best be described as mundane, strangely quiet, and peaceful but carried with it an expectation of some unknown element yet to present itself.

The other nuns were cordial and warmed quickly to Cherise's sunny disposition. Even Sister Leonia dropped her defenses long enough to engage Cherise in a conversation. Skeptical at first, Sister Leonia did her own digging to find out everything possible, including her motivation for coming to Paris.

Strange, thought Cherise, but she decided to put it out of her mind—at least for now. There had been too many memory flashes lately, causing her to be overly suspicious even of Sister Leonia.

Trying to unravel the mysteries surrounding the untimely deaths of her grandmother and her parents had taken a toll on her psyche. Voices in the tunnel kept coming back to her—a new development since her counseling sessions with Father Pierre had opened those areas for exploration.

As difficult as it was to pretend, she was anxious to make friends with the entire group. Who better to start with than the one with the greatest reluctance to let her into the convent? She managed to corral her natural suspicions, even scolding herself, since, after all, weren't these women of great faith? Maybe someday she would be more trusting, but prudence dictated that she must protect herself and her loved ones until such time as all the enemies were brought to justice.

The days passed quickly in the confines of the convent, and Cherise resigned herself to accepting her new identity.

Sister Mary had gently told Cherise of the need to find a flat but was defiant with regard to the time frame imposed by the Mother Superior. Coaching Cherise in the role she now played, Sister Mary was determined to help this woman-child build her defenses to a level that could withstand scrutiny by anyone. That Cherise was so bright, precocious even, did not compare to her inner strength of will. This was not a girl to be taken lightly!

There was definitely an ethereal quality about Cherise, one that could elude the smartest of men, but Mary was prepared for the task of grooming her. Self-awareness blending with a calm, controlled exterior gave Cherise a demeanor that pulled people into her center like a magnetic force. Mary noticed even the hardcore sisters melted in the face of her smile.

The unfortunate business of finding a suitable place for Cherise to make her permanent home seemed to fade into the background. Her appreciation of the sisters' original unwillingness to provide her this home, however, did not escape Cherise's thoughts for long, and she was determined to leave as quickly as possible!

The next week brought increased activity in all areas of the convent. New young women were brought into the inn as quickly as the space would allow. Some had been badly mistreated, and it pained all the nuns to see the degree of inhumane treatment inflicted on their sisters. Girls and young women readied for service to the highest bidder for a life of sexual slavery were particularly needy upon their arrival.

It fascinated Cherise to see how the nuns worked through their daily chores yet still had time to minister to all the girls—each in need of her own counsel. There was one new girl in particular who caught her eye—a young, dark-skinned beauty. She wondered what brought her to Paris, what drove her to come to the convent. Her demeanor defied logic, certainly not indicative of having been abused and sold into slavery. The girl's accent was melodious, a blend of French and an exotic, rhythmic-sounding language. After inquiring about the girl's background, Cherise found out her name was Gabrielle and she had just arrived from Morocco.

"I wonder why she would travel so far from home, knowing she would have no other place but a simple convent!" Cherise muttered. "I must find out what led her to Paris!"

Cherise's natural curiosity moved her to introduce herself to the new girl. What was it about this girl that nagged at the very core of her sense of security? Pleasant and friendly, Gabrielle welcomed Cherise's overtures of friendship almost immediately.

"I would like very much, Mademoiselle Cherise, if you would share my table at dinner tonight," said Gabrielle.

Hesitating at first, Cherise offhandedly answered, "Well, of course, certainly, I'd like that, Gabrielle." Cherise was unhappy for second-guessing everything that was said. She looked for any clues that might show why Gabrielle had come to this convent, even what her motives were for being so friendly. It was not like her to be questioning someone who had shown such kindness. After all, hadn't she made the first overture to the new girl?

Would every chance encounter with people who might seem out of character or place always be suspect to her?

"It was just—oh, what's the use—I'll be trying to figure this out until I'm either mad or manage to run off a potential friend," Cherise spouted, oblivious to the possibility of anyone hearing.

One of the last serious conversations she had with Father Pierre before leaving for Paris had everything to do with the Duvalier link, the conversations in the tunnel, and the urgency of keeping a vigilant eye out for any suspicious activities as she made her way in Paris.

Even up until the last day at La Nuaz Belfort, the complete story was never mentioned and Cherise was certain that Father did not realize how much she had heard in the tunnel and, through her perceptiveness, from the nuns. Reading between the lines with Bernard during his visit gave her another dimension to work from. Gradually, she would uncover all the truth and deal with it at the proper time.

In the meantime, she would be diligently aware of her surroundings and whatever work she could find would help her cover some of her activities, particularly those pertaining to her investigative work.

The evening meals were almost always held in the main dining room, overlooking an expansive inner courtyard adorned with statuaries which suggested a Paris of long ago. The surroundings would give Cherise opportunity to watch and wait for signs of any questionable activity. Burial vaults were ensconced in the far wall, housing those who she imagined had shed blood in wars ill-fought. They gave way to the garden pathways lined with fountains bursting forth their precious water—symbols of life, hope, and reassurance to all who came to drink.

Dinner was pleasant and any suspicions she might have had disappeared quickly, especially after Gabrielle explained how she happened to come to Paris and the convent. Even though her parents were still alive, she had been abandoned while a young girl by a mother who could no longer care for her and a father who abused his young wife. She wanted to believe that her mother's actions had saved her the same fate.

After spending the last twelve years living with a family in Morocco, much as a servant or slave at times, a kind nun had helped her escape and come to Paris. Life had been very hard for Gabrielle, but her great spirit belied that fact.

Cherise, three years younger, was fascinated by Gabrielle and vowed to become her friend. There was much she could learn from this young woman.

Finding Meaning

If ever two souls clicked, Sister Mary and her young protégé became solid friends. Even beyond the bond of friendship, there was the unspoken loyalty of family—not by blood but life experience.

In the beginning, Cherise had found she sought counsel with the sister and warmed to her almost immediately. There was some mysterious indefinable connection which surprised her at first but comfortable, as if finding a lost member of her family.

When she first broached the subject of her respect and affection for Sister Mary, she was greeted with a big bear hug, assuring Cherise the feeling was most mutual.

True to her word, Sister Mary excitedly pulled Cherise into her office a few weeks later, exclaiming, "Beautiful girl, I have news of an opportunity, one you will find very rewarding!"

"What is it, Sister Mary? Please tell me or I will burst with curiosity!"

"Ah, that will be my little secret until we can introduce you to what may be your future." Mary was being playful, and Cherise could tell this was going to be a fun adventure!

"My future, what exactly will that be?" she laughed happily.

"Put your best dress on and we'll take a little excursion to the Avenue des Champs-Elysees, the very heart of Paris! Our path may even bend to the whim of the Etoile."

"If you have found something for me near the Champs-Elysees, I would be so grateful." She remembered for a moment the days of joy spent with her grand-mère, helping in the antique shop, asking a million questions—all of which were graciously answered as if Marie had only time for her granddaughter. There was always a feeling of warmth and love of a special time and place.

Cherise could spend hours studying the patina of the wood adorning the chests so lovingly crafted by an artist's hands, her thirst for knowledge encouraged by Marie Chevais.

Sister Mary recognized a melancholy taking hold of Cherise and dared ask, "What are you thinking, my dear, that you have such a longing in your eyes?"

"It's the memories of those I've loved and lost, but in remembering them, they give me a feeling of tranquility and peace." She decided not to dwell on her very intensely personal recollections but instead give a more cryptic response.

Aside from having personal ties to that area of Paris, Sister Mary was certain it would be such a pleasure for Cherise to spend time among the bountiful beauty defined by the stately trees forming their natural arches over each street, the finely chiseled statuary lining lush landscaped grounds of each residence and, not to be forgotten, the remarkable architecture that only the centuries-old brownstones could possibly claim!

Chuckling, Mary was confident now her hunch had been right—Cherise was going to meet her destiny and in a big way.

Hurriedly, Cherise changed into her best dress, pulled her thick hair back, and tied it with one of her best silk scarves, one of crimson and gold she had saved for a special occasion. "I wonder what Sister Mary has found that she is so mysterious about."

Arriving in the Eighth Arrondissement, the smiling and giggling duo could have been mistaken for best friends out looking for fun in Paris. The sister had changed into her one and only civilian frock just to maintain the secrecy—more for Cherise's safety than that of engaging in the frivolity she was giving into at the moment.

"You are right, my chérie, this is so much fun!" laughed Sister Mary. The truth was she would continue this little charade for as long as they walked the streets, hiding any particular mission she might have from those who might have followed them. Was she overly cautious?

They were close now, and Sister Mary could feel her heart racing, a rhythmic beating in her chest. She thought, I must be very careful to go past the shop and around the block to the Museum of Art. Just beyond the fourth block, she saw their first destination and stepped up her pace.

To Cherise, the charade had been almost comical, but now there was a definite tension and sense of urgency to Sister Mary's pace.

"We will circle around and then make our way through the back alleys to camouflage our destination in the event of watchful eyes."

In preparing for her trip out of the convent, Sister Mary confided their departure time to the Mother Superior, being careful not to divulge where they were going. Instead, she cautioned Mother Superior not to mention to anyone they were leaving, an extra insurance that their little adventure would remain a secret.

Circling now and closing in on the museum, the happy twosome moved through the crowded sidewalk, barely able to contain their excitement. Sister Mary was as excited as Cherise and hoped that her charge would be pleased with the opportunity to work among the people who had loved Marie Chevais. Yes, she was sure this was the right thing to do.

Being careful with her path and making certain they were not being followed, the sister entered the museum and gracefully moved around some of the displays of ancient books, all the while moving toward the back exit with Cherise in tow.

Totally breathless now, Cherise asked, "Why are we going into the museum? Is this where I'm going to work?"

It was time to tell her the news and allow the information to sink in before taking her to the shop of Marie Chevais. "My sweet girl, you remember that the part of the landholdings lost when your parents died in the train wreck were those included in your grand-mère's unsettled estate. Before anything could be done with Marie's holdings, the horrible tragedy befell your family."

She looked over just as a slight sigh slipped through Cherise's lips. "Why are you bringing this up now, Sister?"

"It is part of what I must tell you before we reach our destination," she hesitated ever so slightly before continuing, "and bears significantly on your future. As you already know, the holdings were given to Duvalier by a court of law under suspicious circumstances, supposedly to satisfy old debt. Duvalier had many resources and contacts where he could dispose of the most immediate property and valuables."

Cherise was looking incredulously at the nun, wondering what in the world might be coming next and afraid to hear any more. "Please, Sister Mary, I do not want to hear of the evil work of Duvalier on this happy day," she begged.

Sister Mary pulled her close and quietly whispered so no one could hear, "Dear girl, do not fear because my news is good. I am only explaining how and why we have arrived here in this area, a distance so close to your beloved grandmother's shop. I must show you there are good and decent people in this world."

"What do you mean?" It was beginning to become obvious to Cherise where they were heading, and all the emotions that had been pent up for the past five years threatened to overpower her. Fighting hard now, she managed to control those raw feelings, displaying a measure of her fortitude. She stood quietly waiting for the nun to continue the story.

"You see, Duvalier left the sale of your grandmother's shop in the care of the court to be sold quickly. It was folly that in his greed, he cared only for the money that came from these holdings with no notice of who would purchase and how the properties would be attended. The first group purchased the shop on Rue de Rainier, not for themselves but for one known as Olivier Gereaux."

Sister Mary paused to assess how her charge took in this information before continuing down this path.

Unable to contain the mounting tension any longer, Cherise tearfully said, "I should have recognized how close we were, but it has been a long time and the scenery has changed with the years. Are we going to the shop now?"

"Yes, right now, as soon as we move through the rear of the museum, but first, I want to try to make you understand what this means to you and Andre."

"I still don't understand any of it, and how did you know about this, Sister Mary? Does everyone at the convent know about my past?"

"No, my chérie, Father Pierre told only the Mother Superior, who included me for reasons I will now share. Because we needed their support, three of my Sisters were informed, and what they were told was abbreviated from the entire story. It was necessary in the beginning to form a circle of protection around you.

"Olivier Gereaux was a well-known philanthropist and connoisseur of fine art and antiquities. Careful to keep his identity hidden, he hired a good friend to run the shop and took great care to protect intrusion from any outside capital, even if it had to be run at a loss. The business has prospered for many years, and even though Olivier is no longer alive, his legacy is how he protected your grandmother's place, making sure it would remain in pristine condition until the day it could be returned to the rightful heirs."

Cherise was awestruck and nodded her head in silent understanding. "The manager's name is Monsieur Dominic Broussard, and he is my first cousin! Olivier's hope was that one day you and your brother would return to claim what rightfully belonged to you, and he entrusted Dom with the task of not only keeping everything in pristine condition but also finding the grandchildren of Marie Chevais."

Openly weeping now, Cherise was unable to contain the rush of emotions—joy and sorrow mixed with a sad sweetness born of love known and deep loss endured. "Come, my dear, it is time to meet your destiny."

To any curious outsider, the duo appeared as happy friends walking arm in arm, enjoying the weather and chatting about the frivolous aspects of life. Who could guess that a new day was dawning for the young woman in the bright bandana?

Sister Mary was deep in thought. *There would be plenty of time to share the details with Cherise. When she has time to absorb all this new information, she'll want to know how we found her and my involvement. Cherise will be most curious how I came to the convent and established myself as a serious nun. All in due time, she will know all.*

She couldn't help but drift into that time when Olivier came to Sister Mary's parents, asking for their help in saving what rightfully belonged to the Pontifi children—the shop. As it happened, they were more than willing to be of service, but health limitations would impede working in the shop and committing to the day-to-day activities required.

At that time, Sister Mary was still a teenager but was anxious to do her part in this "adventure." Timing was critical, and the only person they could turn to was Sister Mary's cousin, Dom. Another challenge was finding the children. Rumor had them in a convent near Switzerland. It was Mary who volunteered to become a nun at least for two or three years in order to find out information that would lead them to the Pontifi children.

It was interesting now to reflect on her journey to becoming a nun. Mary acknowledged that, at first, the decision was a frivolous one made by a young woman not ready for such a serious move. Through prayer, along the way, Mary was absorbed into the convent's way of life and became the devout Sister Mary.

It was God's intervention, she thought. Her role now was one that she relished and cherished along with her commitment to God and the Catholic church.

Freedom

PEERING OUT THE window of her flat, Cherise noticed the group of street vendors making their way to the Plaza. "Oh, I love the smells of a Paris morning, just after the first batch of croissants is pulled from the ovens of the patisserie below. She could almost taste the melting butter laced delight with the generous mounds of fresh berry marmalade. And I would not want to miss the sweet fragrance of the morning glory blossoms as they spread their arms in joyful praise of the early dew, settling on the landscape like a blue mist."

Stretching her gaze beyond the park below, she noticed how the dawn breaking lay claim to the darkened alleyways branching out from each plaza, as if to paint an earth-grounded sun over each square mile it covered.

The promise of fresh-baked goods and piping hot tea along with the beauty all around her gave Cherise a warm, settled feeling. It proved once again her decision to come to Paris had been right.

Content to talk to the birds perched on her windowsill while soaking up the morning smells, Cherise lingered for what seemed like only ten minutes, but in fact, it was more like thirty. Aroused from the reverie, she hurried to jump into her clothes, stumbling as she pulled on the crisply folded pinafore while balancing books with the finesse of a novice acrobat just learning her trade.

To an outside observer, it all would have seemed awkward and laughable at best, but Cherise was used to juggling multiple tasks while balancing inanimate objects. Running down the stairs, she almost knocked over the baker, Raphael, carrying his first batch of bread and rolls out to one of the many vendors.

"Cherise, mon petit, you are always in a hurry. Slow down and come have your favorite croissant before it grows cold, a special one I made just for you!" It was hard for Raphael to bring a harsh word to bear upon the delightful young woman even if some of her habits were annoying.

She had come to them four months prior looking for a place to live and had so impressed him and Mrs. LaPorte, captivating them with her charming smile and adultlike vocabulary. Instantly, they had sensed she was special.

Ordinarily, they would never consider a woman, let alone one of her young age, as a suitable tenant. There was a certain aura surrounding this one, almost as if she had the Holy Spirit guiding her every step of the way. Plus the nun, Sister Mary, had vouched for this young woman.

It had taken her several weeks to find this flat and then many attempts to persuade the landlord that she was capable of maintaining it just as any man could—and in her estimation, better.

The reality of her situation as a young, single woman in a city the size of Paris never escaped Cherise, and even from the first day of her arrival, it had served to heighten her senses. Though daunting at first, there had also been an element of excitement.

She was reminded how those raw, basic instincts included hiding from Duvalier's henchmen even though she vowed not to live in fear of the past. Besides, she reasoned, it was wise to have anonymity as a single woman on her own, or she might be thought to be working in one of the professions in which upstanding ladies would rather be caught dead. Covering her tracks and moving among the masses, she was certain to be lost in the maze of avenues and cross streets.

But back to the present. Cherise quickly decided that it was better to accept Raphael's kindness and not risk upsetting him even though she would be late for her class. "Thank you, monsieur!" she squealed. "I don't know what would become of me if you hadn't embraced this simple girl from the hills!" Plucking the special croissant from the heaping pile, she quickly plopped herself down at one of the tables lining the sidewalk café, basking once again in the warmth and beauty of the Paris morning.

It had been a very busy six months since her arrival at the convent in Paris, followed by her near-perfect job. Now she could breathe, feeling for the first time her identity as an adult. Sister Mary had been a wonderful godsend. She was there to pick Cherise up at the critical junctures where her gentle spirit made a difference between Cherise continuing on her chosen path or otherwise giving in to the depression that, at times, had threatened to overwhelm her.

After Cherise confronted her family's legacy and started dealing with the painful memories of the void left by their very absence, it was Sister Mary who proved to be her guardian angel, lifting her beyond the simple elements of dealing day-to-day with living in the past.

Her days were now filled with happy thoughts and fulfilling moments shared along with the art objects of the gallery, some of which graced her own family's lives in ways that told stories long forgotten.

What was that chest used for if not as a historical reference to the lives of those whose memories were to be stored within its drawers? Each object carefully placed upon the satin lining reflected its owner's place in immortality by enriching life and bringing joy to those of the next generations who happened upon them.

Or what of the ornately carved daybed covered in a red velvet so soft only a true weaver of fine cloth could know the love and care given in the making of it? How many of her ancestors had warmed to its luxuriousness while indulging in a brief afternoon nap? Perhaps even dreaming of meeting the loved one to share this space and time.

Were there now any so dedicated artisans as to spend hours and hours carving the tea table that had once been next to her mother's bed? She could envision the quiet conversations her mother might have had in the early morning hours while sipping tea brought by the faithful servant of the manor. Each piece brought back good memories of times spent at the manor with family and friends.

There was a charming locket the size of a hazelnut, cast in the beautiful antique gold characteristic of seventeenth-century France that reminded her so much of the one her grandmother wore with a miniature picture of her beloved Henri inside. When she first spotted it in the shop, her heart fluttered, thinking perhaps it was Marie Chevais's but then remembered seeing the locket encircling her grandmother's neck as she lay in the casket. Even so, when no one was looking, she had to satisfy her curiosity by taking a peek.

Cherise's inner dialogues often left her emotionally drained, but strangely, of late they were having a cathartic effect. Sad as some of these memories were, they also gave her the sense of being with her loved ones. Day by day she felt stronger.

It proved to be a consequential decision to move away from the convent after only two months. Her friendship with Sister Mary was self-sustaining, but unknown interferences from outside the convent had influenced what little relationship she had formed with Sister Leonia and Gabrielle. She couldn't put her finger on it, but it seemed to be that their encounters around her were very strange, almost as if they were hiding a secret from her. The continued whispers between Leonia and Gabrielle whenever they were together, sometimes in her presence, bothered Cherise. It also disturbed Cherise to realize how little she trusted these two, yet Sister Mary had encouraged her to listen to the inner voice.

Gabrielle was mysterious and intriguing, so perhaps what appeared to be strange and unusual behavior was not so much secrets hidden from Cherise but more to do with her own difficult life prior to the convent. Cherise's good intentions of befriending Gabrielle had stalled in the face of the changes taking place in her life. Once she added her studies at the university to her full work schedule at the shop, there was no time to cultivate trust or build a bridge.

The part-time schedule she had chosen at University of Paris quickly added to her workload, but to Cherise it was a joyous dilemma. There was no time to indulge her paranoia, so she elected to continue the status quo and silently wondered about Gabrielle.

The final break had come when Cherise noticed Gabrielle talking to an oddly familiar-looking man who aroused in her a feeling of danger. When she questioned Gabrielle about the stranger, her indifferent response was anything but comforting, almost defensive, and did nothing to help assuage Cherise's fears.

Although Cherise didn't mention the incident with Gabrielle at the time, Sister Mary had sensed there was something new and disturbing in Gabrielle's manner toward Cherise. She made a mental note to keep a close eye on Gabrielle.

Dom proved to be a source of strength to both Sister Mary and Cherise. Careful to protect his young charge, he sometimes imagined himself to be her father and was fiercely loyal to Cherise in keeping her identity a secret even to the close-knit staff. It amazed him at times, watching her and imagining what her early life must have been, the joy of her family all together, only to be followed by such traumatic events! Surprising the fortitude and strength of will for one so young, beautiful and, as he quickly reminded himself, in need of his dedicated protection. He had sworn to Olivier before his death that when the time came if any of the remaining heirs should become part of the shop once again, not one word would leak from him as to their real identities.

Cherise was an arresting study for any red-blooded Frenchman, a young woman of effortless poise with a total disregard for her looks. In fact, she was totally unaware of the effect she had on the stronger sex. The once-beautiful child was now a statuesque young woman whose deep auburn hair fell almost to her waist when not secured by a hair bow. Dom could not help but notice the color of her eyes—a brushed green tint with a hint of golden flecks that gave them almost an amber tone.

Dom was a handsome young man—debonair, most of the young women of society might say—but given to proclivities such as reading and studying in his leisure time. He was not particularly interested in the silly self-absorbed women who found him mysterious, which naturally made him the target of many a determined maiden.

He was devoted to the shop and, when not working, studying for an advanced degree in French literature. Literature and art might have been Dom's first love, but he had an uncanny knack for business, especially the noble trade of fine arts and antiquities.

It was no accident that Olivier had handpicked the talented young man to be his first-level manager at Madame Chevais's shop. Sister Mary's parents had been his confidants for many years and his savior when the time came he had to finally deal with his demons. Oliver had carried the guilt of his early involvement with Duvalier even though he had washed his hands of the misdeeds planned.

There had been a special connection with Sister Mary before she fled to the convent. Even now remembering brought him pain. She knew his story, the connection to Duvalier and the part Olivier had played in the destruction of the Chevais-Pontifi fortune. He had been used in his trust of Duvalier but did bear some of the blame for which he would have to atone.

There had been enough stories of Duvalier and how he had destroyed the Chevais-Pontifi family to satisfy Dom that there was an extreme urgency to protect Clarice, now formally called Cherise. Before having accepted his older friend's offer to manage such a prestigious antiques store, Dom had done some investigating on his own.

It seemed that the children of Augusto Pontifi were lucky to be alive and still fairly well hidden from the perils their parents faced. Dom was well aware of the danger in dropping his guard where Mademoiselle Cherise was concerned, and besides, he found himself more and more enamored of her every day. Strange, thought Dom, to be this concerned about someone other than family, yet he had to admit a feeling of real apprehension whenever she left the safety of the shop. He couldn't let the likes of Duvalier bring harm to Cherise.

Seeking to repair the damage wrought on the Chevais-Pontifi family's good name, Dom had his own plans for Duvalier and he was determined to find a way to intervene in time. He had to carefully plan his next move. Though altruistic in his actions, Dom also had other reasons to eliminate the threat of Duvalier from Cherise's future.

During his investigation into the past ten years of the family's history, he recognized where the real threat was to Cherise and Andre. Proof there was a significant amount of money in Swiss Bank's left unaccounted, plus additional properties, disturbed him to his core. His discovery of a document hidden within the shop's deeper recesses, specifically a letter taped to the back of a drawer in an armoire used for business files, could put him and his loved ones in a dangerous situation. It didn't escape him that somehow it would affect Cherise if she knew of his discovery, so he decided to keep the information quiet.

There was no way to approach this dilemma openly without endangering others. His motive was not driven by greed, or so he thought, but rather a mission to ensure justice prevail. It was his duty not only to protect his share of the shop, willed to him upon Olivier's death, but the portion belonging to the Pontifi heirs. At the right time, he would have to confront Duvalier.

Cherise and Andre would inherit their rightful estate, as it should be, and perhaps feel some sense of vindication. He could not do less than this for Olivier.

It was time for Dom to explore exactly what he needed to do to get loose from any perceived hold Duvalier might have on him. It happened so quickly and easily he did not have time to react to shut Duvalier down immediately. His offer of help seemed more of a friendly gesture thrown out upon meeting someone new instead of a concerted effort to interfere in the business and personal dealings of Dom.

When the first large deposit showed up in his bank account, he immediately went to his banker, demanding to know where it came from. That the bank could not tell him, yet had put this money in his account, disturbed him deeply. It could only have been done at the hand of Duvalier.

It was obvious any of the trail leading back to Duvalier had been wiped clean, but the note he had received a few days later was explicit in its demands.

Dom was to help Duvalier find the grandchildren of Madame Chevais and report any movement of artifacts that could possibly lead to the children.

He tried to send the money back to no avail. After a while, it seemed easy enough to just hold on to it. Perhaps he could eventually funnel it to Cherise. It was at this point that Dom's surreptitious, deceitful behavior began.

In the meantime, it was common knowledge that Duvalier was still waiting and looking for the Pontifi children. It had been several years since one of Duvalier's scouts had supposedly found the children hidden away in a convent, then had mysteriously disappeared in the mountainous region of the Beaufortain Alps.

A misunderstood, little-explored area of France where *civilized* Frenchmen claimed to have endured frightening encounters with the locals, this isolated region remained secure from the nosy neighbors to the north and south.

Duvalier's scout had intercepted a message bound for Bernard through a fluke and had already charted a course to La Nuaz. Just as suddenly, the scout disappeared, leaving no trace or information to uncover.

Duvalier searched for his scout after word had somehow leaked out that a big giant of a man had visited two children high in the alps in an area particularly difficult to find, let alone enter. The children were thought to be the heirs of the Chevais-Pontifi families.

Before Duvalier could mount a campaign to retrieve the children and possibly kill Bernard, all had disappeared—just as if they had never existed. It was to Father Pierre's benefit and the safety of the children and adults housed within La Nuaz Convent that Duvalier, at that very time, was battling other political enemies, unable to spare any manpower. Even though it was a very disturbing time in France when loyalties seemed to dissolve with the amount of money that could be paid to anyone willing to be used for prurient reasons, Duvalier's reach was dwindling.

It had been folly to bring Bernard to their place, but it seemed to be the only solution. Father Pierre had risked much, and now he prayed Clarice was safe under the watchful eye of Sister Mary.

Bernard would know how to hide once again and that only left Andre. If those who were intent on harming him were led to believe Andre was gone along with Clarice, it would be possible to dilute their interest in the convent and Father Pierre.

That the place was like a fortress didn't escape the least of them. Perched high on one of the most rugged peaks in France, the history of the region had long held that the inhabitants would come down from the mountain only to trade for wives and exchange goods once a year. Protecting their beloved priests and the nuns of the garden-enclosed enclave became the people's mission in life. Legend held that those who breached such a barrier had been hung on a stake and burned to death. The faint of heart would never dare trespass in this area of France.

Andre was definitely in good hands, tucked away from the civilization that would do him harm. Father Pierre would make sure his precious charge was well protected. For as long as history had been recorded, in every period and especially now in France, there were those who would be the hunters as well as those who would be the hunted. If he as a priest could not keep one small boy from harm, then what good were all the prayers and rosaries spoken to his God on behalf of the hunted?

He worried about Clarice so far away in the heart of Paris, but at least he could feel that she was self-sufficient and somewhat protected among the masses. Sister Mary, he was confident, would hover over her charge and not allow anyone to come close enough to find the secret. That freed his mind to deal with the problems on hand, namely keeping his fortress safe and his own charge, Andre, away from inquisitive eyes and ears.

In the meantime, he would do his best to keep Andre under wraps and maintain minimum contact with Sister Mary. The time would come when Andre would have to join his sister in Paris. Until then, he would be his tutor.

The Divide

Summer of 1897

Cherise had been pacing until finally Dom stepped in front of her. "My dear little Cherise, whatever is bothering you, tell me and I will help you!"

"Dearest Dom, it is so complicated that I don't know where to begin. Have you ever tried to make the right decision and yet faced with truths having a bearing on what that decision should be, ventured down a treacherous path in spite of them?"

"That is a serious statement for one so young. I beg you to allow me to counsel you. Whatever reason you are unhappy here, Cherise, we can work through it. We knew working so closely with your past you would have to deal with the demons and also the memories of your family."

"Do you remember I came here to Paris a year ago to start a new life?"

"Well, yes, Cherise, my dear, but what has that to do with your unrest? I thought you were content here in the gallery and with your studies at the university." Dom, sensing where this line of conversation was heading, tried to steer it in a different direction.

"Part of me still wrestles with the death of my parents and the revenge that I so dearly wanted. Along the way, I have come to realize there are more important battles to fight, battles for which my parents tried to prepare me. They would not want me to waste my life in pursuit of revenge. However,

I do understand while my true identity is hidden, I'm safe. Once I leave the safe harbor, then the fight may come to me!"

"It sounds as if this is too heavy a load for one so young. Whatever you are considering as your course of action, tell me. Allow me to help you determine your best course." Dom continued to plead, his words falling on deaf ears.

"So what do you plan to do, Cherise? You cannot divulge your true identity—not yet at least." His apprehension mounting, Dom could not help but be impressed with her display of courage. He winced, thinking of his own lack of courage in dealing with certain individuals who were trying to undermine his good intentions.

"My greatest desire is to repair the damage that has been done to my family's name, their honor, and to the cause of justice for people maligned, including those of Alsace-Lorraine." She didn't tell him one of her passions was also to help her fellow women in their fight for equal rights. It occurred to Cherise that this would have to come after restoring the family name and rightful heritage. There was still much work to be done before she had the ability to pursue her causes.

"Perhaps, Dom, the answer to your question lies in the right course of action for the people. Don't you think it would mean more to embrace my heritage? I have been part of both cultures and in the lives of the people of Alsace-Lorraine and the Parisians. Couldn't I speak for all French men and women?"

Dom looked at Cherise sadly, assessing her sincerity and acknowledging to himself with amazement the look of determination in her eyes. He couldn't help but admire his young charge while also worrying for her safety.

"You certainly have picked a difficult road to travel, given the depth of animosity that still remains with some Parisians and Frenchmen as a whole. If you cast your identity aside, you know you may become an immediate target of Duvalier and his henchmen! This sounds like the murmurings of a sophomore student at the university who has been recruited into the latest movement without thinking through the ramifications of this course of action."

Dom knew he was being harsh and appeared uncaring of Cherise's idealistic views, but he had to impress upon her the seriousness of any decision that would put her in harm's way. "You must consider Andre's safety, if not your own."

Hesitating ever so slightly, Cherise took a deep breath and proceeded to lay bare her deepest desires to her friend and confidante. "If I could but hold to my ear the beating heart of my mother while enwrapped in her arms for one last time, knowing I must say goodbye, it would not change the mission for which I was cast. I believe all that has happened to my family was for a reason greater than that for which we live and toil."

He looked at her wondering if this was how she planned to justify her parents' deaths and sincerely hoped she may have found her life purpose. Perhaps it would give her life a deeper meaning even though her goal was somewhat misguided.

Seeing the look on Dom's face moved Cherise to say, "Do not despair, my friend, for I now know my destiny. Bid me to help those who have no strength to fight for what is right. The very act of piracy Duvalier perpetrated upon my family was the act of a very weak man, preying on those who would instinctively trust their fellow human to do the right thing. If I help those with less fortitude, perhaps I can save a few who would help kindle the good in mankind."

"Dear Cherise, how do you propose to take on the world as you so aptly describe your new mission in life? Do you really think that one young woman can make a difference in the way that each region of France views his fellow man? Frenchmen are divided among their own kind and cannot agree on a direction toward peaceful coexistence."

"I believe, Dom, that by living in my own way, the example I set may spur others to action. Along the way, I will quietly do things which can bring change. You know my grand-mère was a very independent, strong woman who viewed life from the perspective of a man. She was unafraid to do those things which were viewed as man's work or a man's place. It was her spirit that has instilled in me a sense of fairness for not just women but for all people, especially my wonderful friends back in Mulhouse."

Cherise could see that Dom was in a state, one mixed with fear for her safety balanced with an admiration so raw in its truth as to inspire a greater purpose for her life. "That I am a woman only means I have a greater sense of determination in seeing my mission take shape!"

Yes, she was sure now of her path, one cast many years prior, before the catastrophe, or murder, that took the lives of those she loved. What she could not see was her own naivete and Dom's own plans for her life. As she had pondered how to make a difference in the world and still be true to the memory of Augusto, Aurelia, and Grand-mère, she had a recurring dream, one that showed a vivid picture of the manor house in Mulhouse all draped in black.

Unsure at first of the significance, Cherise worked it around in her mind over and over. Could it mean that, if left alone, the tarnish of her family's good name would remain like a coffin in the grave, forever buried but leaving the blanch of whispered traitorousness to be shared among the French nationalists? She could not, nor would not, allow the taint to remain upon the Pontifi-Chevais families.

It definitely was a sign, one she could not ignore. Was she brave enough to follow her heart? Cherise could only hope that whatever the ancestral spirit embodied within, it would help complete her mission. Some would question her motives, even her sanity, but for all the naysayers, Cherise could count on supporters to help finish whatever tasks might fall to them.

Most Frenchmen had a connection to someone in the Alsace region, even if but a passing friend, enough to cause them to hesitate before casting stones. Besides, she would still be involved part-time at the university with her studies and soon working her other job. A pang of regret hit her at that moment, a longing to keep the status quo and the comfort of working in her grand-mère's shop. She had to admit it was a time of content—staying busy by day, studying by night, and going home to her lovely flat.

It was another six months before Cherise was ready to make the changes necessary to go underground and begin her journey. The information she shared with Sister Mary and Dom was scant, orchestrated in a way to provide just enough for reassurance but not enough to put them in danger. It was Sister Mary who informed Father Pierre to expect changes in the frequency of information being sent to him since the time Cherise left the convent in La Nuaz. She also warned that it might not appear as from Cherise but Sister Mary would do her best to keep him informed.

Her flat was the one luxury she regretted leaving, but she was forced to close out her lease with Mr. and Mrs. LaPorte. When questioned about her decision to leave, Cherise was forced to lie, a regrettable action toward people she dearly cared for and respected.

The story was, as she boldly told them, "I must return to Milano, the city of my father's family. Of course, I'll write to you often, and it is only for a short while until my second cousin's wife can get on her feet!"

It sounded hollow even to Cherise as she spun her yarn. She was certain that they could see right through her but was determined to maintain her secret.

Andre

Defining an Era

Meanwhile, Father Pierre, although worried about Clarice, had another dilemma to deal with and that was the younger Pontifi. Even as he read Sister Mary's letter, he was distracted by thoughts of Andre.

Never a robust child, Andre had appeared frail lately, and Father sent him more than once to the infirmary. After worrying the nuns to death over the state of Andre's health, they too started noticing how pale and drawn he seemed. There was the nagging cough that seemed to consume him every time he tried to carry on a conversation. It caused them to wonder if they had paid enough attention to their young charge and also at which point his cough had become abnormal.

Andre was the boy with the big smile, pulling on the heartstrings of those who were lucky enough to encounter him. They left his presence a little more caring, perhaps even kinder for having been around his sweetness. *Angel Boy*, as the nuns would refer to him. A handsome youth, he captivated young and old, males and females, with his boyish innocence.

It was Sister Francine who finally came to Father Pierre with fear in her eyes. "We must summon the doctor, Father. Andre is becoming weak and listless, and everything we have given him to strengthen his little bones has had little or no effect. There has never been a time when he was so sick that he did not protest staying in bed, but now he seems to have no energy—even for his animals."

Father walked into the infirmary where the now fifteen-year-old lay on one of the specially placed cots—those reserved for Sister Francine's *special* patients, the ones she deemed in need of God's sunshine to assuage their fears. He wasn't sure who was more frightened: Sister Francine, Andre, or even himself. Andre was especially loved for his kind heart and nurturing spirit.

Just recently, Andre had come to them with a baby deer that he had found in the lower gardens. Seriously injured by a large predator, he had nursed the fawn back to health. It pained him to see any of God's creatures suffering in any way. He made it his task each day to look for all types of living beings that were injured or in danger.

On that particular day, he quietly pleaded, "But, Sister Francine, he is so small and needs our help. Look at him. His eyes so sad and frightened, yearning for his mother but so alone!"

Father could not help but think of Andre's past and his present nurturing of the animals. No doubt he was trying to fill the void left when he lost his parents and, more recently, his beloved Clarice. How could any of them consider turning Andre away with his injured brood? It was becoming a chore, however, trying to find places for all these animals. Soon they would be overrun.

Thinking about Andre now, Father Pierre would have welcomed a zoo full of animals if he could only see the life in him. Perhaps after the doctor checked him over and prescribed some good medicine, he would be fine again.

This recent news from Clarice had not pleased him, and now what if he must summon her back to the convent? He would wait and see what the doctor said and weigh the risks involved with Clarice coming back. Even with a clean bill of health, he made a mental note that he must bring Clarice up-to-date on Andre's frail state.

Clarice had promised him she would stay in touch through the communication channel they had established when she left the convent. Although she had sent a steady stream of notes and letters upon first arriving in Paris, her communications were growing less frequent.

It infuriated the normally mild-mannered priest that Clarice was preparing to venture into a very dangerous and foolhardy pursuit when so many people had sacrificed for her safety to allow her to study in Paris.

How could she even consider going after Duvalier, particularly with the risks involved? Her naivete amazed even him. What of this business of the greater good in pursuit of equality and justice for the Alsace-Lorrainers? This whole business was very troubling: a young woman unclear on her direction in life, most certainly still being pursued by Duvalier and his band of thieves, and now this risky behavior on her part. What she needed was a good scolding, which Father Pierre was perfectly willing to provide.

His concern for Clarice was deep-rooted; there was no turning back for Duvalier, and the fact they had not seen or heard from him in quite some time was equally disturbing.

The following day, the local doctor arrived at the convent. After an hour of examining young Andre, he beckoned a very tense Father Pierre and Sister Francine to meet for a consultation. Nervously they followed him into the library where both sat as instructed, much like their own students, waiting expectantly, hoping for words of encouragement.

Clearing his throat, Dr. Martimbeau paused to gather his words. As gently as he could, softly, almost in a whisper, he said, "Father Pierre, Sister Francine, I am sorry to tell you that young Master Pontifi is gravely ill. Have you ever heard of consumption?"

Sister Francine gasped and clutched the doctor's hand. "But this is impossible, you can't be right! Are you saying Andre has tuberculosis? He did not appear to be that sick until recently, and there has never been anyone around here with any kind of symptoms such as these. Furthermore, we have a very clean, safe environment here at the convent." Her words trailed off as she clutched her rosary.

Father Pierre, although shaken, soothed the distraught nun. "Francine, let us allow the good doctor to continue. There may be something we can do to help Andre. Dr. Martimbeau, what can we do?" implored the priest.

After the two collected themselves Dr. Martimbeau continued, "Tuberculosis has been called consumption because it consumes people from within, with a bloody cough, fever, pallor, and long, relentless wasting. Tuberculosis is spread through the air, when people who have the disease cough, sneeze, or spit. Another theory is that it may be transmitted from eating cow's meat, a theory not proven, I might add."

"How can you be certain this is what plagues our beloved Andre?" Sister Francine interrupted.

When the disease becomes active, three quarters of the cases are pulmonary tuberculosis. Symptoms include chest pain, coughing up blood, and a productive, prolonged cough for more than three weeks. Other symptoms include fever, chills, night sweats, appetite loss, weight loss, pallor, and often a tendency to fatigue very easily.

"His symptoms fit the disease, but obviously, we cannot be certain. One of the ways we protect the others around an infected person is to isolate the patient. The best course of action for our young patient is to send him to the treatment facility in Paris where there are already studies underway to find a cure for this debilitating and often deadly disease."

"Certainly, we will do whatever is necessary to save Andre, but..."—and here Father hesitated—"you need to understand it is very dangerous for him outside of this area. Are there no other options than to send him away?"

"I must tell you, he is very fragile. The disease, if left untreated, will kill him, and even catching it now, the percentage of survival is low. I can't be sure and do not want to alarm you, but it may be a strain that is particularly virulent, and we must act fast for any chance to save him!"

It was a very sobering few minutes while the priest and nun absorbed all that had transpired. The foreboding of a few days ago had now been replaced with the reality that Andre's illness was much worse than they could have imagined.

Dr. Martimbeau suddenly broke the silence. "Perhaps there is another place, one not far removed from here near Switzerland. I recently heard of this facility where they were doing wonderful things to cure what would otherwise be terminally ill patients. I'm not promising to find you a spot, but I'll do my best."

Father Pierre was still quiet. There was so much to absorb in so short a time. He must get word to Clarice right away that her beloved Andre was critically ill and soon to be on his way to a sanatorium. Certain that Clarice would alter any radical plans she might have entertained, his other thoughts became lost with the planning and changes that he must make to save Andre's life.

Finally, he spoke, "Doctor, how do we know this other facility is as good as the one in Paris?"

"We don't, Father, but if you are truly concerned regarding the safety of young Andre, you have the option to send him to this one."

It was difficult thinking through this with Clarice in Paris and possibly in trouble.

"How much time do we have to make this decision, Dr. Martimbeau? I am in the midst of making a trip to Milano and while there, would like to visit a facility prior to deciding on the right course of action."

"Time is of the essence, but it will not change anything to wait a week or two. It will take that much time to wait for a space, and we will prepare documents for both facilities to ensure entry into one of them as quickly as possible!"

"Thank you, Doctor," Sister Francine softly whispered. It was apparent to the doctor they were all under stress and deserved a rest. He only hoped that the news he had delivered would allow them be hopeful for a while. They deserved that. The truth was much grimmer and he determined this wasn't the time to reveal it.

Awareness

July 2005

God, why did her head hurt so badly? Why won't her eyes focus? Why were there people in her room? Wasn't she supposed to be saying something? Everything was out of proportion, moving in and out like gray matter with no form. She couldn't make out the figure next to her bed, but the voice was familiar.

The soft, slightly Southern voice urged, "Mom, Mom, your eyes are fluttering. Wake up, please wake up. It's Loraine, your daughter, and I need you ...Need to talk to you. It's been so long, Mama, and you were doing so well, and...please wake up!" Loraine implored the figure on the bed.

Of course, it was Loraine. Where had she been? Wasn't it just yesterday that they had talked on the phone? Something wasn't quite right, and yet she had no energy to think beyond the fringe of her conscious mind. Why was it so important now for Loraine to talk to her? Perhaps she should try to open her eyes just for a minute to see if her daughter was okay. Her lids felt so heavy, though, almost as if they were glued shut.

"Are you okay, Loraine?" Jackie asked the stunned young woman. "Why do you seem so intense, honey?" The voice was raspy, but there was no doubt that she had just spoken out loud for the first time in six long months. Loraine leaned over and looked at her mother. Her eyes appeared closed, but perhaps she could see out of that little slit. "What are you looking at?" Jackie grunted.

The hair on the back of Loraine's neck stood up as the chills ran down her spine. *Oh my god*, thought Loraine. *That is just like the mother I used to know.* Without thinking, she gushed, "Hallelujah, Mom, do you know where you are? Do you realize what happened and how long you've been asleep?"

Gradually Jackie's eyes opened, but she couldn't quite make out her daughter's features, just her voice. Nothing seemed right; most of all, her damn eyes wouldn't focus! "My head hurts…What happened? Where am I?" Jackie asked belligerently.

Loraine grasped at the words coming from her mother, as if her life-blood had been restored. "Mom, Mama, you really are back!" she cried. "We've been so worried, and oh my god, you've been, well, it's a long story."

Adjusting to the light, she could now see her beautiful daughter clearly. In what was her typical fashion of trying to maintain control of her environment, Jackie made a valiant effort not to appear confused.

Something was wrong with this picture, a fragmented scene much like some of those from her youth. Why was she in this room? It even looked stark, sort of like being in a hospital: very white and sterile with the sporadic splashes of color from cheaply framed prints giving the room a small dollop of warmth. What looked like a bouquet of flowers was limply hanging over the rim of a bright orange vase giving the otherwise near-dead flowers some life.

As if she knew what her daughter was talking about, Jackie casually replied, "Well, you know how time gets away from me, and I've been really busy." The shocked look on Loraine's face spoke volumes, and she hesitated, wondering how ridiculous her response had been. "Ah, well I guess you may have to tell me what's going on. I can't remember why I'm here," she added sheepishly.

Was it just Jackie's imagination, or did the heaviness hanging over them indicate that something serious had happened? Whatever it was, somehow, she had to get over this little bump. As she always tried to do in the past, Jackie's efforts at controlling a situation took on obsessive overtones.

Thinking back, she had a glimpse of her great-grandmother Clarice as a young woman. How strange to be thinking of her right now, and what significance could that possibly have on her situation? *I must get control of my thoughts and figure out what is going on*, she decided.

Jackie had not spoken in what seemed like five minutes, but in reality, it had only been a minute at the most. Closing her eyes to bring clarity to the wild thoughts moving around in her mind, Jackie concentrated all of her efforts to focus on the present situation. She might be damaged, but instinctively she knew her mind would pull her back out of this mess somehow. It was the one place where she had comfort from all the strangeness.

Loraine misinterpreted the quiet as a sign her mother was slipping back into that dark world where she had lived for the past six months. "Mom, Mom, where are you? Come back please!" begged Loraine. "Don't leave again. We have missed you so much! You have to stay with us this time!"

Pulling all the strength she could muster, Jackie spoke up, "What's going on here, Loraine? Where am I? Is this a hospital?"

Loraine's breath seemed suspended in a slow-moving vacuum as she tried to respond nonchalantly to her mother. Sucking in, she replied, "Yes, Mom, you are in Carolinas Medical Center. There was an accident and…" Hesitating, Loraine continued, "Well, I don't know how to tell you this, so I'll just say it. You were badly injured in the crash and left in a coma! Do you remember anything at all about what happened?" Asking the questions would force her mother to engage her mind. Besides, she wasn't ready to tell her mother how long she had been here at the hospital.

Her mother's face clouded over, giving the appearance of someone moving into a self-induced hypnotic trance, and it soon became obvious that Jackie was not tuned in anymore; she appeared to be caught up in her own fantasy. "No, but Clarice is missing. We must find her. Andre is so sick and Father Pierre is beside himself. We've looked everywhere for her and cannot find her. What are we to do? You know I've been spending time in Paris recently with Clarice. You remember the stories of my great-grandmother, don't you?"

There had been other time transformations, but they had taken place when she was still considered to be in a coma; and gibberish was a by-product not to cause undue concern, the doctor said. Loraine, somewhat taken aback, decided it was time to be blunt.

"Mother, you've had a bad accident, and over the past few months, you have been slipping in and out of a coma, and even when you were out of the coma, you had a form of amnesia. You have to try and remember. It's December 2004." Loraine didn't have the heart to tell her mother it was now July of 2005. Not that she'd understand.

"What accident?" Jackie said suddenly. It was obvious now that she was moving rapidly in and out of the different times of her life and also the lives of her ancestors, much visited through the stories her beloved grandmother had shared with her as a young girl.

Before Loraine could relate the details of the accident, an anxious voice said, "I'm so confused. Where is everyone, and how come Craig isn't here?" There was real fear in her eyes now.

The tears started rolling down her cheeks, and Jackie started sobbing softly, like a little girl, much to Loraine's surprise and concern. Her mother was a softhearted woman, braced by an outward demeanor of stoicism, the visible side never giving in to tears. "It's okay, Mom. You're here, not in Paris. Everything will be okay," Loraine reassured her.

"But it was so real and she is, or was, so courageous. I need to speak to her again and…Oh, what's the use?" Exasperated and tired, she finally said, "You really can't understand where I've been and what happened, but someday I hope to make some sense to this journey."

"Maybe this is a message for you to bring back into the twenty-first century, Mom. You know there are strange things that happen, and God has certainly intervened to bring you back to us!" Loraine was the devout child, always believing that her life and those around her were especially blessed by God.

"Somehow, I feel as if I shared the same space with Clarice, but that's not possible, is it? I know it sounds crazy, but I was there."

"Mom, you're not crazy, but you've been through an extreme trauma, and I'm sure your mind played all kinds of tricks on you as you were fighting your way out of the coma."

Gently, Loraine took her hand and just held it for a moment, taking time to let her mother digest everything in her surroundings before continuing. She understood at a deeper level the need to slow down. Besides, she had just called the rest of the family when her mother showed signs of awareness and possibly coming out of the coma, but they had not arrived yet.

Deidre would be the most hurt if her mother slipped back into the foggy world, and she did not have a chance to talk to her. The baby of the family, she had always clung to her mother. It had been particularly hard on her, especially with the havoc Deidre's former husband had been wreaking on her. It might have thrown her over the edge had it not been for the family rallying around her and their mother.

The doctor had warned of the possibility that Jackie might have permanent brain damage and lingering bouts of amnesia. He did not say anything about the possibility Jackie might think she was in another time.

"Mom, why don't you tell me about Clarice and what happened while you were there? What was it like in Paris around the turn of the century?"

Jackie had stopped crying and looked up with a childlike smile. "Oh, you would not believe how beautiful everything was in the city. There were people everywhere and music and laughter—"

Just as abruptly, she changed back to the somber voice, once again reliving a trauma from another life. "But Clarice has so much weight on her small shoulders she has to carry every day. It does not seem fair."

As she was telling the story of Clarice, she drifted back to the streets of Paris. It was 1897 and the city was in the midst of change. So much had happened since the revolution when France lost Alsace-Lorraine once again.

It was an exciting time. The mood was one of expectation. Plans were already underway for the Paris World's Exposition in 1900. Paris would become the stage for the greatest inventions and brightest ideas for the twentieth century. There were detractors, however, and they were building opposition.

Paris in Turmoil

CHERISE COULD FEEL the tension in the air as she made her way through the alleyways of the Third Arrondissement, sneaking a look over her shoulder each turn. “Whoever may be watching will not get the upper hand with me,” she voiced out loud. It was more to ease the nervous energy rather than to scare a possible attacker.

“I’m being a little bit silly,” she thought out loud. There hadn’t been a sign of any of the old demons from the Pontifi past, and her identity had been well hidden the past nine months, thanks to Sister Mary. She was her godsend.

It had been difficult leaving Dom and the shop this morning. Even as the excitement increased for what she was about to undertake, the thought of missing the ever-impassioned conversations with him led her to consider whether she had chosen the right path. Was this the most prudent step to take right now? she wondered.

She had never questioned why or even if she should undertake this *mission of redemption*. Why was she so driven to rectify the wrongs perpetrated against the people of Alsace-Lorraine? Was it, as Dom had alluded to in one of their more heated conversations, a sham and her motive was more in keeping with revenge for her family’s deaths?

Perhaps I have been deluding myself all along, and this dignified justification in the name of honor of Alsace is a lie, she thought. The people seemed to adjust easily enough with whatever changes were cast upon them. Can I honestly pursue this righteous cause with a pure conscience, or must I admit to the pursuit of a selfish vendetta with no possibility there could be a good ending? What of Andre, sweet Andre? How can I remove myself so totally and have so little regard for his feelings?

Whatever the cause became, snaring a public indictment of Duvalier's reputation and exposing the crimes committed then yes, she would have her revenge.

I must do this for Andre, if for no reason other than to protect his future from a life of constant fear. Yes, there is justification in the cause of finding freedom—a freedom from fear, a freedom from hiding and running, and a freedom to reclaim his rightful heritage.

Why does man dehumanize his fellow man? How can one man claim the rights to another man's heritage in the name of a so-called cause only to rob him blind and take away his honor and that of his family?

She was tired and it would be easy to give up, go back to the shop and Dom.

It was interesting that she should immediately think of him instead of Sister Mary and some of her other friends.

Dom, she was beginning to realize, was a steadfast man in her life. There had never been any impropriety on his part, but she detected a longing in his eyes and, in a small way, reveled in the idea he found her attractive. She had never allowed such personal selfishness to interfere with her *chosen* mission; nevertheless, it gave her a sense of belonging. Not sure of how or why exactly, but in some way, Dom had become part of her life and she of his. Yes, it was definitely comforting to feel his presence, but even so, this was not the time to indulge her fantasies.

The nagging persisted, and she finally gave into it, her mind jumping back to Andre again. How could she ignore his needs just as he was coming of age and, she assumed, would want to join her in Paris? What was it Father Pierre hinted at in his last letter that had caused her concern? There was a subtle mention of some weakness, or perhaps it was illness? At the time, she dismissed it as Father's solicitousness.

Determined to quietly research Andre's status once situated, she added that to her list of priorities. Maintaining her identity might be a little tricky considering she had to keep it hidden. Her new identity—one within an identity—would be cloaked so brilliantly within the underground elements of the seamy side of Paris life that she was reassured thinking about it.

There was no time to turn back now. The decision had been made, and her destiny was cast like a ship of mercy setting sail into the fierce wind, unsure of reaching the next shore but secure in the righteousness of its voyage.

Ever inquisitive, Dom had not guessed what she was about to undertake, and for just a moment, she had hesitated, sighing at the weight of her duplicity in lying to him. There would be time to make it up to him, she thought. *I just can't turn around now.*

The landscape had changed—now appearing washed with a gray-hued and dirty mist. Where there had been tree-lined streets of jaded green and cascading lilacs providing pops of color down each alleyway, there was now a sparseness that she could feel as if the life had been pulled from this area of Paris.

Where gaiety and laughter had been the tone on the other side of the Seine, here the tone was one of despair; the downtrodden bowed and shuffled their way through the alleys. The cobbled streets were streaked with trash and, occasionally, a lone animal skeleton stripped bare of any meat. There were the remnants of expensive luxuries long gone as the less fortunate begged for the basics of life.

Turning the corner, Cherise could see the stained-glass windows of the old church refracting the rays of color-tinted light through their expansive panes. Shades of cobalt blue and shiny gold intermixed artfully with the brilliant red and emerald-green figures that were etched within the asymmetrical partitions of the windows, providing the only respite from the dismal gray of the surroundings.

The garden next to the St. Mary's invited all who came to this side of Paris to enter and find their quiet place with God. Looking at the garden wall, Cherise could see the weeping willows hanging their bows low over the rugged cobbled streets. To be in such a place in this forgotten part of Paris had to be the same as entering heaven, she thought.

Heaven would have to wait, and if the Holy Father was watching her now, she might never make it through the gate. Her nerves were definitely on edge; nevertheless, she had to complete this mission. Who was this mysterious woman she was supposed to meet in the garden, and what was her reason for aiding Cherise? Her friend mentioned the name Janene, and she would be flashy in appearance but told her not to worry, it was only a facade.

Curious, thought Cherise. What would *flashy* consist of, and would she recognize this woman? As she wandered through the lush garden, she thought once again of Dom and all that he had meant to her the past six months. "I must stop this nonsense once and for all!" Cherise said to anyone and no one, hoping for some impact yet not sure what that might be.

Sitting alone, quietly contemplating and yet vibrantly alive, she felt at peace with all the decisions even though her loved ones might suffer from fear for their sweet Cherise.

So often her imaginings were shattered by the actual event and so it was when Janene appeared in the garden. Almost as an apparition, she glided to a stop in front of the pensive-looking young woman. Cherise, startled at the sudden appearance of this strikingly beautiful woman, was immediately and uncharacteristically rendered speechless.

"Bonjour, Mademoiselle Cherise," the apparition spoke. "You are somewhat surprised at my appearance?" With a low guttural laugh, Janene swept away the leaves spreading over the bench and sat down next to her new protégé.

Finally, Cherise spoke, "You are not what I expected from a…mistress of the dance, so I was surprised!" She studied the face of her new trainer for the telltale signs, but there was nothing that might have signaled Janene's real avocation. "It's just that you look, well, you look like an angel!"

"It affects everyone like that, my dear. Sometimes it's fun playing with them, especially the men! You must remember you too will be participating in what some of the genteel society would say is only for the *lady of the eve-*

ning, but you mustn't draw such a conclusion without knowing the background. There are many in the fold with nothing but the best of intentions. They long for their place in society, but circumstances have forced them to the dance."

"Please, you misunderstand, Janene. I beg your forgiveness for it is so kind of you to aid me in this quest," Cherise whispered.

"Think nothing of it. Come, let us start our journey through Paris, but first you must put on this cape to safeguard your identity." The ragged cape, crafted from faded brown sackcloth, lay dark and heavy on Cherise's shoulders. She was sure it made her stand out even more. "You will be well-protected once we arrive at the palace, but until then, it must appear that you are my servant."

The duo walked off down the Avenue du Roc to journey the distance across Paris, where Janene would begin the tutelage of her young charge.

The Dance of the Dark Folies Bergère

Into the Fire

CHERISE WAS STRUCK by the amount of heat coming from the gas lanterns in rows along the floor of the stage and ringing the perimeter. How do they manage the glare and all-consuming heat? she wondered. Poised to begin the 207th Folies Bergère can-can review, she was grouped in with the shorter more voluptuous of the *ladies*, some of whom she now counted as her friends.

It had been an interesting and sometimes shocking initiation into what had become her secret life. After her meeting with Janene earlier—and oh, what a meeting—her days moved quickly into the dark world of what morally-upright citizens considered as the seamy side of life. It had taken Cherise a couple of months to blend into the ways of her new family.

There were the harsh, repetitive sessions at the ballet post. Muscles which had never been used were made to perform as a well-tuned machine. There were tears and moments in which Cherise was certain she could not go on, but in the end, a dancer was made.

It was the knowledge that her goal was more important than the method she had chosen to achieve victory that kept her rooted in this environment.

What was still unclear in her mind was whether her ultimate mission was directed at the type of destructive evil perpetrated by Duvalier or saving the dignity of the people of Alsace-Lorraine or perhaps toward a more altruistic endeavor, furthering the cause of women in France. It was becoming clear that exposing the oppression of women was the greatest area of need. At least this gave her the opportunity to explore her own motives and develop her plans.

In her naivete, she had only imagined life in this other world. From a perch where she could not conceivably have known to what lengths most of her *compatriots* had to go even to survive, prejudices and random thoughts were formed, most of them from what she heard among the nuns about the scantily clad women of the Folies Bergère! It did not take long for them to die as swiftly as the first dance in which she participated wholeheartedly.

Funny, she reflected, after being sheltered in the convent with Father Pierre and the nuns, and having viewed life from a perspective driven by the pure of heart, to then be thrown into an environment fraught with prostitutes, opium dealers, and petty thieves. The dancers were considered artisans, removed from the worst of the beggars and thieves, yet there was a sense that one slip and they could easily become one of the fallen. There was a thread of camaraderie among the dancers, but it was there solely on the strength of the dependency one dancer had for another in the course of the dance itself, a realization any missteps could result in dismissal.

Cherise had been transformed. Janine had convinced Cherise to change her hair color to a bright reddish blonde. Along with the face paint she now wore, it would have been difficult to recognize the old Clarice. What would Father Pierre think, or Bennie? Wistfully, she had managed to put thoughts of Andre and the convent out of her mind.

Upon first arriving at the beautiful Palace de Folies Bergère, a place where young women had danced to packed audiences over the years, Cherise could not help but take in the grandeur of the old building. Her love of antiques had come rushing back at that moment. Taking in her surroundings, she noticed the old plank floors, burnished to a deep patina only the years of love and care could produce.

There, built into the main dance hall, were all the intricate details of the master craftsmen of earlier days, carved into the heavy wood moldings, framing the stage and the boxes within the balcony. The opulence of the gilded etchings on some of the boxes and on several panels on the front of the stage gave a golden luster to what might have been old and tired looking.

Peering out beyond the edge of the stage, she could make out some of the special boxes, those with exceptionally ornate carvings and ultra-thick gilding, where they said the rich men would gather to gawk at these scantily clothed young women. It was even said that one of the girls had been swept up in a relationship with an older man, following him back to his home in the Orient.

The Palace Hall of the Folies Bergère was now in a somewhat run-down part of Paris, no longer the lustrous place that had heralded the noblemen and the rich gentry of years past, resplendent in their fine silks and delivered to this destination in their gilded carriages.

The first act was ready to begin, and Cherise, as usual, was tense. Her first crutch, Janene had disappeared a month after her arrival. It was always the same, she thought, but once she immersed herself in the chorus line, it was as if she was born to dance.

She whispered to Rochelle, her line partner, "It is funny, but I do not feel any shame when I let my body give in to the dance, Rochelle. Does that mean I am a depraved woman?"

Rochelle was humored by Cherise's question. It always amazed her—the innocence of this young woman. How she arrived here was a question they all might have had, except for the fact many of them had started with much grimmer circumstances. Depravity was a weapon in their arsenal to be used at will, for it was only the dance that had saved them from the fate of the common prostitute.

But still there was something much different about this beautiful young woman, which, in spite of the harsh makeup and bright hair, she could see in her eyes. She decided to learn more.

"My dear, you are a natural dancer. It must have been in your blood. We all can see that you have the talent of a doyenne, one who has been dancing all her life! You must tell me your secret."

At that bit of news, Cherise giggled nervously, wondering if, indeed, she had a wild side buried within her. There was always something a little uninhibited with the women of this family, intriguing her from the time she was old enough to understand what her grand-mère had to deal with in maneuvering within a man's world.

As the signal to begin the countdown was given, Cherise took a deep breath and exhaled as the music began. She was enraptured with the sounds of the guttural music of the can-can and swish of the cloth as the girls began to throw their legs in high-strutting moves and kicks. Feeling the muscles pull and tug against the gravity of the high kick gave the young woman pleasure, much like the thrills she once enjoyed as she rode bareback on her mare.

Moving now as one unit, the chorus line swayed with the sounds of the accordions and flutes, accompanied by the virtuoso playing the grand piano. Interpreting the flow of the music into dance, the women were caught up in the rousing routine. Simple and forthright in its dance presentation, the can-can was not only popular among the common laborer lucky enough to find a ticket for entry into the grand hall but the middle-class artisans and professional men of Paris. Of course, the occasional aristocrat could still be found hiding in the select boxes, away from the view of the general audience.

The traditional can-can was regarded as a physically demanding music hall dance performed by a chorus line of female dancers who wore costumes with long skirts, petticoats, and black stockings. This particular burlesque differed from the mainstream Paris can-can when at the sound of the gong the girls would suddenly discard their skirts with a flick of the wrists, bringing the excited men to their feet in joyous approval. Shy at first and a little ashamed, Cherise had tried to hide behind the larger women, shielding herself from the view of the audience. The raucousness of the all-male audience even frightened her a little but soon became so routine that she even relished it, teasing certain of her favorites with just the right movement and coquettish glance.

There in the audience was one Monsieur Bonnebeau, a small, slightly round man, certainly not handsome but one could say comfortable looking, the kind of man that a lady could be happy with and never fear of depravity. The type of man who perhaps her grandfather had been when first her grand-mère had spied him in the shop. Yes, comfortable, not a handsome, dashing sort of gentleman but one that a woman could love.

Cherise found herself looking for him each night, and when not finding him in his usual seat, she experienced a lingering disappointment. "This is foolish of me to look for this stranger as if he was the one who would be my soul mate," she confided to Rochelle one evening.

"Ah, sweet girl, perhaps you have the heat for this man, no?" Rochelle inquired.

Blushing, Cherise spat back, "I have no such thoughts, Rochelle! And even if I was capable of these thoughts you speak of, I have a friend left behind to whom I owe my heart!"

It was foolish of Cherise to even have such a discussion with one of her fellow dancers and, under the circumstances, could be dangerous. Lonely, she was longing to have a conversation with the friendly dancer without having to watch every word. Throwing caution to the wind did not seem such a big deal at the moment. Besides, why couldn't she tell Rochelle of Dom, no harm in talking of things superficial?

Her immaturity was showing and Rochelle wasted no time in manipulating the conversation to her advantage. For those whose livelihood depended on the meager pay of the dancer's life, the bounty promised on information for any unusual conversations was indeed very attractive, especially information from the crop of new dancers coming into the line.

"Uhmm, so you have a beau, Miss Cherise, one of established means perhaps? Why are you here if you have such a man? I don't believe you, for loneliness is like a wildcat, clawing, leaving its marks upon your face for all to see."

"Oh, Rochelle, you are right about the loneliness, but what you see in my eyes is the pain I have caused by leaving the one man behind who understood and cared about me." Guiltily, she had to admit to herself that much of her loneliness came from leaving Andre behind at the convent. Dom and

Father Pierre she missed, but not with the scorched aching that pervaded her whole body when left to her own thoughts.

"I fear he will not wait for me the length of time it will take to complete my mission" Cherise stopped abruptly. Realizing too late that she may have offered too much information even though exaggerated to appear she had a love interest.

"Your mission? What is that?"

Trying to cover her tracks, Cherise quickly added, "You may have guessed, I have not had the exciting life that you have, but the mission of which I speak is to live my life to the fullest intention with every breath in me, wasting no precious time. The only way to find the meaning in my life is to explore beyond that which is the accepted way of a single maiden. Focusing too soon on the likes of one man can only leave me wondering what may be out there."

The words sounded hollow even as she spoke them. Pausing briefly, and as shallow and difficult it was for her, she forced herself to say, "Perhaps you are correct. I have lust for this man!"

Rochelle was not totally convinced and made a note to mention the conversation to Raoul. Cherise might want to appear worldly, but her good character and noble bearing made it a hard story for her to sell. It amused Rochelle somewhat how she had tried to cover up her goodness by almost choking over the word *lust*. Not that she didn't think Cherise capable of lusting after a man!

Perhaps she should concoct a little test. It might be entertaining! After all, isn't that what got most women into trouble in the first place? Men were definitely her weakest link, and Rochelle sometimes wondered why she had been cursed with such passion. She would make it a point to watch Cherise more closely because ten gold coins would be the reward for information leading to a missing orphan.

The story was that this *orphan girl* had absconded with important documents that traced ownership of a fortune back to the great ancestors of

Napoleon III. One Joseph Duvalier was paying informants in gold coin for the return of his rightful property.

Raoul had bedded Rochelle many times in the past year, but it was during an episode of sordid excess with wine and opium that he made the mistake of bragging to her of his relationship with the prominent lawyer. It was well-known in circles out of Rochelle's sphere of influence that Joseph was ruthless and would spare no expense to bring all the heirs of the Pontifi and Chevais dynasties to pay their debt to the coffers of the Duvaliers.

Yes, she would definitely keep her eyes and ears open. It was very strange the way this girl had come to them, obviously sheltered and not from the same environment as the other dancers. Experienced at the raw side of life, most of them knew the pain of hunger, the loneliness of being on the street, and the will to survive at any cost.

Prayers for Andre

Father Pierre was pacing the breezeway, making no attempt to hide his dismay at the recent turn of events. The doctors had done all they could for Andre, and now he was in God's hands. Circling back one more time, he did what he had done every ten minutes on the hour—looked in on the frail boy, said a couple of Hail Marys, and asked for God's divine intervention.

Noting that nothing had changed did not keep the father from continuing with his quest for intervention, certain it was only through their prayers and by God's grace that Andre remained alive. The nuns were doing their part by keeping vigilance over Andre just as they had for the past several months, praying to the Holy Father for grace and healing of their special boy.

He had quietly turned sixteen, and they marked it with a little celebration for him. Andre never awakened from the coma, which, in the past forty-five days, had finally eroded any awareness he had of his surroundings.

"Where is that girl?" Father Pierre cried out loud, not caring who might hear.

"I fear she may never see her brother alive again, and dear Lord, it would kill her for sure!" Almost a year had passed and no word had come directly from Clarice, a situation he had once encouraged. Clarice had protested vehemently, pleading with him to allow messages to come through to Andre. Yes, he had to blame himself, but it was for their welfare.

Even Bernard could not contact them once leaving the grounds. The communication had stopped, both ways in fact, to prevent any breach of the secrecy surrounding the Pontifi children. The only messages were those Clarice gave to Sister Mary to be coded to the father and those had stopped completely four or five months ago.

Sister Francine, listening in the corridor, responded to the father's outcry. "When will you finally send a messenger, Father?" she pleaded. It had been his firm stance that no one was to utter a word of Clarice's whereabouts or whether she was dead or alive; in fact, they were to keep all communication among only the three of them. Sister Mary was the only other nun besides herself to whom the father had entrusted Clarice's whereabouts.

"You must keep your voice down!" Father Pierre sharply admonished the young nun, forgetting his own outburst of a few moments ago. "We can only hope that all are trustworthy here in the convent. Clarice would be in grave danger if information of her location should be found out. We risk not only her safety but that of everyone here!"

"I beg your pardon, Father, but it is a sad day that Clarice has not even seen Andre since leaving here. My fear is that somehow her void may have contributed to his illness."

"The scourge was upon him before Clarice left, but you are right. Malaise has affected Andre's ability to fight this battle. But what choice did she have?"

"We must find her and bring her here at any cost. It may save his life!" Sister Francine pleaded. "He is not strong enough to make the trip to Paris."

Father Pierre looked deep into Francine's eyes before speaking. Gently taking her hands, he said, "You must accept that Andre may never wake from the coma and we may not have him much longer. What we hope to do is save Clarice future anguish by bringing her here! I fear for her sanity if she does not see Andre before…" And there he hesitated, unable to finish his dire prediction.

Francine gasped. "Father, that sounds so cold. How can you give up on Andre?"

"I'm a realist, dear Francine. Other than divine intervention, Andre is so sick that to expect him to recover is wasting time, which could be well spent finding Clarice, bringing her back and sparing her a life of guilt!"

"There will be divine intervention. I know it!" She stamped off to check on Andre once more.

Sighing, Father Pierre thought of all the times he had known Clarice was watching him, safely hidden among the pews, while he moved through the rosaries. It had taken so long to bring her back from the hideous loss of her parents. Could she, as an adult now, be better equipped to deal with Andre's death? He doubted it even though her ability to cope with tragedy might take a different form, one he would not want to deal with—the cynicism of the soul.

Clarice was so pure of heart and gentle of spirit he could not imagine facing her anguish at such a loss. It would at least ease her pain to have the chance to say goodbye to Andre.

It was settled then. He would get word to her through the convent in Paris where she had last stayed. Not long after, through the Paris convent's intricate communications system, he was able to send a couple of messages before she disappeared. They had notified him of her disappearance the very next day, assuring him it was of her design.

There was a man named Dom, he believed. Perhaps Dom knew her whereabouts. Would he give the information to Father Pierre? He thought that he was related to Sister Mary of the convent in Paris. It was time to make the journey.

PART SEVEN

Spring Lake, North Carolina (Spring of 1955)

It was just one of her many trips to the ice-cream shop, stopping to look in the store windows, daydreaming about her favorite movie stars and how she would someday be famous. Jackie always ended up buying hot dogs for herself and her brother, Bill, and the luscious chocolate milkshakes for which the Dairy Barn was known. Funny how the money her father had given her, a stack, most of it in one-dollar bills, had ended up being used the same way every day!

Jackie figured this was her reward for the many months of babysitting at fifteen cents per hour, accumulating a fortune of forty-five dollars. But somehow this day was different once a stranger handed her an innocuous-looking card. "Freedom Baptist Church, All God's Children Are Welcome," it said! The anonymous man had kind eyes, and she instinctively had trusted him despite her parents' admonishments to the contrary!

"Hmm, maybe I'll just go visit this church and see what it's all about. I sort of remember going to Mama's church in Ohio when I was a young girl!" she declared to her little brother. "Would you like to go to church with me, Bill-Bill?" Billy was just shy of seven years old, and anything his older and adored sister said was okay with him!

Even though not quite eleven, she was always on guard and aware. It was almost as if she had been born in tune with life and whatever it brought to her. Or maybe it was the subtle way her parents indoctrinated her to be self-reliant, never to totally trust anyone. Hadn't she been the victim of a kidnapping already? her mother had lamented to friends. "We'll not let that happen again ever!" Doris had whined to her best friend, Betty.

"We almost lost Jackie to one of the black market thieves of postwar Germany, and I will never totally trust that my family is safe and secure again!" It was always the same conversation, carried on whether anyone was listening or not. Even Jackie could recite what her mother would say in any situation. She supposed whatever had happened must have really scared her mother, but worrying was not going to be in her life!

The next Sunday, according to her plans, Jackie set out to find the Freedom Baptist Church of Spring Lake, North Carolina. Her brother in tow, they set out early to make sure they would have time to find this place.

After leaving the security of the trailer park, the adventure began by first crossing the railroad tracks that ran perpendicular to Spring Lake's only major highway, Fort Bragg Boulevard—a feat by itself! As she pretended to defy death, boldly jumping the rails one at a time, she could hear the wail of the train's whistle in the distance.

"Hurry up, Bill-Bill! We must beat the train and win the game!" Jackie giggled. Bill's eyes signaled his terror as he grabbed onto his sister's hand. It was always an adventure when he could go with her, but sometimes she did scare him!

"Billy, we're going to church today!" exclaimed Jackie. "This will be a new adventure for us! Are you excited?"

Ignoring his sister's announcement about church and her question, he wanted to know about lunch. "Can we go to the soda shop and have a hot dog?"

"Yes, we can as soon as church is over! Don't you want to know what church is for and why people go there?"

"I don't wanna go to church," he whined. "Why can't we just go get a soda and hot dog now?"

"It's a beautiful place where fancy people go all dressed up in fine clothes. I think they sing in those places and talk to God. At least that's what I think. Mama had a church in Ohio, and I went to it with her one time. Then she didn't want to go, so I went by myself. There is a Sunday school class where you can learn about the Bible and draw pictures and listen to stories. It will be fun, Billy, I promise! Besides, the soda shop won't open until after church!"

He was quiet, and Jackie wondered what was going on in that little mind of his. They had managed to cross the big highway with no trouble and had only six more blocks to go.

It occurred to her that she was scared, not sure if her fear was of meeting all the new people or standing out as different. She had found the best dress in her closet, but even that was tattered and showed some wear. It was her special red velvet dress, now missing the white rabbit fur collar that had once adorned it. Her grandmother had surprised her with it on her eighth birthday; the package arrived right on time to Jackie's excitement.

Oh, how she had loved the dress and had even taken to wearing it in the house for no reason until her mother had finally encouraged her to keep it for special occasions. It came with them back to the States, a little smaller and worse for the wear. That the dress was designed for the cold of winter did not matter to Jackie this particular day.

Her mother had helped her get ready this morning and even encouraged her to go. She wondered why her parents didn't go to church; perhaps she would convince them another time after she had checked it out.

One thing for sure, she loved the idea of going to such a place where all the townspeople gathered, and she could pretend that she belonged to something better than the trailer park although she was appreciative of having a home instead of living on base in an apartment.

Looking at Bill now, his little suit all cleaned and pressed, his hair slicked into the butch so characteristic of the military boys living around and near the base, her maternal instincts kicked in. Wrapping her arms around him, she said, "Billy, I promise to take you to the class where the other boys and girls are playing and I'll come back and pick you up just as soon as the service is over!"

His little lip started to quiver, and the tears rolled down his cheeks as they marched down the hall toward the class. Wiping them away, he gave a sigh, the signal to his sister that he was a big boy and would do what she asked. Bravely, he followed his big sister into the Sunday school class.

The teacher greeted her in the fashion of a sweet little Southern Baptist lady, welcoming both Jackie and her little brother to the class. "My, what a big boy you are." She smiled. "And what is your name, young man?"

"His name is Billy, ma'am. He's shy, so he may not talk for a while—that is, until he gets to know you."

"Well, Billy, my name is Miss Spring, just like the time of year we're in now! Would you like to come and have milk and cookies while I read Bible stories?"

"Oh, he would love that, Miss Spring!" exclaimed an excited Jackie. "Can I pick him up after church is over?"

"Who are you going to church with, my dear…Uh, what is your name?"

"I'm Jackie," she replied. "Bill's older sister. Is it okay for me to go to church, ma'am?"

"Well, of course it is, my dear, but you're so young! Where are your mother and father? Normally we don't see children coming to church all alone, but you are always welcome in God's house. Wouldn't you like me to have someone take you up to the sanctuary?"

Why did she sense that her visit to this church and the community was something other than a normal routine for Miss Spring? There was an undercurrent of something else too. Was it pity? Jackie was determined to keep her head held high even as the kindly Sunday school teacher wondered where the tattered-looking waif of a girl had come from.

She was used to people's questioning looks when she went into town, unaccustomed as they were to children making their own way from the trailer parks across town. They knew she was one of those *military brats* who occasionally showed up but always with one or more of their parents. Since they knew everyone in town, the strangers stood out like a sore thumb.

Once she had even heard the soda shop owner whispering to his friend, "She's been coming in here almost every day for a month, hungry as a lion that one, all alone or bringing her little brother. I tell you, she acts like an adult most of the time—that is, except when she's gulping down those hot dogs and shakes as if she hadn't eaten a lick in days!"

She wanted to scream that it was okay. Her mom knew where she was and loved her. Besides, it wasn't as if she was a baby!

Ms. Spring had been talking to her, and Jackie realized that she hadn't heard a word. "I'm sorry, ma'am, what did you say?"

"I asked if you had a ride home after church."

"Billy and I will be just fine. Besides, I promised to take him to the soda shop for a treat! Really, I'm older than you think. Just had my twelfth birthday!"

She didn't mean to lie, but Miss Spring wasn't going to let it go and Jackie wasn't about to let someone take them back to the trailer park.

"Well, okay then, but remember I'd be happy to help you, Jackie!"

"Yes, ma'am, but it's really all right." She scurried away before the curious woman could ask her any more questions. "See you after church to pick up Billy!"

Sitting in the sanctuary, she was awed by the beauty of the paintings on the walls, adorned with crowns and surrounded by angels. Wondering if heaven could be so beautiful, she vowed to be extra-special good and quit her lying ways! It brought back memories of Paris and the trip they had made before coming back to the States not too long ago. Not as fancy as some of those paintings in the big cathedrals but pretty anyhow. The altar in the front of the church was laden with the most beautiful flowers she had ever laid eyes on. Arrangements of hydrangeas in deep blue purple, roses in colors of sunshine yellow and burgundy red sprinkled with the stark white lilies were arranged to pay homage to the season.

The dapper ladies and their mates sat positioned to hear every word that Pastor Bob had to say. They had come to pay their respects to this God that lived somewhere in heaven, and she was sure it was directly above the church. The choir began to sing the melodious songs in the old hymnals, blending their voices and shouting to the congregation. "Hallelujah, hallelujah, Christ is risen today!"

The congregation wasn't kneeling to pray as she remembered doing when she went to church with her mother a long time ago. They seemed to be bowing their heads. Well, she could do that too. In her own way, she wanted God to know how happy she was to be there and that if he let her come back, she would always pay her respects to him—and be a good girl.

The service went on, and Jackie got caught up in the music and prayer, feeling a sense of belonging. Gradually, the little bit of dread gave way to joy! She couldn't describe it, but there seemed to be a sense of relief from something, but what? The loneliness?

Warm and enveloped in a bundle of love, that is what she felt. Her endless fears and the gnawing she always had in the middle of her stomach were gone! What had been a constant longing for something unknown was lifted off her tiny shoulders in the instant she understood there was this God who would protect her at all times. It might have been that the pain of rejection was replaced with total acceptance and belonging.

"Oh, this is wonderful," she whispered. It was a feeling of being lifted by a spirit, picked up, and moved on angels' wings. "This must be what happens when you believe in God!"

Jackie was not sure exactly what happened to her that day, but from then on, she never felt totally alone.

It occurred to her that she might appear odd to her parents. Would they understand? she wondered. *It seems so sad not to share this wonderful feeling with them, but I'll just keep this to myself for a little while*, she thought.

Paris

Into the Dark

The music stopped, the constant beating of the drum dying away like the end of a thunderous storm. Cherise could feel her cheeks burning, her breath coming quickly as she fought for more air in her lungs. The exhilaration she felt could not be described, for the moment was truly magic. It was reminiscent of a time in her childhood when she glimpsed a meteorite shower, flashing brilliant lights over all the sky in bursts of magnificent gold.

Surrounded by hundreds of clapping hands and yelling voices of an audience of virile men gave her a thrill she could not understand, yet she expected and needed every time she danced. It was as if she became one of them when she was in the dance—a suggestion originally made by Rochelle and discarded by the then-innocent Cherise.

Ah, innocence. She was moving closer to a loss of some part of her innocence, an unanticipated yet much-yearned-for event much to her surprise. Thinking about it now, she could hardly remember a time when her body was not alive with the rhythm of the dance and the suggestion of the music. It mildly bothered her that she had these longings of what she was not sure—passion, perhaps, or some sacrificial offering to the *god of lust*?

The guilt did not linger long, for it was often overtaken by the longing for a man's touch. Oh yes, she finally had to admit there was the lust just as

Rochelle had predicted. What she didn't know was that very lust may have saved her from a worse fate.

Rochelle had been watching her of late, waiting for more information to feed to Raoul, but all she could tell was that Cherise was indeed *hot* for the old man in the audience.

She had decided there was not enough information for him to be summoned from afar and bedding him had not appealed to her of late. Rochelle would rue the day if Duvalier's informant made a trip for nothing—a folly for a less wise woman.

Cherise sensed that Rochelle was eyeing her every move, and in spite of her innocence, she was smart enough to stay one step ahead. What puzzled her was why her so-called friend would be willing to cause her harm.

It started out as an innocent game to keep any curiosity seekers from looking too hard into her background—an obsession with the movements of the dance, capturing her from the moment she entered the stage until she left the dance hall late at night. Then and only then did reason come spiraling back into her conscious mind.

No, she did not like what the other side was doing to her psyche and each time vowed to eliminate the lewd thoughts, replacing them only with loving thoughts of Andre, Father Pierre, and even Dom.

Wasn't it Dom she wanted after all? She was unsure; maybe he merely represented the big brother she never had. After much soul-searching, Cherise came to the realization that the men in the audience were a sad replacement for the emptiness she felt.

Her much-thought-out reasoning only seemed to fuel the need to display her feelings openly during the dance, perhaps as a way to capture a small part of the passion she might have had if she had stayed with Dom.

Pushing it aside had been easy for the first three months, but after she left the university, it was difficult to fill the void, leaving too much time on her hands. Her studies part-time at the university had kept her busy, and hiding the fact from her dance partners meant any studying was done after leaving the dance hall.

She now had more time to think and plan for the inevitable confrontation with Duvalier. Wasn't that the real goal in all this? For some reason, this did not give her the comfort she yearned for and expected. "It is of no consequence for me to cut myself off from those I love if I lose sight of my goal in the middle of a dance floor!" she declared to the sky.

Thinking now beyond the tedious daily routine which had become her life, Cherise wondered about Andre and his health, Father Pierre, and, of course, her beloved Bernard. She had neglected all of them for some grander mission and for this a price had to be paid.

Most assuredly, Cherise's price had been to give away her dignity and then lose her sense of purpose, all for revenge masked as her causes. Perhaps it was not too late to continue on a corrected path, one of prurient purpose and noble cause. Somehow, she would pull out of this cycle of degradation and right her course.

She knew what had to happen, but how to change it all would take more time. In the meantime, she must continue the dance but prove that she did not need the thrills she enjoyed from displaying her body to an audience of lustful men.

It would be a challenge, but with her rosary tucked under her garments and the blessed Mary to help, she would overcome this period of sinful behavior.

As she made her way backstage, one of the managers stepped in her path. "Mademoiselle Cherise, I have a note for you from one of the gentlemen from the *special* section," her cue indicating this was a wealthy, probably aristocratic, connoisseur of the Folies Bergère.

"What do you want me to do with this?" Cherise asked Gerard, the manager. She had seen him spying on her, and it made her very uneasy that he was now blocking her way.

"We expect our girls to be professional, but at least meet these gentlemen to offer their friendship! This one in particular has a great interest in you." It gave him lascivious pleasure to leer at the younger, more naive of the troupe. If he had his way, this one would be his too.

Her face paled as she realized what was expected. Well, if he thought she would prostitute herself for the dance, he was sorely mistaken! As she turned to walk away, he grabbed her arm, causing her to wince. "Leave me alone! I will not do what you ask!"

"We'll see about that, my dear," Gerard said in a menacing tone. At that moment, Mr. Bonnebeau came around the corner. Quickly, Gerard dropped Cherise's arm and backed away.

The encounter had not escaped the watchful eyes of the older gentleman. Up close now, she could see he was not so elderly, merely distinguished and perhaps only ten to fifteen years her senior. "Monsieur Gerard, please introduce me to this nice young woman. I have been a big fan of hers!"

At that moment, Cherise was so thankful to see the kind face of the gentleman she had been flirting with all along that her sigh of relief could not be hidden.

"Oh, I was just explaining to Cherise you would like to meet her, Mr. Bonnebeau. Cherise, this is Mr. Henri Bonnebeau."

"At your service, my dear." He bowed to the young woman. "I am so impressed with the way you dance. May I so boldly ask for the favor of your company at dinner tonight?"

Cherise had not stopped staring at the kindly gentleman and finally found her tongue. Stammering, she said, "Well, I…I think that would be fine. If you would be so kind as to allow me time to dress and prepare for dinner, I'll meet you out front."

Henri bowed and took her hand to give her a gentle kiss. "It is my extreme pleasure, mademoiselle, and I assure you that I'll bring you home right after dinner." It was important for him to make her feel comfortable; after all, she was a prize and he could afford to move slowly.

"Why don't you take as much time as you would like, and I'll return for you at half past seven?" Cherise didn't know why, but the same magnetism he seemed to exude when she looked at him in the audience gave her a feeling of warmth and well-being. Somehow, she did not believe he would be party to hiring a prostitute, and she would make sure to inform the vile Gerard that their relationship was above board.

Gerard had left them standing there to discuss what he assumed were the terms on which she would be engaged by Mr. Bonnebeau. Oh yes, he would have his way with that one. There was too much gossip surrounding her to leave it alone. He had heard the whispers, not fully understanding what they meant but knowing that there was someone looking for her. The idea definitely aroused his interest—so much that he was determined to find who was looking for her!

In the meantime, with a voice of certainty, Henri whispered to the delicate Cherise, "Do not worry about Monsieur Gerard, my little one. He will not touch you again." With that, Henri turned and moved to make his way back to his waiting carriage.

Still flushed from the encounter with Gerard and then the meeting with her admirer, Cherise scurried away, a part of her wanting to hide and the other exhilarated at the prospect of her first *date*. She was noticeably nervous as she entered the dressing room and would have preferred not to run into Rochelle.

"Ah, my dear, you seem to be on edge. Could it be because of a man, perhaps? Is it the older gentleman in the audience who has been eyeing you for the past three months? I saw you with him in the hall. Tell Rochelle all!"

"It's nothing, Rochelle. I am merely going to dinner with the kindly Mr. Bonnebeau."

"Did you say Mr. Bonnebeau? It has to be Mr. Henri Bonnebeau of the House of Bonnebeau!" Rochelle was panting with excitement now.

"Why yes, his name is Henri and he seems harmless. Really, Rochelle, it is just a dinner date, and thankfully he saved me from Gerard."

"Mark my words, dear Cherise, you will not be able to resist his charms! They say he brings women to a point of adoration, and then, well, he either discards them or they become his *queen* for a while. It all depends on how well you treat him, my dear."

"That is not my intention, ever, Rochelle. I'm merely accepting his kind invitation to dinner, this one time only. Besides, if he had not appeared there is no telling what Gerard would have done." She could feel the sweat rolling down her back even as she tried to hide her excitement.

Escaping into one of the private dressing rooms, Cherise could think more clearly without the continuous stare of Rochelle and some of the other dancers who had wandered into the main dressing area. The whole affair was unsettling. Having the time to think away from the gaze of the others would help her prepare for the evening.

It bothered her that she so willingly agreed to the dinner with Mr. Bonnebeau when only an hour before she was proclaiming her fondness of Dom and her promise to think only pious thoughts to God. It was silly to think that one dinner would matter! When it was all over, she could thank Henri for everything and offer to return the favor by cooking for him sometime. Yes, that is exactly what she would do!

The Underground

Father Pierre had taken care to store his robe in the village of La Nuaz at the home of his friend, Monsieur DeBeur. His secrecy could be counted on even to his death, of that Father Pierre was certain. Leaving the inn before dawn and climbing on board the train, the father took comfort in knowing his departure would be safe from the same elements who had been searching for Clarice and Andre.

It was precisely eleven thirty in the morning as he prepared for the arrival of the train into Paris, just as he had planned. Coming into the outskirts of the city and disembarking at a little-known stop had been the perfect choice; only a pair of nuns, one old man, and a woman with three children were leaving the train.

He wondered if the nuns could sense he was a priest, but no, that was his imagination. Now he would make his way to meet Dom at the entrance to the underground tunnel system winding beneath the Sacré-Coeur. A Roman Catholic church, it was located on the highest point of the city in Montmarte. The plan was to build the Baselique Sacré-Coeur at some point, but for now, the old church held her head high, waiting for the time when she would be replaced by a much grander structure.

The tunnels, or more accurately the sewer system, were left over from the time of the Norman invasion when the only place to hide was buried under the streets of Paris. He and Dom could make their way into the center of Paris and escape any chance of being seen. Father Pierre had thought perhaps he was carrying the safety precautions too far, but after his correspondence with Dom, it was clear Duvalier still had his henchmen looking all over Paris for Clarice. Dom had also encouraged the extreme measures to ensure their safety and that, ultimately, of Clarice.

Father Pierre wondered if there would ever be peace for the kind-hearted Clarice. It pained him to think that because of her birthright, she was forced into hiding her real identity. The thought of her forced identity change reminded him to start using her new name, Cherise. It seemed strange to him, but it was necessary! Going forward, he would not utter the name Clarice.

Now the recent turn of events had catapulted her even deeper into hiding; where, he could only imagine. Concerned for the young woman he now knew as Cherise had caused him many sleepless nights the past few months.

Still, Father Pierre managed to quell his fears and keep his sights on this trip to Paris. He had allowed Dom to make the plans even though he was not totally convinced of Dom's loyalties to Cherise.

Aside from the grave state of Andre's health, he now feared for Cherise's soul. If the rumblings he had heard from Dom were true, then they must find her and save what was left of the goodness he knew was inside. A message had made its way to Dom from a good source that there was a young woman dancing at the Palace de Moulin Rouge; an angel with bright hair, the messenger declared.

The color of her hair might have thrown anyone else off track, but Dom had heard Cherise mention more than once that she wished to have golden red hair. The fact that this dancer was drawing a large crowd nightly and seemed to dance on the wings of an angel while going through the bawdy routine only served to confirm that it might be Cherise.

While she was growing up at the convent, it was apparent Cherise had something special in the way she moved and carried herself, as if floating above the ground. Father Pierre always thought that a peculiar habit, but now it gnawed at him from somewhere within.

Was Cherise capable of becoming a lost woman, jaded by the glitter and attention of these men? No, he would not allow that type of thinking. If, in fact, it was Cherise, she must be desperate to be dancing in a common dance hall where the men undress the women with their eyes then take what they want for themselves after the dance. He only hoped that had not happened to his little Cherise!

It was eleven forty-five, and the church was still several blocks away. Yet he was calm in the knowledge that Dom would be waiting for him, and since God was his pilot, nothing would stand in the way of finding and saving her.

As he contemplated this line of thinking, a beggar jumped into his path. "Father, would you be so kind as to give me some food? I am so hungry and haven't eaten in days."

Father Pierre's instinct was to stop and help the simple beggar, but how could he know he was a priest? There was something very strange about the way in which this one approached him and also the way he looked—more like a man cloaked in a costume. He stopped only momentarily to address the man. "I am not a priest, but if you are in need, my son, go to the Chapel of the Invalides and there you will find all that you need!"

It hurt Father to move away from anyone in need, but his intuition told him this was not a man of need but one with questionable motives. He feared that Duvalier had possibly sent this beggar. But then he admonished himself about worrying unnecessarily of so-called hidden dangers that didn't exist. It unnecessarily inflamed the tension he felt. There was no question that a danger did exist, but surely his imagination was working overtime now.

Nevertheless, he wondered if his decision to move past the beggar would prove to be prophetic—at least it was another safety measure. If they could ever be normal again, life would be open to live freely for all of them. It was an absolute truism that no one in the Pontifi circle could claim autonomy, no less the father himself.

It was not for himself that he worried, but for Cherise and Andre and all the people at the convent who had surrounded them with love and care.

There also were the nuns and friends of Cherise in Paris who had sheltered and loved her without concern for their own welfare.

Dom himself could become a victim if circumstances allowed. It was apparent his concern and care for Cherise moved beyond an employee-manager relationship. Father Pierre made a mental note to question Dom about his involvement with Cherise. After all, he was like a real father to the girl.

As he brooded over this knowledge, Father Pierre could see a figure rounding the corner wearing garb that identified him as Dom. He was relieved he could put to rest this unsettling train of thought, at least for the time being.

After the prearranged greetings were exchanged, Dom spoke first, "Greetings, Father, I'm so glad to see you made it safely. Even now I have concern we are being watched!"

"Rightfully so, you are smart to keep your eyes on your back. I had an unusual encounter with a beggar a few blocks back. Unlike any beggar I've seen, this one appeared to be in costume, panhandling for food or coins with manicured hands. His shoes appeared to be those of a man with means."

A strange look crossed Dom's face, but just as suddenly he said, "We must move quickly to avoid being followed! There are many tunnels under the city, and we can move from one end of Paris to the other. The danger lies in being followed into the tunnels because, once inside, there are constraints of movement."

"Okay, my son, I trust your judgment and God's wisdom in allowing me to continue on the trek with you as my guide. He would not have put me on this path, if you were not a man of faith!" Father Pierre declared to the appreciative Dom. He would question Dom later on how he came to find out about Cherise's real whereabouts.

Moving in tandem now, they swiftly found one of the lesser-known entrances to a series of tunnels that ran parallel to the main corridors. This would be a safer way to travel and assure them they might have enough warning if their space was breached by others. They could move through parts of the city underground and, on occasion, come to the surface to make their way yet again to another tunnel until arriving at their destination.

They made their way through gray-dark tunnels illuminated by the occasional gas lanterns and the bursts of daylight filtering down at the exit and entry points. Moisture captured on the stone-laden walls and floors from underground rivers proved to be slippery at best and treacherous to anyone who dared tread lightly. It further heightened the musky smell emanating from the dampness surrounding them.

Keeping their wits was the key to their safe passage, and only fools took the underground for granted. The stone pathways cut through the underground resembled those of a quarry under construction; uneven chunks of rock waited to trip even the most able-bodied who dared make the trek. Those unlucky enough to take the wrong turn or falter among the rocks could end up as food for the sewer rats.

Dom's thoughts turned to Cherise and his continued search for her after finding out she dropped out of the university. It was the only bit of information she would allow him before she left, and even then, he was not given any notice of her intent to depart. Instead, he had been able to track her down to the university. At the time, he thought it would be in his best interest not to alert her that he knew of her whereabouts.

Once he found out she was no longer at the school, his worry turned to alarm. Her disappearance was either meant to keep him from finding out what she was involved in or some dreadful mishap had befallen her. The latter thought he couldn't bear.

Laden with worry, he arrived at the only place where he might make his connection to Cherise—the convent. He had hoped to enlist Sister Mary's aid, but after finding out she too had lost touch and was equally worried, he had asked around the convent.

Several days passed and a message had arrived from Gabrielle, the mysterious orphan Cherise had mentioned to Dom. He had scoffed at her paranoid concerns about Gabrielle.

Now it nagged at him that Gabrielle may have had information on Cherise's whereabouts. He was so anxious to find Cherise that he jumped at the opportunity to meet with Gabrielle once she had contacted him. He did not trust her, but how else would he find the information he so desperately sought?

Danger

SHE COULDN'T RESIST; it was in her blood to move toward the unknown, the thrill of the path less taken. Her father had known, as he knew himself, that she was an adventurer with the courage of a lion. If he had lived, he could have watched his charge even if he'd had to keep one eye closed to most of her adventures. To stifle such a daring spirit would be to unhinge the very essence of what made Cherise so special.

Henri arrived as promised at half-past seven, bearing a dozen red roses as he entered the dressing area. He expected the flowers to trigger questions about his motives, but her response surprised him in a much deeper way.

"Monsieur Bonnebeau, I cannot accept such a lavish gift from you. It would be shameful, and furthermore, I'm afraid you have misjudged me, sir! Do you think me a common tramp?" A very indignant Cherise stood, hands on hips, glaring at the roses in Henri's hands.

Perhaps seeing the delighted look on his face softened her outrage while puzzling her all the same. Not content to let this misunderstanding go any further, Cherise motioned for Henri to sit down. "Monsieur Henri, there is not enough money in the world or flowers to buy my affection. Whatever you may think of me for dancing here in the hall, I am not the kind of woman that allows herself to be bought and paid for."

He had to admit to himself there was more to this young woman than he first thought. And yes, he expected to win her favors through his normal charm even though he suspected her to be of a better class.

Watching her night after night, he imagined many things of her but never that she might be common. There was something very special about Cherise. She possessed an almost-untouchable grace and style, setting her apart from the rest. That she stood out among the crowd was no accident.

"Mademoiselle, I beg your pardon. You have surprised me with your resistance to my charm, unlike what other women might express. It serves you well, my dear."

Still a little indignant, she paused briefly before blurting, "Well, I'm glad you understand, and now if you don't mind, I will be making my way home."

"But, my dear, there is no reason why we cannot go to dinner. You are totally safe with me. There is no deception in my invitation. It is the natural quest of a man who admires a beautiful woman. Wanting to touch the work of art does not mean that he will. Please share dinner with me, and I promise to see you safely home!" Henri implored.

Cherise found that she was being swayed by his honest admission of his motive. *It couldn't hurt to just have dinner with him*, she thought.

Her response was laced with a tinge of aloofness and slight hesitation. Sighing audibly, she said, "All right, Henri, we will try this again. The roses really are beautiful, and if you honestly do understand I only want to be your friend, then we can go to dinner, but only dinner!"

"Oh my dear, I will be the most circumspect of gentlemen. My only wish is to please you by escorting you to a most sumptuous feast."

Having been satisfied his motives were at least somewhat above board, her youthful vigor returned as well as the color in her cheeks. Henri could not stop staring at the beautiful young woman. Cherise was a picture of loveliness, and now, unadorned by makeup, her natural beauty took his breath away. Even more interesting, he took note of the way she carried herself and wore her clothes, garments that he believed were designed to hide her attributes and protect her modesty at all costs.

Certain that Cherise's bright tresses, like her stage makeup, were part of the image she crafted for the stage, he could only speculate about her true hair color.

"Is something wrong, Monsieur? You have been staring at me for a few minutes, and, well, it is unnerving!"

"No, mademoiselle, I beg your pardon. It's just that you look different without all the makeup." The truth was that her beauty threatened to sweep him off his feet, but he was wise enough to know that voicing such a thought would terrify her.

"Well then, let's go find this sumptuous meal!" she smiled, relaxing now. Yes, there was something very comforting about Henri even though she could not figure out why she felt that way.

He's almost old enough to be my father, she thought to herself. *In some ways, Henri favors him, a crazy thought even for me!*

Quietly perched in his carriage, Henri wondered what Cherise was thinking. He would have Charles, his manservant, do a little digging as soon as possible. There must be much to learn about this little dancer and he would make it his mission to find out.

Traveling silently, they passed the Champs-Elysées with its beautiful weeping willows lining the twelve avenues, illuminated the latest discovery in gas lanterns, and anchored in the center by the Arc de Triomphe de l'Étoile.

"Do you know the history of the Arc de Triomphe, my dear?"

"Only what I've learned in the history books at the convent and from my grandparents." Cherise hoped Henri had not picked up on her mention of the convent but decided it would not hurt to admit some connection to Paris since she would not reveal any real identities or names.

"In 1806, Napoleon I conceived of a triumphal arch patterned after those of ancient Rome and dedicated to the glory of his imperial armies. It is a product of late eighteenth-century romantic neoclassicism and has become an emblem of French patriotism. The arch also serves as a reminder that Chalgrin was a pupil of Etienne Louis Boullée, the father of visionary architecture. The most famous of its sculptural reliefs is La Marseillaise (1833–36) of François Rude."

"It is so beautiful here, a tribute to Paris. As a small girl, I would visit my grandparents and we spent time walking the avenues, admiring the architecture of the buildings. They loved the antiquities, so we would go in and out of the shops looking for special pieces for their collections."

"So you are from this area?" Henri's curiosity was pushing him now, intruding on his promise to himself to be very cautious and maintain a slow, steady pace with the distrusting young woman. But she had opened the door with the personal information, and it took all his reserve to stop his questioning.

"My grandparents were Parisians, but they are gone now. I don't like to talk about them," Cherise stated emphatically.

Without acknowledging her response, Henri proceeded to give additional instructions to the driver. "We are close to the restaurant now, my dear. You will be pleasantly surprised to see where we are going."

Arriving at 17 Rue de Beaujolais, they were met by red-coated, white capped attendants waiting to greet the important guests of Le Grand Véfour.

"It's not a wax museum, but you can soak up a bit of history in this institution where Bonaparte, Josephine, and Victor Hugo were among a panoply of others who have dined and whose names are to be seen on the engraved copper plates above the very formal red velvet benches."

He gently helped Cherise from the carriage and admired how she delicately twirled her petticoat in such a way as to bow down to his gentlemanly gesture. Her gaze left him a bit unnerved: hazel green eyes framed by long black lashes waiting expectantly. Waiting for him, perhaps?

Henri vowed that he must maintain control and not be pulled into a relationship that would be dangerous, much the same way that any confirmed bachelor might have concerns. Something about this one was unlike any of the others before.

"If you are hungry, my dear, there is no better place than Le Grand Véfour. Monsieur Dumas's menu grows more inventive by the day, with such exceptional creations as almond milk flan in sorrel bouillon, lightly cooked salmon terrine with eggplant aspic, and rosemary shortbread topped with candied fennel. The milk-fed calf's sweetbreads studded with truffles and gently cooked with a broad bean jus, though more in keeping with traditional homestyle fare, are a true chef d'oeuvre!"

Reciting part of the menu gave Henri a brief respite from the tension he felt from being in such proximity to Cherise's feminine charms. So young yet so sensual and unaware of what power she has over men!

They were escorted into the restaurant by the owner, Paul Dumas. Only the very respected and elite patrons of Paris were treated to the personal assistance of Monsieur Dumas.

"Monsieur Henri, it is such an honor! We have not seen you since… well, in a long while, sir. And you have a friend with you, I see, and a very lovely one at that."

"Monsieur Dumas, I would like to introduce Mademoiselle Cherise, uhm…just Cherise."

"Good evening, sir!" Cherise extended her hand to the obviously awe-struck owner. "You have a very lovely establishment, and Monsieur Henri tells me the food is wonderful!"

Dumas couldn't quite put his finger on it, but there was something vaguely familiar about this young woman. Some other time, perhaps, and he would place the face. A face such as hers could not go unnoticed for long. His friend, Henri, had made a very good selection this time unlike his last choice. But that was another story, one better left unspoken.

"Oh, mademoiselle, it is such a pleasure to have you as our guest this evening. I will make certain you and Henri have all the special items for your pleasure. I will join you later if Henri does not mind sharing your attention!" He smiled mischievously as Henri looked over at him. Cherise noticed the exchange of looks and chuckled, inwardly delighted that she was the object of attention from these two charming men.

Perhaps Rochelle could see into her soul. Quickly, she dismissed this sobering thought. Yes, she would enjoy this evening. After all, wasn't it time that she allowed herself the pleasure of being a woman?

The Unmasking

In the Dark

Father Pierre paused to catch his breath as they stood at yet another set of stairs leading to the surface. It had been like this for the past two hours, moving quickly through the tunnels only to find they had to ascend a set of stairs and boldly face the bright day's sun.

"Hurry, Father, we must make haste to our destination before the end of the day, and we still have many miles to go! It is not safe moving around the tunnels after the sun sets on the Seine. Not so much for the light of day forever missing below but what lurks above once the dark consumes the sky. It becomes a fight for survival."

"You paint a gloomy picture, Dom. How do you know your way through this maze?" asked Father Pierre.

"Let's just say that survival came early for me. As a small boy, I was orphaned and learned to survive on my own. Making my way through the tunnels was one way I had to avoid the wrath of the bullies living on the street."

"But I thought you were raised by Sister Mary's family—your aunt and uncle."

Dom hesitated ever so slightly, wondering if he could share enough information to satisfy the father. "No, unfortunately, we were only reunited once I entered the parish school. The priest knew my family history, and once he was able to put two and two together, finding my cousins was just a matter of course."

"That must have been very gratifying for you as a young lad to finally find someone of your own blood," exclaimed the father.

Dom continued pushing through the tunnels so swiftly that speaking was becoming more difficult, forcing Father Pierre to give up his questioning. "Umm," feigned the less fatigued younger man, "tell you later."

Abruptly they came to the end of the tunnel they had been traversing, a hellish hole covered with narrow, tumbled stones waiting to trip them at every wrong move.

Finally, thought Father Pierre. *Perhaps a chance to breathe*. A blast of fresh air from above gave his lungs a break from the putrid mass that lingered below the surface. When I have time to think, I'll ask Dom a few more questions, maybe even have a heart-to-heart with him. After all, Cherise's welfare and our concern for her motivate us both.

As they journeyed, Father Pierre sorted through the background he knew to be true.

Olivier Gereaux, philanthropist and connoisseur of fine art and antiquities, had purchased the shop of Madame Chevais and hired a good friend to manage the shop, Dom Broussard, the trusted second cousin of Sister Mary. No outside capital was solicited, which was a decision intended to keep nosy strangers from knowing of the business. It had prospered for many years, and even though Olivier was no longer alive, he made sure to keep everything in perfect condition for the time when the rightful heirs, the living grandchildren, could claim their share of the property. He assumed Dom would also have his share as the manager.

What was it Dom knew that he would not or could not share with the father? Hadn't Dom made the first overture to him with the urgent message of saving Cherise from the dregs of society? Father reached out to him for help finding Cherise before embarking on his trip to Paris. Why did he even need his counsel? It puzzled and, frankly, concerned him that Dom was being less than honest in his motives.

Dom could sense the father's concern in the quiet of the tunnel. He must push on and make sure that they rendezvoused with Gabrielle, who had agreed to show them where Cherise was dancing. Gabby, as he called her now, had surprised him by her reluctance to say anything of a negative nature regarding Cherise. Perhaps Cherise had been wrong about Gabrielle's motives.

Gabby had come to him from the same convent where his cousin, Sister Mary, resided. Although he had not checked her credentials, Mary said she was okay. Ever cautious, he was also desperate to find Cherise. It was no secret he needed help in the store and maybe she could lead him to Cherise.

Once they found Cherise, he could clear up any questions that Father Pierre had concerning his motives. He just hoped it would not be too late to save her from further foolishness. Once under his control, he would make certain any stumbling blocks would be removed from executing his plan.

"Are we almost there yet, Dom? I fear it is growing dark and my concern for our dear girl is growing with it."

"There is only one more short tunnel and we will be in the area of the city under the Ninth Arrondissement, the theater district and home to the Folies Bergère."

"Tell me about this place, Dom. Is it as wild as they say, and how is it you have an inside track to information behind the scenes?" The questions Father Pierre had stored for the entire journey under Paris could no longer be contained.

"Father, I beg your forgiveness, but there are many reasons for what I do, all of them with a pureness of heart, I promise. For now, it is better that you remain ignorant until we pluck the dear Cherise from the hands of the devil."

"Very well, Dom, but make no mistake, I will not walk away without knowing all the answers to this puzzling disappearance of Cherise. It is the only way I can deal intelligently with her and try to help her control the impetuous nature she has inherited."

"If it will help pass the time we have left," Dom said, "I will tell you a little of the geography and short history of the Folies Bergère."

Dom made a mental note that he would have to tread lightly with regard to the plans he had for Cherise. It would serve no good purpose for Father Pierre to ever know the whole truth. He could cover up the ugly side of it later once they were back on track.

"Built in 1869, the Folies Bergère started out as the Folies Trévise and was patterned after the Alhambra music hall in London. Originally, the fare included operettas, comic opera, popular songs, and gymnastics. Because the shows catered to popular tastes, they began featuring more nudity and played up the exoticness of persons and objects from other cultures.

"The name was selected from the adjacent street Rue de Trévise but later changed because of the displeasure of the Duc de Trévise, a prominent nobleman. Once the venue became more closely associated with a bawdy dance hall, it was changed to Bergère, a nearby street." Dom could hear father mutter under his breath, obviously not pleased.

Why was it that Dom's words seemed to ring hollow? He had no reason to distrust the young man who, after all, had come to him in distress at learning of Cherise's whereabouts. It would have served no purpose for Dom to participate in a charade that would do harm to her.

Dom was also fighting a mental battle, armed only with his infatuation for Cherise but battling against the pull of temptations from outside. Yes, he had been lured to the edge by those who would willfully hurt Cherise. He hoped that he could satisfy all the elements with a little reason, especially where she was concerned. It had occurred to him she was more than just a little headstrong, and any semblance of his cavorting with the enemies of the Pontifi and Chevais families would send her immediately away. Delicate was the balance between honest ambition and partial deceit. How would he craft the story to grab her attention before she could adversely react?

He had worked long and hard! When he had been approached by Sister Mary, it was as if God had sent him a messenger. Toiling day and night in the shop had seared a drive so strong in Dom for greater material wealth that he could easily be pushed down the wrong path.

The spark of greed began when Duvalier found him there. Curious as to what the old codger, Olivier, had done since he bought the shop and always on the prowl for information leading to *Clarice* and her brother, Andre, Duvalier decided to cultivate a friendship with Dom. It was after several visits to the store and winning his confidence that Duvalier struck a bargain with the young man.

Yes, thought Dom, Cherise would just have to let him explain how his plan would help her win this personal war she had been waging against Duvalier and, at the same time, give them all the riches they both deserved. The large bank deposits had been a mistake he was still trying to change. She would have to understand or else. In his greed and excitement, Dom accepted at face value what Duvalier had promised with regard to Clarice.

After all, Joseph had assured him that he only wanted his fair share of the remainder of the Pontifi-Chevais estate. They would settle up with Duvalier once he could convince Cherise to provide him with the code from the seal and the key to unlock the riches in Switzerland. Duvalier promised to split the proceeds with Dom.

After much soul-searching, Dom decided it would be best for all of them to go along with Duvalier's proposal. It would stop Duvalier from hunting Cherise and her family for the rest of their days, and he, Dom, would be left with great wealth. Surely, Cherise would see the light and accept his actions as a way for them to be together and still have all the riches they deserved.

Enraptured Bliss

August 2005

JACKIE PEEKED OUT from under the thick fur-like lashes long untouched by mascara and not subjected to the natural fluttering that would thin out old growth. In fact, these lashes had become something of a topic of conversation to the visitors streaming in and out on regular intervals.

Where am I? she wondered, still groggy from her dreamlike state. Fighting to wake up from what she assumed was a good, hard-won night of sleep, her unfamiliar surroundings were hardly a source of comfort.

"Okay, Jackie, calm down. You've been dreaming and you're groggy," her inner voice screamed. "Clearly, this is not reality, only a stage for one of your *roles*." What was it that nagged at her consciousness—a past memory of her daughters talking to her, even imploring her to remember? But what was she supposed to remember? Confused, Jackie grew agitated and threw her arm over to one side, inadvertently ringing the call bell for the nursing staff.

The nurse on duty was startled to see the light go on in room 2203. "Uh-oh, this is not good!" she muttered to herself. Eager to finish her shift without encountering an issue with a patient, Carol grudgingly moved to see what precipitated the unexpected call from *Snow White*.

The name they had given the beautiful woman in room 2203 came from the fairy-tale depiction of a maiden who had been asleep. Jackie had become their version of the fairy tale. In a coma for nine months now, her hair had gradually turned completely white, which only added more interest to the story of Snow White.

It wasn't that she, Carol, lacked compassion for the patient and particularly for the family, but they had all held out hope too many times to expect that this bell ringing was anything more than a mistake. It was just last week everyone thought she was back and once again slipped away leaving her family very upset. Since it was three forty-five in the morning, she knew the family was not here and that could only mean that Jackie had fallen out of bed or worse. There was always the chance that her heart had stopped—God forbid—on Carol's watch.

Struggling to get out of bed, Jackie had somehow wrapped the bell cord around her wrist and was now flailing like a calf caught in the noose of a lasso. As she rounded the corner, Carol could hear the woman crying and begging to be set free.

Carol patted her gently. "Jackie, Jackie, it's okay. You're in a hospital and have been heavily sedated. Wait while I untangle you and then we'll take this slowly." She couldn't believe how alert her patient seemed this time.

There had been other times when she had awakened but would drift in and out of consciousness. Something was definitely different about tonight. The look of panic on Jackie's face wrenched at Carol's heartstrings, a weakness she would just as soon hide. Hurrying over to the frightened woman, Carol soothingly said, "Here we go, sweet lady. I have freed you from your constraints."

She lovingly patted Jackie's hand, inwardly acknowledging her affection for the woman they called Snow White. Funny how she had become attached to a comatose patient but acknowledged at the same time that there was something magical about this woman.

Jackie had come to them in bad shape, a critically injured patient devoid of hope for any kind of normal life. What the staff couldn't believe was her will to live and strength of spirit.

It was gratifying she had a devoted family unlike so many of the patients Carol had cared for over the years. Not only did Jackie have two daughters and a son who seemed to worship her but a husband who stayed by her side for the first couple months. Granted it had eased up, but life does go on, after all.

The nurses had talked about him, a handsome charmer who, no doubt, would eventually move on. They had seen it before: intense devotion followed by intermittent loving care and then a gradual lessening of the visits and attention, followed by no contact. They were surprised he was still coming at least twice a week to spend an hour or two with the sleeping beauty.

One time, Carol even heard him talking to Jackie, and it touched her in a way that lingered for weeks. Perhaps her jaded experience had soured her on the promise of love forever, through thick and thin.

It was obvious that he worshipped this now-stilled figure, a mere wisp of the woman depicted in pictures around the room. And this one was taking longer than normal to gradually move away. "Ugh, stop it, Carol. You know better than to get your hopes up on the human race!"

"I remember my daughters talking to me and coaxing me to do something, but what was it, nurse? Umm, I'm sorry I didn't get your name. Why am I here in this hospital? And where is my family? I need to see my family now." Jackie was becoming unsettled again.

"Okay, Jackie, I'm Carol and I've been taking care of you for the past few months and…oh, ah, since you've been here."

"Few months? What do you mean?" The now-lucid Jackie was coming back to life. "Why am I here and what happened?"

"I'm sorry, let me start over and explain a few things to you," implored Carol. "I shouldn't have dropped so much on you all at once. Please forgive me! Trust me, you are fine now, and it's wonderful to see you awake and alert!"

Just as rapidly as the information had been bestowed upon her, the panic hit her, again and again, like waves washing over at high tide, the force pushing her into the long-forgotten memories of that day. The revelation of what happened left her trembling, holding on to what sanity she could muster.

Time stopped for what seemed like hours. In reality, it was but a few minutes as Carol patted Jackie as if she were caressing a child and comforted her with soothing words. Looking at the pictures of her family spread around the room gradually pulled her into a calming cocoon of well-being, a reflection of the inner strength that she always could pull from in difficult times. "I made it. I'm alive," Jackie's inner voice shouted.

She remembered as if it was yesterday, a day that had started with the anticipation of living fully in the moment. After many ups and downs, it wasn't hard for her to bask in the simple joys of life: a beautiful flower, the smiles of her children, a hug from a friend, and always the embrace of her passion—Craig.

"I have to know all the details, nurse, and please, where is my family?" The anxiousness was looming, ready to grab for Jackie's attention, pulling her in ways she could not have known.

The long-ago day was supposed to be a special day for her, the celebration of many years of hard work finally recognized by her peers and the honor given by Queens College. The part that remained fuzzy and demanded more than her lethargic mind could wrap its arms around began at the point where she was stopped at a traffic light near Queens. What happened in the time after that was still a puzzle.

Concentrating now, she could see the light changing to green. "Yes, I'm waiting to make the turn and—oh my god, I remember! The truck! No!" she screamed, startling Carol.

"It's okay, it's okay! You're alive, and your family will be here in a few minutes!"

"Tell me, Carol, please what happened after the truck hit me? How long have I been in a coma? And what other injuries did I suffer? Am I disfigured or crippled?" The questions tumbled out so rapidly that Carol had not had time to answer the first one yet.

As if on cue, the door burst open, and what appeared to be a small army of smiling people rushed into the room. The family had arrived, and it was no small coincidence that their entry had been synchronized.

All were greedy for a glimpse of Jackie's alert face, the one they knew, not the facsimile they'd seen in that hospital bed for months on end. What they never could have conveyed to a stranger or even this kindhearted nurse was the depth of love they had for their mother, daughter, and wife.

Was she any different from yesterday's loved one down the hall, the one who had passed into the void of night, only a memory in the making? Yes, they would tell you, their beloved a special one, unlike every other patient lying in the sterile beds of every hospital in every city.

She, the one who could make her eyes appear to look into your soul or appear to be drinking in the sunshine on a glorious day, oblivious to the problems of the world, or to appear to understand everyone else's problems with empathy and solvable ideas or appear as an angel to help the least of those with the greatest of needs. Yes, Jackie was all those things: one of a special breed people naturally gravitated to in the hope of drinking in the positivity that she exuded.

"Mom, oh, Mom." Deidre was the first at Jackie's bedside, the youngest of her brood, the child who could feel her mother's pain as if her own. "You're back for good," she cried, unable to contain the tears of joy.

Loraine, who understood her mother on a deeper, more spiritual level, pushed her way over, flung her arms around her mother's neck, and gasped, "We have waited for this day so, so long, and it has finally come!"

Craig, her husband of fifteen years, the one who made her heart stop even after all this time, gazed at his beloved wife from a distance, allowing time for their daughters to embrace her. Their mother had always been their life force, giving them strength and optimism during difficult times. They were so dependent on her positive vibes of life that they had suffered the most during the past six months.

Doris, Jackie's devoted mother, had just returned from Florida for the third time. There was no doubt she had spent the most time nursing her daughter, coaxing her and practically bullying her back to life. She was most content to allow the family their time with her before she took charge once again.

Wrapping her arms around both of her daughters, Jackie kissed them lovingly. "I'm back, darlings. Now let me kiss the rest of you! Where's your brother?" Jackie asked impatiently.

"He's on his way, Mom," Loraine said.

Doris moved to Jackie's bedside, gave her daughter a peck on the forehead, and quickly retreated so Craig could finally have his own reunion. With that, Craig moved up for what was their first embrace since the morning of that infamous day.

"Hello, sweetheart, I've missed you so much!" Craig whispered gently, kissing his wife's tears away. "You're not going to leave me ever again."

She looked intently at him, soaking in his ruggedly handsome features and noticing the extra gray in his hair. It had always been a joke with them, and she couldn't resist even now. "You've got more blond highlights in your hair!" She giggled. With that one sentence, the entire room heaved a sigh of relief long held at bay.

Just as everyone relaxed and the conversations were flowing freely, a worried young man bounded in the room. "Mom, you're awake. Thank God!" Jackie's eldest, never one to show emotions, surprised her by dashing over and planting a big kiss on her forehead.

"I may have to do all this over again for the kind of attention I'm getting today," she declared. True to form, her questions once again came in rapid-fire motion. "Give me all the details. I need to know everything! What exactly happened, and when can I go home? How long have I been here?"

"In due time, all your questions will be answered along with most of the details," Carol interjected. "For the present time, you still have to be observed now that you are awake. Dr. Martimbeau will want to run some tests tomorrow, and part of the brain wave exercises will be to measure your responses to conversations related to the accident. At the same time, he'll test your brain functionality to see how everything responds. He may let you go home in a few days as soon as he evaluates those tests."

"When will the doctor come in to discuss this with us?" Craig asked. "I'd also like to take my wife home as quickly as possible, and I'm sure the rest of the family would like that as well. We've waited a long time for this day!"

"Of course, Mr. Hancock. I can understand your eagerness, but you've all waited this long. Let's make sure everything is okay before taking this last big step!"

Jackie piped in as if on cue, "It's okay, everyone. I'm fine now, and I'll never leave you again. Besides, I have a big story to tell you. In fact, I may even write it as a book!" They were all looking at her curiously now, wondering what was rattling around in that brain and perhaps maybe even a little concerned that all wasn't just right.

Loraine remembered one other time when her mother had tried to come out of the coma. She had been shouting and ranting about their great-great-grandmother, Clarice, and trouble with someone named Duvalier. It had all been quite puzzling at the time, but as long as it didn't resurface, they wouldn't have to worry about their mother's mental faculties.

Jackie just smiled like the old Cheshire cat in the Alice in Wonderland fairy tale, the one that lounged around, always smirking at the foolishness of those around him. She would keep all this under wraps until she got out of this place. It would serve no purpose for everyone to think her mind was gone.

No, it was clearer than ever—an awakening in more ways than one. She would write the story, and at the same time her life would be transformed. There was enough material, and no one would ever have to know she lived it herself.

Yes, the story was ready to be written, and it would be the family legacy. Triumph and tragedy, alike in so many ways, traveling the same pathways but turning one way for a tragic outcome or the other to be blessed with a triumphant ending!

Revelations

The Magic of the Eve

The evening was delightful, and the company of one Henri Bonnebeau enveloped the young and exuberant Clarice in an embrace of magical expectation.

Dining on all the delicacies Henri could order in one grand feast proved to be a gastronomic adventure she had yet to digest. The food was one thing, but the attention Henri lavished on Clarice did not go unnoticed. The whole evening became an event extraordinaire, a production that might threaten to weaken her resolve.

Henri could see how delighted she was, and he appreciated her pure joy at each new dish and discovery. No, he would not take advantage of her in this way and risk losing her trust permanently although it took all his resolve to keep from moving toward her.

They had been moved into one of the private dining rooms reserved for royalty and the greatest of dignitaries. Windows draped in red velvet framed the paintings of their illustrious past diners, such as Monet and Gauguin, and candles were strategically placed to illuminate the best features of each diner.

Adjacent to the windows was a beautiful limestone fireplace; regal Louis XIV gold-gilded chairs flanked each side, and a brocaded chaise perpendicular to the fireplace separated the area from the dining table. Ornately carved high-back chairs adorned with the same red velvet covering the windows were positioned across the table, creating an intimate setting for two.

It was no accident that Henri had chosen this room when he made the reservations earlier, but now he wondered if it had been a mistake. He was falling deeper under the spell of this child-woman. Every minute that passed threatened to destroy the resolve he had upon entering the restaurant.

"You are so far away, Henri," Cherise said softly. "Am I boring you with my conversation? I pray not, for you have been so kind to me. More than kind, actually. Much more." The warmth was spreading through her body, filling her with happiness.

He couldn't think clearly, and he wouldn't respond even though it was a simple statement of appreciation from someone who was taken with the surroundings. Henri wouldn't be duped into thinking it was more than that. *Silly old man*, he thought.

Cherise sensed that Henri was conflicted and instinctively reached across the table to grasp his hand. "Henri, I am more than just grateful. You have made me feel like a woman, one that I myself can respect. Do not fear showing me you care, for I believe you are a good man."

Henri paused long enough to catch the air and breathe again. This was certainly not what he had expected, and although her attention was welcome, it caught him by surprise. There were so many contradictions to sort through where young Miss Cherise was concerned, now prim and somewhat moralistic in her behavior with him, in complete contrast with her image projected at the Folies Bergère.

He held himself in check, prepared to fight off the intense feelings that were threatening to overtake reason. The candlelight flickered just enough, illuminating Cherise's face so that he could see her obvious warmth, capturing her look of admiration for him.

If he didn't move away now, he would be pulled further into that gaze, one he didn't want to imagine was of lust for him. He honestly believed that she might still be chaste, especially after watching her all evening.

"Henri, I have many roads to travel and much to experience. As you may have surmised, I am inexperienced in many ways of the world but have lived many lives in other ways, some too painful to recount."

Finally catching his voice, Henri spoke softly to the young woman. Afraid that he might break the incredible spell in which they were cloaked, he gently said, "My dear Cherise, I am honored that you have given me your trust, and my hesitation to speak is out of fear my words might alter your openness. You have bestowed upon me your trust, and for that I'm deeply grateful."

"Henri, I want to experience what it is like to be a woman, to feel the touch of a man and to feel the desire that drives women to give of themselves willingly to a man. I have only dreamt of what it would be like to be held by a man."

Ignoring her obvious overture to him, he replied, "My dear Cherise, you will have many opportunities to meet the right one, but you must consider giving up the dance. The type of men you will encounter will not be of your caliber. It has become very clear to me that you do not belong there, and I will help you start over."

Surprised at his response and a little hurt, Cherise was quick to answer, "You don't understand at all! I am not a captive but have chosen this profession for many reasons, most of which I cannot share at this time. Believe me when I say that most of the dancers have a higher purpose than what is visible to you."

Distraught at the thought of losing her new friend, Cherise could not contain the tears. All the years of pain and the grief she had experienced gave way to the raw emotions long buried by a girl too strong to cry. Sobbing openly now, she buried her face to hide it from Henri.

In one spontaneous moment, Henri came around the table to embrace her. "Cherise, my dear, you must trust me enough to tell me why you hold this pain so deeply. I can help you, my dear." Henri lovingly patted the top of Cherise's hair, making sure not to intrude too far into her space but far enough to give comfort. He had to admit that if in this circumstance too long, he would be lost.

Cherise looked up at Henri and could see the concern in his eyes. The moment would come when she could tell him all, but now was not the time. Pulling herself together, she had to prove to Henri and the world she was capable of handling her affairs and conducting her business without interference from the outside.

Looking sheepishly at him, she spoke the words that, earlier, he might have longed to hear, "Would you teach me how to make love?"

In his ignorance of naive love, he laughed softly. It had not occurred to him that his action in response to her question might damage the spirit of the young woman.

Cherise stole another look at him, uncertain she had heard the sound. Wounded to the core, her demeanor changed almost instantly, her back stiffening along with her gaze at Henri. In the place of her warm sweet smile was a mask of coldness—her veil of armor.

Henri sensed the change in the young woman. "My chérie, I was not laughing at you but merely expressing my pleasure at your innocence. Forgive me for my lack of sensitivity."

"But of course, Monsieur Henri. It is no problem as I too was playing with you!" She completely understood now how little he thought of her as an adult. Yes, it was clear and she would not let this happen again. Never, never must she lose sight of her ultimate goals, and this interlude with Henri, as pleasant as it had been until the last ten minutes, was merely a fraction in time. In a moment of weakness, she had almost crossed over the line from *playing a role* to actually *becoming the role.* No, she would replace him too.

"Please take me home, Henri. I'm very tired, and tomorrow will be a busy day for me in the theater. There are other people depending on me, and I must be fresh and ready for the new day!" Cherise stated with more emphasis than necessary.

It was very clear to Henri that he had not handled this interaction with his usual finesse, but then nothing was normal around this child-woman.

"Cherise, I do not want to take you home while you are upset. It grieves me that I have hurt your sensitivities. Please forgive me, dear."

"Oh, you have not done anything of the sort. I have just realized how foolish my behavior must seem. There is no offense taken, and we can leave as friends." The finality of her statement was not lost on the distressed Henri, but it was apparent that he wouldn't win this argument tonight with the headstrong Cherise.

As they were leaving the restaurant, Monsieur Dumas casually addressed Cherise, "Mademoiselle, I have been thinking all evening that you remind me of someone who was very near and dear to me for many years. Are you, by any chance, related to the late Madame Marie Chevais?"

Visibly moved, Cherise gathered her wits about her and quickly—too quickly—responded, "Why, no, monsieur, but I know the name. It is kind of you to think that I might be of such breeding." With that, she spun around and marched out to the waiting carriage.

Henri lingered for a moment, more curious than ever. "Monsieur, why do you ask that question of young Miss Cherise? Are you referring to the famous Chevais woman who people believe was murdered by a band of thieves?"

"Well, yes. She was a friend of mine and a good customer. Her husband and she were good customers for many years before he passed away. I must tell you that your young protégé has an uncanny resemblance to Madame when she was a young woman."

Momentarily ignoring that his friend had given him a great deal to think about and information to feed to Charles, his manservant, he proceeded to thank Monsieur Dumas for his great hospitality with promises he would bring the beautiful Cherise back again soon.

He silently resolved to get to the bottom of the mystery surrounding his young charge. And charge she certainly had become. He would ensure no harm would befall her. It wasn't totally clear, but somewhere he felt a part of him was already lost to her charm.

The Arrival

The Same Evening

It was wearing on the father, he could tell, but they were almost at the rendezvous with Gabrielle. This was no time to slow down if the information he had been given was accurate. The race was to keep Cherise from making a terrible mistake. But greater was the need to keep her out of the clutches of Duvalier, a problem to which he had contributed.

Yes, it was one thing to connive to win Cherise over for the purpose of furthering his own wealth and property holdings, but to expose her to potentially deadly risk was unthinkable. Further complicating matters was his realization that he did, in fact, love the beautiful young woman.

Now he must find a way to protect her and still have what he wanted: the part of Duvalier's fortune taken from the Pontifis. He could then begin to methodically search for the spoils from Duvalier's pilferage of his own family's properties so many years before. In spite of how wrong the father may find this entire situation, Dom believed he could justify all his actions in the end.

"Father Pierre, we have one more turn and then we'll be able to exit from this underground maze! See, the stairs are just ahead. Gabrielle will be waiting for us above ground. You may remember she is the young nun who replaced Cherise in my shop at the recommendation of Sister Mary."

Still puzzled by the discrepancies in Dom's story and alarmed at the increasing number of people who had been made aware of Cherise's existence, Father Pierre sharply said, "Make no mistake, Dom, we'll have our conversation once we arrive at the dance hall before any words are conveyed to Cherise!" Father Pierre's demeanor had changed; his tone surprised Dom, but not enough for him to change his plans.

Father Pierre could be a force when in pursuit of a cause or defending a principle. Beyond those two were his loyalties to the Pontifi children, and any breach or threat where they were concerned could summon his inner beast. Troubling enough was poor Andre lying in a semicomatose state, unable to speak or move; but even as worrisome was what Dom had told him regarding Cherise's whereabouts, the company she was keeping, and her wanton disregard of her brother's state of health.

Becoming angrier by the minute, Father Pierre stepped up his pace as if to squash the demons that threatened to overtake his good sense. Climbing the steps now, they could see the streetlights of Paris casting a glow into the darkness of the underground. As he reached the last few steps, and breathing faster, he said a little prayer to God, asking for his guidance and patience in dealing with Cherise. It was, he argued to himself, not the end of the world if she was a dancer in the Folies Bergère, as Dom had indicated. If he could only reason with her before some other force grabbed onto her and pulled her further into the lifestyle. He shuddered to think what may have already happened.

As planned, Gabrielle was standing under the lamppost at the next corner just beyond Rue Richer, waiting with anticipation. Brooding one minute and anxious the next, Gabrielle went over the last information she had been given. If what Rochelle had said was accurate, they could make the evening show and then the fake would be exposed for what she was. She, Gabrielle Aroonia, would ultimately have what she wanted and, at the same time, gain Dom's loyalty. He would then give up his infatuation with Cherise.

Now closing the distance, Dom greeted the young woman from Sister Mary's orphanage with a warm embrace. After all, Cherise had lied to him, hadn't she? And Gabrielle was the one helping him now.

Gabrielle had her own thoughts of this charade perpetrated by Cherise. It was a waste of time considering Duvalier would find her through any means. She fancied that by helping Dom bring her back, this was enough to keep Duvalier at bay. Foolish, of course, considering that she, Gabrielle, had her own agreement with him, a pact agreed upon with a promise made in blood.

There were other considerations where Duvalier was concerned. She had her own designs on reaping the reward for finding young Miss Cherise. And that old batty Sister Mary would not get in her way!

It had not been easy to convince the sister of her *best intentions* for finding Cherice, a ploy designed to pull at Mary's heartstrings. The silly old woman had been crushed by Cherise's disappearance.

Father Pierre was more standoffish and a little suspicious in his greeting of Gabrielle. "How do you do, Miss Gabrielle?" Father said. "I trust Sister Mary is doing well these days!"

"Yes, Father, she sends her regards and asks that you come to the orphanage to stay with her while here in Paris! In fact, she insists on it!" declared Gabrielle.

"We'll see. We now have more serious business to take care of, and that is finding my young charge in good condition." His face belied the fear he felt at what condition he'd find his beloved Cherise and a new fear for his friend, Sister Mary.

Father could not help but paint a picture of Gabrielle in his mind. In it, he envisioned a dark aura of Satan encircling her while intermittent bursts of flames provided an eerie brightness. He experienced a momentary feeling of sadness for her lost soul but quickly moved beyond Gabrielle to focus on his objective.

Father Pierre was careful not to venture too far down that path lest he let on to Gabrielle his suspicions of her duplicity in this arranged meeting.

He also worried what Dom's role was in this little charade; although he didn't think him capable of the same malevolence emanating from Gabrielle.

Concerned once again for Sister Mary, Father casually asked of Dom's friend, "Why didn't Sister Mary come with you? It's curious I haven't heard from her in a couple of months. Is her health okay?"

"Yes, Father. Her duties at the orphanage have been too numerous as of late, and she sends her apologies. She also instructed me to take good care of you in your quest to find Cherise."

Of one thing he was certain: Sister Mary would never trust anyone but the father with the type of knowledge Gabrielle was alluding to. Even Dom, her cousin, would possess limited information as to Cherise's whereabouts, particularly if she intended to keep her distance from him.

In due time, he would have his conversation with Sister Mary, and he felt certain it would prove to be a different version from that which Gabrielle shared.

However, if the information Gabrielle gave Dom was correct, they were closing in on Cherise and he would soon be able to embrace his beloved girl. It also didn't escape him that Gabrielle had obviously acquired her inside information from her unsavory contacts or, even more troublesome, those who might want harm to befall Cherise.

Confrontation

The apprehension she felt was pervasive—an ever-present blend of fear and some magnetic force pulling at her, beckoning her to continue down this unknown path. Why did she feel so compelled to go back to the dance hall, a place proven to be, at best, a haven for young women on the fringe? Henri had made it very clear what he thought of a young woman dancing in the Folies Bergère and tried to warn her of the dangers she faced by continuing on that path.

Why had she allowed him into her consciousness? It nagged at her even as she rode in the carriage back to the Moulin Rouge. She had to admit that he had gotten under her skin, more than somewhat, and in spite of her murmurings to the contrary, it bothered her that he disapproved of what she was doing.

Henri could feel Cherise's angst in the small confines of the carriage, and it grieved him to know he had contributed to her sadness. It was difficult taking the high road even when he knew in his heart that it was the only way to save her from a more nefarious fate.

It continued to nag at him that his young friend was hiding something and needed help. What could have forced her to engage in this risky situation? None of her mannerisms fit with the typical dance hall women. Her very demeanor was of the well-bred young women of the day.

Why did she pursue this folly of dancing among the thieves, prostitutes, and beggars? His curiosity continued to nag at him, and deep in thought, he was caught off guard when Cherise shouted out, "Stop! Stop the carriage! Let me out now! Right now!"

Startled, Henri tried to reason with Cherise. "Please, my dear, wait until we are back at the dance hall. It is only three more blocks!" Yes, he had been hard on her before leaving the restaurant, but he wanted to do the right thing where young Miss Cherise was concerned. There certainly had been many times when taking advantage of a young maiden had been second nature to him. However, she was different, much different, from the common dancer in the hall.

He experienced a tremendous need to protect her, a feeling that would be paid for later and at whatever cost it could exact from him. The evening had already left him drained, and even though he could easily become desensitized with most of the women, whether he bedded them or not, he was rapidly becoming disturbed at her display of despair. He had not expected this turn of events.

That Cherise wanted to jump out of the carriage upset him deeply. Regret must have been mirrored on his face when Cherise turned to him once more.

"Henri, I am so sorry, but I must leave now—immediately. Please don't ask me to explain. It has nothing to do with you."

Unsettled, he said, "Very well, my dear. I can't keep you, but please don't do anything rash. There is nothing in your past that would make me think less of you. It is obvious you are not the same as the others!"

With that, Henri instructed the driver to halt the carriage, and he gently hoisted the independent young woman out of the carriage. Cherise was gratified at Henri's kind words but hurriedly departed the carriage nonetheless.

She would have to cover her tracks better in the future. There would not be another opportunity for him to get so close to her vulnerability again, not after her humiliating display at the restaurant. Cherise's cheeks flushed at the memory and how she had come so close to offering herself to this man. Still, there was something reassuring about him, and whether she liked it or not, somehow she knew her path would cross Henri's again.

Her thoughts turned immediately to the group she spotted—now a couple of blocks back. She didn't get a good look at the lone female, but there was no mistaking the other two. It wouldn't do for Father Pierre and Dom to see her like this. "What in the world are they doing here?" she wondered out loud.

She saw them three blocks from her destination, walking briskly, and she was certain they were looking for her! This was not good! Were they heading to the dance hall? Why was Father Pierre here in Paris? Everything was becoming too complicated. Why couldn't they leave her alone?

As she silently spoke the words, the long-held pain of loss and separation buried beneath in her many layers threatened to overwhelm Cherise. Why did her knees want to buckle? Her strength of will seemed to be fading at the thought of embracing the father. Dom, on the other hand, was another story yet untapped. *I mustn't give in to this weakness of spirit; my resolve to finish my task must remain strong!*

The fear gripped her again, this time unrelenting as the panic set in. There was no mistaking Father Pierre and Dom had teamed up to find and confront her. But why? What could bring Father to Paris? "Oh, dear God," she uttered. "What if it is Andre?" The ache she felt at voicing his name challenged any hesitation or rationale Cherise had for not seeing Father Pierre. Gathering her wits, she moved away from where the carriage had been and skirted behind a building housing an old wax museum. She must watch them first and then figure out a way to get into the dance hall without being seen.

She darted between the buildings, clinging on to the lamppost that framed the abandoned doorway into the museum. An old sign proclaimed, "Get your ticket here! See Marie Antoinette in her last hour!" A mental picture of Marie's head rolling off the grandstand gave Cherise a moment of pause. No time to worry about what happened so many years ago.

Cherise stationed herself so she could see down the narrow alley leading to the side door of the dance hall, waiting to ensure no one was lingering and, most of all, that she was out of view of the unwanted visitors. From her perch behind the museum loading dock, she waited anxiously for the first sight of the group, mostly of her beloved Father Pierre.

Longing to touch him triggered memories of times past and loved ones lost. Thinking about her loved ones, particularly Andre, caused her to feel the sorrow once again at the way her life had to be conducted. Living in the shadows had deeply taken its toll on her sense of belonging.

In a moment of self-pity, she could easily ask, "Why me?" But Cherise never allowed herself the luxury of letting simple emotions interfere with her master plan, at least when the plan was at stake.

"Dearest Dom, why did you bring them here?" Cherise spoke to no one, yet everyone; hurt and anger welling up from the past. And how did he know where she might be? "I mustn't think less of him. After all, he has my best interests at heart! But it does trouble me that even with my strongest admonishments to the contrary, he would follow me into my secret world. Why now? What is his motivation?"

Precisely at that moment, the group passed by the alley view—Dom, Father Pierre, and Gabrielle! Gabrielle, she gasped silently. How could they do this to her? It was all becoming much too clear. That Gabrielle was among them meant only one thing: she was the one who had found her out and was exacting revenge for whatever perceived slight she felt at the hands of Cherise.

The tears ran down her face, uncontrolled along with the silent sobs that threatened to give away her hiding place. *Oh, not Father, not Father. Surely, he does not believe her to be trustworthy. And Dom! I thought he cared for me!*

The thought of Dom's duplicity in searching for her through his contact with Gabrielle disturbed Cherise enough to rapidly change the despair she felt into a searing anger. It burned through her like a fire, consuming all in its path. It was enough to erase the tears and change the sobbing woman into a ferocious adversary for any who would cross her path uninvited.

Pulling herself together and gathering her wits about her, Cherise watched as they approached the front entrance to the dance hall. Certain they had not seen her and that she could make it across the alley way to one of the unused back entrances, she quickly made her way over to the door.

If she could gain entry into the costume supply area located in the back, she could safely hide away and still sniff out who and what had brought them here. The seamstresses toiled during the day but were gone by night, so it was the best option she could think of at the moment. She was not expected for the late performance, so with any luck, Father Pierre and Dom would move on after assuming she was not one of the dancers.

But what if Gabrielle has an inside connection? She must see for herself who gave out information about a girl fitting her description. It would be hard for any of the dancers to figure out she was the missing young woman, especially with her gawdy bright hair and heavy makeup.

She must get a grip before sneaking inside. Carefully she pulled open the door and, after giving a cursory look, made her way down an unlit stairwell ending up behind the main stage. There was much activity inside the dressing rooms and waiting areas, but she was able to move behind the curtains to make her way over to the sewing room.

Once inside, she breathed a sigh of relief; a small tremble worked its way down her spine. Shaking it off, she vowed to find out what Gabrielle was up to and deal with the consequences. If it meant leaving the dance hall, so be it. She had a foreboding this was somehow connected to Duvalier, just like the premonition she had in the convent.

It was time to leave the sewing room and work her way above the staging area in an area often forgotten—the lofts created by the permanent stage sets. A person could wiggle through the narrow space and situate himself where he could see into a couple of the rooms.

Just as she positioned herself above, Rochelle appeared with Gabrielle in tow. "Well, dear old friend, what mischief have you been creating in the name of God? Or should I say, what farce are you perpetrating on the innocent people you've dragged in here?" Rochelle asked.

"You mentioned there was a girl here that, at first, fit the description of a young woman for whom one of your rogue friends had been looking! She had changed her looks so dramatically the first week you did not want to risk his ire by notifying him in case this was not the one."

Recalling the conversation, Gabrielle continued, "She didn't belong in the dance hall, a young woman of breeding and refinement, reluctant at first to take to the stage. Do you remember, my dear Rochelle?"

"And what is your interest in this so-called unknown woman?" Smelling money and the hint of betrayal, Rochelle pressed on. "Why, Gabrielle, what could you, a fledgling nun, possibly have to do with us common dance hall hussies?"

"There is a priest who would pay handsomely to find his young charge, a child really, who left the orphanage and made her way to Paris for supposedly idealistic and lofty reasons," said Gabrielle.

"Humph, there is no one here that could belong to a convent! There is the one I told you about, always making friends and winning over the other dancers, but that she could be the one of whom you speak is ridiculous."

Pacing and thinking only deepened the furrows in Rochelle's brow. "My sources, on the other hand, tell me that the one you describe could be the one Duvalier's henchmen are looking for, and that is far more attractive than giving her up to a mere priest!"

Gabrielle looked at her friend incredulously; she underestimated Rochelle. Although she buffered her scheme with the premise it was all for the sake of winning over Dom, she also had a large stake with Duvalier—a holdover from her dangerous voyage from Morocco to Paris.

Gabriel's motives were purely selfish: eliminate the competition from all areas of her life and rid herself of the charade. Cherise pulled too much attention from everyone around her with her sniveling good humor and supposed pureness of heart. She was sick of it!

Even Dom had been like a lovesick cow, pining away since Cherise had been gone. Yes, it was far better to cash in from the priest than Duvalier because the priest would take her far away. And besides, Dom would feel honor bound to *rescue* her from the clutches of someone like Duvalier. She would be free of her pact and any wrath he might have would be directed at Dom.

Didn't Dom say she had a very ill brother? That would send her back, if nothing else.

No, she would not play along with Rochelle even though it was tempting since Rochelle thought Gabrielle less cagey or intelligent. Muttering under her breath, Gabrielle said, "There is not time to worry about my superiority over this dance hall whore. I'll just have to maneuver around and find Cherise myself before she is cast over to Duvalier!"

Wondering what she would look like and remembering the comments about the brightly colored hair, she set about making her way to the dressing rooms.

Escape

CHERISE STIFLED THE scream. Using every ounce of willpower she could muster and unable to move for a few minutes, she pulled herself together. Shaken to the core, she gained strength from the sheer desire to fight back. She would not let them have their way!

"I will show them I'm not so easily fooled! There can only be one reason Gabrielle is guiding them to me. She has made a pact with Duvalier or one of his followers. Her motive for helping Father Pierre certainly could not be altruistic. Perhaps I can isolate Father Pierre and get a message to him." Defiantly, she declared that "under no circumstances will I leave with him though!" Cherise made up her mind to follow Gabrielle from the loft above until she could see the father once again. Somehow, she would get word to him.

Would he betray her? If she told him in the note not to give her away, she had to believe he would keep her secret. But how could he throw his lot with the likes of Gabrielle? Perhaps the nun's facade had convinced him she was to be trusted.

Where did Dom fit in this equation? Had she ever totally trusted him? It was strange, his story of how he happened to be managing the shop. Was it her naivete that freed him to build his story? *No*, she silently cried. *I cannot believe he would use me this way.*

"Oh, Lord," she cried, "help me to find my way!" The lump in her throat caused her to stifle a sob. "Help me, God, I beg of you!" she cried.

It was at that moment that the solemn priest entered the room where she had been hiding and knelt to say his prayers. Praying to the Holy Father, Father Pierre begged for help in finding his beloved Cherise. As he began his lament, a small voice whispered behind him, "Father, forgive me for I have sinned. I am unworthy of God's love and…" Turning suddenly, Father Pierre almost dropped his rosary. There standing behind him was the vision he had prayed for—even though she looked like a dance hall girl.

He swooped the trembling Cherise into his arms. "Oh, my dear Cherise, we were so worried, and when Dom wrote me of your supposed whereabouts, I had to come find you. Let me look at you!"

"Father, Father," she cried with joy. "I am so sorry to have made you worry." Hesitating slightly, she quietly said, "It's just that, well, it's complicated, and I am just a foolish girl."

Brushing her comment aside, he said, "We must find the others and let them know you are safe."

"No! No…you can't!"

He could hear the panic in her voice, almost a wail of desperation. It stopped him in his tracks; the reality of her situation and the vulnerability she must feel gave him a new level of understanding. Holding on to her, he soothingly said, "My dear sweet Cherise, they were only trying to help me find you."

"But you don't understand, Father Pierre, Gabrielle has made a pact with the devil himself, Duvalier, and you have led her straight into my hiding place!" she cried.

"It was she who led us to you. Dom and I both wanted to find you. Dom knew only of bits and pieces from Gabrielle, and it was he who alerted me the necessity of finding you to save you from yourself, my dear."

With that, Cherise slowly turned to look into his eyes, the reflection of a man of the cloth shouldering the weight of one whose flock had gone astray.

The realization pained her. "You think me a lost woman, don't you, Father?"

"Oh, my little one, I am not holding judgment of you. You will always be my sweet little Clarice."

At the sound of her given name, she flung herself into his arms, sobbing once again. "It isn't what you think. You must trust me. Yes, there are those here who would do me harm, as also in Dom's world. There may not be a safe place for me, but as long as I'm here, the world looks upon me as one of the many *invisible* women.

"It was enough for a while to give me the freedom to work toward my ultimate goal—clearing my family's name. Now with this parade of so-called friends and associates, I fear my identity may be compromised and…" Her voice was now rising to a crescendo. Just as suddenly, the father cut her short.

Angrily he spoke to her. "There are others to think about, Clarice. You can't always act as a solitary individual without responsibilities to those who love you! Have you not wondered about your brother the past few months?"

As he spoke, it pained him to think of what he must tell her. Softening now, he took her by the hand and led her to a quiet corner where they would not be readily seen and he could discuss the situation with Andre.

"Father, tell me please. What is wrong with Andre? I'm so sorry that I have been self-absorbed. Tell me he's okay, please, Father."

Even now as he agonized over what needed to be said, Father Pierre knew that the words he would speak would forever alter Clarice again. If God could only change the course on which young Andre was destined, he would do everything in his power to heal him.

"Tell me, Father. I beg you!"

"Sit down, Clarice." With that, he gently pulled her to the bench in the corner. Taking her small delicate hands into his and looking into her eyes, he started to deliver the news that would change the way she looked at him. It was no small feat, but he must tell her the truth.

"Andre has a form of consumption and has been ill for a very long time. At first we hoped for the best and did not want to worry you. In fact, we considered sending Andre to a sanitarium in Milano known to do wonders for prolonging life of the…well, terminally ill."

"Terminally ill? Father, please no, not Andre! Tell me he will be well in time."

"Andre is not in pain, Clarice. You must take comfort in that. He is now in the final stages in a comatose state and looks closely at the face of God." He said the words as gently as he could, but there was no easy way to deliver such news.

The low guttural animal sound that emanated from her shocked even him. God help them all. Where was the mercy? Where was his God now?

Surely, God would give Clarice the strength to weather the loss of her brother.

"I must see him!" she gasped. "I must see Andre!"

He didn't have the heart to tell her it might be too late. Instead, he cradled her in his arms, finding strength in the knowledge that he might be her only refuge for a long time to come.

Just then, the group arrived en masse, a mélange of people each with their own agenda. One or two of them clearly had designs on taking advantage of the bereft young woman.

Dom, the self-appointed leader of the pack, was clearly preparing to take charge of Clarice's life for the time being. Speaking to the priest, he said, "Father Pierre, I will take the responsibility for making sure Clarice is out of this environment and back into sane society. After all, we have much catching up to do."

The priest made a decision at that moment altering the course of her life for years to come. "The journey is over, and my dear little Clarice is too distraught to speak to any of you this night. It is enough that she was tracked down like an animal and I bear some of the blame for this, but she will not be exposed to any more humiliation from any of us."

Before they could reply, Father Pierre spoke directly to Dom and Gabrielle. "Thank you for your help, Dom, and your kindness to Clarice—Cherise as you know her—while employed with you. Gabrielle, if it hadn't been for your information, Dom would not have reached out to me, and for this I'm grateful. But now it's time for Clarice to heal and the road will be long."

"But when can I see her, Father?" Dom asked. "I have much to say to dear little Clarice."

"Now I am taking Clarice to an inn to rest and will speak with you tomorrow of my plans. Please do not interfere this evening."

Dejected, Dom nodded ever so slightly and turned to walk away. It didn't matter that he loved Clarice; in the father's eyes, he was the vessel for the danger she now faced.

Burying his face in his sleeve to hide his emotion, the once gallant yet weak man finally came to the realization his selfishness may have cost him the love of this selfless young woman. He might never forget his lapse with Clarice, but he wouldn't forgive himself if what he worked so hard for was sabotaged by his own actions. There was no denying securing the Pontifi fortune still held by Duvalier had become his obsession.

Clarice would have to come around. He was narcissistic enough to believe she could not live without him and, in time and with enough prodding, succumb to his charm. He had not pursued her when she was in the shop, allowing her the chance to learn and grow on her own accord.

He would go away now, but this journey wasn't over. It would be easy once he had her out of Father Pierre's clutches. In the meantime, he would find a way to speak with Cherise and tell her of his feelings.

Looking from a distance, the priest thought he detected a skip in the once-dejected man's step. There was something about Dom he had never trusted and that hadn't changed. Now he had more important things to deal with, namely, Clarice's mental health, her welfare, and not only her future but also that of the entire convent back in La Nuaz.

Vanished

For what seemed like the tenth time, the staff at the Folies Bergère assured Henri of Miss Cherise's departure with a priest and that all had appeared to be of free will. The only real information they could give him was that it appeared there was some connection from inside, through their own Rochelle, to a woman in the group named Gabrielle.

Henri was shrewd enough to know there were other ways to extract the information he needed, plus he had an insider who could filter through the gossip, delivering just what he needed to find Cherise.

While Henri's motives in looking for Cherise were to help her, others had motives more deceitful. The noise from the night she disappeared, now over a month ago, had not escaped the ears of the manager, Monsieur Gerard. He knew how to manipulate Rochelle to find out everything he needed. And now he was most interested to see that Monsieur Bonnebeau was still digging for information, giving him a new possibility to find a way to cash in.

The activity Cherise's disappearance had created was remarkable in that it was centered on what some would consider an onerous woman, one who, after all, was only a dance hall girl. It infuriated Rochelle. After all, she, as the reigning queen of the burlesque, should not be subjected to imbecilic, incessant questions. Why would they think she would know anything about the peasant girl; furthermore, why would she care the girl had left?

Even Gabrielle had been insulting with her stupid questions and insinuations. Of course, she did not know what had happened to Cherise and did not care. She had led Gabrielle to the girl only because it was better for Rochelle with her gone. Monsieur Gerard even threatened her if she didn't give up the information.

The only one who had been halfway decent, in fact very nice indeed because of the money he gave her, was the little-known pianist from the late-evening performance, Xavier. She decided on the spot to give him the little tidbits she had remembered of a conversation she overheard between the priest and Cherise.

There had been too much pressure, expecting Raoul to come any day to check up on her and find the girl. Rochelle was almost certain Cherise was the one Duvalier had been seeking. It wasn't her problem, and she made sure to distance herself from the disappearance. Besides, the reward would not be good enough considering Raoul would only take advantage of her and keep the money. No, she would not play his game anymore.

When Gabrielle had come to see her a couple of months ago, it was a hidden blessing by a pseudo nun—an irony in and of itself! The farther away Cherise got, the happier Rochelle became.

In the meantime, Henri was doing his due diligence and closing in on just the right information to track down the one who made his heart race. It amazed him this young woman could extract such emotion from a seasoned bachelor such as he. If in the affairs of the heart there is one special lover, he may have just let that one go, at least for the short term.

He had vast resources of wealth and connections he could easily tap into, but something kept nagging at his resolve. It was curious, but there was a part of him that respected her wish to hide her true identity. At a deeper level, he understood her need to keep him and any who would interfere at arm's length. It only seemed fair to give the girl freedom to choose her best life as much as he would have wished it to be with him.

Yes, he would spare her the trappings of his wealth and power by allowing her to be free. It was a decision which caused him considerable pain, but it was in her best interests. There was no denying his affection for Cherise, and given time, he fancied she might have had an honest desire for him.

It was in this moment of clarity that he made his choice: a quick break. Summoning Charles, he barked the orders, "Take all the intelligence you have gathered and put it away in a safe place, hidden from all and not the least of me. Under no circumstances are you to allow access to this information! Is that understood, Charles?"

Stunned, Charles reluctantly agreed. "Yes, sir. I will guard the secret with my life, but wouldn't you at least like to know some of her history or where she might hide?"

"No, the book is closed on this story. Whatever happens will, in spite of my efforts. There are still too many people who know from whence she came, and my hope is her guardian will keep her safe far away from where she is known. Any knowledge of her whereabouts at this time will just create more danger for her."

Charles knew the finality of his employer's tone, one which gave no room for discussion, and any attempt he made would fall on deaf ears. It troubled him because he could see the love Henri had in his eyes for the strange young woman.

Henri never told him to discontinue his own search. He knew there would come a time when it was vitally important to his employer. Charles would be ready to help. Everything he had, and his very life, he owed to the benevolent Henri.

In the meantime, away in his hiding place, Bernard paced as he read and reread the wire from Father Pierre. Troubled, he continued his back-and-forth movement around the perimeter of the large room. To a stranger, he might have seemed a curiosity—the giant man, slightly bent with age, able to move so quickly around and around the room.

Feelings of joy were intertwined with waves of fear for his little Clarice. What had happened in Paris for Father to break open Bernard's hiding place? He knew the dangers of contacting the gentle giant, and yet he must have felt it necessary to take the risk.

If Bernard hadn't been so excited about the news of Clarice's imminent arrival, he would have been more troubled. Whatever happened, they would deal with it—directly and swiftly! He had a few complications of his own to deal with but would make quick haste in dealing with them.

Above all else, he would make a safe haven for her where no one would find them. He would give immediate notice to his employer but only that he must take a leave of absence for health reasons. Never trusting anyone but Father Pierre, Bernard had built an insular existence with his new family.

He was keen enough to understand that Duvalier's spies were everywhere and, quite possibly, had infiltrated his current employment. If it all seemed paranoid, so be it. With little maneuvering, he could quickly move his base of existence and easily set up a secure place for Clarice.

They would go to his safe place. It was the one area where Duvalier would never look, and for that reason, it housed the great secret therein: the Chevais family seal's exact location in Switzerland.

The priest had once asked him why not destroy this object of man's greed and be done with it. If the elusive seal was disposed of in its entirety, there would always be unanswered questions to provoke the hunters to keep searching, leaving no earthly rest to the hunted.

No, even the hunter's best odds of finding the holdings and remaining wealth would be to allow Clarice the opportunity of turning twenty-one years of age. After that time, she would lead them to the fortune or other methods would be used to force her hand.

Bernard could thwart those attempts by keeping Clarice in a hiding place, removed from any of her former homes and cut off any connection with her current base of friends. It would be difficult but necessary for the time being. Even Father Pierre would have to be left unaware of her exact whereabouts.

Picking Up The Pieces

It had weighed heavily on him, the knowledge Andre was dangerously ill with little hope for a cure. So much so he almost broke rank to race back to the convent once again.

After much convincing, Father Pierre recognized the current situation might just force him to release Andre into Bernard's care. They could not risk Bernard's appearance among them, so Father did agree to try moving Andre to the new location. If Andre could be moved, bringing him with them was the only choice left to make. If they could keep Andre alive long enough, nursing him would give Clarice something to live for beyond her current obsessions.

It was all so strange, not so much the vendetta she still carried against Duvalier but more so the twists and turns in her route. He did not doubt her ability to come to grips with the person who had been Clarice; however, the road might be long. It was most fitting that through the melodrama that had become her life, she would end up becoming one of the nurturers and not the nurtured.

Bernard would make sure both of the Pontifi children would thrive in their new environment and perhaps even take back their rightful place in Paris. There was no thought in his mind of Andre's imminent demise, an idea too foreign for him to even consider.

First things first, he must prepare for Clarice's arrival with Father Pierre and then quickly lose any of the curious along the way. He had it all worked out, and even the priest had marveled at the expediency with which Bernard made all the arrangements.

It was agreed that after he deposited Clarice, they would work out a plan for Andre, which first included his move to a sanitarium run by monks. There, Bernard had friends who would assist with the nursing and care in order to strengthen Andre for the move to the safe house.

The monks knew how to cure all manner of illness, and consumption was no exception. The strange herbs and spices they used were thought to work magic on even terminally ill patients.

Bernard feared for Andre, but if there was any hope at all, this might prove to be their best chance. Even Clarice in her current mental state would have to feel positive about the chances for Andre.

The time was right; they would have the pieces of their lives put back together again. He was certain!

At that moment, he spotted the carriage with Father Pierre and what was once his lovely Clarice coming around the bend. "Sacrebleu! What has she done to her hair? It does not look like my little Clarice…just a pitiful girl."

Eyes cast downward, the once-vibrant young woman had lost her battle with the ghosts. Dark circles ringed her eyes, giving her the look of a street mime. The wild mane of hair was fighting with her at the moment; several strands blew into her eyes while the rest swirled around her neck.

Deep in thought, she ran through her recent litany. "When does it all end? How can I live with the knowledge that I let my brother down not once but twice? Is there any person as low as me? What of my lusts and those still remaining? How can I ever look Bernard in the eyes?"

The carriage pulled up to the back of the hostel, and there she could see her beloved Bernard looming like a bear waiting for his missing cub to come back into the den.

Her heart beat faster as her time of reckoning approached. "What will he think, Father? Does he know where I've been?"

"No, Clarice. There is no need for you to explain to Bernard. It will be your choice whether to tell him or not. Mark my words, it will not change his feelings or love for you. I must have a word with him alone first."

At the priest's words, a feeling of calm came over Clarice. It was at this point an inner dialogue began much like that time in the garden when she came to confront her demons and gained the courage to move out of her cloud of despair.

There had been the angel bringing the voice of her father, Augusto Pontifi, a divine intervention perhaps. This time Clarice had a clear vision of the woman she was to become. Sitting in the carriage while Father Pierre greeted the anxious Bernard, she began to think about the future.

Why should I be afraid to embrace the love that is so freely given? There has always been a deeper purpose for my actions. The time has come for me to embrace my family, absorb all the love they have to give and move on to completing my mission in life.

It does hurt me to know I have neglected Andre, but sometimes the choices we must make are for the greater good! By tasting freedom, even though tainted, I have found my inner strength, and whatever else I accomplish in my life can be attributed to my growth as a woman.

There are no fears from which I must run and hide. If I must be stored away like some hidden chattel, then it will be temporary! I will live my life as I see fit and, along the way, accomplish those goals which are of value.

My first mission will be to help my frail brother become well and all else will wait. After which, I will make certain my family will never be hurt again even if it means giving up everything.

Yes, I can take the power away from those who are intent on hurting us. Once I have secured the family, I will begin my quest in earnest to assist the plight of women in France! The revenge for the Pontifi family is not mine to take.

To the amazement of Father Pierre and Bernard, a calm and collected woman stepped from the carriage. Bernard was now transfixed by the transformation of the dejected-looking woman who had arrived just minutes earlier.

The hair was still wild-looking, but the eyes belied the appearance. "Oh, Bennie, how I have missed you," Clarice declared. "You are a sight for sore eyes." With that remark, she laughed and everyone else did too, breaking the tension from a few minutes ago.

"My sweet little girl, or should I say young woman, I have counted the hours since Father Pierre wired me." With that, he lifted her up into his big arms and gave her one of his famous bear hugs until she gasped for breath.

"Oh, I'm sorry, Clarice. I'm so excited to see you! You are safe, little one!"

"Ah, Bennie, my transformation has already begun, and you mean well with your protective ways! I do feel loved and secure with you, but no longer afraid for I have a deeper purpose driving me. Never will I be imprisoned by anyone for being who I am." Pausing, she continued, "You do not have to fear for me, gentle giant, for I am now an independent woman. Bennie, even if you knew it could be a difficult and risky challenge trying to make an impact in people's lives, wouldn't you always take the risk?"

Both men looked at her in stunned silence. Father Pierre was the most surprised at the change. There was no denying a woman was standing amid them. A sense of deep pride warmed Father Pierre as he beamed at his long-time charge.

Perhaps he could fear less but to fear not would be folly in spite of the bravado Clarice displayed. At the very least, he would remain cautious and expected Bernard to watch over her carefully.

As if on cue, Bernard piped in, "Be that as it may, Clarice, we still must exercise caution if only to protect the others around us. It would be folly to throw caution to the wind, wouldn't you say?"

"Of course it would, Bennie. What I meant to say is you will not have to worry for my mental state or how I embrace life going forward. Certainly, I will not be foolhardy, and my first priority will be to see after Andre until he is well enough for me to leave."

Father Pierre spoke up, "Clarice, my dear, you know he is very ill and you remember the conversation we had in Paris. Because of his condition,

Bernard and I have arranged for him to move into the St. Bonaventure Monastery where he can have around-the-clock attention from the monks."

"But, Father, I can take care of him. It will be much better for him to be with us at Bennie's safe house!"

"She is right," Bernard spoke up. "We have a better chance of his survival with Clarice nurturing and caring for him. I am prepared to give him my full attention too."

"Very well, but do not forget you will be keeping them safe at the same time, Bernard."

"Do not fear. I can handle those duties with the utmost of confidence. I'll arrange for one of the monks to come to us and bring the herbs and spices which will make Andre well."

"Clarice, what if Andre does not improve? Are you willing to accept you did all you can for him?"

"Yes, Father, I am more prepared now than I have ever been. If Andre has only a few months, weeks, or days left, I will make sure they will be the most special time for him, and in that quest, I can take comfort. Is there anything more important?"

"You have grown up, my beautiful Clarice!" With those words, Bennie put his massive arm around her and guided his protégé to the waiting carriage. For the first time since before the death of her grand-mère, he was satisfied his *little girl* would be just fine.

PART EIGHT

The Plan

As THEY APPROACHED the humble-looking dwelling, Clarice could see the smoke coming from the chimney. The cabin appeared to be made entirely of stone—a small fortress nestled behind what appeared to be a series of small hills juxtaposed along a natural ridgeline.

It was built that way, Bernard explained, to keep intruders at arm's length and give the inhabitants plenty of warning of any approaching visitors—welcomed or not.

She gazed in amazement at the quaint little cabin, wondering all the while how Bennie could always foresee every possible twist and turn in their lives. Giving him her undying gratitude could not begin to compensate for what he had endured for Clarice and Andre.

That he blamed himself for their parents' deaths was certainly a travesty of the worst kind. He had given so much in trying to save them all yet could not. Clarice knew he agonized over every detail, again and again, each night until he would finally fall into an exhausted sleep.

The demons were kinder to her now or perhaps she had grown beyond them. It was time to make further plans, and as soon as Andre was well, she could proceed. It gave her a moment of excitement to think of all there was yet to experience.

She had been quietly contained long enough and could no more resist the outburst than a bloom bursting open when exposed to the heat of the sun. "Bennie, is that our new home? It looks so inviting and yet mysterious all at the same time. I can't wait to busy myself in the ways of making it a home for all of us! It has been a long, long time, and we won't waste another minute of it. There is so much I must do!"

Bernard chuckled at the raw enthusiasm and promised quietly not to impede his protégé's desires to undertake a little homemaking. His little surprise notwithstanding, it was his normal penchant to take charge and assign servants to their various tasks, but it would be interesting to see what Clarice did to define her surroundings. It certainly couldn't hurt and would help her to heal.

He had been surprised at how quickly she rebounded from the fiasco in Paris. After a couple of days traveling to his special hideaway, there had been ample time to discuss her newfound freedom from the past. Any ghosts she had stored were quickly exorcised as she and Bennie renewed their well-grounded ties to each other and the past.

"Bennie, do you believe that God puts us each here for a purpose beyond one of self-gratification?"

"It's a heavy question you ask, Clarice, but I will give you my short answer. If we all were of a grander purpose, there would be no wars, strife, or hardships. Love would abound and every face would have a smile.

"But think of this, if you have no evil, how can you have goodness? What becomes the measure of goodness, and how would you know the difference? Even more important, who would be left for you to save with your mission?" He chuckled as he said this and saw the confused look on Clarice's face.

"Why do you mock me?" an indignant Clarice demanded.

"Ah, my dear, I am only teasing you for fear you will lose your sense of reality. You have a noble mission, but as in all undertakings done in the name of God and rightness, we can become too serious and lose our perspective on the end goal. It is important for you to recognize those pitfalls along the way. You can tackle your life's passion and still have enjoyment and pleasure from life. Do not let your path stray too far from what is real and tangible, like a husband and children, for example. You have to trust your core values, those taught and also inbred from your parents. As long as you have the trust, you will never have to worry about losing your way."

"As always, Bennie, your wisdom is sound. I will incorporate your words into my daily prayers for guidance."

The carriage pulled up to Bernard's hideaway cottage just as a couple of eyes peered out from window, from the face of a welcoming committee of one. "What do you call this place?" asked Clarice.

The committee of one burst through the door at that moment and exclaimed, "Welcome to the Pontifi Manor, Miss Pontifi!" The shock of hearing her name silenced Clarice momentarily. Unable to respond, the portly old woman feared she had committed some faux pas and quickly grabbed the unsuspecting young woman in a warm embrace.

"Why, why, thank you, Miss…uh, I don't know your name."

"I am Patrecia—Bennie's wife."

Another surprise! Her eyes widened as she looked over at Bennie just in time to see the look of endearment in his eyes as he acknowledged Patrecia's presence. Ever the circumspect manservant, he did not move to embrace his obviously much-loved wife.

Glancing over at Clarice, he cautiously made the formal introduction. "Patrecia, please meet Miss Clarice Pontifi. Patrecia and I were married two years ago but have known each other since we were young. Now we can all catch up later, but Patrecia, be a dear and fix us some tea, would you? I'm going to show Clarice to her room." It was a subtle way for him to usher his wife out of earshot.

Curiosity no longer contained, Clarice had to find out about this new development. "Bennie, when were you going to tell me of this good news?" she asked.

It did not escape Bernard that she said good news. "I have not had the opportunity to tell you of my great news, Clarice. There were more urgent issues to deal with and, well, it seemed frivolous to bask in my own contentment with the serious decisions yet to be made."

"Oh, Bennie, I am so very happy for you. She's lovely and seems so right for you."

As expected, the two women became fast friends, and the addition of Patrecia proved to be a godsend. With Andre arriving in five days and the monk, Brother Ange, who was selected to help assist the ailing boy, arriving in three to four days, having another trusted advisor for Clarice eased some of his burden. There was much to do and so little time.

His mission now would be threefold: keep the Pontifi dynasty safe from harm, support Brother Ange in bringing Andre to wellness, and set the stage for Clarice's freedom and ultimate return to Paris. Wouldn't she be surprised to know his forward thinking? He chuckled at the thought.

Clarice's Plan

Several days passed as the group anxiously awaited Andre's arrival. The monk, Ange, had arrived three days after Clarice, and she had been fascinated by his herbal concoctions. The highlight of his medicine making came when he broke silence long enough to tell her of the healing powers of one particular brew, and yes, after much pleading from Clarice, it would cure her brother. Dare she dream of it, Clarice wondered.

It was the fifth day when Andre's carriage finally rounded the turn at the base of the hill. Robes flapping in the air, two monks sat perched upon the carriage seat, directing the horses to slow up. There was a feeling of euphoria in the cabin upon Andre's arrival, Clarice caressing his hands and wiping his brow as she whispered words of love to her brother. Out of a coma for the past two weeks, he looked much better than she expected and wondered if the few days at the monastery had already begun to work their magic.

Their reunion was bittersweet, a by-product of the years of longing for his sister's touch. Rather than embrace Clarice with his whole heart, Andre held himself in check, waiting like a wounded animal to see when she planned to leave him again. Physically weakened by his disease and emotionally drained from the times his sister abandoned him, Andre could no longer initiate the display of affection so willingly given in the past.

True to her nature, Clarice worked her own magic, and although Andre was reluctant at first, she managed to weave her way back into his good graces. Fearful yet hopeful, he could not hold back his unbridled affection for his sister. His very nature was one of goodness and mercy. He could forgive and possibly even forget in time.

They doted on Andre, the team of Clarice, Bennie, Ange, and Patrecia, watching as the life seeped back into him. Time passed slowly, but each day the young man grew stronger as the dutiful Brother Ange worked his magic with the potent herbs and spices brought from the monastery. Andre could sit up in bed for periods of time, and the relentless coughing that marked his malaise started to subside.

Clarice was certain her brother was growing stronger. All the while, the sun moved out of the sky more slowly as the early buds of spring came peeking through. The skies were brighter, and the days were magically moving into the evening hour.

But as Andre improved, she experienced a sense of unease. The March winds were beginning to blow, and she could feel her restlessness building. Pacing became her only outlet, and with the last of the winter snow melting, she could finally venture outdoors. The wilderness had a way of beckoning her to come and mingle with the freshness of the dew's breath in the early morn. It always amazed Clarice how clear her thoughts became when outside with nature.

It was evident Andre was on his way to being cured and didn't require the attention from his older sister he once had. She had the shell of her plan already crafted, but filling in the details required much more thought and walking the property would be just the right fix.

Bennie had cautioned her to be realistic about her plans, and although she believed in his good sense, it was time to finish what she started, but in a way that could have the optimum results. After all, she had been here four months now and it was time to look forward.

She paced relentlessly for the next couple of weeks. How was she to tell Bennie, her guardian angel? He had been watching her and Clarice sensed it, understanding the connection they had. Leaving would hurt the kind and gentle giant, but what was becoming very clear was the intense pain she felt every time her mind moved forward to that day of departure.

"Oh, I cannot go on like this, pacing and walking, constantly moving to keep from facing the obvious truth. I must tell Bennie of my plans." A determined young woman marched into the house that evening, planning to bare her soul to the one man who knew her like a book. She also trusted him as she did Father Pierre, but the father never totally understood her complexities the way Bennie could.

As she opened the front door, Bennie was there to greet her. "Bennie, we have to talk!"

"Ah, yes, my dear Clarice. I could see this coming just as the winds were blowing to the East. Come with me into the library where we will be undisturbed." Bennie left to bring them some hot tea and give her a moment to collect her thoughts.

The comfortable room did nothing to dispel Clarice's feelings of anxiety. Warm and enveloping, the room had a shabby elegance to it. Weather-beaten antiques and comfortable overstuffed chairs covered in leather crackled with age filled the room. An ancient Oriental rug sat squarely in the center. A blaze was roaring in the fireplace to quell the chill in the room at the end of a blustery day.

She could feel her cheeks burning, a combination of the wind chafe and the quick warming from the chill outdoors. The pit forming in her stomach from the conversation about to ensue might have something to do with it too, she thought. "I might as well get this over with," she half mumbled.

Bennie returned with tea and crumpets. Just perfect for their summit, she thought. "Thank you, dear Bennie."

"You are fearful, Clarice. I can see it in your eyes and hear it in your voice. Do not fear telling me your plans, for I've known this day was coming soon."

With those words, he could hear her breathe a sigh of relief.

"Oh, Bennie, you know how I love you and Andre. I'm also very fond of Patrecia. It's just that I have much to do and little time to accomplish my tasks."

"Tell me of your plans, Clarice." Bennie settled back into the largest of the leather chairs, making himself comfortable, yet staying attentive to what Clarice was about to say.

"I must leave as soon as it can be arranged, Bennie. Andre is on his way to wellness, and he has all of you to help him now. Besides, we have made a pact that no matter where we travel, we will always be of one heart."

She waited for a response, and when none came, she continued, "My plan always had its roots in helping others less fortunate and finding a way to eliminate Duvalier's hold on our family. There may be a way to take away his power by taking away the object of his obsession—our supposed remaining fortune. He does not need to know there is little."

Continuing in a rapid fire, Clarice half pleaded, "The only way possible to even plan in earnest is to be in Paris, which will allow me to explore all my available options as well as draw Duvalier out in the open. And no, do not fear it will be some time before I'm ready for that bold move.

"After I witnessed the plight of many of my friends in the Moulin Rouge, I started thinking of how easily it would be for them to fall further into a life of depravity and despair. My heart was heavy listening to some of their stories and knowing I could help but did nothing. To establish a place of refuge for these disadvantaged women and those on the fringe of society, we could help change the direction their path might inevitably take. By providing a place for them, we can keep them from the dance halls and, even worse, working the streets."

"So, my dear Clarice, I hear you and am proud of your motives, but how does your plan protect you while you are pulling all this together? The minute Duvalier gets wind of any activity on behalf of the Pontifi-Chevais, he will lunge. And where will you stay during this planning phase? Have you thought through these details, my dear?" Bennie's eyes twinkled even though his heart was heavy. He too had been planning for this time.

Exasperated, Clarice lashed out, "Bennie, I don't have all the details but certainly have the will of the spirit and can find a way. Surely, Sister Mary will have some ideas for me, and perhaps we can explore those options together.

I trust her almost as much as I trust you. There are many good hiding places in Paris, and my disguises are many."

"It just so happens I too have a plan, Clarice. You see, a wise man once told me to expect the unexpected and you will never be caught off guard. While you were on the way back from Paris, I made some overtures to a couple of our mutual friends and also an old friend of mine."

"Why, Bennie, you are teasing me now."

"No, my dear, I knew it was only a matter of time before you would leave again. It is in your nature, much like the wise man I quoted, your father, Augusto Pontifi. You have the wanderer's spirit much like him, but he always expected the unexpected and, even though caught in a trap, had made plans for the end, understanding the danger whenever that might come."

"Tell me of your thoughts, Bennie. I will listen."

After spending a couple of hours together in the library, many plans had been drafted, some of which Clarice would follow and some to be discarded. Bennie did not need to know and worry unnecessarily. Her interpretation of what had been openly discussed and decided upon would have to remain flexible, just as she would.

"Come, Clarice, let's go feed our stomachs before we perish. We have had a good meeting of the minds, my dear!" Bennie was content. Clarice seemed to be agreeable to his slant on the plans, and even if she veered off the path some, he believed he could keep tabs on her.

Arm in arm, they marched into the dining room just as dinner was being served. The announcement was made to those at the table, and Clarice would tell Andre later. She was to leave a week hence.

The End of the Journey

Jackie (2005)

As Jackie sat staring out the window, random thoughts swirled in her head.

The similarity of this day reminded her of the one at the beginning of her journey.

It had been more than six months since her release from her own prison with a freedom of spirit she hadn't felt in over forty-five years. You could say Jackie had been reborn not only of the spirit but also of the flesh. If only others could understand what it's like to live inside the walls of your mind, unable to communicate or function as a normal human being.

Her broken body healed except for a few scars and the slight limp from a crushed left leg. She had endured many months of physical therapy, and even while in the coma, therapists would work her limbs to bring them back to full function. Yes, she had been given another chance, and for that, she was first grateful to God and then to the countless people who helped her.

Now she must repay her debt by finding a way to help others in need. It was part of the randomness of her thoughts, every day exploring a new avenue but not quite finding the right answers. Perhaps she should look back to Clarice and see the path traveled in her final move to Paris.

There were daily routines now that gave her a great sense of being part of the family again. In the beginning, each one of the children would take turns coming over to stay and help Craig. There had been so many friends streaming in and out it required one of them to handle the visitation flow. Controlling the amount of food coming into their kitchen had taken more than one of them.

They had looked at her strangely at first, Craig and the children. It finally didn't seem to matter to them whatever gibberish Jackie wanted to spout; they could still hold on to her and love her no matter what.

Doris made an appearance after Jackie had been home a couple of months and, in her usual fashion, took charge. The crusty old woman seemed to understand all of Jackie's gibberish, but then she had the connection too.

Jackie tried to explain the connection she had with Clarice during her *absence*. It was the one inspirational thread that kept her moving toward full consciousness and would become the foundation for the book she would write.

Of course, it seemed strange to others, but then wasn't the mind the creator of our reality? Perception became reality even in Clarice's world. It took an accident that almost killed Jackie to show her a different reality. She could do anything the mind could conceive.

It was funny now, thinking back to the day she was to give the speech, how those same words had floated in her mind while practicing in front of the mirror. Would she have changed that day if she could? An interesting thought and one she wasn't sure could be answered with a straight yes or no.

Today she was more aware, more alive, more in love, and, most of all, very appreciative of all that had been given to her in this life. Never again would she take life for granted. Understanding and enlightening others to live each day was her challenge now.

How could she help others find their inner souls and live life to the fullest and then enlist them in the quest to help those less fortunate? It was only when a person found inner understanding that he or she could begin to look outward.

Clarice had become a humanitarian at an early age, sacrificing many years of self for the betterment of mankind. Her idealism managed to follow her into adulthood, and the early tragedies gave her the strength of commitment and courage needed to pursue her course of action.

It would require some digging, but Jackie was certain there was information buried somewhere that would chronicle Clarice's moves and actions from the year starting 1894 and continuing to 1897.

In the meantime, she would continue to do her best to help the family adjust to the *new* her. It had been a bit of fun playing little tricks on them, hiding in her imagination and pretending to lapse back until breaking down in giggles. Sometimes they laughed with her, but most of the time they admonished her for giving them a new scare.

Finally, time had passed enough that seeing her every day and the strength she displayed gave them a sense of relief. They could relax and enjoy the renewed woman. Color had come back into her cheeks, her hair had been dyed a beautiful warm brown with golden highlights, much like before, and the eyes were brilliant. There was something definitely different in those eyes, still a beautiful hazel but with more depth.

Clarice's Encore

The days leading up to and the final departure had been filled with emotion; on the one hand, there was a sense of joy for the future but also one of dread for a past destined to follow.

Clarice had prepared her brother well with Bennie's help, and now all she had to worry about was what might be waiting in Paris. Her excitement was building, a curious mix of anticipation and fear of the unknown!

The plan was in place. Bennie was well-informed except for a couple items that, for his sanity's sake, she did not elaborate upon, and Sister Mary was ready for her arrival. Yes, she was coming back full circle.

On the day of her arrival, Sister Mary greeted her tenderly, wrapping her in one of the embraces for which she was famous. Clarice grinned at her, happily acknowledging how she missed the dear nun during her time away. There was a fleeting look of sadness in Sister Mary's eyes quickly to be replaced by her natural warmth and vibrancy.

Clarice's absence during the last six months in Paris had caused Sister Mary pain, a state for which she would have to bear the guilt and make amends. It was not so much for the deed but the lack of trust Clarice had in not confiding with her friend.

Her justification, if there was to be any, was in the difficulty of sharing details for a plan still in development. Her other reasons were not justifications but rather the shame of her dancing position at the time. There was no need in causing Sister any more anxiety where she was concerned. There had been enough already.

As it had been with Bennie, she was ready to confide all the details to Sister Mary, lest she put her through any more stress. With this cleansing though, it was especially important to share everything with the sister in the event Clarice lost her way or even her life. She was a vital connection as a trusted friend who could reach out to Bernard. There were details she didn't share with him and reasons for not doing so.

"We'll get you settled and have a nice long talk, Clarice." It was nice to hear her real name coming from the nun. "I'm sure there is much you have to tell me, and I'm eager to hear more of your plans. Bennie has shared some of them with me."

"I, too, am eager, dear Sister, to share all with you. This time, I will not hide behind a half-truth. My regret is deep at not keeping in touch with you during my, shall we say, dark period."

"Ah, Clarice, do not think too much of where you spent your time or to whom you gave counsel or not. You only have to answer to God, my dear, and He will forgive all your transgressions."

Clarice chuckled. "Sister Mary, I hope my transgressions were more those of a naive young woman out to save the world."

"Of course, my dear. Those of us who know and love you understand full well what you have had to deal with the past few years. In due time, you will even forgive yourself. Now why don't you unpack and settle in and I'll call you for dinner?"

Stars that could normally be seen by this time of night were shut out by the rapidly forming clouds, promising a spring storm to all those thirsting for the rain. As often happens, night had come abruptly, dumping its dark veil over the sunlit day, much like snuffing out the only candle bringing light into an otherwise dimly lit room.

Looking out her window, Clarice thought she saw a flame flicker across the courtyard below. She wondered if this was an omen—good or bad. A beginning of the end to the Pontifi story perhaps? Her thoughts were interrupted by Sister Mary's gentle knock on her door. "Clarice, dinner is served in fifteen minutes."

"Thank you, Sister Mary. I will be down promptly." Pushing aside her ominous thoughts, she finished her preparations for dinner. With great resolve, she made her decision to give the sister all the details later this evening. There would only be the two of them, and the time was right.

Why did she feel so anxious? Even if her friend tried to talk her out of it, she had made her choice. Upon entering the cozy dining room and smelling the aromas of Sister Mary's comfort food, she started to relax. As dinner progressed and the casual easy chatter that characterized her relationship with Mary became more subdued, Clarice sensed it was time.

She addressed Sister Mary, "As you know, I have come with a plan in mind, Sister, one which carries some risks. Although somewhat fragmented, I am resolved to follow through with the main ideas, so please do not try to dissuade me."

The nun was looking directly into her friend's eyes and could tell she was very serious in her mission. "Oh, my dear Clarice, I promise to hear you through and not utter a word if you will allow me to speak when you are finished."

"Fair, enough. You will hear all, and there is even more than what Bennie knows!" She noticed the frown on Sister Mary's face and took a deep breath before speaking. "My trust in you is no greater than my trust in Bennie, but you have an ability to understand what I'm to tell you without worrying needlessly."

"You give me a lot of credit, my dear," the sister offered as a last statement before Clarice began to unfold her plan.

"First, I must find a way to work back into the position at the shop with Dom, gaining his trust, of course with your help, Sister Mary!"

Sister nodded, staying true to her promise of silence. Gaining confidence and momentum, Clarice continued, "It is my plan to work my way back into a position of trust with Dom, charming him to win him over. As you already know, our friendship was strained when Dom allowed Gabrielle to gain his trust in the ruse of finding me.

"When I left Paris abruptly, he became angry, more for his loss of connection and easy access to the Pontifi fortune than his desire for me. Under the circumstances, I chose not to explain my time dancing at the Foles Bergère or my lack of communication with him. So when I left, there was no other choice but to cut off communication with him and everyone else, except you. We could not risk exposing Andre to anyone in the outside world, much less one with ties to Duvalier, an innocent victim or not." Mary was momentarily startled at Clarice's assessment.

"Knowing Dom, there is a good chance his ego might have been deflated as well, and it is his vanity I'm counting on to enable me to reenter his life. This time, it will be with deliberation, a chance to form a more intimate relationship." She glanced over at the sister, wondering if she was shocked at the direction the conversation had been heading.

If the sister found any of this information disturbing, her face never gave any indication. Clarice continued, "Of course, I will never marry Dom, but at least the activity will bring Duvalier out into the open to claim the rest of the Pontifi estate. My wish is to come to some agreement even if most of our worldly goods disappear. Dom can have whatever it is he now pines for and for which he is willing to give up his soul."

Sister Mary was surprised at the depth of understanding Clarice had gained regarding her erstwhile cousin. Although of the same blood, she had lost any semblance of trust in him during the events that transpired in their quest to find Clarice. He had strayed from the moral core of his family's values.

Clarice continued, "I will no longer be a slave to the material wealth which breeds the evil within man. It is important for me to retain only enough to start the work for which God has entrusted me. You know what my passion has become—to open the home for women in trouble and in need, like those unfortunate ones from the Foles Bergère. Life has dealt them a blow from which they can rise above if given a helping hand at a time when they are most needy. It's a difficult road, but one which they can travel with God's help. Watching them struggle not only inspired me but also gave me the strength to fight the demons which threatened to rob me of my senses. It was the love of others who saved me when I came so close to falling. You included, Mary. It is for these reasons I must follow this course."

Peering at the sister once again, Clarice noticed the tears in her eyes and look of acceptance on her face. "You do understand, don't you?"

Clearing her throat and gaining her composure, Sister Mary addressed Clarice, "My fears for you are small compared to the admiration I have for you and the work you are preparing to undertake. Yes, I will worry, but your mission is far more important than the trappings of living a life of well-meaning intentions with no accomplishment of acts."

She continued, "I will do everything in my power to help you along the way, and your mission will also be my mission!" With those words, Clarice wrapped her arms around the nun and openly wept.

It was a different reaction from what she expected, but one for which she was profoundly grateful. Now her path seemed even clearer, and having the sister's support buoyed Clarice's spirits.

The evening became one of joyous celebration with plans being made and even some girlish gossip to share in together for the pure fun of it! Perhaps it was one too many glasses of wine, but her world seemed to be opening up and even the sky appeared to be glowing with radiant splendor.

"Tomorrow will come soon enough, my dear, and we must have serious discussions by the light of day so we can make the most effective decisions."

"You're right, Sister Mary. I am tired and will see you in the morning. It has been a very full and rewarding day." Pausing one more time, she said, "Thank you for being there for me. I love you, my sister."

"God will bless and keep you, Clarice! Fear not for he is with you."

Dom's Return

THERE HAD BEEN enough time to prepare. At last count, there were 323 wooden pegs securing the wood flooring within the circumference of her bedroom at Sister Mary's, a calculation she made while walking back and forth hundreds of times the past week. Planning for her next move and with Sister Mary's urging, she allowed the practical side of her nature to win the first round.

Clarice would first transition into her new role by helping part-time in a home for wayward young women. As she became acclimated to the environment and her confidence increased, she would then approach Dom and ask for a second job in the shop. It would be hard for him to resist, she reasoned with Mary, because her knowledge of the history of the building and artifacts within would ensure Dom of a successful business.

Beyond the actual clerking job, Clarice also knew he couldn't resist moving closer to her again if for no other reason but to gain access to the remaining spoils of the Chevais-Pontifi fortune.

They had discussed the many pitfalls of what could happen if Dom had easy and immediate access into her personal life. It was for that reason the idea of first becoming entrenched in the job of helping disadvantaged women and possibly even starting classes at the university once again became her chosen plan of action.

Sister Mary knew Clarice was ill prepared for dealing with a man like Dom in an intimate and personal way. It would be all too easy for her to succumb to his charms and lose her way again, this time permanently. She might think of herself as an independent and strong young woman, but to a manipulative master player like Dom, she was no match.

This was the morning the carriage was to pick them up and transport them for their initial visit to Les Beaux Jardins de la Grâce, a home to help women in trouble. In spite of Clarice's protests, Sister Mary was also determined to help at the home. "But you do not have to worry about me, my friend. I'll be fine!"

"Silly girl, I have too much time on my hands, and after all, isn't this what a nun is supposed to be doing? After you described the despair and degradation these poor young women had suffered, it seemed preposterous not to help." Secretly, Mary hoped that, by staying close, she could limit the amount of exposure Clarice might have to find herself in trouble.

As much as she trusted her young friend, she worried about the bravado that could carry her deeper into a relationship with Dom and further danger. It would be difficult to keep him under control. After all, Clarice was a Chevais and Pontifi with the passions of the French and Italian blood coursing through her veins.

"Well, of course. How foolish of me to think otherwise! Please accept my sincerest apology, Sister Mary. I am even more excited now!"

"One more thing. Bennie has a friend, Charles Beauchamp, who has arranged for his carriage to pick us up. Do you know him, Sister Mary?"

"I'm afraid to say I've never met him, but if Bennie trusts him with your life, he must be exceptional!"

"The carriage driver's name is Frederic, a man of great discretion, also according to Bennie. It is a wonder how he manages to keep up with his friends on such a personal level." Clarice chuckled, thinking of the man who she loved as a father. It gave her a warm feeling to know the love of this man would always be with her no matter where they traveled.

As promised, the carriage arrived promptly at half past nine, and Frederic couldn't have been more efficient in his ministrations to the ladies.

It was odd, she thought. He had a familiarity, yet she didn't recognize him as anyone from her other time here. Curious yet if he was Charles's trusted driver, then who was she to question it?

"Monsieur Frederic, please extend to Monsieur Beauchamp my deepest appreciation for his assistance and for also allowing us to have such an able driver. Tell him we must meet someday."

"Yes, mademoiselle, I will be most happy to share your greetings with him. He speaks highly of your Bernard. You may rest assured he will make himself available to you as you need him."

During their visit with the director of Les Beaux Jardins de la Grâce, Frederic had steadfastly maintained his position outside the home. He had insisted on waiting and escorting them back to Sister Mary's house, much to Clarice's irritation.

The tour of the home reconfirmed Clarice's desire and resolve to move her passion in this direction, educating and ministering to the women in need. Adorned with pictures at every turn and colorful furnishings, albeit well-worn, it was obvious the staff had tried to give the women something from their own homes that they lacked.

Clarice already had a vision for making the home beautiful by enlisting and then guiding the residents to share in the design plan. With her ability to teach these skills, she already had one of her goals in sight.

She would give them the tools they needed to make a home and to teach the proper ladies' skill sets for their future lives. Yes, she could see it coming together, and as her imagination grew, so did her excitement.

Meanwhile, they made their way inside the dining wing where the kitchen emitted smells of freshly baked breads and cinnamon-laden pies, sending an invitation for all to join and share in the bounty of the home. The aromas reminded Clarice of earlier days in the manor.

Cheerful greetings and the warm welcome gave Clarice an instant feeling of homecoming. Although somewhat worn and shabby, it clearly represented a place of safety and love for the women housed therein. Yes, there was much she could do to help them.

They were chatting excitedly as they approached the carriage, and in her enthusiasm, Clarice started sharing her new opportunity with Frederic—a slip perhaps, but given from the heart.

He noted the information but said nothing, a learned skill passed on from his experience with his employer. It took years for him to work his way into Henri's good graces, and he was determined to find out everything he could without spooking the delightful young woman.

Although Frederic would not be the courier directly to Henri, he was a valued employee nonetheless. Charles screened all information shared with Henri and would be compelled to give Henri this latest scoop.

It had occurred to him Clarice might recognize his outline from behind, but so far he didn't think she noticed any similarities to the driver of the carriage the night she and Henri dined at the Le Grand Véfour. After all, it had been dark and he kept his face forward.

"Frederic, we have had the best visit within. My heart is so full of joy at what I'm about to undertake it makes me want to break into song," a giddy Clarice burst forth.

"Very nice, Miss Clarice and Sister Mary. And what, may I ask, will you be doing to help?" He couldn't resist the temptation to ask and it might be important for later.

"Sister and I will be working part-time in the home, teaching the young ladies how to manage their lives. We will help them with their studies, teach them how to be *ladies*, and give them the encouragement they need to go out into the world unafraid. It is so much more than the immediate care we will be providing. We will be building a platform from which they can dare to dream while developing the self-confidence to pursue those dreams to reality."

It was apparent this young woman had a passion to help others, and he could see why his employer might be taken with her. Troubling still was the way he had met Clarice, and Frederic wanted to make certain that no stone would remain unturned in his quest to find out all the truth about her past.

Charles, a man who rarely disclosed secrets, seemed to be content with his knowledge of the young woman and her background. Frederic still wanted to know a little more.

Delivering them safely back at Sister Mary's manor, he proceeded to make a side trip. It wouldn't do any harm for him to find out more of this Dom person. His ears might be old, but they could still hear, and the inferences he could glean came from many years of experience dealing with people. If there was anything of concern, he would be able to capture it within the first few minutes.

In another part of Paris, Dom was in his shop, preparing the books for his investor to dissect, after another unsettling day with very little trade. He hoped Duvalier would go easy on him because, after all, he had given him just enough information of Clarice to satisfy him, hadn't he?

It didn't feel right, but a man had to protect what was his and she left of her own accord. He was certain she would return; the time and day were unknown to him, but he had his feelers out even now. He had heard rumblings that Miss Clarice was in Paris at this very moment and staying at the home of Sister Mary.

He was a patient man, and the time was near when he would make his move.

First, he had to confirm the little tease's whereabouts and then have one of his hired men watch her every move. If she lingered too long before coming to him, he had his plan ready.

Admittedly, he let her get under his skin so that thoughts of her as his mistress sent waves of fever throughout his body. He pictured her naked skin, silky and smooth, touching his as the heat of the moment rolled over them, leaving her begging for more. He remembered the deep auburn hair, long and lustrous, imagining his fingers wrapped through the coils and pulling her tight to him. Of course, this was before the abominable behavior she had exhibited before leaving Paris.

Wasn't there a time, he questioned, when he would willingly have married Clarice? Undoubtedly, he had a painful moment remembering her sweetness. How could she have degraded him in the fashion of a common street woman? Oh, enough, he mumbled under his breath.

She proved to be just another wench, and I will have her bend to my will. It is all so perfect, a setup fit for the most appropriate revenge, along with gaining the rest of the Pontifi fortune, which rightfully belonged to him. Atonement was near.

Frederic couldn't help but notice the handsome young man, definitely a catch for any woman who would give him everything he wanted. There was something else about this man whom he instinctively knew was the mysterious Dom. If he could just engage him in conversation, Frederic was certain to pull more from this encounter.

"Excuse me, sir, where did this beautiful Louis the XIV armoire come from? What is this small engraved crest of arms inside the drawer? Can you give me a little information about this please?"

The sudden conversation coming from this stranger startled Dom. "Uh-oh, my apologies. I did not see you in the store." It was apparent Dom was angry rather than apologetic, a slip that did not escape the eyes of the wise old man. There was definitely a link between this Dom and Clarice; something very dark lurked in between. It was imperative he dig into this affair.

His question hung in the air like a trapped bumblebee searching for an escape. There would be no answer now. As if to reinforce his concern, a cloaked man, best described as fanciful, came in from the street and commanded Dom's attention. Duvalier, with no words spoken, had managed to create in his silence a dramatic entrance.

There was a moment, almost imperceptible yet inescapable to Frederic, where he could see the fear on Dom's face. He could feel the tension in the air and the smell of blood, a mixture of cold steel being tested under the weight of the executioner's blade as it sliced through living tissue.

Very disconcerting indeed, thought Frederic. His questions would have to wait for now as his concern for the fair maiden grew. His report back to Charles would contain his observations.

The Mystery

In her naivete, Clarice failed to recognize the many faces of greed at work in their quest to uncover the hidden documents detailing the remaining Pontifi fortune. These valuable pieces of her history would ultimately lead to the Pontifi treasures and land holdings. Her trust in Dom had been nullified a long time ago, but in her haste to pull together her plan, she neglected to factor in all the possibilities and elements which could influence the outcome.

No doubt Dom's charm had once captivated her and his persuasive manners could again convince her of his loyalty. Unknown to Clarice, however, was the significant influence Duvalier had over Dom. Somehow, he was involved, but she could not picture how or when he might show his face. There were too many pieces of the puzzle, and Clarice just wanted to be done with all of it.

It had been several weeks since she had begun her part-time work at Les Beaux Jardins de la Grâce, and the days had flown by quickly. The immersion into her new routines had been almost too easy, and Clarice sensed a growing restlessness. "Oh, why do I always yearn for the unknown, the mystery of that yet to come?" It was a curse she could not shake, the wanderlust inbred from her grand-mère. She had heard enough to know her proclivities for risk taking had been inherited from a long line of Chevaises.

This time she would be more careful. The Folies Bergère was an aberration, one that could have had grave consequences. Clarice could not allow such a misadventure to occur a second time. She owed those she loved a strong commitment to keep the covenant as proposed in her last meeting with Bennie.

It was time to make her move. After much deliberation, Clarice ventured out with a specific goal in mind, one that could have far-reaching consequences. She would do this alone.

Arriving at the shop, Clarice waited a few moments before making a move to enter. Taking a deep breath and gaining courage, she approached the front door with bravado only someone passionate for his or her mission could accomplish. As she entered the shop, she could see his outline at the rear of the store.

Careful not to startle him, she gently called out, "Dom, are you there? It's Clarice. I want to talk to you." She forced her voice to sound calm and easy. She had lost sight of him and carefully made her way to the back where, she recalled, his office was located.

She shuddered when thinking of the office, once a beautiful example of Marie's decorating genius and where she had spent many hours looking over ledgers and books. Now the stale smell of winter's smoke lingered within the layers of fabric hanging from the tall windows. A gray haze seemed to float above the artifacts, and beautiful old antiques gave way to occasional dust covers draped over the older pieces.

She could almost believe that it was now haunted by her ancestors. "Serves them right," she said out loud. Clarice perked up at the thought that even Ma Mère's spirit might be lingering in this place, perhaps waiting for her family to return and claim its rightful position within these walls.

At that moment, Dom came up from behind, startling Clarice. "What are you doing here, Clarice, Cherise, or whatever your name is today?" he snarled. If she was thinking he'd make this easy, she was very mistaken. He would use this opportunity to get what he wanted.

"Oh, Dom, you startled me! I did not want to frighten you."

"Frighten me? I think you have a fanciful idea of your power, my dear Clarice."

She wasn't quite sure if he had softened or was still playing her with his sarcasm. Cheeks burning from the sting of his words, she could feel her tenseness turn into anger, but Clarice would curb any thoughts of lashing out at Dom. This was not the time for her to become defensive or to invoke a sense of self-righteousness; no, this was a time to win him over for the good of her plan.

Softening her voice again, Clarice spoke, "Dearest Dom, we have much to discuss, and I beg you to allow me the chance to explain a few things in due time. Yes, I know it has been a long absence, but my reasons were sound."

He looked at her in wonder. Did she really think him so stupid as to not see through her ploy to charm him? Perhaps it would be fun to play her game to see where it led. He had his own ideas, but a little dalliance along the way would not interfere with his ultimate goal.

It had only been a few weeks since he had gotten word of her whereabouts; his people had done their job well. It was interesting that just now she came waltzing back into his life. Suspicions aside, he would have to consider whether there was any significance of the timing to his plans.

"Very well, Clarice. Why don't we start with your reason for being here? What could you possibly want from me or the shop for that matter? You can see the general state of disorder, and I doubt there is much here you'd be interested in!"

Seeing her opening, Clarice jumped at the chance to explain her motive for today's visit, and perhaps later she could tell him enough about her exit from Paris to satisfy his curiosity.

"Well, to be quite direct, I need to make some money for a project that is close to my heart—the support of Les Beaux Jardins de la Grâce, a home to help women facing starvation or worse." She stopped and quietly watched for any reaction on his face, but there was none. Perhaps he would be incapable of warming to her.

She quickly continued to keep from losing her nerve. "With my university studies and helping at the home, there are only enough hours to help a merchant part-time. I immediately thought of you, Dom, and the fondness we both have for this place." Looking around, it was obvious the shop needed a woman's hand.

Dom was still quiet, thinking through this new bit of good news. She had come directly into his domain, and he could take care of many of his problems all at once. With the Pontifi fortune right at his fingertips, he could anticipate the time when the name Duvalier would no longer haunt him. His constant, pathetic fear of the viperous old man would finally end. He would have it all: the treasures, Clarice if he so chose, and the end of the intimidation from his nemesis.

"As you may, Clarice, I could use some help here. Make yourself useful, and we will have a meeting later to go over your duties and my expectations." With that, he abruptly turned and walked away leaving her standing, bewildered but pleased at the news.

It seemed too easy but sweaty palms served to remind her of the reason for the initial fear at approaching Dom. She would be foolish to assume that he was going to be willing to let the past be forgotten and her disappearance as not a deliberate slap at him. But whatever else he was now, Dom could make her feel all soft inside and question why she could ever distrust him. At one time, he had been a trustworthy employee of one of Ma Mère's oldest friends, and for that, she must give him a small pass.

They had their meeting that afternoon, he outlining his expectations and her agreeing to the terms of employment. It seemed almost surreal, yet here she was in the shop, walking out with a new job and cautiously, a new excitement in her step!

It hadn't been easy to sit through Dom's nonemotional and cold assessment of her previous lack of experience with a real job. His insinuations of her potentially missed calling at what, perhaps, she might be best at; dancing half naked in front of lusting men, cut through her like a knife. She bit her lip until it bled but was determined to keep the meeting professional and show him she could rise above her past.

"Very well," he had said, "you can have the job!" It was at that point she jumped up and hugged his neck, dropping her guard and showing her lovable nature. It took him off guard for just a moment, but then the mask came back, covering his excitement at having her so close.

The days were full and each had their own routines, the latter taking Clarice just a few days in which to adapt. It was enough to keep sufficient space between them and continue with the status quo.

At times she could see him polishing and gently handling the artifacts as delicately as possible with love and admiration. It was during those times that she felt the connection to him. As much as she tried not to think about Dom, he was all too present in her mind. "I must stop this nonsense and get on with my job at hand. My plans do not include Dom and certainly the life I want to live!"

In spite of the constant battle she played with her mind, she was having great success with the home for displaced women. With Sister Mary's guidance and direct involvement, she felt comfortable the home was on the right footing and many young women would be helped to a better life.

Dom, in the meantime, couldn't help but notice Clarice's physical charms and beauty. He refused to think about how she had managed to get under his skin, simply putting it off to his own weakness of spirit. It was during one of the times they were thrown together on a cleanup project that he realized just how far she had gotten into his psyche.

She had been cleaning the frames of the paintings for several hours and they managed most of the time to ignore each other, Dom stopping occasionally to assist a customer.

It was after one of these intermittent breaks that he became aware she hadn't stopped for two hours. What could she possibly be thinking of all this time? His curiosity got the better of him, and he approached Clarice from behind.

"Clarice," whispered Dom, as not to scare her but he did, enough so that she practically fell back into his arms.

"Oh, you startled me. I was deep in thought and was not expecting you or anyone for that matter. Actually, I was quite oblivious to anything beyond my immediate vicinity." It was a little lie, but there was no sense telling him that her thoughts were mixed between Les Beaux Jardins de la Grâce and Dom.

There was something in her eyes that belied her thoughts. He couldn't control his emotions anymore and pulled her into his arms. With that one movement, he also tried to kiss her as she struggled to move away. Clarice's resolve to keep her distance failed as she gradually gave in to feelings of love and lust. Their lips met with such pent-up passion, long held in check, she had to muster the strength to pull away, gasping for breath.

"Clarice, I know you want me as much as I want you! We need each other and you need a man. I saw that in you from the time you were in the Foles Bergere'. You could not have danced and pranced the way you did without the lust, my dear."

The brutal way of his words served to douse the burning flames she had just minutes ago. It was just enough for her to come to her senses! God, what was she thinking? That he may have actually cared for her?

She tried to pull away, but it was no use. Dom was too strong for her, and he continued his assault upon her. "Stop fighting this feeling, Clarice. You know you want this too."

"Stop! Stop! You are hurting me, and I want no part of being your concubine, which is what you think me to be!"

At that moment, the bell signaled a customer's arrival. It was perfect timing as Dom would never allow anyone to see this side. "We are not through with this, my dear. You will at least listen to what I have to say." With that, he loosened his grip and she moved away.

"We will continue our little discussion this evening over dinner," Dom half sneered as he spat out the words.

A chill ran up Clarice's spine in contrast to the exhilaration she also felt; it threatened to overtake her common sense. *What am I doing?* she wondered.

It was too soon to allow this level of intimate contact knowing the inherent danger that awaited her. *Why am I so excited at the prospect of being wined and dined by a man clearly on a mission that could only lead to trouble?*

Thoughts of Henri burned through her as if a new torch had been lit. He was the first and only man who had swept her off her feet so suddenly as to have left her breathless and yearning for more. But hadn't he doused the fire as quickly as it had been lit? She was hopelessly caught up in the moment remembering how he had tried to make amends by assuring her it was only for her protection.

The truth was that she felt most alive and excited during these moments of heightened fear. Just thinking of Dom's motivation and her willingness to make the leap into the lion's den warmed her in ways only a man could. The Chevais curse was again extending its viselike grip, holding her until she either acted upon the desire it presented or managed to replace it with the common sense she inherited from her father.

Fortunately, thoughts of her father sufficed to calm the fire that Dom briefly had kindled. It had been a long time since she had that sense of anticipation over being wined and dined by a man, one who clearly was on a mission that could lead to trouble. Henri had captivated her once, and she managed to escape. Would she be so fortunate this time?

Of course, she was over dramatizing the situation. Hadn't she just had the same lascivious thoughts of him?

This might be a good time to simply have a serious discussion with him to explain the particulars of why she had been working as a dancer in the Foles Bergere'. She would expound on her sudden departure from Paris.

Her reasons for not reaching out to him prior to leaving or even shortly thereafter were more difficult even for her to understand. Should she say it was her shame at seeing him again after the joy she derived from the dance? God, she wanted to forget everything that had transpired. No, she would not allow her obvious weakness to intrude on their discussions and leave her more vulnerable.

Yes, I plan to talk to you, Dom, and you will be most interested in the proposition I have waiting for you at the right moment, Clarice thought.

Henri

CHARLES MADE HIS way into a rather stark-looking apartment building, so plain that it had appeared to be uninhabited for many years. It became almost transparent in its sameness, mirroring all the others on the avenue. If not for the beauty of the tree-lined streets and the obvious attention paid to the pristine exteriors, an outsider would have mistaken the area to be for those of lesser means.

Relaxing among low-hanging fruit trees within the courtyard of the otherwise bleak exterior, Henri was surrounded by lush greenery, the type normally found in the tropics. Birds of paradise were in abundance, along with their live-feathered friends peeking out of gilded cages, curious about all visitors who might wander in. A setting like this could be found only among Parisians of means, those whose fortunes would allow such extravagances.

The first hint of what waited around the corner came in the form of the relaxing smell of lavender with a subtle hint of mint. Those wonderful fragrances, coupled with the sound of the bubbling fountains, usually soothed Charles, but his mission demanded that he maintain a certain edge. He had been collecting information on the whereabouts of Mademoiselle Clarice ever since her sudden disappearance last May.

In spite of Henri's admonishment to the contrary, it was now time for Charles to bring him what Frederic had collected. Conveying this new information to his employer without alarming him would take all the resolve and energy he could muster.

Those who knew Henri understood his deep need to be one with his environment. His youth had been spent in an institution for patients enduring long bouts of consumption. Through the good care of his family and the money they could provide, he slowly improved until the day he walked out a young man free of disease.

"Henri, may I have a word with you?" Charles inquired of his employer and longtime friend.

"Of course you may, Charles. What is on your mind? You look as tense as a fox in a henhouse, pacing back and forth that way."

"It is time for me to open the wound you have so aptly covered." Not hearing a response, Charles continued, "It seems Frederic has followed our mademoiselle into a situation which may be of imminent danger for Miss Clarice. She has ventured directly back into the hands of one Dom Broussard."

Glancing at his employer now, he continued, "I cannot stand by and ignore the danger that is waiting to ensnare her while protecting your feelings." Charles looked at his employer to see if he could gauge any reaction to his harsh statement. Although an employee, Charles had Henri's ear and his trust. It might bruise his employer short term, but Charles knew it was best to be forthright.

Henri had ample time to brood about the young woman. If he honestly cared about this woman, he definitely needed to step up and take command of the situation. His complacency where Miss Clarice was concerned had bothered Charles greatly.

Henri was a powerful man even though his demeanor would belie the fact. The years spent fighting to get well gave him a perspective on living humbly and with gratitude. Quiet and calm in his actions, he could be mistaken for a weak and easily intimidated man, but this was a mistake only the foolhardy would make.

The same tenacity and will to survive also gave him the fortitude to fight for those things he cherished. He rarely allowed anyone to penetrate his wall of emotional protection. The causes for which he fought rarely involved specific people but a broader right to exist and enjoy freedom from fear and hunger.

Where was Charles trying to go by delivering this new information? Henri had to admit the mere mention of her name had awakened long-held latent feelings, a mixture of pleasure and lost possibilities. He sat quietly, digesting everything and composing himself before responding to Charles's obvious irritation with him.

On the one hand he could choose to be angry with Charles for disobeying his direct order, but that would be like telling him to turn a deaf ear to his own cry for help. On the other hand, his assistant's insight into Henri's heart couldn't be dismissed so easily, and perhaps he should explore why he had so willingly walled himself away from Miss Clarice Pontifi. He had to admit it was easier than being rejected by her.

Ah yes, he knew full well who she was, but not until he let her get away. It was in a moment of clarity after her departure that he realized what the restaurateur, Paul Dumas, had recognized in the young woman. His own inquiries among a few close confidants gave him all that he needed to understand what had driven the young woman.

"Charles, in your diligence not to share anymore information of our mysterious young woman, you have stumbled upon some very disturbing information and seem compelled to tell me!"

"Sir, I only mean to keep you informed and also help her if possible. I do not mean to disobey your orders, but—" And before he could finish speaking, Henri interjected by first waving his hand.

"It is of no importance, Charles. You did what you thought best under the circumstances." In a rare moment of candor, Henri shared new information with his protégé.

"After Clarice left, I did some investigating on my own and found out exactly who she was and why she had been in Paris in the first place. The reasons she may have been dancing in the Folies Bergère became rather clear to me, but with this knowledge, I could only assume her heart lay elsewhere.

To think she could possibly open up her heart to an old fool such as me was folly."

"I had no idea," Charles said. "Why did you ask me to keep tabs on her but never give you any information that could open the door again?"

"Ah, my old friend, strange is the working of a man's heart. I fear that my pain got in the way of good reason. Now I must confront certain demons and open up to the possibility of more pain and distress where our young friend is concerned."

"It doesn't have to be all or nothing, Henri! You of all people know that there are many facets to the heart, and to have a dear friendship may be the best of all. But one thing I do know is that we must act fast or you will not have an opportunity to reestablish this *friendship*."

"You are right, of course, Charles. Tell me what you have learned and we will make a plan." He wondered if he could protect her and still give her the opportunity to grow and become what she was meant to be.

"You should see her, Henri. She is a different young woman from the one you watched doing the can-can." Charles peered over at his employer to see if he had stepped too far. Henri never knew to what extent Charles protected him, but with his efforts to gain information on the lovely Clarice prior to their *date*, he had a firsthand view.

"Well, tell me about her then. What does she really look like? I never thought the bright and wild hair fit her." Henri laughed, breaking the ice.

"The difference is dramatic. Mind you, I've only had a brief glance at her. It is Frederic who has her confidence and drives her to this *new employment* almost every day."

Becoming somewhat impatient, Henri demanded to know. "Okay, then what color is that hair, Charles?"

Charles laughed. "It is dark auburn and flows down her back like the waves of the river. Frederic says her eyes sparkle like green emeralds speckled with flecks of yellow diamonds. Her laugh is so infectious it pulls you into its warm embrace like a mother caring for her child."

"Aside from your obvious admiration, she sounds like she has special gifts. Do you think she is well suited for a role with this home for young women?"

"Yes, Henri, I do, but she may now be in grave danger."

"Let's not jump to conclusions, Charles. Dom Broussard may be greedy and easily controlled by the wrong element, but what I learned about our mystery man has far more complexity. He is Sister Mary's cousin, and somewhere in his psyche, there is a good side to him. He seems to have a fondness for Miss Clarice. When I said her heart lies elsewhere, it's possible this Dom is the key."

"There may be a way to engage him." Pulling out a notepad, Henri surprised Charles once again by handing him a list. "I want you to take care of investigating a few of these items."

"Of course, Henri. I will take care of these items promptly!" Just as quickly as he had entered Henri's world, he departed with his mission in hand. His employer had a way of gently leading him and others to do his beckoning.

Seduction

SLIPPING AROUND THE corner of Rue de Guerny, she could see the front door clearly, the lackluster patina a reminder of yesteryear's care. Now if she could only pull this off, the rendezvous she had pictured for so long was imminent.

She arrived at the shop slightly past six, well after closing. Palms sweating and feeling lightheaded, Clarice tapped on the front door to let Dom know of her arrival. Breathing deeply, she tried the handle and the door opened. It was too easy and, although causing her a moment's hesitation, did not deter her from entering. "Dom, are you here?" she asked.

In the ensuing silence, there was that one brief moment where she could change her mind and alter the course she had taken. Clarice, her legs feeling a little like rubber, continued to move forward. She could not control the growing excitement she felt.

Just then, Dom came around the corner, startling her. The sight of him took her breath away. In a much different approach than the last time they met, he lovingly pulled her to him. "I have been waiting for you, Clarice."

In one instance of weakness, she reached up to touch his face, lifting her own toward his to look into Dom's eyes. Was it her imagination or did she see warmth and love in his eyes? Quickly shaking her head, Clarice managed to pull herself together. It had shaken her to realize how weak she had become in his presence, a lapse she couldn't allow again.

Dom, aware of the effect he was having on Clarice, softly said, "What are you afraid of, ma chérie?" He used the term of endearment that her father had used when talking to the women he loved. Once again, she was unnerved by Dom. Sighing, she turned to him.

"Dom, there is much you don't know or understand of me, what drove me to leave and stay in seclusion for so long. You have expressed anger at the way I left Paris so suddenly and with no contact. You, of the many people involved in my so-called rescue, have caused me to question and doubt what your real motives are in making these overtures of friendship."

Looking directly at him, Clarice said, "Perhaps there is even more for me to worry about." There, she had said it directly and honestly. Ma Mère would have been proud of her.

His eyes did not betray his flash of anger. No, he was too smart to let a few words interfere now. "Ah, my little Clarice, you have much to learn about me as well. Perhaps we need to start fresh and get to know each other." Was there a growing respect taking hold?

The first time she had come back, it caught him by surprise. What was he thinking? Looking at Clarice now and marveling at her beauty, he knew the answer, but why complicate his life? There was much to gain but also much to lose. He assured himself that he could handle it.

His ticket to freedom from Duvalier was standing right before him, but why did he feel so troubled at the idea of deceiving her even if for what he considered a worthwhile cause?

In an effort to maintain her composure, Clarice said, "Dom, I assure you we will have plenty of time to understand each other and find a way to communicate more effectively. I only want to earn a fair wage, and if by chance that includes working in a place I once loved so much, then I am the luckiest girl in the world."

Not hearing a response, she stammered, "Very well, Dom, we will go to dinner and get to know each other better. Thank you very much for the invitation."

He smiled knowingly. Going to dinner with him would be fine. It was just a matter of time and he would have what he wanted.

"Well then, shall we depart, mademoiselle? I have chosen a restaurant perfect for the occasion—Le Grand Véfour. A most beautifully fitting place for you."

Stifling a gasp, Clarice looked at Dom in disbelief. Could he still be playing with her, and was she so blind as not to see? She felt dizzy. Quickly composing herself and determined not to display any emotion, she simply nodded in agreement.

Her reaction to the restaurant did not escape him. He had to admit he was a bit puzzled and might have to explore this development further. In spite of the unfortunate Duvalier situation, he had, for the most part, long-term good intentions by bringing her here. But to Clarice, her world seemed to be turning upside down.

That Dom wanted to share one of his special places with her was a way to ignite her affection once more. It would help make her feel more comfortable in his presence and make the meeting he planned easier.

"You will love the fare, and the owner was a friend of your grand-mère many years ago. I thought you might like to connect with him, and you both could share some stories from before...well, when your grand-mère was the toast of Paris!"

Clarice looked straight at him. "Dom, it sounds lovely, really! I have heard many wonderful stories of its history and the famous people who have dined there. I just don't know what to say because it sounds so extravagant."

"It is only fitting that we start our new relationship off with a celebration!"

The carriage picked them up promptly at eight thirty, and for the first time, she started to relax. Perhaps she had misjudged him after all.

After their earlier rocky start, Clarice had busied herself organizing a space in her grand-mère's old office while Dom finished his bookwork for the day. Admittedly, she had been surprised at Dom's offer of the space. He seemed to be trying to please her.

Finally, they arrived at Le Grand Véfour, and memories of another night came flooding back. Silly, she thought. It was an infatuation at a time when she had lost her direction. She would not give it any more weight than to remember Henri's kindness and be thankful for his intervention with the despicable manager at the Moulin Rouge.

Entering the restaurant, she momentarily hesitated at the memory of an enchanted time. It seemed a very long time ago, but had it only been a year since the man beside her had interrupted her world? The irony did not escape her.

Two men, two worlds, and the road called *Life* ahead. The night in the restaurant with Henri had been special, yet she had refused to allow a minute of their time together to enter her heart or mind until now. Her thoughts were like an avalanche, cascading over her. "Stop it!" Clarice spoke out loud.

Dom looked over at her, surprised at the outburst but also keenly aware how the surroundings had affected her. It was the second time this evening that Clarice was visibly shaken, and it had something to do with coming here. He kept his silence, and they proceeded to enter the restaurant.

"Monsieur Dom! What a pleasure to see you again. It has been so long." Paul Dumas was coming toward them now.

"Ah, Monsieur Dumas, it has been awhile, my friend." Being careful not to use her full name, Dom made the introductions. "Please, let me introduce Mademoiselle Clarice to you."

"I am so very charmed, my dear. You are welcome here. I must say Dom did not prepare me for your beauty!"

Embarrassed, Clarice extended her hand. "Why, thank you, sir. I am flattered, but you must say that to all the young ladies!"

"No, believe me, Mademoiselle Clarice, only to the rare beauty. As a matter of fact, you remind me of another young lady who was here not too long ago."

Clarice held her breath but could clearly see Monsieur Dumas did not recognize her from the night with Henri. If he did, she hoped he would be discreet and not share that information.

Ushered into one of the private dining rooms, Clarice was relieved to see it was not the one she had shared with Henri.

"You will have Jervais as your attendant this evening, and he will see that you are well cared for, Mademoiselle Clarice and Monsieur Dom."

"Why, thank you, Monsieur Dumas. It is lovely!" Clarice almost whispered. Immediately, her senses were aroused by the strong aroma of Casablanca Lilies. Tingling, she turned to look at the somewhat familiar room. It was almost like before; even the smell pulled her in.

Similar in size and furnishings to the one she had shared with Henri, this one had been cloaked in royal blue velvet and gold braid, giving off an aura of an aristocrat's hideaway. In the center of the far wall was the fireplace, but this one was of cut limestone etched with the same gold used in the braided edges of the divan. Something else was different, yet Clarice could not put her finger on it.

Whether it was the headiness of being in these beautiful surroundings with a handsome man or just the memories of Henri, Clarice felt warm all over. She knew Dom was looking at her, and although she could not see him, Clarice could feel the proximity of his body.

At just the perfect moment, Dom came up behind her and carefully wrapped his arms around her. Whispering in her ear, he said, "Clarice, we have this room to ourselves, and we can spend the evening getting to know each other. You do not have to fear me, my dear, for I care deeply for you."

Could it be? she wondered. Clarice had to admit all other thoughts faded away once Dom's arms encircled her. His smell—an aphrodisiac of blended spices, musk, and the natural scent of his body—drew her closer. *Why can't I break away? What is this spell he has cast upon me?* The ripples were moving over her at a fast pace now, and Clarice was afraid she might be lost at any moment.

"You must be starving," Dom said as he dropped his arms abruptly, breaking the spell. Shaking it off, he said, "I will summon Jervais and give him our order. Then we can sit by the fire with some sherry and talk about your dreams, my dear. You will be surprised how easy I am to talk to!"

Dom had already surprised her this evening by behaving like a gentleman when, clearly, she was ready to succumb to his charm.

Clarice had thought of Dom many times but only to rehash and wonder of his involvement in all that had befallen her family. Now as a woman coming into her prime, could she escape his charms? Sizing him up, he had the look of a thoroughbred: muscular and lean, tall with broad shoulders, and a thick mane of dark hair. There was a lusty masculinity to him that unnerved her. It was something she could not describe other than a desire to know him more intimately. It made her warm all over.

Shaking off those thoughts, she said, "Dom, you were always my friend first, and it was you who shared in my initial plans, supporting and encouraging me. You were the one worried for my safety yet did not stand in my way. For all those reasons, you have my gratitude."

"Well, maybe I should have stopped you. Had I known what your ultimate plan had been, Father Pierre and Sister Mary would have been immediately alerted."

Protesting now, Clarice said, "My ultimate goal was never to end up at the Folies Bergère. However, my contact for the work that would have paid for the university and my bed and board led me down a different path! My plan was to help the young women who are thrown into that life of degradation through no fault of theirs!" Her voice growing increasingly louder, she said, "You can be sure, Monsieur, that I never became what you are now implying!"

He sighed, and for the first time since her so-called rescue, she heard him reaffirm what the old Dom would have said, "No, I would not think so of you, Clarice, but it was easy to assume you had chosen the dance hall for some experiment."

Before she could relax and linger in the warmth of her sherry and more encouraging words from Dom, he continued, "You were easily misled, my dear. I could picture you as the naive schoolgirl yearning to taste the forbidden fruits on the other side of society! It would have been easy for you to slip and enjoy your lusty nature."

Lusty nature! How could those two little words succeed in getting under her skin? She was angry enough now that Dom could just sit there and rot before she'd utter another word! Why did he have to ruin the moment? But part of her knew what Dom implied was not far from the truth.

Settling in with an aged sherry, he looked at her. Why did he feel so out of control? She was still so young. Could he not keep his tongue silent? He wanted to believe her, but what he saw with his own eyes and surely what Gabrielle had told him did not support what she was telling him now.

What was the mystery of Clarice that provoked and teased at his emotions, those he never allowed to surface? He could not let his plan be derailed. It wasn't greed anymore although he had to admit it was the catalyst for his current predicament: the balance between a good life and the possibility of losing everything, even his own life.

Dom was shrewd but no match for Duvalier's group or the man himself. He had a conscience and a sense of right and wrong carried over from his upbringing and time spent with Sister Mary. Admittedly weak, he hated pulling Clarice into danger but couldn't stop what he had to do.

Yet when he was with her, all reason failed and he could not focus on their predicament.

"You still sulk, my dear Clarice, but you know that you could have come back to me, to all of us, for help and we would have gladly given you what you needed to continue your education."

Clarice had to turn at the moment to look at this man who, just a few minutes before, had all but caused her to lose her temper yet now was so sincere in what he spoke that his gentleness lay bare for her to see.

She could understand his rationale. Is it possible that she did long for the wilder side of living? Was it true, also, that her lineage of passionate women somehow cursed her to become one who would never be satisfied with the mundane and forever fight the wanderlust within her soul?

Would one who is pure in heart have those stirrings she felt more often than she dared to count?

She sighed and looked at Dom. "You may be seeing things in me that I cannot admit to myself, but I will tell you this, Dom. My life will be devoted to helping young women avoid the pitfalls which could lead them into a life that would only bring them shame and regret."

"I do believe your intentions were and are honorable albeit misplaced." He pushed aside his own dishonor. No time to think of it now.

"Perhaps God has given me a small light of understanding of how easy it could be to fall prey to our lusts, especially when we are in need of sustenance and a roof over our head."

"Dear Clarice, I do not hold you in contempt. You were born to be a passionate woman and will make your mate happy. I may have allowed my anger to cloud my judgment when we first found you at the dance hall. But if you will allow me to start fresh, then I will also forget and forgive any transgressions you might have had."

"Very well, Dom. You may never believe that I had no transgressions, at least of the sort you have in mind! If you will move beyond this part of our lives, I, in turn, will forgive you for trying to sell me out to the devil."

Dom was startled at her last statement. Could it be she knows of my arrangement?

"You look a little pale, my friend. Did you think me so naive that I could not see the little signs all around me? I'm also smart enough to realize that you were duped into helping Duvalier and you have been trying to save the shop. For this, I do not blame you, but your dishonesty with me soured my trust in you."

With great clarity, Dom realized the folly of his ways and the price he paid to dance with the devil. At least it appeared she did not know the rest of the ugly truth.

He barely whispered, but when he did, all he could say was, "Clarice, my love, you have carried this and still chose to forgive me all the while knowing that I might be pulling you into more danger?" It was all he could do to keep his head up while looking at the woman who pulled at his heart.

"Oh, Dom, we all make mistakes, and I read enough of my grand-mère's records that it became obvious to me how Duvalier manipulated people to do his will. Once you came to work at the shop, you were marked. You were being pulled into Duvalier's clutches through the blackmail he resorts to when he cannot have what he wants legitimately!"

"My life was lived in a bubble of fear that he created for those who love me. But I will beat him at his game and give him what he wants and it will free you!"

In that moment, he knew. He knew without a shadow of a doubt what Clarice meant to him and what he had done. The pain and regret he felt in that instant was unbearable. How could he put her in this position and all the while pretend as if all was well? He looked at her again and thought his heart might break.

Tears flowing gently down her cheeks, she sat there gazing at him. It was a sight that overwhelmed his senses. He made his way over, knelt down at her feet, and looked her in the eyes. Could he ever make amends? he wondered. Grasping her hand, he gently said, "My darling Clarice, please forgive the sins of this egotistical man and know I have loved you from the moment you entered my life."

For the first time, all the veils were removed and she saw clearly that Dom Broussard was more than a friend. It was beyond friendship although it did not dissolve the anger at what he had done to her and indirectly to the family she had lost. Could she totally forgive this man? she wondered. He had so embedded them with the very enemies who had her family killed. It would take more than loving him to get beyond the pain of his transgressions to forgive him.

"Dom, I can forgive most things, but I need some time to truly believe that your words are sincere and if there is real penance to be done. Please give me time to think through this and whether we can move past our history."

Holding her close, he gently kissed her lips. If only they could shut out the world. They would enjoy each other this evening and then he would deal with them before she found out. She would never understand.

His lips found hers, and the hunger they had for each other could wait no longer. She was oblivious to the outer world as time stopped. The only thing she was aware of was the passion invading her body like a fire she had never experienced. Dom took his time as they explored each other, Clarice begging for more and finally consummating their love.

They spent the next hour in the wonderment of what had happened, touching and kissing as they could not get enough of each other.

Sacrifice

At around eleven, a carriage rounded the corner and stopped in front of the restaurant. The three gentlemen appeared as if coming to dine but did not leave the carriage; rather, they waited for the greeter to come up to the carriage. After a few words were exchanged, the carriage left.

The threesome had assembled earlier in the day, bringing all the collected information with them for their meeting with Monsieur Duvalier. It had been a long time since they had all been together, a direct result of the orders that the man himself had given them many years ago.

It was curious after all this time, they would even need to meet. They had taken everything of value from the family, including their very lives. Their sole purpose had been to carry out orders given by Duvalier, which would strip the Chevais and Pontifi families of all they owned. The others, unlike Robard, had not been aware of the order given to kill Marie Chevais and, later, the family members.

Robard was feeling anxious again, the result of his direct responsibility in all the misdeeds that had befallen the Chevais and Pontifi families. Now he was dealing with a crazy loon who could easily wipe him out as well. How did he know the others weren't going to turn on him?

Ultimately, the task of killing Paul Marchand had fallen on him too and one he had carried out willingly, but since that day, things had changed. Perhaps it was a bit of conscience now that he was a father of two young boys. In his last confession to the priest, he had told him of his misdeeds, being careful not to mention names. It had shocked the priest, and Robard ended up feeling more anxious than ever.

He was tired of being held captive these many years as Duvalier's henchman and wary of what his employer could possibly want with targeting this innocent young woman, one of two remaining descendants of the Chevaises and Pontifis. It did not bode well, and Robard vowed to move away from his reach as soon as he could. In the meanwhile, as the leader of this last mission, he would find out more from his two teammates.

"Gentlemen, we will come back after Dom has had his belly filled with wine and food. My contact has indicated he will be eating shortly, and we will wait to make sure he is weakened from his wine and lust of the lady in his company. We will take no chances on losing them. Our orders are to take both of them back to Duvalier tonight in one piece. What Duvalier does with them is not our worry."

"Robard, why do we even pursue this folly? What of Dom Broussard? Does he not work for Duvalier and have his trust?"

"My orders are clear. Dom is to be taken captive along with the fair maiden. It isn't our problem, do you understand? We have no choice in this matter, so I will not discuss further!" Robard continued, "We will catch them by surprise at their weakest moment and finish our mission as ordered!"

In the meantime, Clarice was enjoying Dom's company, and it had become a magical evening. No doubt, Dom was confused as well. At the start of the evening, she did not completely believe his intentions were all good even though it would appear so.

Dinner was served, and they set about the task of savoring the remarkable meal, one that obviously had been handpicked by her new suitor. Pheasant under glass appeared with bits of orange and truffles arranged artfully on the tray. Along with the beautiful display came the freshly baked breads for which the French were famous. The aromas were overwhelming to the senses.

The presentation of cheeses after the main course were too numerous to name. Small petit fours followed them as they moved to the sofa, their bellies full and appetite satiated in every way.

Warming by the fire, they shared the full-bodied Beaujolais Dom poured for them. It was delightful, and she could feel her senses being lulled into a mellow yet expectant state of anticipation once again. *Anticipating what?* she thought. She was already basking in the newfound sensations of love and lust. Was it that she wanted to feel the touch of his lips again and even more? She could feel the heat rising from her belly, and as she was enjoying the moment, Dom suddenly moved away to stand by the fire.

Dom looked at her and shook his head as if to break the spell. He had been lulled into this false sense of security by his own lust and inability to stop from falling further into the web of her charms. He had to be totally honest and lay himself bare to her once and for all. He never expected this to happen, and now he must protect her at all costs even if it meant losing her.

Yes, he had agreed to play with the devil and would have to pay the price, but he was determined she would not suffer for his sins. His hope had been that by winning her over he could convince her to give up the remainder of her estate to Duvalier and he, in turn, would be freed from his bondage.

He did not know at the time that she wanted no part of the estate, other than the shop and enough to help support her volunteer work and, of course, Andre.

It was not too late to turn back, but he'd have to convince Robard that Clarice had full intentions of turning over everything to Duvalier. He just needed some time to gather what Duvalier wanted. Tomorrow he would make it a priority and set everything right once and for all.

At that particular moment, there was a knock on the door. "Monsieur Dom, forgive me but I must have a word with you." Stepping outside and pulling the door as not to alarm Clarice, Dom listened intently to what Monsieur Dumas had felt was so urgent as to interrupt his evening.

"There is a rather, well, obnoxious person out here demanding to speak with you and the mademoiselle. I would not have interrupted, but he threatened to cause trouble if I didn't do as he asked. He also had two other gentlemen with him." It was obvious Monsieur Dumas was ruffled, an unusual circumstance for the normally collected restaurant owner.

He miscalculated Robard's sense of urgency, one which had been forced upon the hapless man by Duvalier. He had been told that a meeting was imminent, but he assumed it would be in the shop and in a civilized manner. This invasion of his space did not bode well.

Stalling, Dom asked, "Did he give his name, Paul?" At that moment, Clarice opened the door with a worried look on her face. Dom turned to Clarice and said, "Do not leave the room."

"What is wrong, Dom?"

"I must go speak with these men, Clarice. Please remain here and I'll return in just a few moments. If for some reason I do not return, Monsieur Dumas will make arrangements to see you home and I will meet you later!"

"But you can't just go out there! What if it has to do with Duvalier? You will be in danger and all this for things that have no value to me! I heard what Monsieur Dumas said. They want to speak with me also." She was clearly distraught, yet resolute.

"Shhh, my Clarice. I know what must be done to break the chain of bondage that hampers me...us! My fear has kept me constrained for too long, and it is time to break free. Remember that I love you, Clarice." With that, he brought Clarice to him and kissed her passionately, long enough to raise the ire of the one outside the door, yelling for him to come out. He turned and hurried away, fighting to maintain control and confront what awaited him.

"Dom, please come back!" There were loud voices and a shrill holler followed by scuffling with what sounded like an army of men outside the door. Her instinct was to go to him, but her common sense prevailed at least for the moment.

After a few minutes, she had enough and tried valiantly to follow him through the door, but another set of hands pulled at her. She could feel herself struggling to maintain balance, and suddenly the room started spinning.

All she could remember was those hands, vaguely familiar but not those of Paul Dumas. The hands had a pleasant scent of spice that tugged at her nostrils. She never saw her assailant before passing out.

The next day, she awakened to the sun blazing through the window. A tray of food was sitting next to her bed, uneaten. The sound of Sister Mary reading softly from her Bible had stirred her from some faraway place.

"What happened, Sister? Why am I here?" Panic then set in as she remembered the night before. "Where is Dom, what happened to him at the restaurant?" an anguished Clarice begged Sister Mary for answers.

"Shhh, calm yourself, my dear. Everything will be okay in due time. Dom is just down the hall, and I will bring you to him shortly."

"Down the hall? Where are we? What happened, and why isn't he here in front of us?" Clarice demanded. The sick feeling in the pit of her stomach continued to spread, the fear gripping at her very being. "I don't understand."

"You need some more rest and then we'll pay him a visit. He is sleeping peacefully after a very difficult night."

"It's beginning to come back now. Dom left me in the dining room because some men were trying to cause trouble—Duvalier's no doubt! Please tell me he is all right! I could not bear it if Dom, in his gallantry to save me, was harmed."

Sister Mary looked at her young charge with a knowing glance. It was obvious Miss Clarice was smitten. It might not be too good for her to see Dom at this point. He had taken a horrendous beating and was in very poor condition. The doctor had reassured the sister that, with the right care, he might improve enough to have a somewhat normal life, but the head injury had damaged him permanently.

"It would do no good to tell you he was fine. Duvalier's men did indeed try to take him and then would have come after you if not for the fierce battle Dom put up. Because of his bravery in trying to protect you and fight them off alone, he sustained multiple injuries, one of which was a head injury."

Before Clarice could catch her breath, Sister Mary hurried on, "His efforts did not go unnoticed, and several of the restaurant patrons, along with the manager, jumped in to help. They were able to block the group's entry back into the dining room."

"I must see him now!" She tried to step out of the bed and hit the floor as her legs crumbled beneath her.

"Whoa, whoa. Let's get you back into the bed. You need your rest right now. Dom is sleeping fitfully, and in due time you will be able to go to him."

The evening's events had proven to be too much for the young woman, and she started to cry softly. "How did I get here? I don't remember anything that happened after being forced back into the room."

"A stranger came to your rescue, one to whom Monsieur Dumas paid great respect but would not give us his name. He alone entered the room and quietly disappeared out the back, carrying you ever so carefully over his shoulder."

She looked at the sister, and as she started to speak, the faint memory of those strong hands with the gentle hint of spice stirred something deep within her. What was it about the scent, the hands and the man, one whose face was covered with a scarf? Everything was so confusing. Maybe the sister was right after all; she needed to close her eyes for a few minutes just to clear her head.

Remembrance

A WEEK PASSED and she still hadn't seen Dom. The sister had assured her that he was mending slowly but still in a semicoma state of awareness. He could hear but could not respond. They had been able to coax him with stimuli to move his hands and even limited yes-and-no conversation, but speech did not come so easily.

Clarice, after a couple days languishing in bed, managed to come out of her own hiding and take meals with Sister Mary. She didn't know why, but she couldn't find the energy to venture down the corridor to Dom's room. Even though her body was in good condition, a fear gripped her like no other had since the time of her parents.

Conversing with her mirror image, she spoke from the heart. *What is wrong with me?* she wondered. *I need to go to him and tell him how I feel. How do I feel? I must face my feelings. Even Sister Mary had asked if I wanted to see him now. This man saved me by risking his life for me, and I'm now acting as a coward? No, I will not become something I'm not—a weak, fearful woman.*

It was time and she would make her move to see him. Tiptoeing down the hall, afraid of being heard, she inched closer to his door. Hesitating, she slowly opened it and peeked inside. She hadn't expected to see him awake and looking right at her.

It unnerved her momentarily, but she pushed open the door and made her way to his bedside. Sitting down next to him, she cautiously took his hand and started stroking it. "Oh, my dear Dom, what have they done to you? I am so sorry that I could not help you in your time of need."

He stared at her for a moment, and then his eyes softened noticeably as he recognized her for more than just a caregiver. What was it about her? He tried to pull it from his mind but was stopped by the dark wall. It was always the same when he tried remembering; the wall came between him and the clarity for which he so desperately searched.

There was something warm and soft about her though. She must be someone special to me. He read her eyes and could see she was struggling, and in that moment, he reached his hand out to touch hers. Uhmm, it was so soft and she was so inviting even in the tentativeness of her actions. He wanted her closer.

The small gesture of mutual understanding aroused something in her only a woman in love could understand. She set aside her inhibitions and leaned over him. In a matter of minutes, Clarice was kissing his lips, softly and slowly, as if she had been seduced by the connection flowing between their outstretched hands.

She suddenly realized what she was doing and pulled away. Clarice could see the puzzlement in his eyes, but there was something else too. Was it a look of love and admiration? Perhaps she was reading too much into this.

It was time to leave before she did something to regret. He was still holding on to her hand and would not let go. Oh, she must break this spell. Looking him in the eye, she said, "Dom, my dearest, I am just down the hall and will be back later, tomorrow, and however long it takes for you to become totally whole." He seemed to relax then and closed his eyes.

Clarice left the room and went to find Sister Mary. She had finally come to grips with her surroundings and knew her way around the small monastery. There will be a time when we must all leave, but for now this may be the safest place for us all.

The days turned into weeks and Dom had slowly come to life even to a degree that was more surprising than originally predicted. It was in the last week they were there that Dom's memory returned, not completely but in bits and pieces.

The monastery had planned a farewell for the one they called the raven-haired princess. It was obvious that Clarice had won their hearts as she seemed to have the ability to do with all who came into her life. She was excited to be making the move to the university but also sad to be leaving Dom behind. It was a confusing time for her, but she agreed with Sister Mary the time was right to move on.

The brothers at the monastery assured her that they would continue to take good care of their new friend, Dom. He was healing nicely, but they needed more time to work with him on his memory.

She had been emotional all day thinking of her final visit to Dom's room to tell him goodbye. It had taken much resolve for her to even venture down the hall to his room. But venture she did.

Knocking gently on his door, she could hear him moving about. He had been walking in his room and sometimes down the halls with her or Sister Mary. "Come in, dear Clarice."

As she slowly opened the door, her eyes immediately took in the room. She didn't see him at first and then she looked over and saw him peering out the window. Gasping in surprise, she realized what he had done for them.

Positioned in front of a small fireplace in the corner of the room was a small settee with an inviting fire caressing the corner of the room with its softly lit glow. An array of freshly cut flowers from the monastery's garden was placed on a table beside it, along with a bottle of champagne and two glasses.

He was wearing a different robe from the one that had been his uniform for so long. Slowly he made his way toward her and, with great care, embraced her. At first she pulled back stiffly, but his gentle pressure was like a magnet pulling her to him.

She finally reached up and opened her arms to him, and time stopped. With one swoop of his arm, Dom had managed to capture her in his strong embrace. His kiss made her feel like being enveloped in a warm cocoon with all her senses on high alert. She first allowed and then welcomed his strong hold, abandoning herself to the passion so long held in check.

They spent the day and night together bodies intertwined as only two people in new love could do. It was a magical time with Clarice, vowing not to let the moments disappear into the abyss of the ordinary. She did not want to break the spell and finally left Dom to go back and unpack her suitcase.

Not forgetting her other commitments, she vowed to make good on her promises to continue with her work at the university and with the young women to whom she owed so much. This period of time would be her way of helping Dom come out of the prison of his mind, and then she would move on to the next phase of her life.

Later, when she was alone, she could languish in the sweet remembrance. The passion, a blend of love and lust and the tenderness, freely given, would bind her to him for eternity. This interval would supply her with the memories that, even months later, would warm from within.

They rendezvoused every night for the remainder of the time Dom stayed at the monastery. Clarice had endeared herself to the monks, and they allowed her to stay as long as Dom was still there mending.

Her heart was full and, in spite of her earlier musings, could see a future for them together, painted in a beautiful landscape. It never occurred to her they might part. They even discussed ways to deal with Duvalier once and for all. She was prepared to offer him everything he ever wanted, except that which would be used to help others and the care needed for her brother.

All the broken pieces from her past were neatly falling into the puzzle frame and smoothing out into a present of hope and promise. Could it be possible that she had found the missing pieces with Dom?

Yes, she could finally allow herself to laugh freely, love intensely, and relax in her newfound happiness, so much so that the day he left stunned her; the shock reverberated throughout the monastery. She found his room empty and then the note.

"My dear Clarice, please forgive me and understand that I must go away for all our sakes."

Could it be possible? Had she done something to send him away? None of it made sense. She stopped breathing as time stood still. Taking a breath before daring to read on, the letter continued, "It is with great sadness that I must leave you. There is much you do not know of me and what entanglements I have had the past four years. You are so young and innocent I cannot drag you down to the depths of my degradation. Just remember that I do love you and always will. My sacrifice is in leaving the one good thing in my life and that is you."

She could not read on, crumbling the note and tossing it onto the floor. Tears blocked her vision, and she gave in to the sobs that racked her body, crying until, hours later, she collapsed in exhaustion.

The monks knew the young man had left in the night and sensed Clarice's need for privacy and solitude. Sister Mary had departed several weeks prior, going back to her own routines, and they were not going to intrude on the young woman.

It took five days and finally bringing Sister Mary back to talk Clarice out of her room. It was only then she could begin to heal.

Sister Mary had her own inner dialogue to deal with after recent events. There would be plenty of time to share the details with Clarice. When she has time to absorb all this new information, she'll want to know how we found her and my involvement.

Clarice has the right to know how I came to the convent and established myself as a serious nun. All in due time, she will know all. Mary had much to share with her young charge.

The New Life

It was hard remembering before. Everything seemed so different now; a sense of calm had come over her life like a veil made of delicate cloth, fragile and beautiful, yet strong enough to withstand the tug and pull of many hands.

She rarely went back in her mind to that day or the following days and months. It was strange how she had finally arrived at this place and point in time. How long had it been? Four years?

Everything happened so quickly, she tried to remember—the feelings of love, joy at new revelations, then the fear, and finally acceptance. Moments in time broken only by the people traveling through them, assembled ultimately into blocks of life either well lived in love or as lost souls searching for a missing link.

Clarice forced her thoughts to Dom. It was only fair to occasionally give him the respect of her time if only to acknowledge the role he had played in helping her to move beyond what had been a tumultuous young adulthood.

She suspected she had loved him, but not in the way a woman can truly love a man.

Dom had been weak, but he did love her in his own way, shallow perhaps, but sincere from his perspective. She could now forgive this man whose life became dispensable because of his own doing.

Fulfilled as a woman with a wonderful man by her side now, it was hard to even imagine what a life with Dom would have been like. Grateful that she was with her one and only true love, she thanked God every day for her blessings.

Troubled at first, she had worried about what had befallen Dom but imagined that he had talked his way out of the situation with Duvalier. He had seemingly disappeared but would occasionally drop Sister Mary a note to let her know he was doing fine and traveling the world.

She dared not think about what she had to give up in the interest of all involved. It was still painful, but time had helped heal the void. It was the right thing to do, and God alone would be her judge.

Sister Mary had finally opened up to her and shared the rest of what had been the missing piece. She had been enlisted as Clarice's guardian angel many, many years before by Bennie and then monitored by Father Pierre.

Although not of the same religious order, she moved into the convent specifically to watch over her charge. Mary had been a good steward with respect to taking care of young Miss Clarice. Her lapse was in confiding in and trusting Dom to also protect her while working for him in the shop.

The shop had been sold not long after, and the new owner had turned the business into a brisk enterprise. Surprisingly, it only took her three months to work up the courage to enter the shop, but once inside, she could feel the warmth and love the new owners had given to it.

Yes, everything was as it should be—life perpetuating life. It brought a smile to her lips as she relished the knowledge of how love had found her at last. Life was good, and she felt fulfilled. There was little Giselle, the apple of their eyes, a miniature of the courageous Marie Chevais. She felt a swell of motherly love at the thoughts of her toddler lying quietly beside her.

Looking at their beautiful child, she could quell the guilt of giving up Dom's child. It was a heart-wrenching decision but one made out of love. At the time, Clarice's future was still unknown and to keep the child would have been a selfish act. She took solace in the knowledge that the baby was with a good family and would be raised with love.

Then there was her husband, a man above all men. One who could make her heart skip a beat at a simple glance or the soft touch of his hand.

At first it had surprised Clarice, and she had difficulty wrapping her arms around the idea that Henri was her passion.

He had been the one who ultimately saved her, but it wasn't just gratitude that she felt. There was genuine love and respect for the kind of man he was, one much like her father.

Bennie and Father Pierre had rejoiced at the announcement of their engagement. She remembered the day well. It had been almost three years to the day when she had been rescued from the melee at the restaurant, including the year spent in healing within the walls of Sister Mary's new convent.

They were celebrating their first anniversary of being together. Henri had surprised Clarice by bringing in Bennie, Father Pierre, Sister Mary, and even Andre for their special night.

She was overwhelmed with joy at seeing her family, and before she could come to grips with it all, there in the background were some of the nuns from the convent. If it had been three years prior, dark thoughts might have taken over, but this day all was joyous.

In front of everyone, Henri asked for her hand in marriage. The tears on that day were those of joy, and nothing could have ruined the occasion.

She learned much later that Henri had watched over her for a very long time. It was he who had saved her from danger and had been one of her guardian angels along the way.

She decided it would serve no purpose to tell him of the baby she gave up for adoption. It was not a fear of rejection but rather the knowledge that Henri would be honor bound to find the child who belonged to his precious Clarice.

Henri had his own joy and would never divulge all that he knew and had known about his Clarice. He loved little Giselle and cherished the time they spent together as a family. This was life as it should be, and as long as he had breath, he would protect them.

Yes, all had turned out just the way he planned. The other annoyances had already been taken care of and buried so deep that no one would ever find out.

Forever Thread

JACKIE HAD BEEN writing the story now for several months, determined to find and solve the mystery of Dom's disappearance, Clarice's missing inheritance, and Clarice's life between the years of 1898 and 1904. That was the year her dear grandmother Giselle was born.

The pull was tremendous as they had been connected by more than a birthright and Jackie's mother, Doris. Even though it appeared that Clarice's story came to a happy ending, World War I had become center stage in their lives, creating a backdrop of death and destruction. The years were difficult, and the only solution was to send their daughter, Giselle, to America.

It was time to move into the next part of her story, the one about Clarice's daughter, Giselle, Jackie's revered grandmother, her mother, Doris, and all the years since.

Every day, Jackie thanked God for allowing her to live and write the stories of the women who came before. She knew that the story of her grandmother's sacrifices would pull at her heartstrings, but it was important to share the history with her own grandchildren.

The story of Doris would bring her the most pain: a woman before her time, tough and resilient yet fragile and easily broken. She was the rebellious one, fiery to the end—either fighting for the underdog or digging her heels in to maintain her independence.

Then her story, one that almost ended too soon. She would share most of it, but carefully. There were a lot of pitfalls that could be encountered in writing about oneself, a veritable minefield of missteps made and lingering journeys yet to be taken.

It was on one of her writing days that the letter came. Innocuous enough, it looked like an official document, but upon closer inspection, Jackie could tell that it was from France. Excitedly, she opened the envelope, hoping it contained a response from the consul's office to her request for information.

Upon further inspection, she could see the card within: a small white card simply written in English. It read, "Madam, I am the great-grandson of one Dom Broussard. It is my wish to meet with you and discuss a matter of great importance. I will be in your area two weeks hence and will contact you."

Card in hand, she felt that old sensation of exhilaration. She had to admit that this bit of news titillated her senses at a time when she was feeling restless. It was exciting to think she might actually come face-to-face with a descendant of her great-grandmother's suitor and protagonist.

Why the suspense and secrecy? Why now? She had to admit her intense curiosity about what happened to Dom after leaving the convent. Yes, she would welcome his ancestor. Perhaps this will reveal more of what became of Clarice's baby.

About the Author

An Army brat, the author was raised primarily in Europe where her father was sent after serving in World War II. The family moved from Germany to Austria and then on to Italy giving her insight into her European heritage. Judy is married with three children and nine grandchildren. She lives in North Carolina with her husband Robert.

In her early thirties she had her first brush with entrepreneurship, owning and managing two hardware stores. She then launched a career in the telecom/technology field becoming one of the founding partners of a telecom start-up company.

A past president of Charlotte Chapter National Association of Women Business Owners, she helped start a mentoring program for floundering businesswomen called Extreme Mentor, a platform to steer women to success.

Giving motivational speeches to women inspired her to write this book, incorporating some of her great grandmother's story. She spent fifteen years writing *All the Seasons Never Lived,* a tribute not only to the strong women in her family but celebrating women everywhere.

CPSIA information can be obtained
at www.ICGtesting.com
Printed in the USA
LVHW050028080222
710297LV00006B/195/J